# resistance

## j.f.r. coates

# j.f.r. coates

Text copyright 2021


Cover by Ilya Zyor

www.artstation.com/ilyar


Resistance

978-1-922061-73-7

J.F.R. Coates

Queensland, Australia

# acknowledgements

I would like to thank my husband Jamie for supporting me while I wrote this book (and Heretic). Without his support, these two books would have taken much longer to complete.

As always, I must also thank my family. When growing up, my parents always encouraged me to keep reading. That love of books has fuelled my desire to create my own stories for many years now.

I must also thank those who support me on Patreon. Your financial support has been most appreciated. Thank you for being there with me throughout this entire process.

And I must also thank you all – my readers. For every review and comment, thank you. They do more to help me than you could ever imagine. I hope you enjoy Twitch's story.

Human or starat.

Warrior or mechanic.

We can all make a difference if we put our heart to it.

J.F.R. Coates

# about the author

J.F.R. Coates was born and raised in picturesque Somerset, England, but he moved out to Brisbane, Australia as a teenager. He grew up reading from a young age, starting with Enid Blyton's *The Famous Five* and *Secret Seven*, before finding his calling with J.R.R. Tolkien's *The Hobbit*. Speculative Fiction has gripped him ever since, and now he calls amongst his favourite authors Maggie Furey, Phillip Pullman, and Neil Gaiman.

He still lives in Brisbane, where he lives with his husband and – as seems ubiquitous for authors – his two cats.

You can follow him on Twitter at @jfrcoates, or Facebook at /jfrcoates.

He also has a Patreon, which allows for sneak-previews of what's to come, as well as additional stories that fit in around his novels. All support is always gratefully received. https://www.patreon.com/jfrcoates

J.F.R. Coates

# chapter one

Twitch cowered in the shadows. There was almost nothing but darkness clinging around the starat, robbing him of his sight and filling him with fear. The planet surface was far above his head, and no light from Prox came so deep. At least, Twitch reasoned, the shadows should help keep him hidden from unfriendly eyes. The starat still struggled to understand how he had come to be in such a situation. Humans patrolled through the darkness up ahead, but they were not the nice, friendly ones Twitch had come to expect on Centaura. These were cruel, twisted humans who were more like those back on Ceres, before his life had been changed by Captain Rhys.

These humans were part of the Inquisition, and their fervour reminded Twitch of the Vatican officials in the empire. So did their hatred of starats and all things that weren't part of their small view of humanity. Twitch had been sent up against them, and in his desire to strike back at the human who had wronged him, he had agreed to this foolish mission. Now he was in the dark, deep inside a hidden lair controlled by the Inquisition, without any idea of what to do now.

He turned his head to the left. At least Twitch wasn't alone. He had hidden amongst a pile of supply crates with David, his beloved partner and strongest friend. David had been by Twitch's side for years, and he knew he could always rely on his partner. For now, though, the coffee-furred starat looked as nervous as Twitch felt.

Despite that fear, a comforting hand rested on Twitch's shoulder. The two starats had barely spoken a word since they had descended from the hidden passage beneath the church, almost half an hour

7

earlier. They didn't dare, for fear of being seen or heard. Twitch knew that starats weren't expected to be down here, in an Inquisition stronghold. No free starats, at least.

Looming over everything was the reason Twitch found himself in such a situation. A great machine towered over all the surrounding underground structures. Even in the low light of the great cavern, it shone brightly with its own illumination. A Denitchev drive, many hundreds of times larger than any Twitch had seen before, providing a steady glow throughout the cave. They were usually found in the heart of spaceships, used to fuel the transition into faster-than-light subspace travel. This particular drive was as large as some of the skyscrapers in Caledonia, larger than many of the ships they were usually housed inside. It towered over everything inside the vast cave, even the crane directly in front of it.

A prickle ran down Twitch's synthetic tail. He couldn't be sure exactly why the Inquisition needed such a massive device, but he knew he had to find some way to stop their plans, if he could. He glanced across to David. The two starats nodded to each other. It had been a few minutes since they had last heard a human come close to them.

Twitch slowly rose to his feet. His toes pressed down against the smooth concrete floor, and through them he could feel every blemish and impurity in what looked like a perfectly flat surface. The sensitivity of his artificial legs was something he was gradually trying to get used to. With a shake of his head, he forced himself to focus. This was not the time to let himself get distracted.

The underground facility was mostly shrouded in darkness, with only a few small areas lit up brightly with floodlights. The storage warehouse was kept in shadow, but close by was a long platform running alongside magtrain tracks. There was no train present at the moment, though Twitch had seen one of the magtrains leave not long after they made their way down to the lowest levels of the cavern. The tracks only went in one direction; towards a tunnel at the far end of the cave, lit up by a few small flashing red and green lights.

Beyond the station was a cluster of small buildings where most of the activity seemed to be centred. The logo of two crossed golden swords shone brightly above the largest of these buildings, which Twitch had come to believe was the insignia of the Inquisition. A little further beyond the buildings was what Twitch was really concerned about. The Denitchev drive filled up most of the remaining space in the cavern, rising almost all the way to the distant ceiling. Pipes and tubes spread out in a wide network from the top third of the giant machine. Some led to what appeared to be storage tanks, while others plunged into the rock either side of the drive.

Twitch took a deep breath. He squeezed David's hand before releasing it. He pried his fingers into the top of one of the storage crates, lifting away the heavy lid. He was barely able to move the lid, and he quickly needed to release it again, but he had seen what he needed to know. He almost sneezed at the overpowering scent of cinnamon that came from the crystals. He quickly closed the lid and buried his muzzle in the crook of his arm.

"Denitchev crystals," Twitch said quietly, once he was confident that he was not about to sneeze. His throat was dry, but he tried to keep the quiet whimper out of his voice. "Fuel for the drive. There's so much of it."

"Can we destroy them?" David asked, just as quietly.

Twitch shook his head. "No, not without drawing attention to ourselves." The starat paused, resting both hands on the edge of the crate. He craned his neck to look up towards the top of the drive. "I need to have a closer look at that and see what it's for."

"We can still find another way out," David said, hope in his voice.

Twitch hissed softly. "We can't do that. Not without knowing what they're up to."

David sighed in resignation. He didn't argue with Twitch. They had already had that conversation before they had been forced to descend from the church above their heads. There was no way but forward. They had to pass on information to Amy.

No one cried out in warning as Twitch slowly crept out of their hiding place. What little activity had been around the warehouse had moved away again. In the distance, he could hear a few humans shouting and calling out to each other, but none of it seemed to be coming in their direction.

Unfortunately, all of that activity sounded like it was between them and the Denitchev drive. There didn't appear to be any easy routes around the cluster of buildings either. They would have to go right through them, risking running into a hostile human.

Few of the humans looked like soldiers. Most wore standard civilian clothing with no visible weapons, though there were a couple of armed guards in light armoured vests. Most were Centauran humans; short and squat, barely taller than a starat. Twitch counted three Terrans amongst them.

Twitch breathed in deep again. He let the air out in a slow exhalation as he tried to slow the racing beat of his heart. Then he started to move before he gave himself the opportunity to back away.

It was easy to keep to the shadows. There were so many of them, with so few lights to illuminate the underground darkness. The few floodlights positioned around the cave were static, pointing down to one single spot on the ground beneath them. They lit up the station and the buildings, but they kept most of the rest of the cave in gloom. Dark fur allowed the two starats to better blend into the shadows.

Twitch led the way, creeping towards the low buildings. There were about half a dozen of them, all relatively small. The tallest of them was only three stories in height. A few lights were on in some of the windows, and a couple of armed guards marched around the perimeter. Twitch had never fired a gun before. He'd never even handled one, but he would have felt a lot safer if he had some kind of weapon to rely on. Tooth and claw provided little defence against bullets.

The two starats moved slowly and quietly. Twitch kept his eyes forwards, while David focused on behind them, making sure no one was able to sneak up from the rear. Every footfall that reached Twitch's ears caused his heart to skip a beat, but they slowly crept forward unnoticed by the humans.

David's hand squeezed tighter against Twitch's.

Twitch glanced back to see a flashlight beam in the distance, further back on the path they had just walked down. His breath caught in his throat. Either side of them was open and exposed, without anywhere to hide. They had no choice but to keep moving forward and hope that the shadows behind the compound would be enough to hide them.

Ahead of the starats was the low buildings, which provided the opportunity to provide a little more cover from whoever was following behind, but also the risk of more humans. The shadows played tricks with Twitch's eyes. He imagined dozens of humans leaping forward from the darkness, but none did so.

The wide path to their left narrowed as it approached the buildings, which were located in the middle of a small, shallow hollow almost in the centre of the cave. A wire fence ran around the perimeter of the buildings, with a narrow gateway open at the path. There was no one guarding the gateway, and it was secured open by a loop of chain. To either side of the mesh perimeter fence was a sturdy, more defensive wall. Large slabs of concrete were stacked in front of the fence, waiting to be installed in the defences. If they wanted to get through to the drive, they would have to pass through the compound.

A nudge from David drew Twitch's attention to something just above the gate. There were a couple of small cameras there. One looked out onto the path, while the other looked inwards to the compound. Twitch flicked his tail. If they had people monitoring security, then someone might already know they were there.

Twitch hitched in his breath. They would have to be quick. "Come on," he mumbled to David, pulling on the hand of his partner and leading them both through the wire-mesh gate.

Despite Twitch's fears, no one shouted out as they passed through the gate. All remained silent, and the two starats darted off the main path to slip between the first and second of the low buildings. None of the structures appeared to be made with any permanence in mind, as they were all constructed of the same cheap, prefabricated metallic components.

Twitch placed his hand on the smooth metal of the closest building. It felt surprisingly warm to the touch. He lowered his hand again as he heard a deep growl coming from inside. His ears flicked up at the sound, recognising it as one of the native creatures he had seen outside the city. "They have dragons in there," he whispered to David, leaning close to his partner so he could keep his voice as quiet as possible. "Think we can use one?"

David just stared at Twitch, his mouth agape. Eventually, there was a small shake of the head. "Are you nuts?" the larger starat hissed. "They're far too dangerous."

Twitch shrugged his shoulders. "Worth a thought," he mumbled. Secretly he was quite glad that David had shot down the idea. The dragons had been scary enough from a distance. He dreaded to think what they might be like up close.

Movement back on the main path caught Twitch's attention. The starats crouched down as two humans walked past, from the direction they had come from. Both humans carried a flashlight, and they wore a golden pin on their collar. Twitch was too far away to properly make out what the pin was, but he assumed it was of the crossed swords. Neither human looked towards them, and after a few moments they were both out of sight.

"We should keep moving," Twitch mumbled. He squeezed his hand around David's again and tried to ignore the feeling of his heartbeat hammering in his throat.

"If we must," David replied. This time he took the lead, and he moved further away from the path so they could skirt around the inside of the perimeter fence. There was a couple of metres gap between the prefab buildings and the fence, and it kept them away from any prying eyes on the main path.

Evidence that humans did sometimes come to the back of the buildings was scattered across the ground. Food wrappings had been discarded on the rocks, and Twitch almost kicked a metal flask before he was able to lift his foot in time. Thankfully, there was no one currently there, allowing the two starats to hurry between the buildings.

As they approached the Denitchev drive, Twitch began to truly understand just how big it was. The device was gigantic. Even the crane in front of it was massive, but still dwarfed by the machine. He could only begin to imagine how long it had taken to design and build. If the Inquisition were able to make it work... He didn't even know what they could do with it, but he was sure the plans had to be dangerous.

Surrounding the base of the monstrous structure was another wire mesh fence, which looked pitiful and useless compared to the Denitchev drive it protected. On this side of the compound, both the gate out of the small hollow and the one into the drive were both locked. Twitch could see the chain and padlock holding the gates closed.

"I thought they'd have more protecting it," David whispered, tentatively placing his hands on the fence.

"They must be really confident no one can find this place," Twitch said, speaking under his breath. He lightly bit down on his lip and flicked his tail to the side. "That means they're either really dumb, or much more capable than we think."

"Let's act as though it's the latter and get away before it's too late," David hissed softly.

Twitch sucked in his breath and looked around. There wasn't another way out from within the fenced compound. Running along the top of the mesh fencing was a strip of razor wire. They had nothing to cut through the wire fencing, and nor did they have time to search for something. His eyes moved up to look at the razor wire. Then he glanced down to his feet. He tensed his toes, before he crouched down to feel over his claws. They were sharp, but he didn't know if they'd be sharp enough to do what needed to be done.

"What are you doing?" David asked, crouching down by Twitch's side. The larger starat kept his eyes sharp, looking around them for any potential danger approaching. Though there were humans just the other side of the prefab buildings, none of them were moving closer. They were talking amongst themselves, but too far away for Twitch's ears to pick up on the exact words being shared.

Knowing that David had his back, Twitch was able to tease his fingertips to the base of the claw on his right big toe. It felt so natural, so real, that Twitch still had a hard time believing that everything from his hips down was cybernetic. He pinched at the claw, then twisted his fingers around until he felt something give. It didn't hurt, but there was a twinge of something that pulsed within his foot. It wasn't quite discomfort, but Twitch wasn't sure he liked the feeling.

Twitch moved his hand back and opened his palm, letting the claw he had just pulled away fall into it. He felt his gorge rise for a moment, before his body caught up to the fact that he felt no pain from pulling it free. Instinct still told him that it had to hurt, and it put him in the memory of Captain Rhys's ruined, clawless hands.

The broken-off toe claw was much sharper than anything on Twitch's hands. He lightly touched his finger to the sharp surface, and it almost cut through his skin with only the softest contact. It would be enough to cut through the fences.

"Did you have to do that?" David whispered, distaste evident in his voice and the way his muzzle had scrunched up.

Twitch shrugged as he pressed the claw against the wire fence. He pulled down, and the metal snapped apart with a soft twang. The starat glanced around in alarm at the sound, immediately freezing, but there was no response from the nearby humans at all. Letting out the breath of air he had been holding in, Twitch slowly began to cut through the metal again.

One link at a time, the mesh began to break, until there was soon a gap large enough for the two starats to slip through. Twitch held the metal apart for David to squeeze through, but even so some of the jagged edges snagged against the larger starat's fur and clothes. A few red lines of blood welled up on the starat's thigh as he staggered through.

Neither starat commented on the small cuts, though David hissed softly and pressed a hand to his thigh as he tested his weight on his leg. The starat grimaced but did not limp as he started to walk again. There was only one more fence to go now, but there was a small, open climb before they reached it at the top of the hollow.

Twitch glanced back a couple of times, but through the gloom he couldn't see if any humans had seen them. No flashlights were aimed in their direction, so he could only hope that their presence still went unnoticed. Most of the moving lights of the patrolling guards were on the other side of the compound.

The second fence proved just as vulnerable to Twitch's claw as the first. Once more, the thin but tough wires broke with a gentle twang, snapping away as the claw pushed down through them. A beam of light from a flashlight swung in their direction, but it didn't illuminate them, passing by a few metres from the starats and the sliced fence. Twitch pulled David down, fearful of the voices that drifted through the darkness. Only after a few seconds did he feel comfortable enough to rise to his feet.

They were inside now, with just the crane between them and gigantic structure of the Denitchev drive. Around the base of the crane were large crates, all filling the air with cinnamon. This close to the drive, Twitch could see all the various vents and intake pipes that criss-crossed over the entire machine. Thick cables ran across the ground, connecting the machine with the nearest of the buildings behind the starats, presumably providing power for the colossal construct.

"What are you here for?" Twitch said, speaking to himself as he placed a hand on the machine. Close by there was a ladder than ran up onto a spindly scaffold that appeared to run all the way up to the far-distant summit. His eyes dropped back down to David. "There has to be something down here. Can you see anything?"

David winced, pressing a hand to his injured thigh. Blood came away on his fur when his hand moved, but he didn't appear to be bleeding too severely. His tail tucked between his legs. "What's that there," he said, pointing towards the base of the drive.

Twitch's eyes followed his partner's finger. He hissed and grinned in satisfaction. There was a small handle and a door. Twitch scampered across and pressed his ear against the door, making sure there were no sounds coming from inside. When he was confident all was quiet, he pulled the door open. He was blasted by a strong gust of icy air, rippling his fur as he stepped inside.

Most of the small room was taken up by a bank of computer terminals, with a holographic screen projected onto the far wall. An idle animation played over the holograph.

"A control room," David said quietly, stepping into the small room behind Twitch. He pulled the door closed behind them. There was little light but for the computers. "Do you think we can do something from in here?"

"Maybe," Twitch said uncertainly. He moved forward, waving his hand in the hope of finding the sensors that controlled the holographic screens. To his surprise, the screen flickered on. Whoever the previous user had been had left themselves logged in. Twitch grinned.

The starat's eyes moved quickly as he browsed through the options the screen gave him. He expected the drive to have a remote control, so there would be little permanent damage he could do, but he was sure he could find some way to delay activation.

"What can you see?" David asked, lingering close to the door with his hand resting on the handle.

"Most of the critical systems can only be physically reached from the very top," Twitch said with a hiss of frustration. His tail tip curled down. "We're not going to be able to get up there without being seen."

"Then we have to do something down here," David said. He leaned back on the door, ensuring that no one from outside could open it and surprise them.

Twitch hissed softly. There had to be something more that he had not seen. He flicked his hand to the right and his eyes widened. A schematic of the drive flashed up. "Can you see a datastick anywhere? We need to save this for Amy," he said, but his words slowly trailed off as he noticed something on the readout. His eyes were drawn to a cluster of systems less than a quarter of the way up the drive. Amongst them was the Denitchev crystal conversion control. If he could sabotage that, then he might be able to do more damage to the drive.

Twitch stepped away from the holoscreen. His eyes flicked around the small room, but he could see nothing that could be used to help in his sabotage. "Will you be alright down here without me?" he asked, turning back to his partner.

David nodded. "I'll be fine. I'll do what I can to save as much information as possible."

"If you can mess around with the sensors and data they have saved, then do what you can," Twitch said. His lip trembled. He bit down on it, hoping to hide the involuntary movement from his partner. He leaned in close, nuzzling against David's cheek, then lightly kissed him. "I'll be back soon."

"Be safe," David replied. He returned the kiss and held his arms around Twitch for a few moments. When he released the smaller starat, he had a weak smile on his muzzle.

"Only if you are too," Twitch said, forcing his voice to come across as bright and without a care in the world. His ears flicked, listening out for danger as he shuffled around his partner and pushed the door open. The low whine of a magtrain grew louder, and a few humans shouted in response to it, but no one else was close by. He tried to smile without fear as he pulled the door closed, but he couldn't quite manage it. He heard David bar the door from the inside.

Twitch squared his shoulders and looked up. It was just up to him now. Armed with nothing but a broken synthetic claw, he had to bring down a Denitchev drive the size of a skyscraper. The weight of his task threatened to crush him. He could not buckle. It was time to climb.

The starat was easily able to pull himself up a nearby ladder that connected to the scaffold above him. His toe claws clicked against the metal more than he would have liked, but all was quiet nearby. One side of the drive was exposed to the darkness of the chamber, but the towering structure had been built in a natural alcove. Three of the sides faced onto rock, with only a few metres of distance between them at the closest points. Twitch stayed to those sides as much as possible, only climbing the exposed side when there was no other way up.

Each level was almost identical. Cabling ran the outer walls of the drive, with venting pipes at regular intervals. Twitch knew he would not have to climb all the way to the top, but he was still daunted by the climb. Whatever the Inquisition were planning, Twitch needed to slow it down.

Occasionally, Twitch heard voices drifting up or down to his level, and he pressed himself flat against the drive every time he heard someone close by. No one noticed him, though one time he could see the shadow of a human pass over him as they walked on the level directly above him. On that occasion, he had quietly scampered away to find a new ladder to climb up.

The distant summit seemed to get no closer, no matter how many ladders Twitch climbed. His legs never got tired, but his arms and shoulders were weary as he hauled himself up; the rungs just that little bit too far apart to be a comfortable climb.

Twitch could see what he needed to reach. A large platform extended out on the exposed side of the drive, towards the crane beside it. On a ship, a regular sized Denitchev drive would be loaded with crystals semi-regularly, but this drive looked different. Twitch could see that the crane would lift massive crates of crystal fuel to the platform, which would then be inserted into the drive. Everything was set up like it needed to be a constant feeding of the drive's internal conversion chambers.

"What could they need that for?" Twitch whispered to himself, pausing for a moment on the last ladder he needed to climb. He could hear no one around, though the sounds drifting up from below made him cringe with fear. Every moment he delayed he risked being seen, or for someone to find David locked in the terminal room at the base.

Twitch's ears flicked as he hauled himself up onto the platform. A wide conveyor belt took up much of the space, with wide metal struts supporting the belt from both sides. Though it was switched off for the moment, the starat could see how it was used to feed crystals into the cavernous mouth of the drive. Everything inside the drive was dark and still, though the stench of cinnamon almost drew out another sneeze from the starat. Small fragments of Denitchev crystal were embedded into the rough surface of the belt.

There were no humans on the platform as Twitch glanced around. He took a moment to rub his aching upper arms, before hurrying towards the wide, cave-like entrance to the drive. The starat knew that it led through to the conversion chambers, where the crystals were pulverised into the Denitchev particles that were so critical to subspace travel. His ears curled and his tail shivered. The Inquisition had to be planning something troubling. The starat felt like he was overlooking an obvious fact, but he had no time to think what that might be.

Instead, Twitch hurried across the belt towards the opening of the conversion chambers. If he could find a way to sabotage the belt, then the Inquisition would struggle to keep their drive properly fuelled. It wasn't about destroying the drive. He could only damage it long enough to buy time for people like Amy to intervene.

The drive was not a standard design, with nothing like the belts being seen on drives of usual sizes, but Twitch was not surprised to see a control panel for the belt on the drive wall. He dug his claws into the side, prying it open to expose the electronics inside. There was nothing he could do with the control panel that could not easily be fixed. The starat's ears curled as his muzzle scrunched slightly. He turned away. There had to be something more.

Twitch's attention turned to the conveyor that would be used to feed the drive with its crystals. He slowly moved into the darkness, his feet cautiously testing out every step before he committed his weight. The belt had a little give to it. Ahead of the starat, there was only darkness. None of the limited light from inside the cave reached far into the drive. The powerful scent of cinnamon overwhelmed Twitch's nose.

Still cradling the broken claw in his hand, Twitch crouched down. He tested the claw against the belt, finding it managed to cut through the rough surface easily. He allowed himself a brief grin before he started to slice through the belt, creating a deep gouge through the tough material that he hoped would not be detected until the machine was powered on.

With his ears alert for any sound of movement on the platform, Twitch slowly worked his way across the entire width of the belt. When he made the final cut, he could feel the tension in the belt slacken, but nothing fell away just yet. The starat hurried onto the metal strut closest to him, not trusting his weight on the belt anymore.

He had done something, but Twitch wasn't sure if that was enough. His eyes turned further into the darkness. Slowly, he crept along the small strip of metal that supported his weight, feeling for the far end of the belt. He could see almost nothing at all, not even his own hands as they groped forward. He crawled on his knees, not wanting to catch himself by surprise and tumble into the conversion chamber.

Even still, the belt's end surprised the starat. His hand fell into empty air as the stench of cinnamon made him gag. He quickly sat back and held one hand over his nose. He wrinkled his muzzle and stuck out his tongue.

Once he had regained his composure, Twitch reached down beneath the belt, gripping onto his broken claw tightly. He groped for the gears that would turn the belt, finding the thick teeth easily. Relying on touch alone, Twitch struggled to find anything he could manipulate into failure, but he was encouraged by the thought that the humans would also struggle to repair it.

Fumbling with blind fingers, Twitch managed to wrench the gears out of alignment and wedge his claw into one of the gaps he created. The belt would fail when it split apart and would need replacing, but the starat hoped that the broken claw would grind the entire thing to a halt again. That might take a bit longer to diagnose and repair the problem.

A prickle down the back of Twitch's neck forced the starat into movement again. He didn't want to wait any longer than he had to. He wrinkled his nose and tried to force out the scent of cinnamon, but he could smell nothing else. His attention briefly fell back on the control panel. He reached inside and pulled out some of the wires, shredding them in his claws and leaving the entire thing unusable. Content that he could do little else, the starat crept back to the platform.

A human voice shouted. The voice came from the level below. Another answered from above.

Twitch swore quietly to himself. He cautiously crept along the metal walkway, keeping both hands against the wall as he tried to keep his claws from clicking with each step. His heart beat high in his throat. The humans were close, but he could not hear them on the ladders above and below the platform yet. They would not be far away.

Though he felt safer in the shadows, Twitch knew he would be quickly discovered if he waited too long. His eyes flicked from side to side. The ladders in either direction would be too dangerous. Humans would already be there, blocking his way down. His eyes turned to the crane at the far end of the platform, just beyond the edge of the conveyor belt. He teased his tongue over the edge of his sharp teeth. There was only one thing he could do. His toe claws extended, gripping against the metal beneath him.

Twitch ran. His ears focused on the sounds of humans above and below, leaving his eyes fixated on the crane at the far end of the platform. His feet thundered across the metal. Voices shouted, but he did his best to ignore them. To listen to them was to allow the fear of being caught to grow. He could not let himself get caught.

Another voice shouted. Demanding Twitch to stop. The starat had to suppress an instinctive urge to obey, forcing himself to keep moving his feet. The crane grew larger as he got nearer, but the gap between platform and crane also seemed to grow. Doubt crept into his mind.

Twitch's feet faltered. He glanced back. Three humans clambered up the ladders. Two more jumped down from the level above. One human carried a gun, but none of the others appeared to be armed. The starat looked forward again.

A crack of gunfire made the starat flinch. He expected a flare of pain, but he felt nothing but heat as the bullet missed him. A squeak of terror escaped his mouth.

The starat tried not to look down. He ran along the metal beam supporting the conveyor belt, and there was nothing to his right but a rapid plunge to the rocky ground. He was over a dozen storeys up, and with the higher gravity pulling down on his shoulders, he doubted he would survive such a fall without slowing himself down.

Then there was nothing in front of him either. Twitch reached the far end of the platform. He did not break stride as he pushed off hard, leaping into the air. His feet freewheeled for a few terrifying seconds as he began to fall, his arms outstretched for the latticed metal frame of the crane. He hooked one hand around the metal, jarring his shoulders as his torso impacted the side of the tall structure.

The humans fired another shot. The bullet pinged against the metal just above Twitch's head, sending sparks across his face. His grip slackened and he began to fall again.

Once more, Twitch got his hands around the scaffold surrounding the crane. His shoulders burned as they took most of the momentum of his fall. He hung for a moment, looking up to see the shadows of four humans looking down at him. None of them dared to follow him over the edge, but he had not bought himself much time. There would be others on the ground who could intercept him. He released his fingers again, falling once more, aiming for a small ledge partway down.

Twitch struck the little platform hard. It splintered and buckled in the impact, throwing his balance off and pitching him over the edge. A scream ripped from his throat as he began to fall with no control. The air whipped around him as the ground quickly approached.

With barely any thought, Twitch managed to snag his toes around the scaffold as it whistled by. His claws scraped into the metal as his arms flailed for something to hold onto. He couldn't get his hands around anything, but his legs shuddered as his fall slowed slightly. He twisted in mid-air, getting his feet down first.

Even as he managed to get some control on his fall, Twitch landed on solid rock with a jolting crack that sent fierce pain through his spine. The anchors in his hips held firm and lessened the force of the impact slightly, but he still felt like he had been punched in the stomach.

Something cracked in both knees and ankles, but the pain he had been expecting never arrived. Rock splintered beneath his feet, but his legs had proven to be strong enough. A small, rasping whimper escaped his lips as he struggled to gather his breath.

The starat knew he had no time to recover. Though his heart still hammered away in his chest, he forced himself to stand upright. His balance felt shaky as he began to move again, and his feet wobbled as he lifted them off the ground. He had done some serious damage to them, but for now they still worked. He could still walk, and that gave him the chance to get away.

First though, Twitch needed to make his way back around to David. He grimaced as he walked, aware that he should be feeling a lot of pain, but his legs were somehow able to mask those sensations. He was grateful for it, but he almost stumbled a couple of times. His feet failed to position correctly as he tried to place his weight down, making him feel disorientated.

Thankfully for Twitch, it seemed most of the guards and workers had already climbed up onto the scaffold to deal with him, and he had temporarily eluded them on his mad plummet down. His ears could pick up the sounds of a chase coming down, but he kept his focus on the ground for the moment. Once he was reunited with David, then he could start thinking about the humans again.

Twitch worked his way around to the front of the drive, and he was relieved to see that the terminal room door was still closed. He lightly knocked against the door three times and waited a few moments for a response from within. He barely breathed until he heard a quiet voice from inside.

"Twitch?"

"It's me. We need to hurry."

The door quickly unlocked and opened. David carried a screwdriver in his hand, brandishing it almost like a weapon. "Did you do it?"

Twitch shrugged, before he reached out to take David's free hand. "I can only hope so. What about you?"

David held up the small datastick and nodded. His jaw tensed. "Got everything I could find."

Twitch breathed a small sigh of relief, but he cringed as he heard a human voice shouting from somewhere above. "Good, but come on. They know we're here."

"Where to?" David asked, following Twitch.

Twitch hissed softly beneath his breath. "Train station. There's a magtrain at the platform. We might be able to sneak on."

David nodded. He offered no alternative options for them to take. Twitch wasn't sure there was any. He didn't even know if the train would be a viable option, but he wasn't going to just stand around and wait to be captured.

This time, the two starats didn't need to slip through broken wire fencing to escape. The human security force had left the gates open, leaving a clear path to safety. Now they were no longer in danger of hitting the drive, a few scattered shots were fired down at the starats. None hit their target, though Twitch could feel the heat of a couple pass by. They had to get to cover, quickly.

David let out a yelp of fear, and for a terrible moment Twitch thought he'd been hit, but the larger starat kept moving just behind him. They clasped hands so they wouldn't get separated, and after a few terrifying seconds, they were able to get amongst the cover of the compound buildings.

Twitch pulled David between the first two buildings. The occasional gunfire ceased, but Twitch knew it wouldn't be long before it started again.

"You're limping. Are you alright?" David gasped.

Twitch glanced down to his legs. Nothing outwardly felt wrong, but he could feel a strange grating whenever he moved his ankles or knees. "I, uh. Jumped a long way down," he said, a nervous smile coming to his muzzle. "Glad Amy built these things pretty tough."

"How far?" David asked, his voice tightening up in fear.

Twitch shook his head. "Fourteenth storey, I think," he replied. His head spun just from thinking about it. His hand tightened around David's. "Hit some things on the way down. Tell you all about it when we're safe. Promise."

David bit his lip and nodded, but he kept quiet. It wasn't far between the small compound and the train station. The magtrain was still at the platform, and it showed no signs that it was about to depart.

An alarm started to wail throughout the cavern. Twitch didn't know how many reinforcements the Inquisition could call on, but he knew that there was already nearly two dozen chasing after them. If too many came then they would be quickly overwhelmed and discovered, no matter how hard they tried to hide.

The magtrain station was little more than a single platform with a low prefabricated metal building to the side. The tracks terminated at the closest end of the platform, and the gleaming white train itself consisted of just a pair of carriages. There weren't any humans on the platform, and nor did there appear to be any on the train either.

Twitch flicked his tail, barely daring to believe they might actually be able to make it.

He didn't see the human until she stepped out of the shadows.

He didn't see the baton she held in her hand until it smashed into his torso.

Twitch doubled over in pain. All the air was knocked from his lungs. He wheezed and struggled to breath. Pressure was placed on the back of his neck, preventing him from rising once more. There was a dull thud as David was also knocked to the ground.

They had been caught.

# chapter two

Twitch and David were both bundled onto the train with their arms and legs bound. Two out-of-breath humans had joined them to stand watch as the train began to speed its way out of the great cavern. Their captors didn't seem to realise the nature of Twitch's legs, as they had used nothing more than simple nylon rope to bind his limbs, but Twitch didn't try to escape. Not just yet. He had no desire to be shot.

They hadn't been questioned, nor searched beyond a quick frisk for weapons. No one had said anything to either of them. Twitch hadn't wanted to speak first. David kept his head down the whole time, his tail tucked in between his legs as he sat awkwardly with his arms pinched between his back and the seat.

Twitch didn't know where they were being taken, or even how fast they were moving. There was no point of reference outside the train, with nothing but pitch darkness outside the windows as they travelled through the underground tunnel. Only the occasional sway of the magtrain gave away that they were moving at all.

The two guards spoke quietly amongst themselves at the other end of the carriage. One of them, with pale skin and deep black hair, lazily held a pistol in one hand, keeping it aimed in the general direction of the starats. Twitch kept his ears pricked up for any interesting titbits of conversation, but they were simply talking about plans for their evening, with nothing particularly giving Twitch any information he needed to know.

Then a word was mentioned that instantly got Twitch's attention. He struggled to keep looking down at the floor, but one of the guards had mentioned 'Cardinal'.

"...said he was getting the first flight out of here."

"What was he even here for? All he seemed to do was scowl and order us around."

"He was looking for someone, I was told. A starat, weirdly."

The pale human scuffed his foot against the floor. His pistol tapped against the side of his chair. "Why would he want a starat?" he said with a growl. Twitch chanced a glance up to see the human's lip curled in disgust.

"Did something back on Terra," the other human said with a shrug. Twitch looked towards her only for a moment. She was dark-skinned. She had tattooed the Inquisition symbol onto the side of her neck. Twitch glanced away again before she looked to him. "I think he lost the starat though, so he's going back to Mars to tell the Vatican how close we are."

"These fuckers better not have done anything."

Twitch lowered his ears and turned his head away. He hoped they didn't realise how clearly he could hear them.

"If they did, we'll fix it."

The pale human raised his voice. "You're not going to win. It's too late to stop us."

Twitch said nothing. He wanted to. He longed to retort back at them, but the meekness was returning. The words felt like they were caught in his throat, and he just turned his head and stared down at the floor. He wanted to be brave like Captain Rhys, but he didn't know how. He closed his eyes and tried to control his rapid breathing.

Before the humans could say anything else, the train began to decelerate. A few lights flashed past the windows as it slowed, before it arrived at another small platform that looked much like the first. From his few glimpses out the window, Twitch could see less rock and more concrete of built-up corridors and rooms.

The guards approached Twitch and David and removed the bonds around their legs, before they roughly grabbed the starats by the collar. They were dragged from the train as it came to a complete halt and thrown to the platform. Twitch whimpered in pain as the impact with the ground jolted his stomach, which felt bruised from the human's baton. Three more humans approached.

"What's the meaning of this?" one of the newcomers barked out. Twitch couldn't see anything about him other than his blotchy red skin and thick black moustache. He wore robes similar to those Cardinal Erik had worn on Ceres. The Martian was mercifully nowhere to be seen.

"These two were caught trying to sabotage the drive," the pale guard said. He kicked out at Twitch, catching him in the ribs. Twitch tried not to react, but he couldn't prevent the whimper of pain.

"Any damage?"

"We're still trying to work that out."

The robed human sighed. "Any ID on them?"

"None. We're not sure if they're erased from the system or hiding their identity in some other way."

"Are they new to the planet?"

"Uh, we haven't checked that yet. We'll get right on it."

"Very well." The robed human snapped his fingers. "Bring them. They'll have to share a cell with another miscreant while we work out who they are and who they work for."

One of the guards grabbed Twitch by the back of the neck. The starat yelped out in pain as human hands closed around his fur and skin, roughly dragging him away from the platform. He didn't struggle. He just let himself fall limp in the human's strong grip as he was taken after the robed man ahead. Being talked about like he wasn't present brought back unpleasant memories of Ceres. He had hoped never to experience that again, and he struggled to hold the dark thoughts at bay.

The corridors all looked much the same. There were no windows to look out of, leading Twitch to believe they were probably still underground. The lights that lit the smooth walls were bright and harsh, hurting Twitch's eyes if he looked too close to them. He kept his head bowed, not that he had much choice with the hand gripped around his neck.

A heavy metal door slid open. Twitch's bonds were cut, but before he could react, the human forcefully threw him inside the cell. David followed just behind as Twitch rolled out of the way. The door slammed closed behind them, almost crushing David's tail in the process. The darkness that followed was absolute, with not a single sliver of light making it around the door.

"You alright?" Twitch asked. He struggled to sit up, with his arms still bound behind his back.

"Little sore, but not too bad," David replied. He shuffled in the darkness. "Got anything to cut these ropes?"

Twitch struggled to get his back against the wall behind him, positioning himself so his feet were able to touch up against David's bound hands. Working in the dark, Twitch was careful with his movements. He didn't want to hurt his partner in the process, but he was able to scratch his remaining claws through the nylon bonds around David's wrists. His claws snagged. With one firm pull, Twitch was able to slice through the rope, which shredded and fell away from David. In a moment, David was able to grope behind Twitch's back to free him of his bonds too. The two hugged tightly.

"Don't suppose you have a torch in there too, do you?" David asked with a nervous laugh.

Twitch patted around his shorts, glad to feel the outline of his tablet still in his pocket. He pulled it out and fumbled around for the button on the side to switch the screen on. It had no service, but the torch still worked. There wasn't much light, but it was enough for him to see David sat beside the wall.

Just a few metres away was another body.

Twitch yelped as he recoiled, almost dropping the tablet as the second person moved. They were human.

"I thought I recognised your voices," the human said. He leaned forward into the harsh white light of Twitch's tablet. Oily black hair fell down over his forehead, obscuring his eyes and nose, but Twitch still recognised who it was.

"Tyler?" he squeaked in surprise. "I thought they'd taken you away."

"They did," the human replied, barely biting down on sardonic laughter. "I'm not exactly here for my good health."

"Thank you for not telling them about us," David said, holding his hand out for the human. Tyler did not take it. David's hand slowly fell down. "We're sorry if we got you in trouble. We didn't mean to cause any problems."

Twitch curled his tail. He wanted to sit down, but he didn't trust his damaged legs. The joints felt stiff. He wasn't sure he would be able to stand up again if he sat down. He swayed on the spot as the sensors down his legs struggled to tell him which way was down.

"I thought you'd be smart enough to run as far as you could," the human said tersely.

Twitch grinned nervously. "We're not always that clever."

"I did say we should," David said hesitantly. His hand rested on Twitch's shoulder.

Twitch sighed softly and nodded. David's earlier advice to go back to Amy was certainly sounding a lot more preferable now. "We should have, yeah. But we needed to know what they're doing."

Tyler ran his hand through his long hair. "Well shit, if that's what you're after, I could have told you that," he said. He looked between the two starats. Even in the darkness, Twitch could see that he looked paler than he had done on the surface.

"Do we want to know?" David asked nervously.

"If it means you'll get off this planet and run as far as you can? Yes, you'll want to know. This planet isn't safe for you. For anyone." Tyler thumbed towards the door. "You saw what they've got back there, didn't you?"

"The Denitchev drive?" Twitch asked.

Tyler nodded. "Then it shouldn't take much to work out what they're doing with it. Think about what the drive does and how it works."

"It emits particles into the air, and then an electric charge contained by an electromagnetic shield displaces everything into subspace when there's a high enough concentration," Twitch said. He frowned. It didn't make sense. Why would the Inquisition need one of those? Then he went cold. "Oh shit."

"What do you mean?" David asked. His voice sounded tight, but Twitch didn't look across to his partner. He didn't even move.

Thankfully for Twitch, Tyler was able to explain things. "Everything within an electromagnetic shield is displaced when there's enough particles in the air and a strong enough electrical current is discharged through it. The drive back there is big enough to coat the entire planet in particles. And the shield..."

"The one that protects the planet from Prox," David whispered.

"They'd push the whole planet into subspace," Twitch said in horror. His tail flicked nervously. He wanted to pace around, but he didn't trust his damaged ankles to support his weight properly. He tapped his fingers against his jaw. "But the shield would still protect the planet from subspace, right? Another electric charge and it would jump back to realspace."

Tyler shook his head. "Not if they trigger the shields to fail a few moments later. The entire planet would be consumed by subspace."

Twitch flicked his ears. He remembered something strange he had found in Tyler's home. A shield emitter strong enough to cover the building. The bunker had been airtight as well, probably strong enough to remain intact in a vacuum. It had been a safehouse to protect against the Inquisition's plan. "Your bunker..." the starat said, but Tyler cut across him.

"Every Inquisition home and stronghold has one. When the time is right, the shields go up and protect the devoted faithful. When the planet is gone, they jump back to realspace, drifting where the planet used to be," the human explained. "A few ships are prepared, ready to pick up the survivors. I doubt we'll be amongst them."

"I damaged the machine," Twitch said. His voice shook, and he grasped hold of his tail in both hands. The synthetic limb felt strange still. The fur just wasn't quite right, and it wasn't as warm as his flesh had been. "I stopped them for now, right?"

Tyler sighed and shook his head. "I doubt you did much, I'm sorry. Last I heard, they were planning to go in a couple of weeks. I don't think you would have delayed them at all."

Twitch whimpered softly. "We have to get out of here. We need to stop this."

"What can you do about it?" Tyler asked, laughing coldly. "No disrespect, but you're just two starats. The Inquisition have been working on this for years."

"Not us," Twitch said. He reached out to grasp David's hand tightly, hoping to reassure his partner that he wanted to do nothing else against the Inquisition. "But we know people who can help. People who are strong enough to stop them."

"Like who?" Tyler said sceptically.

Twitch lowered his tablet, taking away a lot of the light that filled the dark room. "Amy Jennings might be able to stop them. Captain Rhys knows people in the military, when he gets back. Minister Bakir too. She offered to help us before," Twitch said, counting off on his fingers.

"Bakir?" Tyler said, laughing again. "The fucking president has been planning this with the Inquisition. The government isn't going to do shit."

"We don't know that," Twitch said, his voice small and quiet. He stared down at the dirty floor, swaying on unsteady feet.

"I do," Tyler said, tapping at his chest with one hand. His lip curled into a sneer. "Jennings is too pre-occupied with Terra, and the military is shackled by the government. There is no stopping this. There never has been. It's always been trying to stay safe during it. And let me tell you. Right here is not safe."

"We have to do something," Twitch said, his voice trembling at the mere thought of it. Fighting against humans had always been something taboo and wrong. For a starat on Ceres, standing up against humanity meant to welcome death. Escaping the meek starat he had once been was a struggle, but he forced himself to lift his eyes and stare Tyler in the face. His hands clenched into fists.

Tyler gestured around the dark room. "What do you expect to be able to do? They're not going to just let us walk free."

Twitch snarled. He felt David's hand squeeze around his, but he shook his partner away. "You're just going to give up and let billions die?" the starat growled. He shakily rose to his feet, feeling his left ankle almost collapsing beneath his weight. "You'll do nothing?"

"There's nothing we can do," Tyler replied with a resigned sigh. He spread his hands and looked across to the two starats.

"I don't believe that. There has to be something," Twitch growled. He limped towards the door, taking the light from his tablet with him. He flicked his ears and frowned. "When do you think they might open this door again? They have to give us some food or something, right?"

"Maybe, yeah," Tyler said with a shrug. "They haven't yet and I've been here for a few hours. Busting for a piss, but they haven't even let me go to the bathroom.

"Charming," David muttered. Twitch could hear his partner grinding his teeth through the darkness.

Twitch spun around on his toes, trying to ignore the harsh grind in his ankle as he moved. He growled again and felt like throwing something at Tyler. "You used to be with these people," he snarled. Though the darkness, Twitch could see the human's eyes widen in fear. "You know how they work. Help us and we can stop this. Or you can die here, sad and pathetic."

Tyler slapped both hands to his forehead and groaned. "Alright, I'll help you. What do you need to know?"

A smile slowly spread across Twitch's muzzle. "When they open this door, whether to give us food, interrogate us, gloat at us, whatever. When they do that, how many humans will there be? What's the protocol?"

"Two, usually. More if we, er... they consider the prisoners to be particularly dangerous. To be honest, they won't consider us dangerous. Two starats and a disgraced priest. They won't be threatened," Tyler explained. He tapped his foot against the floor.

"Humans always underestimate starats. It's how we're able to get away with so much, isn't it, David?" Twitch said, forcing a small giggle into his voice. He bounced on his toes, trying to hide his fears in manic energy.

"However unjust that may be at times, it isn't now," David warned. Twitch could hear him rise to his feet. "We are unarmed, and they aren't. I don't like where this is going."

Twitch turned around to face the darkness. "I'm not talking about arms," he said. His tail flicked nervously. "I think I have a plan."

\*\*\*

Twitch sat back against the wall, nervously tapping his fingers over the grimy floor. His ears angled forward to listen to the sounds of footsteps just outside. Tyler and David breathed heavily as they waited in position.

The starat pulled himself a bit more upright. It was difficult to get into a comfortable position without his legs attached, and he kept pushing an uncomfortable pressure on the connectors to his tail. The last thing he wanted was for that to disconnect as well. He already knew he was risking himself. He was the bait needed to distract the guards.

The door opened. Light flooded into the room, and Twitch had to bring his arm up to cover his eyes as he was momentarily blinded. His eyes watered. He blinked a few times, trying to clear his vision. Three silhouettes moved in front of him. He looked up to see a robed human standing in the doorway, just behind two armed guards. Their pistols were pointed towards him.

None of them had time to speak. David and Tyler moved quickly. They both struck at the same time, striking the two guards with Twitch's cybernetic legs.

David used an underarm swing to bash Twitch's leg against the guard's chin, while Tyler favoured an overarm movement to club his guard over the top of the head. Both humans crumpled and fell to the floor limply.

The robed human didn't give them a chance to attack him. He turned on his heel and fled, just about evading Tyler's wild swing in the process. David's hand on Tyler's arm stopped the human chasing after his quarry.

"Wait here," David said, his voice raspy as he crouched down next to the human he had felled. His hand pressed against the human's neck, where it remained for a few seconds. He then leaned across to do the same to the other human. "They're still alive, but they're really not going to like it when they wake up. Give me the leg and get their guns."

Tyler crouched down beside David, passing the starat Twitch's leg. The human then pulled the guns out of the fallen guards' limp hands.

Twitch could barely breath as he watched everything, feeling so detached from it all. His plan had somehow worked, though he hadn't counted on the third human escaping. They didn't have long before more humans would descend on them, this time prepared for anything and carrying even more weapons.

David tugged at Twitch's shorts.

That finally brought a reaction out of Twitch, and he grinned at his partner to hide the doubts in his mind. "Not the time for that, is it?" he said.

David playfully swatted at Twitch's ears. "Get these back on. We need to move quickly," he replied. He smirked and lightly kissed Twitch on the cheek, before returning to Tyler.

Twitch sighed softly and started to fit his legs back on. It was a simple process, and he easily found the latches and pushed firmly. He always felt like he was pushing too hard and was about to break something, and he gritted his teeth together and flicked his tail nervously. Then there was a small click and the limb secured against his hip.

Sensation staggered through the limb a few seconds later, and Twitch wiggled his toes to make sure that they still worked. The middle toe didn't move at all, and the others felt stiff. He grimaced as he turned his attention to the other leg. That one was a little quicker to attach, and he was still able to move all his toes when he did, though his ankle felt loose instead. His ears pinned down. He needed to get somewhere safe so he could start fixing them.

David held his hand out to Twitch. "Ready to go?"

Twitch used David's weight to help pull himself up to his unsteady feet. He almost pitched forward as his legs tried to adjust for an uneven ground that wasn't present. Taking just a single step was difficult. His legs rebelled every movement, but after the first few steps, he felt something click and the movements became easier once more.

"They giving you trouble?" David asked in concern.

Twitch nodded and grimaced. "I'd be even worse if I didn't have them," he replied, rubbing his hands over his thighs to check the sensory feedback.

Tyler held out a pistol to the two starats, just between them both. Twitch glanced up to his partner. David's muzzle scrunched into a grimace as he made no move to take the offered weapon.

Twitch warily eyed the pistol, before reluctantly taking it in his hands. The weapon felt unfamiliar to him, and he struggled to work out the best way to grip it.

"You used one before?" the human asked.

Twitch shook his head.

"Just point the right end at any humans you see, other than me. Squeeze the trigger when you're sure," Tyler explained. He corrected Twitch's grip slightly and pulled the starat's finger away from the trigger. "You have enough ammo for twelve shots. Don't waste them."

There had only been two pistols to give out, and Tyler kept the other. David remained unarmed, and he stayed behind Twitch and Tyler as they cautiously emerged out into the corridors. An alarm started to sound, with flashing red lights pulsing over the hard white that usually illuminated the corridors. For the moment at least, there wasn't any sounds of following footsteps, but Twitch knew it wouldn't be long.

Tyler knew where he was going. He took the lead, with Twitch following right behind. David held onto Twitch's hand as he brought up the rear.

The human led the two starats down one of the corridors, before pushing open a fire escape. Concrete stairs branched out in both directions in a squared spiral. Twitch glanced down. The bottom of the stairs was quite some distance away. A quick look up made him realise that the top was just as far.

"We'd better hurry before they try to cut us off," Tyler warned. He gestured up the stairs.

"All of them?" Twitch squeaked.

"All the way to the top, yes. Come on, hurry," the human replied.

Twitch whimpered. His legs barely worked on the flat floor of the corridors. He wasn't sure how they'd react to climbing the long flights of stairs. He struggled to lift his feet high enough. Both ankles were weak, and his foot dangled down limply with each step. He almost stumbled several times, but he was able to arrest his fall before tripping.

Sweat came to Twitch's brow as he climbed. David occasionally gave him a gentle push from behind, but he had to resort to dragging himself up with his hand on the railings.

"Where does this lead?" David called out. They had passed by several closed doors, but Tyler hadn't been tempted by any of them.

"Different levels of the cathedral undercrofts," Tyler explained, throwing one arm out to the nearest door. "Usually used for research and development. Right at the top is a door that opens to the main street. We need to get to that before they realise we took the fire escape. Out there, we can blend in easily."

A door slammed far below them.

"I think they already know," David muttered, only loud enough for Twitch's ears.

Tyler paused and held his hand out to pull Twitch up the stairs a little faster. The door just below them burst open, and three humans sprinted out into the stairwell.

Twitch didn't even think. He lifted his arm and aimed. He squeezed the trigger. The pistol almost jumped out of his hand from the recoil, but his shot met its target. A human fell, clutching his chest. The other two collapsed after quickfire shots from Tyler.

"Go!" the human yelled. The sounds of pursuit were getting closer.

David grabbed hold of Twitch's free hand and pulled him further up the stairs.

Twitch followed numbly. He couldn't think about what he had just done. Not yet.

Another door opened. This time further up the stairs.

Tyler swore. He was able to shoot one human, but there was half a dozen of them already, blocking passage further up.

Twitch lifted his pistol and fired three shots. Only one hit the target, and one human fell back with a wound to his shoulder. Concrete dust puffed up from the wall behind the humans as the other shots missed.

David didn't stop. A shout of warning came down from the humans, but David ignored them as he charged up to meet them. Twitch didn't let go of his partner's hand, though he was thrown clear as David's shoulder slammed against a couple of humans. They fell back and David burst through to the other side, but Twitch stumbled on the stairs and felt a human's foot press down on his back.

Another human tried to grab Twitch's legs. He kicked back and felt his foot impact with their jaw. Bone cracked at the force of the kick, and a muffled whimper of pain was quickly silenced.

The body pinning Twitch down slumped and fell. The starat staggered up to his feet, only to have another guard slam him against the railings. He yelped in fear as he felt the metal railings give slightly from the impact. He kicked up hard against the human's legs and twisted his torso to unbalance his grappler.

The human screamed as he toppled over the edge. His screams lasted for a very long time.

Twitch couldn't think about that yet, either.

David's hand was bloody as the other starat took hold of him again. He had been clipped across the upper arm. His jaw tensed tight; his ears curled low. The two starats had gotten past the doorway, but there were more humans coming.

Tyler had been shot in the chest, but he was able to club the last guard in the stairwell over the head to disable him. The human crouched down for a moment, plucking something from one of their fallen foes. He looked grim as he stared down the corridor. Half a dozen humans looked up, many carrying pistols which were all trained on Tyler.

The voice of the red-faced human called out from the corridor. "Brother Tyler, don't be foolish."

"Go," Tyler said, not looking back to the starats.

"Not without you," Twitch said. He tried to pull away from David, but his partner had a tight grip around his wrist.

"I'm right behind you. Go," Tyler snapped back. He raised his right hand up.

Twitch could see what the human held now. A grenade.

"Run! Now!" Tyler shouted. He primed the grenade and arched his arm back to throw. "Get out of here."

Tyler tossed the grenade down the stairwell and started to turn. The humans opened fire. Blood sprayed as Tyler fell.

David tugged at Twitch's hand again. This time the starat obliged. He turned to run as fast as his damaged legs could carry him.

Twitch didn't look back.

David barged open the door to freedom and sunlight shone onto the starats. At the same moment, an explosion ripped through the stairwell. Flecks of concrete bounced from the walls and drifted down in dust.

Twitch was thrown forward from the blast. His ears were filled with screams, but they fell to silence as the door slammed closed behind them. Smoke drifted out from the cracks around the doorway. He held the pistol up in one shaking hand in case the door opened again, but it remained shut.

Slowly, Twitch's attention was diverted to their surroundings. They had emerged in a small park next to one of the towering skyscrapers of Hadrian. Alien plants swayed in a non-existent breeze. A sticky red tendril brushed across Twitch's shoulder, making the starat yelp in surprise. He rolled away from the grasping tendril and pulled himself up to his feet, batting away David's offered bloodied hand of assistance.

"We should…" Twitch started to say, before he was forced to stop by the building urge to throw up. He took a deep breath and squeezed his eyes closed as he tried to suppress the rancid feeling in his throat. He couldn't get that scream out of his head. Nor could he forget how that human had just crumpled when he'd been shot.

Twitch realised that David was saying his name. He slowly looked up to his partner. "Go…" Twitch said quietly. The immediate urge to throw up had receded, though his stomach remained unsettled. "We should go."

David pulled Twitch away from the door and deeper into the park. He could already hear the sounds of people moving through a nearby street, seemingly unaware of what had happened so close by. There, they would be able to blend into the crowd and complete their escape from the Inquisition. A whimper escaped Twitch's lips as he finally looked back. No one followed them. They were free.

Twitch could only hope that the price to pay was not too severe.

# chapter three

Twitch felt numb. He was back in the semi-familiar confines of the hotel room Amy had procured for their stay in Hadrian. The city glowed brightly out of the window, shining in defiance of the long night. Normally, Twitch would find it beautiful, and though he looked out at the city, he didn't observe anything. He just sat on the edge of the bed, his hands draped across his lap and his tail curled up behind him.

Food didn't interest him. He wasn't sure he would be able to tolerate food. The mere thought of it unsettled his stomach. People had died because of him. He had killed them.

David knelt in front of Twitch and took both of his partner's hands in his own. "Do you want to talk about it?" he said softly.

Twitch shook his head. He talked about it anyway. "I can't stop thinking about his scream," he whimpered. He closed his eyes, but that only made things worse. Now he could see it playing out like a projector on his eyelids. He snapped them open again, staring into David's comforting brown eyes.

David squeezed tight around Twitch's hands. "You did what you had to do. We all did."

"But did it need to come to that? They didn't need to... we didn't need to..." Tears finally came to Twitch's eyes. He didn't try to stop them as they flowed down his face.

"They would have killed us if we didn't," David said. He lifted one of Twitch's hands up to kiss it gently.

"That doesn't make it right," Twitch squeaked. He didn't try to pull away from David, but he couldn't look his partner in the eyes. He looked down and shuddered.

"Right? No," David admitted. He kissed Twitch's hand again, before sitting down on the bed beside the other starat. His arm gently wrapped around Twitch's body, pulling him close. "It doesn't make it right. It made it necessary."

Twitch pressed his head against David's shoulder, remembering too late that his partner was injured. He pulled back from the slight gasp of pain that David tried to suppress. "I'm sorry," Twitch said with a groan. "You're hurt too and I'm making this all about me."

David pressed a finger to Twitch's lips. "I patched myself up in the bathroom a few minutes ago when I called Amy. It was just a glancing hit, so I'll be fine. I'm worried about you."

"You called Amy already?" Twitch asked, his ears flicking up. He was eager for any distraction for his mind to cling onto. Anything that rid his ears of the ringing screams of the human as he fell. His voice stumbled and nearly faded into a silent whisper. "What did you tell her?"

"I told her we've done what she asked, and that we want to go home. She promised to send Mortimer out to pick us up. He'll be here first thing tomorrow morning."

"Will we be safe tonight?" Twitch asked. His eyes drifted back towards the cityscape shining brightly outside the hotel window. In the distance, he could just about make out the lights from the church.

"They didn't know who we were and no one followed us here. They can't find us," David replied. He kissed Twitch on the forehead. "Then tomorrow we'll see Amy and then we'll never have to do anything like this again."

Twitch knew it was a lie, but it was one he was willing to believe. "Promise?" he asked.

"I promise."

Twitch sighed and nodded. He looked down at his legs. They had been what had caused all of this. If he hadn't needed new ones, then he would never have needed to accept Amy's offer for the replacement cybernetics. Now they were broken and all the tools he had to fix them were in Caledonia, on the other side of the planet, or so it felt. "We should never have agreed to this."

David gently rested his hands on Twitch's thighs, his fingers brushing through the synthetic fur. "It was never a choice," he said quietly. His ears drooped as he gently stroked Twitch's legs. "This isn't your fault. None of this is."

Twitch whimpered and bit his lip. The pain of his teeth against his soft flesh momentarily distracted him from the turbulent thoughts that plagued his mind. "Then who's fault is it?"

"Cardinal Erik, for hurting you," David said with a growl, pulling up his top lip. "Amy for sending us here. Me, for not protecting you when I should have."

"It's not your fault," Twitch said with a gasp, lifting his eyes to stare at David. His partner's eyes were watery.

David smiled softly. "I'll believe that if you accept it's not your fault as well."

Twitch exhaled heavily through his nose. He lowered his head again. "I can try."

David kissed Twitch on the forehead, then rubbed his hands down towards Twitch's knees. "Do you need help taking those off?" he offered.

Twitch tried to curl his toes. Only half of them reacted. He nodded sadly. As much as he hated the feeling of having nothing beneath his hips, he knew that he was only continuing to damage the broken limbs by continuing to use them. "Please, yeah. Then can you help me have a shower?"

David leaned in and kissed Twitch again. "Anything for you, my love. Come on. Let's get you cleaned up."

Twitch didn't move as David undressed him, before he carefully removed the damaged cybernetic limbs and rested them against the wall. He let himself get carried into the bathroom. He longed for the cleansing water to wash over him. He could only hope that it would wash away the sins of his actions. Best of all though, it would mask the tears that continued to flow.

\*\*\*

Twitch didn't sleep that night. Every time he closed his eyes and rested his head back on his pillow, he could hear the screams of the human again. He could hear Tyler's last, desperate words to get them to flee. He could feel the explosion on his fur. Tears wetted his cheeks again.

David had been able to fall asleep relatively easily. The larger starat was snoring softly as he lay on his back. Usually, the sound was soothing to Twitch, but his troubled mind found it an extra irritation that stopped him from sleeping.

After several hours of trying to sleep without success, Twitch slowly dragged himself out of bed. He hadn't reattached his legs after getting clean, but he didn't bother putting them on again. He didn't want to go far. He crawled across the floor to the balcony door. It was difficult trying to open the door, as he had to balance himself carefully before reaching up for the handle, but he was able to slide the glass screen open without waking David.

On the balcony was a small coffee table with a couple of chairs so someone could sit and overlook the city while enjoying something to eat or drink. Though Twitch's stomach was beginning to growl with hunger, he had no desire to drag himself back inside to fix himself something to eat. Instead, he just pushed the door closed behind him and hauled himself up onto one of the chairs.

Without his thighs to support him, he had to slump back in the chair awkwardly to sit comfortably. At least the chair was designed with a starat in mind, so he had somewhere to put his tail. The air was cool as it brushed over his fur. The heat of Prox had been chased away by the deepening night, and it would be some time before the star returned to warm the air once more.

Despite it being the middle of the night – both in terms of Prox and what the clocks said – the city was far from quiet. Twitch could still hear the faint whine of the electric cars as they made their way through the city streets, and the light murmur of conversation as it drifted up from the humans and starats walking to and from the towering buildings. Even at night, whether by Prox or by the Terran-style clock Centaura still adhered to, there was always work happening.

Twitch curled his tail around the legs of the chair. He had tried to be brave like Captain Rhys, but that wasn't who he was. He wasn't a fighter or a soldier like the former human. He was a mechanic; a starat who fixed machines. Anything that involved taking a life was not a fight he wanted to be involved with.

The starat looked up to the sky. Clouds had covered most of the stars, obscuring any potential view of Sol. Twitch sighed. It wasn't that he preferred his life on Ceres. Thinking about his time then sent a disgusted crawl through his tail, but it was certainly much simpler. Back then he only had to worry himself with the next job and keeping out of the way of the humans who ran the port. Now, he didn't really know where he fitted in to anything, or how he was supposed to act.

Rain began to fall. It was only a light sprinkling of water from the clouds above, but it brought with it a whole new smell that Twitch enjoyed filling his nose. He closed his eyes and leaned back. No matter how dark his mood or how foul his thoughts, the sound and smell of rain would always be something that brought a smile to his face. It was something he had never experienced on Ceres. There was no rain, no weather, on the dwarf planet. Every rain shower was a delight to Twitch, and he found that he loved going out into the rain and getting his fur wet. For now, he was just happy to sit back and listen to it fall.

The memories of the day were seared into Twitch's mind, but the soothing sound of the rain was able to slow his thoughts. He held one hand out, resting it on the balcony railings. Rain gently pattered against his fur. His head began to droop forward onto his chest as his eyes finally began to close.

***

The next thing Twitch realised was that he was being woken up with David's hand on his shoulder. He jerked awake and blearily blinked a couple of times, trying to clear his vision. The rains of the night had passed, and the dark sky was glistening with starlight.

"I thought you might need this," David said, drawing Twitch's attention back to his partner. He realised David was holding out a cup of fresh coffee for him. He took the cup gratefully, holding the porcelain mug close to his muzzle so the steam drifted over his face to warm him up.

"Thanks," Twitch said quietly. His tail thumped against the back of the chair. It was a rare occasion when David voluntarily gave him a cup of coffee, so he knew there had to be a reason behind it.

"Mortimer will be here in ten minutes. I've already got everything ready to go, but I thought you needed as much sleep as you could get," David explained.

A small smile pulled at the corners of Twitch's muzzle. He knew there had to be a reason why David needed him to wake up quickly. He sipped at the coffee, finding it almost at a drinkable temperature. "Do you mind helping me with my legs again?"

"You wait there and I'll get them for you," David said, patting Twitch on the shoulder before heading back inside the hotel room.

Twitch tried to force out a giggle to reassure David that he was alright, but he couldn't get the sound through his tight throat. His mind felt refreshed by his sleep, almost like the rains had washed away most of his concerns. He could still feel them just beneath the surface of his thoughts, but for now the rivers of his mind had been replenished enough that he was able to keep them submerged. But they were still there, like jagged rocks just below the surface.

By the time he had finished his coffee, David had helped him reattach his legs and finish getting dressed. His legs felt just as unsteady as they had the previous day. If anything, his balance on them felt like it was deteriorating faster. He needed to lean on David for his first few steps, before he could feel the sensors in his tail helping to calibrate his legs once more.

Someone knocked on the door. A shiver of alarm passed through Twitch's body, before he remembered that Mortimer was due to pick them up. He leaned a hand against the wall to support himself while David went to open the door.

Mortimer was alone. He was dressed in his usual smart suit and tie, which Twitch still thought looked a little out of place on the furred body of a starat. Mortimer straightened his tie as he stepped inside the hotel room. "Glad to see you both looking well," he said. His voice was quiet and tentative, as though he was already aware of the troubles David and Twitch had gone through.

David scoffed as he closed the door, but Twitch quickly spoke up before his partner could say anything. "We need to speak to Amy, and we need to speak to her as soon as we can," he said urgently.

Mortimer nodded, seemingly ignoring David's scorn. "I did hear so much. Are you ready to leave? I have transport waiting to take us back to Caledonia."

"We've been ready to leave since the moment we got here," David growled. He advanced on Mortimer, and for a moment Twitch was convinced his partner was about to hit the suited starat, but he just snatched the bag on the table beside Mortimer. "We should never have even come. There had to be someone better than us."

Mortimer held a hand to his chest. He didn't step back at all, despite the fury in David's eyes. "You can take that up with Amy in a few hours, I promise you that."

"Oh, we certainly will," David growled. He held out his hand for Twitch to take. "Now get us out of here."

*\*\**

Mortimer's transport was a car parked just outside the hotel, which took the three starats through to the nearest airport on the outskirts of the city. A private shuttle was waiting for them there, with only a pilot to greet them and no one else boarding. Less than an hour after leaving the hotel, they were in the air above Hadrian and already making the approach to the great ocean that divided the two continents.

Mortimer didn't press for information as they flew across to Caledonia. The starat remained quiet for most of the time, only speaking to offer Twitch and David food and drink from the shuttle's supply. At one point, he offered to have a look at Twitch's legs to see what he could do to run some quick repairs, but Twitch vociferously refused the offer. The topic didn't come up again.

Twitch's appetite still hadn't fully returned. He nibbled at a dry sandwich and sipped a second cup of coffee, but otherwise did not feel hungry. He spent most of the flight staring out the window to the deep darkness outside. But for the occasional glimmer of stars on the ocean below, there was nothing to see, but still he stared past his weary reflection.

Caledonia eventually breached the horizon. The city was heralded by the lights from the expansive network of hydroponic farms that surrounded Caledonia. Twitch's tail thumped against his seat as he saw them. A weight was slowly lifted from his shoulders as the skyscrapers rose from the dark land. A sense of homecoming began to fill him, and he turned to smile at David. The smile was brightly returned, and for the first time since Twitch had woken up from his injuries, the expression reached David's eyes.

Caledonia was familiar. Caledonia was safe. He could forget about the fears they had left behind in Hadrian now. Twitch needed that to be true, and he ignored the quiet voice in the back of his mind that told him he was going from one danger to another. Nowhere on Centaura was safe right now.

Once the shuttle had landed, Mortimer led them out to another car that was waiting to take them into the city proper. As all vehicles were on Centaura, it was a driverless and automated vehicle that responded to the vocalised directions Mortimer gave it. Their destination was the Jennings Tower in the middle of Caledonia. The towering building rose higher than any other around it, with the megalithic letters shining bright from the side.

Twitch wasn't comforted by the familiarity. Though he felt safe, no longer needing to look over his shoulder for the Inquisition, he still felt a prickling unease running down his spine. His heart hammered in his chest as he thought about the long elevator journey up towards the highest level in the tower. Waiting for him up there was the reason why he had been sent to Hadrian. The reason why he had been forced to kill someone.

David placed a comforting hand on his shoulder after they got out of the car and approached the lobby of Jennings Tower. Mortimer led them inside, not once stopping as they crossed the wide-open lobby. Twitch's damaged feet clicked and scraped across the marble floor. His ears pinned down as he tried to ignore the sound, but he couldn't stop the couple of glances in his direction.

Twitch was glad when the doors to the elevator closed behind them, sealing the three starats away from the lobby. Mortimer hummed quietly to himself as the elevator began to rise. It was a tune Twitch didn't recognise.

The slight movement of the elevator as it rose threatened to unbalance Twitch. Without stable and solid ground beneath his feet, his sense of balance was being disrupted. He had to lean heavily into David just to remain upright, and nausea was rising in his belly as his head conflicted with his legs in the sensations they gave him.

Finally, the elevator jolted to a halt and the doors opened. The small foyer was empty, and the doors to Amy's office closed. Mortimer moved ahead of the other two starats and pushed open the doors, then stood to the side and gestured for Twitch and David to go on ahead.

Amy wasn't in her office. The cityscape twinkled and shone in the windows as Twitch approached the deserted desk. He gratefully sat down in one of the chairs, pleased to be off his unsteady feet. David sat down by his side.

"I'll see if she's ready to meet you," Mortimer said. He smiled and bowed his head to the two starats. He didn't go back out to the small foyer, but instead slipped out a small side door at the other end of the office.

Twitch exhaled slowly. "Do you know what you're going to say?" he asked, looking up at his partner.

"I'm not sure yet," David admitted. He shook his head. His voice quivered. "I'll try not to shout too much."

"She probably deserves it," Twitch mumbled beneath his breath. His eyes turned to the cityscape as it spread out through the wide windows. Something flashed bright in the distance, though Twitch couldn't tell whether it was the electromagnetic shield or a distant thunderstorm.

Twitch rubbed his muzzle. He didn't know what he was going to say. He didn't even know how he was going to say it, either. He knew he wanted nothing more to do with Amy, and that any further assistance she offered him was not worth the incredible cost it had taken. No matter what she offered him, he would not be tempted.

They only had a couple of minutes to wait before the door to the side of the office opened again. This time, Mortimer wasn't alone. Amy walked ahead of him. Her dark fur was brushed to its usual pristine standard, and the gold stud of her ear piercing shone in the light. She beamed widely as she sat down opposite David and Twitch.

"It's so nice to see you both back safely," she said. She placed her hands down on her desk and leaned forward slightly. "Did you manage to learn anything?"

Twitch glanced up at David, but his partner didn't seem like he was about to speak. He tapped his broken foot nervously against the floor. "They have lot of guns, and they're only too happy to use them," he said with a soft growl. "We were out of our depth there. It almost killed us. I still don't know how you could have thought we were best for the job."

"I understand it was dangerous," Amy said. Her smile didn't waver. "But did you succeed? Did you find the drive?"

Twitch wrinkled his muzzle. "I found it. Must have been two-thirds the size of this building," he said. He lowered his eyes, staring down at the desk. "I did some damage, but I don't know how long they'll be delayed. I know... I know what they're going to be using it for."

"So do I," Amy said.

Twitch's throat felt dry. He swallowed a couple of times. "What?" he hissed. His hand tightened around his partner's.

David growled. "You knew? You knew what you were sending us into?"

Amy leaned back in her chair and shrugged as Twitch stared up at her. "I've known all along what their plans were. That's part of the reason why Snow has gone to Pluto with Captain Griffiths. I needed to know if the plans and the tech were viable. I needed to know their progress."

"You lied to us," David hissed. His hand slipped out of Twitch's. He rose to his feet and took a step closer to Amy. Twitch struggled to stand by David's side.

"It was never information you needed to know," Amy replied. She shrugged again. "Would you have done anything different if you'd have known?"

"I would never have accepted it," Twitch said, forcing the words out as his throat felt like it squeezed closed. He felt dizzy as he swayed on his broken legs. "This is too big for someone like me. I might have been able to delay it, I don't know. But I can't stop it. How can I? I'm just one starat."

Amy sighed gently. She looked up to Mortimer, who was still standing off to the side of the desk. "Would you care to get some drinks for us, please," she said. She tapped her fingers against the mahogany desk as Mortimer bowed and started to retreat. "Perhaps something alcoholic."

"I don't think we need..." David said, but he was interrupted by a raised hand from Amy.

"You need something. You've been through a lot, and for that I apologise," she said. She looked between the two starats. "I had my reasons for sending you both, and I think your success in halting the drive justifies that decision. But you need to tell me everything else you learned in Hadrian."

"Cardinal Erik wasn't there," Twitch said sullenly as he slumped back into his chair. His immediate anger towards the cardinal had faded. Instead of a rage and a desire to inflict harm on the Martian, he just hoped to never see Cardinal Erik again. His ears flicked as he looked up to Amy. "He's gone back to Mars to inform the Vatican of their progress here. I think that means they were almost ready to activate the drive."

"How long do you think you delayed them?"

Twitch shook his head. "I don't know. Hours. Days. I couldn't have done any more or else they'd have killed me," he replied. His voice had gone a little higher pitched than normal, and his breathing was getting quicker and quicker. He felt worse than he had trying to fight free from the Inquisition facility. Recalling the memories somehow seemed more terrifying than living through them.

"And have you told anyone else about it yet?" Amy asked.

"No one, no. We came straight here with Mortimer," Twitch said, shaking his head a couple of times. His ears curled down.

"I'd keep it that way," Amy warned. She looked up as the foyer doors opened.

Twitch glanced back quickly, but it was just Mortimer returning. The other starat carried a few small glasses and a bottle of a dark liquid. Twitch turned his attention back to Amy. She grimaced and continued, as though she hadn't been interrupted. "We think the government may be helping the Inquisition."

"It's President Shawn," David said, before Twitch could respond.

Amy sucked in her breath as Mortimer placed down the three glasses, one in front of each of the starats. He poured out a small amount of the liquid in each glass. The scent immediately assaulted Twitch's nose. It felt like his nostrils were burning just from the vapours that came from the amber liquid.

Amy's hand shook slightly as she lifted her glass. Twitch could see the liquid rippling. "President Shawn, you say?" she asked. Her voice was tight, but her eyes gleamed brightly. "Do you know for sure? That's not exactly a small allegation you're making."

David nodded. "We found transcripts of conversations between Shawn and leaders in the Inquisition," he explained. He reached down to open his backpack. After a few moments he pulled out a few of the pages they had recovered from Tyler's safehouse. He tossed them onto the desk and let Amy sift through them. Twitch did not see the flashdrive David had filled with information at the drive.

"Where did you find this?" Amy asked. Her eyes gradually widened as she read over the transcripts. She took a sip from her glass, then refilled it.

"In an airtight, shielded safehouse beneath an Inquisition home," Twitch said. He lifted his glass up to his muzzle and sniffed the powerful fumes again. Even that was enough to make him feel slightly dizzy. He sipped at the amber liquid and almost gagged at the burning, slightly sour taste.

Amy's eyes looked up at Twitch from over the reams of paper. "An airtight...? Oh, so that's how they're doing it. Clever," she said. She lowered the transcripts and smiled, though it was more of a nervous grimace. "First time with whiskey? It's a bit of a learning experience."

Twitch wrinkled his muzzle and nodded. He certainly didn't like the flavour, but he did appreciate the burning warmth that trickled down his throat. He took another sip and tried to ignore the taste. "We can't fix this," he said, forcing the words out around the deep breaths he took.

"No, I don't think you can now," Amy said in agreement. "But that doesn't mean you haven't been incredibly valuable. This information is very useful, and any delay you inflicted on the Inquisition gives me a little bit more time to act. For act I will, you can have my assurance, Twitch. I have the resources to stop them, now that I know what they're doing."

"You have to. I don't want to think about what might happen if you can't," Twitch said with a whimper. He stared down into the amber liquid in his glass. He could see his shimmering, swirling reflection in the whiskey.

"Look at me, Twitch," Amy said.

Twitch slowly lifted his eyes to stare into Amy's. He didn't see any fear there. Her ears were perked up straight, and her fingers gripped tight around the glass of whiskey. "I will finish this, once and for all. I've been working on this for far too long to have some fanatical nutjobs get in my way."

Twitch hiccupped as he tried to speak. He held a hand to his mouth and tried to suppress another involuntary squeaking noise. "Just don't... just don't ask me. To do more," he said, struggling to get out a full sentence. He stared down at the whiskey in surprise. He was sure that the warmth spreading through his body was because of the amber liquid. It mellowed his thoughts and chased away some of the shadows that had been brewing at the back of his mind. He liked the feeling. The warmth quietened the screams.

"There's nothing else I will ask of you," Amy said. She rose to her feet, seemingly feeling none of the effects from the whiskey that Twitch was struggling with. "We've already gifted you the legs. Those are yours to keep. A good sum of money has been transferred to your account as well. More than enough to cover any expense you may have for several years at least. I know I put you through a lot, but I hope this will be enough to make it tolerable."

Twitch bowed his head. He didn't answer. He knew Amy was being generous with her compensation, but deep down he knew that nothing would make it worthwhile.

"Thank you," David replied, speaking through gritted teeth and evidently going through the same thought process as Twitch.

Amy clicked her fingers. "Mortimer, make sure they get a bottle of whiskey as well."

Mortimer bowed slightly. "I'll get one right away." His eyes glanced down to Twitch's legs. "Would you care to send those back here and I can repair them for you?"

Twitch bared his teeth. "No, thank you. I'd rather do it myself," he replied. He didn't want anyone playing around with how his legs worked. Certainly not when he was capable of repairing them himself.

"It would certainly be safer if..." Mortimer said, but he was silenced by a stern look from Amy. The suited starat shook his shoulders and began to turn on his toes. "I'll go fetch that bottle of whiskey then."

"Sorry about him," Amy said. She flashed a quick smile before turning to look out the windows. "He likes things to be done the proper way. I'll still be in touch, after this. I'm interested in you both, still. I won't have any other big jobs for you, unless you want them. But I may still call on your services for some insight into how the empire works. I hope that will be alright."

Twitch was inclined to immediately say no to the offer, but the words didn't come to his lips right away. His mouth hung open for a few moments.

David's hand tightened around Twitch's. "You lied to us," he said with a growl. "You sent us to Caledonia, knowing that we would be in danger. It's going to take more than compensation and nice words to make us trust you."

"Please, give us some space," Twitch whispered, lowering his head. His tail tucked close to his legs. Nausea welled in his stomach and he quickly put down the unfinished glass of whiskey before he could be tempted to drink again. He swallowed and grimaced. "I can't do anything more. Not yet."

Amy slowly turned back around to face them. The corners of her lips tugged up in a small smile. "I understand perfectly. You have my word, I shall leave you alone until you're ready to trust me again," she said, holding a hand over her breast. She then gestured down to the desk. "If you could leave behind any more information you found down there, then I can have it analysed and actioned upon. Send through any data you may have to Mortimer."

"Of course," David said. He fell quiet, but his hand never once left Twitch's.

"So, that's all you need from us?" Twitch asked nervously. The whiskey had gone right to his head, and the warmth that had spread through him both relaxed and disorientated him.

"That's all for now, yes. I would advise that you lie low for a while," Amy said. "Don't do anything to pull attention from the Inquisition, or from the government. If you are right, and President Shawn is behind this, then he may look to pull his influence if he knows who you are and what you know. Let me deal with this, and I promise you I'll keep you safe."

Twitch took a deep breath and nodded. "We won't do anything stupid," he said nervously. His tail curled up beneath the chair. "I just want to go home."

"Then go home," Amy said, a kind smile on her muzzle. "You have done more for me than you perhaps realise. Thank you both."

Twitch slowly rose to his feet as Mortimer returned to the office, a fresh bottle of whiskey in his hand. He beckoned to the two starats.

"Oh, and Twitch?" Amy called out, stopping Twitch and David leaving just before they walked through the foyer doors. She had risen to her feet as well. "I know you've met Minister Bakir, but I suggest not seeing her about this. If President Shawn is involved, then chances are the whole government is. Alright?"

Twitch nodded. "I understand," he replied. His ears flicked as he struggled to keep the doubt from showing on his face.

"Until next time then. Goodbye, Twitch."

Twitch gratefully turned around again. He had to walk slowly as he struggled to move his heavy, stiff legs. He felt tired. Two things awaited him. Home, and then bed. Safety, and rest. They couldn't come soon enough.

# chapter four

Twitch slept long into the morning. If he had dreamed at all, then he couldn't recall them as he woke. Though he had only previously slept in that bed while he had been waiting for his cybernetic legs, and all the bad memories that came with that time, Twitch felt comfortable lying between those sheets, not moving until he chose to do so. There was something cathartic about knowing the bed was his and David's. It was theirs. They owned it, just like everything else in the small, cosy house. He had never owned anything before.

Prox still hadn't even started to lighten the eastern horizon as Twitch sat at the small workshop overlooking the back garden. Rust-red plants that looked almost like grass filled the small outdoor area, with a wooden fence opening out onto the parklands beyond.

The starat's workshop was little more than a small desk with several simple tools scattered across the surface. His damaged legs had been partially opened, but there wasn't much more he could do on them without more equipment, which David had gone out to purchase. Twitch had a holographic projector on the desk, displaying the manual Mortimer had provided for his specification of legs, allowing him the chance to study the theory before he began to prod and poke inside the damaged cybernetics.

At his hips were the second pair of legs Amy and Mortimer had gifted him. Unlike his original pair, they were obviously cybernetic with no attempt made to portray an organic appearance. The design was sleek and smooth. There was no artificial fur, though the skin was still dark brown to match the fur that would have covered his legs. The skin felt rigid and tough to Twitch's fingers, with obvious seams where the semi-flexible panels connected. Small gaps in the panelling around his knees and ankles exposed the joints, with rubber segments allowing for good flexibility.

Twitch adored the artificial aesthetic of the legs, but he was nervous about going out in public with them. He knew it was a silly fear, but he was worried about appearing so broken. His tail flicked, and his fingers tightened around his screwdriver as he paused his exploratory pokes. On Ceres, he would never have survived such injuries. He'd have been sold off to the Vatican for destruction.

A knock at the door surprised Twitch. The screwdriver jerked in his hand, and he felt something dislodge inside the detached ankle.

"Ah shit," Twitch muttered to himself. He carefully placed the screwdriver down on the desk, before turning and swinging his legs out to the side. They took a few moments longer to respond, as his inactivity at the workshop had automatically sent them into a low power mode. A tingle of electricity pulsed down from his hips to his toes as they powered up again and responded to his inputs.

Every movement felt so smooth as Twitch walked across to the front door. He didn't limp, and every step was faultless, without any stumble or misstep. They didn't feel natural. They felt better than that.

Twitch opened the door to be surprised by a gasped squeak. Before he knew what was happening, he had been wrapped up in the arms of another starat. He would have fallen back, but his legs quickly adjusted to the extra weight pushing against him.

"I'm so happy to see you!"

It only took Twitch a moment to recognise the dark furred starat embracing him. So much had happened since he had last seen Steph. It felt like months since he had last had the chance to see her. He knew she had come to see him after his injuries from Cardinal Erik, but he could barely remember anything from then. He felt guilty about that. He had come from Ceres with Steph. But for the starats and human crew on Captain Rhys's ship, Steph knew no one on Centaura, just like him. They needed to stick together.

Twitch returned the embrace, and gently kissed the top of her head as she rested it against his collar. He looked up to see Richard and Leandro had come with her, and once he extricated himself from Steph's tight grip, he embraced each of the other starats in turn.

"Why don't you come inside? David's shown you around before, hasn't he?" Twitch asked, forcing his usual smile to his muzzle. He could not allow his fear and weakness to show. He stepped to the side and let the three starats come inside.

"Yeah, he showed us when you were still recovering," Steph said. She bounced on her toes as she looked around, before her eyes drifted down to Twitch's legs. She gasped. "They look incredible. How do they feel?"

Twitch blushed as the attention of the three starats all turned to his legs. He lifted his right leg up, easily able to balance perfectly on his left, and flexed his toes. "They feel good," he said, smiling nervously. The grin came easy to his muzzle. Perking his ears up took a little more effort. "I'm just fixing my other pair after I broke them in Hadrian."

"What happened there?" Richard asked hesitantly. "David was a little light on the details."

Twitch managed to hide his faltering smile as he turned away from the other three starats, under the disguise of leading them through to his workshop. "I'd... rather not talk about it," he said quietly.

"She got you to do too much," Leandro said. His honeyed voice was muted as he followed just behind.

Twitch rested his hands on his workshop desk. His tail tucked between his legs, and he didn't look back to the other three. He felt a hand rest on his back, but he didn't know who it belonged to.

"She got me my legs. Fixed up my tail," Twitch said, trying to speak through a tight throat that threatened to close up completely. "I..." The words he tried to say to ease the concerns of his friends died before he could say them.

"Is there anything you'd like to talk about with us?" Steph said. The hand on his back gently stroked through his shirt. "We're all here to help you, if you need us."

Twitch turned around and sat up on the edge of the desk, letting his legs swing beneath him. He managed to smile again and hide the discomfort swelling deep within his chest. "I'm fine, trust me. Just been going through a lot of changes." He looked around at the three starats. "Why don't you pull through a few chairs to sit down? I'd like to still work on these legs, if you don't mind."

"We don't have to stay if you're busy. We just wanted to see that you're alright," Steph said quickly.

Twitch shook his head. "No, please stay. The company would be nice. David won't be back for a few hours," he said. He draped one of his damaged legs across his lap and stroked his fingers through the soft, realistic fur. But for a smooth silkiness that wasn't present in his natural fur, Twitch could still barely feel the difference between his organic fur and that of his cybernetic limbs.

"We'll stay as long as you need," Steph assured him.

Twitch didn't know if she could see into his inner turmoil, but he was soothed by her words regardless. He smiled at Steph. A genuine smile. He needed more of those.

A few minutes later, the four starats were sat around Twitch's workshop. He had prepared tea and coffee for them all, and a plate of biscuits was slowly being consumed as Twitch got back to work on his legs. He peered at the right ankle, trying to work out what he had managed to dislodge earlier. His eyes flicked back and forth, between the detached limb and the holographic projection of its schematics.

"So, what have you three been doing while we've been away?" Twitch asked. He was still slightly distracted by his work, but his ears were trained on the three starats around him.

"Watching the skies," Leandro replied. He sounded sombre, with his voice losing much of the musical lilt that usually accompanied it. "Captain Rhys will be back in a couple of days with Emile, if everything went well. But I'm worried... Something wasn't right about that mission. There were too many secrets about who was organising it and why they went."

"Something's not right about anything here," Richard said. He drummed his fingers against the desk. "This stuff you've been doing, Twitch. The rumours I've been hearing at parliament. There's something big going on."

Twitch tensed slightly at the mention of parliament. "What have you been hearing?"

"A hidden cult that's secretly running everything and a resistance trying to fight back," Richard said. He wrinkled his muzzle. "I didn't want to believe it when I first heard about it, but Minister Bakir thinks it might be based in truth."

Twitch froze. His screwdriver trembled in his fingers.

"That's what you were sent to find out about, wasn't it, Twitch?" Steph asked. Twitch could see her leaning forward out of the corner of his eye. "That was the deal you did with Amy for the legs."

Twitch's ears curled in. He slowly breathed out. "Yeah," he admitted. He didn't know how much more he could talk about it. The memories were still too raw, the pain too strong in his chest. But he also knew that the starats deserved to know about the dangers they faced. "There is one. That's why Cardinal Erik was here. It's run by the Vatican."

"Shit, I knew it," Richard said with a growl. "Do you know what they're trying to do? We haven't been able to work that out."

Twitch looked up at the starats around him. Richard and Leandro he had not known for long, but Steph had been a part of his life for years. He knew he could trust her. He nodded sombrely. "They've developed a weapon to destroy everything here. The whole planet will be ripped apart if they succeed. I sabotaged it, but I don't know how long I set them back."

A brief silence met Twitch's words. He stared down at the cybernetic leg on the desk and tried to ignore the tears that threatened to spill. "I wish I could have stopped them, but I couldn't. I can't. I'm just one starat. What could I do against them?"

"Should we... think about leaving?" Richard asked uncertainly.

Twitch turned to him. He laughed bitterly. "And go where? I'm not going back to the empire. I won't be a slave again."

"Nor will I," Steph added. She placed a hand on Richard's thigh. "We're free here, and we have each other."

Richard pinned his ears back. "All the same, I'd like to get out of this alive. Can you tell us everything you know, Twitch? I'd like to pass this on to Bakir."

Twitch grimaced. "I don't think that's the best idea. The government is in on it. President Shawn is part of the Inquisition." He turned back to the leg and frowned. His eyes quickly glanced up to the holographic plans, and he focused the view on a part around the ankle. Something didn't seem quite right, beyond the obvious damage.

"Shawn is? Fuck," Richard whispered.

"Bakir's good though. She's on our side," Steph said. Her voice shook around the slight growl in her words. "Do you think Amy is? Do you trust her?"

"Do you know that?" Twitch asked, his voice hoarse. His hand tightened around the screwdriver. "Do you know Bakir is good?"

"I believe it with all my heart," Steph said. Her ears perked up and she held her hand to her chest. "Can you look me in the eye and tell me that Amy can be trusted?"

Twitch didn't answer the question. Instead, he prodded a little deeper with his screwdriver. His earlier fumble had knocked aside a small bundle of wiring, dislodging them from their usual casings. It had revealed a small disc about the size of a single claw that wasn't on the schematics. It was plugged into a small port just above the ankle joint with a single narrow cable. It appeared to be wedged into a place that hadn't been designed for it. A red light occasionally flashed. Beneath the light was a line of miniscule text that Twitch's eyes weren't good enough to read clearly.

"Any of you have really good eyes?"

"How come?" Richard asked, leaning forward to look over Twitch's shoulder.

Twitch prodded the mysterious disc with the tip of the screwdriver. "There's some writing on that. Can you read it?"

Richard sucked in his breath as he leaned in close. He squinted as he tried to make out the tiny lettering. Twitch did his best to lift the little disc up with the screwdriver without unplugging the wire that held it connected.

"JT0986, I think," Richard recited. "It sounds like a serial code."

"Can one of you look up the code and see what comes up?" Twitch asked, glancing back to the other two starats. He didn't let the disc move from the screwdriver tip.

Leandro had already been doing so. He wordlessly moved his tablet in front of Twitch. On the screen was a technical specification sheet for a product with the same serial code as the little disc in his leg. The product was listed as a GPS tracker. It was owned by Jennings Technology.

"They're tracking me? Why?" Twitch asked in alarm, not expecting any answers from the three starats with him. His first instinct was to rip the tracker out, but logic stayed his hand. If it was active, as the flashing light seemed to indicate, then Amy would know if it was disconnected. He would need to be smarter about that.

"Are you sure she's who you should be trusting?" Steph asked again.

Twitch slowly lowered the tracker back down, letting it sit amongst the wires surrounding it. "Maybe it's standard, and it's used so I don't lose them?" he said, but he could hear the uncertainty in his own voice. He didn't believe that, but he didn't yet want to accept the alternative was true.

"Let us take you to see Minister Bakir," Steph said. She reached out with one hand to take hold of Twitch's. "I promise you, no matter what you may have learned about Shawn, she is not part of this conspiracy."

Twitch pulled his hand away from Steph's. His tail trembled. He wanted to believe her. He wanted to put his trust in the starat who had helped make their time on Ceres tolerable. He had never had reason to doubt her judgement before, but bad memories plagued his mind and darkened his thoughts. "Last time I saw her, David and I were chased through the Caledonia Mall by the Inquisition," he squeaked quietly.

"Why did you not tell us this before?" Leandro asked. The grey starat sat up slightly in his seat and leaned forward.

"Because I was scared," Twitch admitted. He couldn't meet anyone in the eye, so he just stared down at the cybernetic leg on the desk. "Because I thought you would think I was lying, and that I was only seeing the bad in humans here. Because here should be perfect and I didn't want you to think it wasn't."

Steph pulled Twitch into a hug. Slowly at first, he embraced her back and let his head rest on her shoulder. "You never have to be scared to tell us anything. You know that, right?" she said quietly. She kissed him gently on the cheek.

"I know," Twitch replied. He pressed his forehead against hers. "Things are just so different now. I'm still trying to get used to what I can and can't do. Or should and shouldn't."

"We all are, Twitch. You don't need to do it alone," Steph said. She kissed him again, then released him. "Will you come with us, though? We can keep you safe, I promise."

Twitch sighed and nodded. "Sure, but I want to wait until David is back first. And I need to see if I can do something about this tracker. Amy didn't want me to go to the government about any of this. She can't know where I'm going."

"Anything you need us to do?" Steph offered.

Twitch flicked his ears. He stroked his hand up the detached leg. "I need a power source and some connector adaptors. I might be able to rig up a port that makes it look like the legs stay in the house," he explained. He frowned and swished the tip of his tail. "First though, I'm going to have to take these legs off and look to see if they have a tracker in them too. Can someone keep me steady? It's hard to balance without them."

"Just tell us what you need us to do," Richard said, rising to his feet.

Twitch felt nauseous as he forced a grin to his muzzle. "Alright. So first, you're going to need to take off my shorts…"

***

There had been a second tracker in the other set of legs. Twitch had found it buried amongst the wires just above the right ankle. There hadn't been anything in either of the left legs that he could find. He didn't know if his solution to the trackers worked or not. He had unplugged the device in his functional legs and quickly plugged it into the rudimentary battery he had been able to quickly construct. The light kept flashing, so he could only hope that it was still tracking, and that it hadn't reported any faults back to Amy.

By the time David returned with the tools and spare parts Twitch had requested, Twitch's unbroken legs had been reassembled and clicked back into place. The situation was quickly explained to David. Though he was a little reluctant to go back to parliament after what had happened the previous time, he agreed to go with them all to see Minister Bakir.

Within an hour of David's return, they were already at parliament. It looked just as Twitch remembered. Though his eyes were constantly wide as he looked around, he could not see any human wearing the golden crossed swords of the Inquisition. He also didn't see Amy or Mortimer, or anyone else he recognised as working at Jennings Tower. No one had been noticeably following them.

Richard and Steph were able to get them into the large, circular building with ease. With their recent work for Minister Bakir, they had been given credentials that gave them limited access to the Centauran parliament. It was enough to get them inside, and have a message sent out to the minister that they wanted to see her.

Twitch sat nervously in the lobby of the parliament chambers while they waited for Minister Bakir. He hadn't had the chance to fix his faux-organic legs, so it was obvious that everything from his hips down was synthetic. He had expected comments about his legs, but none had come. He barely even had a second glance in his direction. No one even cared how broken he appeared.

That didn't stop Twitch nervously running his hands over his legs. Without fur there, he felt strangely naked despite his clothes. The feel of his synthetic skin wasn't at all like a human's, but he did have to wonder if Captain Rhys had felt similarly strange when he first got his fur.

It was not Minister Bakir who came to greet them. Instead, it was Maxwell who arrived. The starat looked with surprise at Twitch's legs, but he didn't comment on them. Instead, he reached out with his cybernetic hand in greeting. David shook his hand quickly, but Twitch's grip lingered a little longer.

"I'm so glad you decided to come back," Maxwell said. He scuffed his bare foot nervously. "I was so worried about you last time."

"We appreciate the concern," David said. He cast a wary eye around the exposed lobby. "Are we able to speak to you and the minister in private? We don't want to be overheard at all."

Maxwell seemed to be a little taken aback by that. "Of course, yes. Come with me. The minister is waiting for you."

The starat led them up into the circular corridor that ran around the outside of the parliamentary chambers. Nothing had really changed from the last time Twitch had followed Maxwell around them. The pictures of the past presidents remained the same. The steady flow of humans and starats walking around in both directions seemed normal, with no sign of any Inquisition influence. The back of Twitch's neck prickled. The accusations he had felt ridiculous, but he knew he wasn't wrong. He knew what he had witnessed. There was no doubt in his mind what the Inquisition was planning, and he knew how deeply the rot in the Centauran government had spread.

He could only hope that Richard and Steph had been right, and that Minister Bakir was not involved in it.

Minsiter Bakir's small office had felt cramped on their previous visit with four starats inside. With seven, there was barely any room to move at all, but the minister still greeted them warmly. There were only two available chairs in front of the minister's desk, and they were given to David and Leandro.

"To what do I owe the pleasure of this visit?" Minister Bakir asked, once she had greeted them all, and everyone had found a place to stand comfortably.

Twitch looked down to David. They shared a quick glance. His partner nodded slightly. Twitch took a deep breath as he readied himself.

"David and I were sent to Hadrian by Amy Jennings to investigate the Inquisition," he said. He leaned back against the wall, resting one foot against it. "We found out that they're at least partially run by the Vatican, and that they plan to end the war against Centaura by pulling the planet into subspace and destroying it."

Minister Bakir managed to mask her initial reaction, but she still tightened her hands into fists. "And you believe this is a credible threat?"

Twitch nodded. "I do. I saw the machine they've built beneath Hadrian. It's a Denitchev drive bigger than most buildings in Caledonia. It will use the planet's shield to act just like an oversized spaceship," he explained. He grimaced and tapped his foot against the wall behind him. "I sabotaged the machine, but they could have it running again soon. Amy knows about it, but I don't know what she can do."

The minister shared a quick glance with Maxwell. "And why do you come to me with this information? I am no one with great influence."

"Because Amy lied to us and we're no longer sure what her motivations are," David said. He clasped his hands together on his lap.

"Worse than that," Twitch said quietly. His voice trembled and he curled his tail to cover the front of his legs. "We believe that President Shawn is working with the Inquisition."

Minister Bakir froze completely. Her green eyes stared up at Twitch in shock.

"This is no small accusation. Do you have proof of this?" Maxwell asked, filling the silence.

David pulled the datastick from his pocket, the one he had taken from the drive beneath Hadrian. "We were able to download plans of the Denitchev drive. I was also able to copy some files we found in a priest's home in Hadrian. Amongst them are communications between Shawn and the Inquisition."

Minister Bakir's hands shook. "May I take that, please?"

David did not immediately pass over the precious information. He hesitated. Twitch placed his hand on his partner's shoulder, and the exchange was completed a moment later. The minister placed the datastick in her pocket.

"We shall analyse this information," Maxwell explained. He shared a nervous glance with the minister. "Should this prove to be true, then you have done us a great favour."

Twitch nodded once. "I wish I was wrong, but I am certain. They have airtight bunkers they can hide in, so that they're safe while the planet is displaced. I'm sure you'll find one where the president can quickly get to safety."

"There's a bunker beneath parliament house, but that's been there for years," Minister Bakir said quietly.

"Does it have a shield generator inside? That will allow anyone in the bunker to drop back into realspace, and a ship will then sweep through the area and rescue everyone left behind," Twitch said. He shuddered and pinned his ears down against his head. "If they find a way to drop the shields, then there's nothing that will save the planet."

Minister Bakir breathed out slowly. "Alright. So the Vatican is moving to destroy us, with the help of our own president? I had hoped the recent protests had been nothing to worry about, but this is worse than I could ever have feared," she said. She laughed nervously and tapped her claws against the desk. "Any good news at all?"

Leandro spoke up. "Captain Rhys is back in two days. He might have learned more on Pluto."

Minister Bakir clicked her tongue and shook her head. "If things are as dire as you suggest, then we can't wait around for ifs and buts." She paused and spun around on her chair to look out the narrow window squeezed between two databanks. "I'm glad you chose to trust me. I don't yet know what I could do, but I will not sit idly on this information."

"Could you expose him? Call him out on what he has done?" Leandro asked, flicking his lone ear to the side and tilting his head.

Minister Bakir shook her head. "Not without definitive proof. That would only galvanise them to act quicker. If your datastick gives me enough, then maybe, but I would not rely on that."

"Who else can we trust to fight back against them?" Richard asked.

Minister Bakir turned back to face them as she remained silent for a few moments, her dark-furred brow furrowed in thought. "For you, no one. Let me deal with this, please. I know how things work here, and I have a better idea of who to trust and who could be involved."

Twitch felt a little flutter of fear inside his chest. It was quickly replaced by a sense of relief that the minister wasn't expecting anything of him. "Will you want to see Captain Rhys when he gets back?"

The minister paused again, before she nodded. "Yes, I think that would be for the best. I will start work as though I will not get to see him, but any input he may be able to provide could be invaluable," she said. She rose to her feet and opened her mouth to speak, but she was interrupted by a knock at the door.

Fear spiked through Twitch's body again. His foot tensed against the wall, and he could feel small flecks of it break away beneath the force of his toes. He tried to relax as Maxwell squeezed between Richard and Steph to reach the door and open it.

A human was standing on the other side of the door. Neatly trimmed black hair surrounded a thin, pale face. Thick-framed glasses perched on the end of his nose. It was a face Twitch had seen before, in this very office, though he had never met the human who it belonged to.

"Having a party in here, Minister?" President Shawn asked. His voice was light and jovial. Twitch could see a brightness in his brown eyes.

"Just welcoming some new starats to Centaura, President," the minister replied, managing to match the light tone and smile from the human.

The president beamed widely as he looked around the room. "You're new here? Fantastic," he said brightly. He firmly shook the hand of every starat but for the minister's and Maxwell's. "I'm so glad to welcome you to Centaura. What do you make of the place?"

"It's alright, I guess," Twitch mumbled quietly. He kept his head down, not wanting to meet the human in the eye.

"Dark," David added. "These nights are much longer than we're used to."

"It can take a lot of adjustment," President Shawn admitted. He rubbed his hands together, then clasped his fingers. "Should you be interested, you should find some time to look up two nightfalls from now. There will be an incredible show of meteors, which I'm promised will be quite the spectacle."

Twitch flicked his tail and kept staring down. The knowledge of who this man was and what he planned made his fur crawl. He didn't want to look into the eyes of the human and see someone normal. He wanted to imagine the monster like Cardinal Erik. The thought that someone so normal could have such horrific ideas sickened Twitch.

"Meteors are cool," David replied. His voice sounded even and neutral. "We had a few of them on Ceres, though there was no atmosphere to light them up."

"Asteroid Belt, right?" President Shawn asked.

Twitch chanced a quick look up. The human was not looking towards him. Instead, his attention was on David. There appeared to be nothing about the human that gave him away as working for the Inquisition; no crossed golden swords, but Twitch didn't expect anything so obvious. He knew that Shawn would hide his true loyalty until he was ready to act.

"That's right, yeah," David replied.

"Must have been tough, being so close to Mars," the president said. He sounded so jovial, so pleasant that Twitch knew he would never have suspected the president, were it not for the information he already had.

David shrugged. "They didn't bother us if we didn't give them reason to." He smirked. "Besides, Terra was closer to Mars than Ceres for about half the year."

President Shawn frowned slightly. He took his glasses from his nose and wiped the lens clean. "I guess you're right," he said, before returning his glasses back to the proper place. He turned his attention back to Minister Bakir. "I can tell you're a little busy for now, but I'd like to speak to you as soon as you're able. Some new policy advice."

"I'll be with you soon," Minister Bakir replied.

The president gave a thumbs up, before retreating out of the cramped office. The warm smile didn't once leave his face.

Maxwell closed the door behind the human. He glanced down at his cybernetic arm. Twitch could see the small computer display exposed on Maxwell's wrist. He could feel the tension drain from the room as the other starat nodded to confirm the human had gone.

"Do you think he knew what we were talking about?" Leandro asked in a hushed voice.

Minister Bakir shook her head. "No, I don't believe so. The walls in this building are perfectly soundproofed. You would never be able to listen in on any conversation from outside," she said. She leaned forward and rested her arms on the desk. "But I think it reinforces the point that you should spend as little time around him as possible. Let me deal with this. I promise you, I will get done what needs to be done."

Twitch bit down on his lip. He looked the minister in the eye. He had heard that before, coming from the mouth of a starat who had just finished lying to him. With the tip of his tail gripped tightly in his hand, the starat nodded. "I trust you."

"I appreciate that," Minister Bakir said, inclining her head. "Should I need you again…"

"No." Twitch interrupted the minister with a harsh word. He winced, not intending to growl so much. He softened his tone. "I know you'll do everything you can. I wish I could do the same, but I just… I can't. I can't do any more. I'm not a fighter."

"I think you've done more than you realise. I shall respect your wishes and not call on you again, unless you tell me otherwise," Minister Bakir said in assurance. She looked up to Maxwell. "Can you escort them all home. To their front door, if you would. I don't want any repeats of last time."

"Understood," Maxwell said, bowing his head to the minister. "Will you not want my presence for your meeting with the president?"

Minister Bakir grimaced. "I think I'll be fine. He's probably wanting to impose new controls on Terran starats," she said, before pausing with a sigh. She looked out the window. "Not that any of that really matters, if he and his Inquisition friends have their way."

"I'm sorry I didn't have better news for you," Twitch said. His tailtip curled and he lowered his head.

"Better you told me than didn't. I don't trust Amy Jennings to act on this in good faith," the minister said. "It is obviously in her interest to stop the Inquisition too, but what else might she do? Ah, I'm theorising again. Best to find out what is actually happening first before I go into the what ifs."

"Is there anything else you need of us, Minister?" Richard asked, gesturing to himself and Steph.

"No, not for now. Tell me if you learn anything new, but don't go hunting for information. Keep yourselves safe," Minister Bakir said. She gestured with one hand towards the door. "Best if you follow Maxwell now. I don't want to keep the president waiting too long."

Twitch held his hand out for the minister. "Thank you for listening to us, and for believing us."

"Thank you for all you've done so far," the minister replied, squeezing Twitch's hand. "I've got this now. I'll fix it, I promise you."

Twitch was glad of the assurances. He knew there was nothing more he could do to change anything. This was all something that needed people with vastly different skills and abilities to what he possessed. He just wished that the pressure pushing down on his shoulders would lift.

Captain Rhys couldn't get back soon enough. He would be able to fix everything. Twitch knew that would be the case. In just two days, he would be able to feel happy and safe once again. That could not come soon enough.

# chapter fiue

Twitch had barely gone outside in two days of endless night. None of the small group of starats had. The five of them had stayed beneath the same roof, despite how cramped it made everyone feel. There wasn't much room, but they were all well used to making the best of a shared living space so small. It meant they all stayed safe together, and they would all be able to learn any new information at the same time.

No one knew exactly when Captain Rhys was meant to return to Centaura, but Twitch knew that without any delays on Pluto, then the former human was meant to return that day. The only way Twitch could keep himself from staring out the front window all day was tinkering more on his broken legs.

Twitch was almost confident the legs had been fixed entirely. Nothing rattled when they moved, and the connectors and joints all seemed stable and secure. He hadn't yet had the opportunity to test them, but he had started to charge them so he could try walking around the garden.

Instead of Twitch, it had been Leandro sat by the front windows, constantly staring out onto the quiet street, which was being lit by the early light from Prox as it finally crept above the horizon. The grey-furred starat had barely spoken in the two days since the meeting with Minister Bakir. He had told none of his stories, no matter how much Richard or Steph had asked it of him.

David had used the time to bury himself in various textbooks and medical studies. He still hoped that, with Doctor Anthony's help, he would be able to study to become an actual doctor at some point. With the doctor travelling to Pluto with most of the rest of Captain

Rhys's crew, those plans had stalled for a short while, but David had wanted to learn as much as possible to impress Doctor Anthony.

Time seemed to go by so slowly. With no more work to do on his legs, Twitch began to pace around the room until he was asked to stop by Leandro. After that, he just sprawled out on the bed and closed his eyes, trying hard to think about anything but what had happened in Hadrian. It was an almost impossible task. With nothing else to distract his mind, his thoughts kept drifting back to the underground facility. The scream still echoed in his ears.

"Someone's coming."

Twitch's eyes immediately snapped open as Steph's voice called through the small house.

"It's William! And... is that Captain Rhys's friend?"

Twitch hurried into the main room. He opened the front door fast enough to almost wrench it free from its hinges. He felt like running out to greet William, but there was no sign of Captain Rhys at all, nor of the Silver Fox. It was only William and Aaron, the human friend Captain Rhys had followed to Centaura.

Twitch may have hesitated, but William did not. The other starat started to run the moment Twitch had opened the door. He broke away from Aaron quickly, and almost barrelled into Twitch. The other starat's arms wrapped tight around Twitch's body. Fresh tears matted William's cheeks.

"Oh, I'm so glad you're alright," William said, his voice shaking with emotion. He took a step back and looked over Twitch, paying close attention to his cybernetic legs. He smiled weakly. "They look so good on you."

"Where's Captain Rhys?" Twitch asked. He felt a cold shiver pass through his stomach.

William glanced back to Aaron, who had just caught up. "We should... we should go inside."

Twitch didn't move. "Where is he? What happened to him?"

"Twitch, please," William pleaded.

This time, Twitch relented. He allowed William's arm to wrap over his shoulder and gently push him back inside his home. Silence met them both, with Aaron following just behind. Everyone had overhead the brief conversation. Everyone could see the tears in William's eyes, and the sorrow in Aaron's.

Something terrible had happened on Pluto.

"Please tell me he's alright," Twitch whispered. He slumped down on the couch, next to David.

William whimpered and shook his head. He dropped down onto one of the other seats and held his head in his hands. His shoulders trembled as he tried to suppress a sniff. "No..."

"He didn't make it back," Aaron said. His voice was tight, and his face drawn. His eyes were red, with dark rings circling them. "He never got back to the shuttle."

"What happened?" Richard asked. He knelt down beside William, holding onto the other starat's hand.

"Rhys got separated from the group. There was a dragon. He released a dragon, which got us through to our target, and then... I..." Aaron said, trailing off uncertainly. A small frown touched his brow.

"He didn't make it back. I don't know what happened to him. No one heard from him," William added. He sniffed again and took a deep breath. "We didn't have time to go looking. Snow told us there was an empire ship coming."

Aaron frowned and opened his mouth, but he didn't say anything. He rested his head against the wall behind him.

"We had to get out of the system quickly," William continued. He slowly lifted his head, doing nothing to stem the tears that matted his fur. His ears folded down and leaned into Steph's side as the other starat gently ran her fingers through his tail fur.

"I don't think there was a Terran ship," Aaron said slowly. He rubbed one hand over his cheek, which was bristled with the growth of several days. "We destroyed their distress beacon. The empire couldn't scramble a ship so quickly."

"Well one got there," William retorted, twisting his neck to look back at the human. "Why else would we have left without him?"

"Was there a ship or not?" David asked. His hand found Twitch's.

William's ears drooped. "There must have been," he whispered, but he no longer sounded certain. He pulled his tail away from Steph and stood up, leaning heavily on his organic leg. The claws of his synthetic foot tensed, scraping over the carpeted floor. "I remember there being an enemy ship, but I can't remember what we did to evade it. Everything must have happened so quickly."

Another voice cut across the room. Leandro had risen to his feet. "And Emile? What happened to my Silver Fox? Why is he not here?"

Aaron swallowed nervously. His eyes flicked around the room. "He... was meant to be on the shuttle. He was never meant to leave it, but he wasn't there when we got back. He might have gone to look for Rhys."

"He might have?" Leandro asked. His ears and tail drooped. He made a noise like a strangled choke, before breathing in deep. "Do you mind if I have a moment, please?"

No one stopped the grey-furred starat as he sombrely made his way through to the bedroom. The door closed behind him, and Twitch could hear him collapsing onto the bed.

Twitch bowed his head. He felt completely numb. He had been so sure that Captain Rhys was going to come back and fix everything, that he hadn't even considered the possibility that he might not return. It seemed unreal, like one of the many nightmares that had been plaguing his nights.

"Why can't you remember what happened to him?" Twitch asked in a small voice. His brief anger had faded as quickly as it had formed. "Why wasn't he able to make it back?"

"He was hurt," Aaron said slowly. "It was that subspace thing he can do. He did too much and hurt himself, so he went back to the shuttle early. Then there was the dragon, and..."

"I don't know what happened after that," William added. "I could barely think about anything but what I was doing." He shifted his feet awkwardly. His cybernetic leg was almost identical to Twitch's in its design. A brief trickle of worry ran down Twitch's tail as he wondered whether a tracking chip was in that leg too. What would Amy do if she knew that William had come to visit Twitch? Surely she wouldn't expect them to stay apart.

"We did everything we could, I'm sorry," Aaron said. He reached out to take Twitch's hand in his own. He laughed bitterly. "Shit, you really do look like him."

Twitch flicked his tail. "He looks like me. Looked." He whimpered softly. "Please tell me he's not really gone. We need him."

"I'm sorry," Aaron whispered again. His head was bowed, and his fingers gripped tight around Twitch's. The starat could feel him shaking slightly.

Steph squeaked softly. "Snow is here," she said in warning.

Twitch jumped to his feet in shock. "Ah shit," he muttered, quickly spinning around on the spot. Fear overwhelmed grief for a moment. On the mantle by the front door were the tracking chips that had been implanted in his legs. He grabbed hold of them and stuffed them into his pocket just as Snow knocked on the door.

The albino starat cautiously stepped inside when the door was opened. Both her hands were heavily bandaged, reminding Twitch of the injuries Captain Rhys had suffered. Her movements didn't seem as confident as usual, and she held one hand slightly in front of her whenever she took a step. Her blind eyes never quite managed to look at anyone.

"I trust you have been told the news?" she asked quietly. Her voice cracked with pain.

"We just told them," Aaron said.

Snow started slightly at the voice, and her sightless eyes swept around the room. "I didn't realise you'd come here, Captain Lee," she said. Her muzzle twitched as she composed herself again. "I just came to pass on my condolences to everyone here, and my sympathies that we weren't able to bring everyone back home safely."

"Do you remember what happened?" Richard asked. He had stood up, though both Steph and William held onto his hands.

Snow shrugged. "I lost contact with him early on. Anything could have happened, I'm afraid. We all knew the dangers before leaving. Him more than others."

Twitch didn't know what to say. No one seemed to know, as a silence fell across the room. William seemed to be on the verge of tears again.

"He died for the cause of making starats everywhere safer," the albino said softly. "That can not be forgotten. He died for us." Snow placed her hand on the front door, which had remained open. She swayed slightly, and Twitch could hear the catch of her breath as she put pressure on her bandaged hands.

"Were you hurt too?" Steph asked, vocalising the question before Twitch considered whether it was prudent to ask.

Snow smiled weakly as she turned to look in the general direction of Steph, but not quite meeting her gaze. "I overexerted myself. It has been a long time since my subspace powers have been tested to their limits, but I will be fine in a few days," she said. Her voice trembled. "I appreciate your concern."

Twitch bowed his head. Even Snow, with all her powers had been pushed to the limit. He hadn't realised the risks that Captain Rhys and the Silver Fox had willingly thrown themselves into. He stared down at his legs. They had stopped him even saying goodbye to Captain Rhys.

Snow tentatively reached out to Twitch. She lightly placed her injured hand on his shoulder for a moment. "I just want you to know that anything I can do for you, or Amy, all you need to do is ask."

"I understand, thank you," Twitch said, turning his head away just in case she could sense the wrinkle of his muzzle.

The albino starat looked sightlessly around the room once more, before she stepped back outside again. In the distance, further up the street, Twitch could just about make out another starat, standing and waiting. The sharply cut suit looked like it could have been Mortimer, but he couldn't quite make out any defining features.

Then he closed the door and the starats were gone from view.

Twitch turned back around to look over the dejected faces. "Well... fuck."

"What do we do now?" Steph asked.

Twitch didn't have an answer for that. Everything had relied on learning what Captain Rhys thought about the situation, but now he was gone. There was no chance of knowing what the former human would have done.

"There's something else happening here, isn't there?" Aaron said. The human looked around the room as he nervously bounced his hands on his knees. "What did I miss?"

Twitch didn't have the heart to say anything. He slowly slumped down to his haunches and leaned back against the door as David started to explain everything that had happened since Captain Rhys had left for Pluto with most of his crew. He barely even heard anything. Instead, he was trapped inside his own thoughts, with fear about what was coming. He had been so sure that Captain Rhys would be able to fix everything. Could he trust starats like Minister Bakir or Amy to stop the Inquisition? Were they even capable of it?

Twitch drifted through the conversation silently. His eyes occasionally followed whoever was speaking as Aaron questioned the starats about what had happened on Centaura. David answered most of them, and for the first time he told everyone just what had happened in Hadrian, though he made no mention to the lives Twitch had been forced to take in their escape.

At some point, Leandro had returned from the bedroom. His eyes were red, and his fur was matted with tears, but he otherwise seemed composed as he returned to his usual seat by the window. Twitch had returned to the sofa as well, coaxed up to his feet by David, who had wrapped his arms around the smaller starat.

The fog of Twitch's thoughts didn't lift as the conversation turned back to what had happened in Pluto. Neither Aaron nor William could clearly recall any events that had happened after landing on the dwarf planet, and their memories often conflicted with each other. William had been certain that they had been forced to leave early because of an enemy ship, but Aaron could recall no such event happening.

William rubbed his hands over his face. "It's stress that's doing it. Maybe the terror of fighting like that," the starat said, in means of explanation why neither could remember what had happened on Pluto. "I'm sure that can do weird things to the mind."

"For you, maybe," Aaron said quietly, shaking his head. "I'm trained as a soldier. I'm meant to be able to remember everything clearly, no matter what trauma I go through. I can understand your memory being unclear, but there's no excuse for me."

"Would you really forget something like that?" Leandro asked bitterly. He tapped a finger to the side of his head. "I remember everything that ever happened to me. The good, and the terrible. I have seen friends killed in front of me for no reason other than we had a cruel owner who gleefully tortured and murdered starats. I remember them because no one else would."

"We're not all brave and strong like you, Leandro," William whispered. His hands were clasped together, and he stared down at his ankles. "No matter how much we try to pretend otherwise."

Aaron turned to face William. He lifted the starat's drooping chin with one hand. "You went out there, knowing the dangers. You didn't run like many would have wanted to do. You were brave. You were strong. Just because you were scared doesn't make that untrue."

William turned his head away from Aaron, knocking the human's large hand to the side. "I should have gone back with him. Kept him safe."

"We all could have done many things, William," Leandro said slowly. He rubbed his cheeks dry, though his fur was still matted and tangled. "I should have told Emile not to go. We both knew he did not have long left, but he wanted to do this. I should have stopped him, but I did not. I hurt because of it now, but I can not change what I did or did not do. I do not think he would have stayed here, even if I had tried to stop him."

"But I could have helped him," William pleaded.

"Maybe you could have. Maybe you would have died too," Leandro replied calmly. He met William's eyes and smiled. "Just be thankful you came back to us."

"He's right," Aaron added. "We may never know what happened to Rhys, but like Snow said, he died to help starats here and in the empire. We can honour his life by finishing this, once and for all. We make things safe for starats everywhere."

Twitch exhaled slowly. He was glad for the protective arms of David wrapped around his torso. "We're not fighters," he said, looking up to Aaron. "We tried that already. What more can we do?"

"I'm a fighter. I'll do it on your behalf," Aaron replied. He looked down to the watch on his wrist. "I will also debrief with everyone on the *Freedom* to see if their memories are conflicting. I will piece together the truth of this no matter what it takes. I know we don't know each other well, but you can trust me. Rhys was my friend, and any friend of his is one of mine. If ever you need me, please call."

"I will, thank you," Twitch said. He tried a smile. It didn't quite fit right on his face with all the turmoil in his head, but it did make him feel a little more like himself.

Aaron returned the smile as he rose to his feet. He then frowned. "Ah, shit. There was one other thing I needed to mention," he said, clicking his fingers. "Major-General Ulrich asked to see you, Twitch. Tomorrow if possible. It was something to do with Rhys's ship."

"She wants to see me?" Twitch asked in surprise. He had never met the major-general before, though he had heard about her through Captain Rhys. His tail quivered as he nodded. "Tomorrow is fine."

"I'll pass that on, and I'll arrange some transport for you," Aaron said. He offered his hand to Twitch, and then to every other starat present. They all took the offered hand. Aaron had been right. He was a friend of Captain Rhys, so he was a friend to the starats. Twitch knew he could trust the human every bit as much as he had trusted Captain Rhys.

As Aaron left, Twitch leaned into David. The warm comfort of his partner's fur grounded his thoughts a little, and it stopped them drifting too far away into the dark corner of his mind. He feared falling into that darkness again. He teetered on the edge, and it was only the presence of the other four starats that kept him from plunging down into it.

Twitch sniffed back some fresh tears as he looked around the room. Again, he forced a smile onto his face. "Anyone for tea?" he asked. His voice sounded high-pitched to his ears as he tried to sound bright and normal. His voice broke into a nervous laugh. "Or whiskey?"

Tea was decided on. Whiskey was considered too dangerous given the fragile state of mind of the starats. Twitch was slightly disappointed. The numbing warmth of whiskey would have helped soothe his troubled mind, but he accepted the advice of his friends. He could only hope that tea and food would help to normalise everything. If he tried hard not to think about Captain Rhys, then perhaps he could overcome the grief he felt bubbling deep inside.

The smile soon returned. The mask was reset. Twitch could feel the cracks spreading through his mind. He didn't know how much longer he could take it all.

He needed some good news.

# chapter six

Twitch put on his brave face. He also put on what he now considered to be his brave legs. They were the legs that showed off their artificial nature. He was a broken starat, but he had been made stronger because of it. The Vatican had taken away his legs, so he had gotten new ones. Better ones.

The empire had stolen away someone very important to Twitch. He couldn't replace Captain Rhys, but he wouldn't allow the death of his friend to bring him down. He would keep living. He would keep fighting in his own way to spite those who would take away someone close to him. He would not let them take another.

Twitch's newly recovered determination didn't stop him feeling nervous about the meeting that was coming. He didn't know what Major-General Ulrich wanted to see him about. Aaron had not been able to provide any more information, and the soldier who had come to Twitch's house to pick him up had not known either.

David had not been permitted to come, with only Twitch being given clearance to see the major-general in the military facility beneath the Caledonia space-elevator. That had led to a mostly quiet journey from the city suburbs, out to the mountains beyond the fields of greenhouses that grew most of the planet's crops. Occasionally, the starat soldier asked a question about life in the empire, but he quickly seemed to be too horrified to learn much more.

The soldier, whose name was Aldred, shook Twitch's hand vigorously when they made it to the space elevator. "You're braver than I could ever imagine," the starat soldier said. "I could never live like that."

"I hope you never have to," Twitch replied. That was all he had time to say, as he was handed over to the supervision of a human soldier.

The comment warmed Twitch's heart as he followed the human into the interior of the mountain. Twitch stared with wide eyes at the soldiers who passed by. He was used to being around the military. He had spent most of his life on the military port on Ceres, though he had originally been raised near the civilian mines on the dwarf planet. He still wasn't used to seeing starats in any uniform other than the dirty overalls he had worn every day of his servitude on Ceres.

Twitch was taken through to a small office that overlooked the greenhouses and hydroponic farms. There was no one waiting for him in the office, but his human guide told him to take a seat. A drink was offered, and Twitch sat down in front of the desk while he waited for a cup of coffee. A rebellious grin warred with his grief and worry. David wasn't here to stop him having the coffee, so he was going to indulge while he could.

The coffee arrived first. It was bitter and strong, but Twitch didn't mind that too much. The warmth of the drink was enough. Though Prox had been above the horizon for almost twenty-four hours, the intense heat had not returned. The outside air was cold, and the air-conditioned interior of the military base wasn't much warmer. His fur was usually enough to keep him warm, but he had never experienced such intense cold on Ceres. There, the temperature had been constantly regulated to a level that humans were comfortable in.

Finally, the door opened again and a starat stepped through. Twitch jumped to his feet as he looked over the newcomer. She was dressed smartly in a white shirt and black trousers, with the military insignia over her right breast. Her right eye was glassy and still in her eye socket, and a scar ran up the side of her face, its presence given away by a line of white fur.

Twitch flicked his tail and shivered. He had forgotten he had not been the only starat injured by Cardinal Erik on Centaura. The major-general had been the first victim of the Inquisition after the cardinal's arrival on the planet.

"You must be Twitch," the starat said. She gestured to the chair, letting Twitch know he could sit down again. "I'm Major-General Ulrich."

"Nice to meet you, Major-General Ulrich," Twitch said, before wrinkling his muzzle. "Bit of a mouthful that. Do people really need to call you that every time? Must take ages."

The starat smiled as she sat down on the other side of the desk. "Only formally. You can call me Nessie, if you'd prefer."

Twitch tried the name out. "Nessie. Nessie Ulrich? You were named after Essie?"

"Afraid not. It's short for Vanessa, but that never worked for me," the starat replied. She tilted her head slightly to the side as she looked over Twitch. "I don't believe starats use last names in the empire. I've been curious about that."

"It's a family name, isn't it? We don't have families," Twitch replied. He grimaced and shrugged his shoulders. "No need for last names."

"I'm sorry. I should have realised," Nessie said. Her one working eye glanced down to the desk between the two starats.

"It's not your fault, don't worry," Twitch said brightly. His tail curled up against the leg of his chair. "I know you didn't mean anything by it."

"Would you take a name, now that you could?"

Twitch had never thought about that. He hadn't really considered it at all, not thinking it to be an option. But he already knew what name he would use. He clasped his hands together beneath the desk. "Griffiths."

Nessie smiled sadly. "I suppose it wasn't going to be long before he came up. You must miss him," she said. She reached out across the desk and took hold of one of Twitch's hands. Her one working eye sparkled brightly.

"I do, yeah. I..." Twitch hesitated. He looked up to Nessie Ulrich. He was tempted to explain what he had uncovered in Hadrian to her; how he had been so desperate for Captain Rhys's help in fixing it all. But something held him back. Though he had not been explicitly told not to inform the military about the situation, both Amy and Minister Bakir had warned him about who to trust. He didn't know Nessie Ulrich. He didn't know how reliable she was, or if she was somehow working for the Inquisition. Just because she was a starat did not mean she was on his side, just like he had doubts about what Amy and Snow were hiding from him. He lowered his eyes and held his tongue.

Nessie sighed. "There's something I need you to do for me, if you're willing."

Twitch tensed. He looked up sharply. His fear must have been obvious.

"It's not much, I promise you," Nessie said, raising her hands. "We need assistance transferring ownership of the *Freedom*."

Twitch flicked his ears. "And how can I help with that?" he asked in confusion. He didn't see how he would be needed for such a task.

Nessie smiled wryly. "Usually there wouldn't be a problem. There would be a first officer or override codes to transfer ownership and captain's privileges to someone new, but the *Freedom* is still a new ship in our armada, and there was no formal first officer. New codes weren't installed, and we don't have access to the Terran ones. We can override it, but it will take time."

"And you need me because..."

"We need Captain Griffiths' voice and fingerprints."

Twitch stared down at his hands. "Of course, yes. What do you need me to do?"

"We need to go up to the *Freedom*. You'll need to access the ship's computer and transfer it away from Captain Griffiths. I'll walk you through the process."

Twitch looked up towards the ceiling. Somewhere, high above them, was the *Freedom*, the ship that had once been named the *Harvester*. It had been there that Twitch had first spoken to Captain Rhys. He almost didn't want to go onboard. There would be too many memories of the captain on that ship. Even so, he nodded. "I'll do it."

"I know it's hard for you, Twitch. We do appreciate you doing this for us," Nessie said. She rose to her feet, and Twitch quickly followed her.

"It will be like saying goodbye," Twitch said. He managed to suppress a whimper, and instead fixed a smile onto his face. It was time to say goodbye to one of the most positive influences on his life. As much as he wanted Captain Rhys back, he knew well enough that there was no chance of that. Death had been a sadly constant presence on those Twitch cared about. To be a starat in the empire was to know that death was a real and constant danger. He knew how to accept it and move on, though he never wanted to feel that again. Centaura was meant to be an escape from all of that. He could only hope that he was finally free from it.

***

The *Freedom* was docked at the Network Central satellite hub orbiting over the north pole of Centaura. The massive satellite had awed Twitch the first time he had seen it, and his reaction was no less wonderous as he stepped off the shuttle. The space elevator up to a neighbouring satellite had been slow, and the shuttle across to Central uninteresting, but everything was worth it as he reached the centre of the web that surrounded the planet below.

Wide windows provided a brilliant view of Centaura and to the field of unfamiliar stars beyond. None of the nearby stars were visible, with Proxima Centauri and the binary stars of Alpha Centauri on the other side of the station. The red light of Prox still gleamed off the few ships Twitch could see docked a little higher above them.

Nessie was not stopped as she made her way slowly up towards the higher reaches of the satellite, with Twitch following close behind. A few soldiers looked towards Twitch, but none spoke to him or tried to stop him. Most were humans, but there was enough starats around to make Twitch feel more comfortable. He wondered how long it would take him to get used to uniformed starats.

Access to the *Freedom* was guarded. Four humans stood at the airlock doors, and they refused to step aside until they had seen identification from the major-general. They held them for a few moments as they waited for confirmation through their headsets that the two starats had permission to enter the ship.

Though the ship had been retrofitted with new equipment since arriving on Centaura, Twitch could easily tell that it was the same ship it had always been. The corridors looked the same, though they were a lighter colour than he remembered. Everything was shrouded in darkness though, with only a few of the lights currently on. The air had a sharp tang to it, and the coolness irritated his nose as he breathed.

Twitch placed his hand on the open doorway through to the bridge. He had rarely gotten to go in there, but he could tell that it had changed significantly since he had last seen it. A narrow stairwell led up to a balcony that had not been there before, and the terminals and stations around the side of the bridge all appeared new. The holoscreens at the front of the bridge, all switched off for now, were new as well.

"Captain Rhys would have loved this ship," Twitch said quietly. He stepped forward into the middle of the bridge and turned around on the spot, looking up to the balcony. He tried to imagine Captain Rhys standing up there, looking down at his crew with that stern and serious glare. It had always been so strange, seeing the mirror image of himself with those expressions that had been so antithetical to his own.

Nessie had hung back, still standing by the stairwell up to the balcony. "I was looking forward to serving with him," she said. She flicked her ears towards the stairs. "We won't be permitted long in here. We'd best get things done quickly."

Twitch reluctantly followed Nessie as she ascended towards the upper level. He had wanted the chance to have one last walk through the ship. It wasn't the same when it was empty, but it would have been nice to see his quarters one last time. It had been the first time he had a room of his own, though of course he had shared it with David. He would also have liked to see Captain Rhys's quarters once more, as that had been where his life had been completely transformed. It had been there that he had first spoken with Captain Rhys, and when he had seen the former human go through an understanding, where he had seen a starat as a person and not an animal.

Instead, all he was able to do was stand atop the balcony and look down over the bridge while the major-general switched on the computer terminal. A few more lights in the darkened bridge switched on with the holoscreens. The quiet hum of the computers filled the silence.

Nessie guided Twitch through a log in process onto the ship's computer that required a fingerprint scan and vocal confirmation.

Twitch had been a little worried that his fingers wouldn't work, after the injuries Rhys had suffered in the escape from Terra, and it took the starat a couple of attempts to put the right tonal inflections into his voice.

Then he was in. The holoscreens at the front of the bridge lit up with the computer interface.

"May I?" Nessie asked. She stepped in front of the terminal as Twitch moved aside.

Twitch's tail tucked between his legs as he looked out across the bridge. There was nothing else for him to do now. He had done his part. All that was left was for Nessie to revoke Captain Rhys's ownership of the ship.

"Ah shit, what's this?" Nessie muttered.

Twitch's ears flicked up as he glanced to the holoscreens. An error warning had popped up, demanding action before the starat could proceed.

*Captain's Authority Required Before Deletion*

"What does that mean?" Twitch asked. He flicked his ears in confusion as his focus returned to the computer.

"I'm not sure," Nessie said with a frown. She tapped at the screen a few times, but the error message refused to be cleared. "Seems like someone tried to delete something from the computer logs. You mind fixing this? Maybe it will respond to your touch."

Twitch returned to the terminal. The moment he placed his hand down on the screen, the error message vanished. In its place was a list of files that were pending deletion. A shiver ran down Twitch's tail. "These are visual records from Pluto. Why would someone delete those?"

"I don't know," Nessie said uncertainly. She tapped her foot against the floor. "It certainly shouldn't have been authorised. They need to stay on record for at least two years."

Before waiting for permission from the other starat, Twitch flicked through the list of entries to find the one that corresponded to Captain Rhys's helmet camera. He opened it, and the holoscreens flickered to life to display the visuals from the Pluto mission.

"We really shouldn't..." Nessie said, but she didn't make any move to stop the video playing.

"I need to know what happened," Twitch whispered. He breathed quickly as he fast-forwarded through the footage. His hand trembled as he watched, trying to find some clue that would give him an understanding of what had happened to Captain Rhys.

Suddenly, the video turned to static. "Shit," Twitch muttered. He rewound the footage to a few minutes before the end of the recording. He stared with wide eyes as he watched Captain Rhys fumble around with a cage. Inside the metal bars was a dragon.

"Why the fuck is that there?" Nessie yelped. Her hand gripped tight against Twitch's wrist. "This is on Pluto, right?"

Twitch had no answers. He could only keep watching as Captain Rhys went completely still, with his hands extended out in front of him. Twitch recognised the stance. Captain Rhys had been trying to do his subspace tricks. Though Snow had tried to train Twitch as well, he had never been able to grasp the abilities as well as the captain. Twitch didn't mind that. Subspace gave him a headache just trying to think about it.

The dragon on the holoscreen slowly started to prowl forward as Captain Rhys released it from the cage. Twitch's breath caught in his throat. There was a flash of red scales across the camera as the dragon's tail lashed out. The camera's view jerked back into a rapidly approaching wall. Then there was nothing but static.

Twitch whimpered and fell back. Tears came to his eyes as he sunk to his haunches. "Fuck," he said. He had closure. Finality. He felt even worse because of it.

"So that's that then," Nessie said softly. She held her hand out for Twitch. "We really should keep going though, I'm sorry."

"Wait, there's one more," Twitch said thickly. He didn't want to do this, but he needed to know. Leandro would want to know what had happened to the Silver Fox. His hand shook as he tabbed back and found the Silver Fox's camera footage.

Most of the footage gave no indication why the Silver Fox had been unable to return. The human had remained in the shuttle for the entire time. Twitch could hear the pirate giving tactical advice and updates from the safety of the shuttle, using a computer terminal to gain access to the port's security cameras.

Then the Silver Fox said something that didn't make sense. "I'm on my way, Captain Rhys."

Twitch's ears flicked in confusion. He looked up to Nessie, but she didn't seem to realise what he had been confused by.

"He must have spent a lot of time with you starats if he called Captain Griffiths that way," she said, smiling.

Twitch shook his head and paused the video, just as the Silver Fox emerged out of the shuttle. "No, that's not it. Look at the timestamp. That's about two minutes after Captain Rhys's footage ended. How could he still be talking to him?"

"Perhaps the timers were out of sync," Nessie suggested. Her working eye glanced down to the terminal. Her ears curled as her tail flicked between her legs.

Twitch frowned. He didn't think that would be correct. He played the footage again, his eyes wide as the Silver Fox made his slow way into the spaceport. Air vented from the corridors, creating a vacuum inside the Tombaugh Station. Twitch yelped in surprise and hope as he saw a starat kneeling alone in the middle of the corridor, not far from the airlocks.

"It's him," Twitch squeaked. "It's Captain Rhys. He was still alive!"

Twitch's excitement then turned to fear and confusion as he watched the Silver Fox removing the damaged, cracked helmet from Captain Rhys's head. Frosted moisture clung to the starat's fur as he struggled to breath in the airless void. Then the view from the helmet-mounted camera shifted unnaturally as Emile removed the helmet from his own head. Vision spun around to look instead to the human.

Twitch couldn't watch. He knew what was going to happen next. He turned his head to the side and fought back a sob. On the holoscreen, he knew that the Silver Fox would be dying, giving his life so that Captain Rhys's could be spared. At least he now had a story to take back to Leandro. The grey-furred starat would be able to know his love had given his life to save another.

But one question remained. If Captain Rhys had survived all of that, then why wasn't he on the shuttle with Aaron and William?

Twitch glanced up at the holoscreens again. Nessie had sped through some more footage, and only returned it to normal speed once Captain Rhys was back in the shuttle. Twitch pinned his ears down as he listened to Captain Rhys's anguish and guilt at losing the Silver Fox, whose body had been carried back to the shuttle.

"He made it back," Twitch said in confusion. He scratched behind his ear and looked across to Nessie. "Snow said he didn't make it to the shuttle. So did Aaron and William."

Nessie didn't have an answer to that. She just stood tensely and kept watching the projection in front of them. There was a short conversation between Rhys and an unheard Aaron. A few minutes passed. Twitch expected something to happen to Captain Rhys to pull him away from the shuttle once more, but nothing happened. Aaron returned.

"He lied?" Twitch asked. He could barely believe it. He had thought Aaron had been trustworthy, but he had lied to them. And so had William. It didn't make any sense.

Captain Rhys was taken aside by Snow. Twitch couldn't hear what the albino was saying, but he could hear Captain Rhys speaking. The former human was getting more and more angry in his words, and they chilled Twitch. It sounded like Pluto was developing the same weapon that had been buried beneath Hadrian.

Twitch's throat felt dry. "Can we get Snow's audio too? I want to hear this."

Nessie rewound the footage back to the start of the conversation. This time, they could hear both sides. It confirmed Twitch's fears, but they went so much further than that. Snow was wanting the weapon for herself. She wanted to destroy Terra.

Then Snow attacked Captain Rhys. She pushed him from the shuttle, and after a brief struggle, Captain Rhys fell back to the surface. In the last moment before he lost sight of the shuttle, Twitch could see both Aaron and William slump limply to the floor.

The video cut out before Captain Rhys hit the ground.

Nessie cleared her throat. "Well shit. Save everything. I don't need to tell you that things just escalated. This is a major crisis," she said. She swallowed and tapped her claws together as Twitch saved a copy of the footage from Captain Rhys and the Silver Fox, making sure to include the audio from Snow.

"You think Snow was the one who tried to delete this?" Twitch asked. His tongue felt thick, slurring his words as his mind raced and tried to process what he had seen.

"I think it's safe to assume that," Nessie replied. "Save two copies, please. I want you to keep one as insurance."

"Me? What will I do with it?" Twitch squeaked. His tail curled down between his legs again. This hadn't meant to involve him in something new. Now he had knowledge that there was a plot to destroy Centaura, and a counter-plot to take down Terra. He felt torn as he debated telling Nessie about the Inquisition plan, but still he kept his tongue.

"You know Captain Lee, don't you? Show him this. Make him understand the truth," Nessie said after a little pause. "You saw how he fell down then? I think Snow did something to his mind to make him forget. I don't believe he's in on this."

"And if he is?" Twitch asked. He didn't get an answer. He sighed. "What will you do?"

"I'm taking this to Fleet-Admiral Bosler. She has to know what Amy is planning. And then I'm going to her," Nessie growled. She clenched her fists up tight. "She's my fucking cousin, and she's planning this? I'm going to give her a piece of my mind."

"You think this is Amy? It's not just Snow?" Twitch asked. He had finished making a couple of copies of the data. He presented a small datastick to Nessie. He pocketed a second one.

"You've been to her meetings, haven't you? She's passionate about ending the war with Terra," Nessie explained. She spoke quickly. "If she was sure that Terra couldn't be saved, then I think she would. Especially if she has someone like Snow advising her. She's dangerous. She always has been, even when we were kits. She's just very good at hiding that behind a smart mind and sweet smile."

Twitch glanced down to his legs. He stretched out his left foot. "I found a tracking device in my leg. I removed it and kept it active, so I don't think she can still track me," he said. He trembled. They had been wrong to trust her, if this was what her plan had been.

Nessie Ulrich took hold of Twitch's hands. She looked him in the eye. "I'll make sure she comes to justice. For what Snow did to Captain Griffiths, and to stop her plans on Terra. I will stop her."

Twitch pinned his ears down. He had heard that one before. He could only hope that the major-general would be able to do something before Amy did enacted her awful plans. But not before Amy was able to stop the Inquisition from doing just the same thing to Centaura. His head spun. He had to say something about the Inquisition plot. The military needed to know what was happening, if they didn't already have intelligence of it.

"There's something else..."

# chapter seuen

Twitch felt overwhelmed as he returned home. Nessie had questioned him for a couple of hours back in her office for all the information he had learned in Hadrian. She had then gone on to meet up with Fleet-Admiral Bosler and sent Twitch home. If she needed more from him, then she would get in contact, but she had chosen against having Twitch recount his story to the fleet-admiral. They had already stretched policy by allowing a civilian access to the *Freedom*'s computer. She didn't want to risk more.

All the starats were still there when Twitch made it home. He had not told them what he had seen on the *Freedom* right away, instead promising that he would explain everything once Aaron and had the chance to join them. Everyone involved in the Pluto mission deserved to know what had really happened.

The truth burned at Twitch's throat, just as the datastick in his pocket felt like a great weight he could not carry. The other starats did not press him with questions, though they did look in his direction often. Twitch could tell the questions were ready to spill out.

To fill the silence, David switched on the holoprojector, but Twitch was dismayed to see a news report coming from the city of Hadrian. Twenty humans, all dressed in the traditional robes of the Vatican, marched through the city streets. They had been met by over a hundred humans and starats to protest their actions.

The crunch of tyres against the road outside warned the starats of someone's arrival. David peered out the window, pulling aside the closed curtains. The holoscreen was left on as David left the living room, moving towards the front door to let Aaron in.

"Fucking idiots," Richard whispered, growling softly as he narrowed his eyes. His focus was entirely on the holoscreen, his teeth bared in anger.

The front door opened and then closed a few seconds later. Twitch turned in his seat, only then realising that the human had not come alone. The starat with Aaron had dark, almost black fur and a strange band of a dull, flexible metallic substance across his forehead. Twitch was sure he knew the strange starat, but he couldn't immediately place where from.

The unknown starat stopped dead in his tracks as his eyes fell on Twitch. His mouth hung open and he nervously licked over his top teeth. "You... I thought..."

Twitch's ears folded down. "That was Captain Rhys, not me. I'm Twitch. You must be Nick, right?" Twitch asked, recalling then where he knew the starat from. He had been present at Amy's Starat Freedom Union meetings. Like Rhys, Nick had gone some way to mastering the art of subspace manipulation.

Nick's tail thrashed behind him. Understanding reached his eyes. "You're the one whose body he took?"

Twitch nodded slowly. His eyes drifted from the black-furred starat to the human by his side. Aaron's jaw was tense as he looked towards the holoscreen. Twitch then reluctantly turned back to see what was going on in Hadrian.

"It's the same here, isn't it?" Nick said with a growl. He gestured one hand towards the holoscreen as he perched on the arm of the sofa.

Twitch stared down at his hands, clutched in his lap. He could feel the presence of Nick and Aaron looming over him, but he did not trust himself to speak. The knowledge of what he had to say made him feel nauseous.

"It's so much better here," William said, filling in the stalled conversation. "Things like that are just a few idiots. We can't control what they think."

"More than just a few though, isn't it?" Nick said bitterly. "It's thousands and more, from what Amy says."

"I wouldn't trust what she says," Twitch said suddenly, lifting his head. He shifted his hand to rest over his pocket, where he could feel the outline of the datastick.

"What do you mean?" Nick asked, his tone turning harsh.

"I learned something with Nessie," Twitch said, rising to his feet. He felt like his legs should be trembling from his worry and fear, but they were perfectly steady.

"It's about Pluto?" Aaron asked.

Twitch nodded. "Yeah, it's about Pluto."

Nick growled. "That shit was a clusterfuck from start to finish. Something really strange was happening there. None of us were told the full briefing."

Twitch pulled the datastick from his pocket. He muted the news report on the holoscreen and turned to face the expectant starats and human. "You've been lied to. This is about Pluto, about Captain Rhys, and Emile." He plugged the datastick into the projector and brought up the footage he had taken from the *Freedom*. He took a moment to compose himself, then began to play it over once more.

\*\*\*

No one spoke as the projection played out in full, showing clearly the fates of Rhys and Emile. None of them looked away, not even Leandro as he got the final confirmation that his beloved human partner would not be coming back to Centaura. Twitch forced himself to watch it all, even if he wanted to look away and cover his ears so he didn't have to listen to Snow betraying Rhys all over again.

The silence lingered for a few seconds after the visuals turned to static. Twitch switched off the recording. He swallowed and scrunched his muzzle as he waited for someone to speak.

"Where did you get that?" Aaron said, breaking the silence at last. His hands gripped the back of the sofa.

"I was on the *Freedom* with Nessie… Major-General Ulrich to help transfer the ship over from Captain Rhys's permissions," Twitch explained. He scratched behind his ear and scuffed his foot against the carpet, making sure he didn't scratch through it with his claws. "We found that pending deletion. We think Snow might have tried to cover things up."

"She changed our memories," William hissed, his ears curling flat against his head. He lifted his legs onto his chair, hugging around them with both arms. "How could she do that to us?"

"She did it because she knew you would ask questions if you knew the truth," Leandro said slowly. His eyes were full of tears, but his voice did not break. His tail thumped against the arm of his chair. "She did it because you have honour like Emile."

"I'm sorry you had to see that," Twitch said quietly, inclining his head and looking down to Leandro's swinging feet.

"Sorry?" Leandro asked. "There is nothing to feel sorry for. I knew in my heart that I would not see Emile again. Now I see that he gave his life to save another. I feel pain from his loss, but I can not feel anger in knowing what he did."

"But we weren't able to keep Rhys safe," William said with a snarl. He clenched his fist and beat it against his thigh, only to wince as he struck unyielding synthetic flesh. "We wasted his sacrifice."

"Do not be so quick to speak as though you have failed," Leandro said, lifting his hand.

Twitch's ears perked up. "You think Captain Rhys might still be alive?" He struggled to keep the hope from welling too strongly within him.

"Have you told anyone else about this?" Aaron asked, speaking before any of the starats could answer Twitch's question.

"No, no one else," Twitch said, his eyes wide as he looked up at Aaron. "Nessie was going to tell someone called Bosler about this, but I haven't said anything to anyone outside this room."

"Why do you ask?" William added.

Aaron breathed out slowly. He tapped his fingers against the wall behind him. "Because the SFU has fingers all through the military and through the government," he said slowly. His eyes flicked towards the curtained window, but Twitch could hear nothing from outside. "Amy's been planning something for years, long before I came to Centaura."

"She plans to use this new weapon against Terra. She plans to destroy it. That's what she's always meant when she says she wants to end the war," Twitch said with a squeak.

"Is that even possible?" Nick asked in terrified awe. "A whole planet destroyed?"

"It's the same tech that the Inquisition are using to threaten us," David said.

Nick bowed his head. He nervously rubbed at the metallic headband beneath his ear. "I barely believed it when Aaron told me about that. You really saw it?"

Twitch nodded. He wished he could deny that it existed; that there was no threat against Centaura, but he could not. He had seen the Denitchev drive, and he knew exactly what it was capable of. He draped his tail across his lap. "I just wish Captain Rhys had been able to make it back. He'd know what to do."

Nick bit his lip and turned his head away, saying nothing. Aaron put his hand on the starat's shoulder.

"Can you play the footage back again?" Aaron asked, keeping his hand still, his fingers surrounded by Nick's fur. "Just the bit at the end there, when Rhys starts falling."

Twitch reluctantly turned back to the holoscreen, running the projection back until the moment Rhys lost his grip on the shuttle. His ears curled at the look of fury and power in Snow's eyes. The recording played quickly, and to Twitch's eyes, nothing was clear as Rhys had fallen in panic.

"Hold it there," Aaron said, tapping a finger against his chin as he approached the projection. The frame on which Twitch stopped the recording showed the barren surface of the dwarf planet below the shuttle. Although the holoscreen only showed a 2D image, Aaron wandered around the projection to get a few different angles of reference. "Gravity is low on Pluto, so he wouldn't fall quickly. I think he would survive that fall without significant injury."

"Do you think he could still be alive?" Twitch asked, hope daring to blossom in his chest again. His tail swished slowly.

"Please don't get your hopes up," David cautioned.

"If he has help from General Carson, then maybe," Aaron said slowly. He grimaced. "But we don't know if General Carson was duped by Amy as well, or if he was in on the plan. Even getting a message out to us will be incredibly difficult. Until we can get back out to Pluto, I wouldn't expect to hear anything from him."

Twitch sighed. He had been foolish to allow that small hope to grow. It withered away as quickly as it had appeared, leaving him feeling drained. "Guess it's all up to us then, isn't it?"

"I thought you didn't want to get involved," David asked, a touch of fear coming into his voice. He rose to his feet and put his hands on Twitch's shoulders, making sure the smaller starat couldn't go anywhere. "We don't have to do anything."

Twitch flicked his tail, unable to meet his partner's eyes. "I know I don't, but I don't want to sit back and do nothing either," he said nervously. He could feel the weight of everyone's eyes on the back of his neck, but he didn't look around the room. "This is too important to do nothing."

"I know you want to help," Aaron said, "but you are not a soldier, Twitch. There are few of us here who can claim that. This isn't your fight."

This time, Twitch did meet the eyes of the human. He stood away from David, reluctantly shaking off his partner's hands. "I don't know if I can do nothing," he admitted, scuffing his foot against the carpet. "If Captain Rhys isn't coming back, then someone else has to step up and do what he would have done."

"You are not Captain Rhys," Leandro said. He rose to his feet too, swaying slightly as he reached out to take Twitch's hand in his own. "Your strengths are not his. You should not go to fight just because that is what he would have done."

Twitch wiggled his nose and scrunched his muzzle. Nausea rose in his stomach just thinking about having to fight, but he could not sit back and do nothing. He looked around the room. Amongst the starats, ears were folded, and tails drooped low. Even Aaron was hunched as he leaned against the wall.

"Let me speak to Major-General Ulrich," the human said slowly. "We can work out what action needs to be taken, and if there's anything we can include you in, I'll contact you again."

"Should we contact Michael as well?" Nick asked, though he offered no explanations as to who he was referring to.

Aaron seemed to know what the black-furred starat was talking about, as he nodded. "Might be worth doing. Until we get hold of you though, then you should keep your head down and not get involved with this."

Twitch curled his right ear down and nodded. He sighed deeply and looked towards the frozen image on the holoscreen. The thought of fighting filled his ears with the scream of the dying human. He resisted the urge to pull down on his ears, not wanting to reveal the turmoil still in his mind. His thoughts kept returning to Hadrian though, and the menace that lay beneath it. The machine that only he and the Inquisition had seen. A new thought speared through the gloom. "Actually, I think there is something I can help you with right away."

"What were you thinking of?" David asked warily.

Twitch tried to grin in a carefree manner to placate his partner. He didn't think he managed it with the usual precision, but he put in a passable effort. "I know how the Denitchev drives work. I'll be able to calculate how many particles in the atmosphere will be needed to trigger the jump to subspace, and I'll work out how quickly that drive below Hadrian can produce it. If we get enough sensors around the planet, then we'll be able to work out when the danger is critical. Give us a little warning."

"You can definitely do that?" Aaron asked. He sounded suitably impressed.

Twitch nodded eagerly. "Yeah, I certainly can."

"Good. I'll let the major-general know. I'll speak to her as soon as possible and we can work out a plan going forward," Aaron said. He started to pace around the room, making sure not to tread on a starat's foot or tail as he did so. "As much as I'm worried about what Amy is planning, we have to focus on the Inquisition first. Does that sound reasonable to everyone else?"

"Amy has to be throwing everything into stopping the Inquisition as well," Steph said with a frown. "If they win, then we all lose."

"Unless she is counting on us to clear this up for her," Leandro said with a growl. He rubbed the side of his muzzle and stared down at the floor. "We must not give her a free pass to carry out these plans of her. Someone has to speak to her."

"No, don't approach her about this," Aaron said sharply, pausing his pacing and turning to look down at Leandro. The grey-furred starat bristled, but he said nothing in response to Aaron's rebuke.

Twitch unplugged the datastick from the holoprojector, finally removing the still image of Rhys tumbling out of the shuttle from the screen. "What should we do?" the starat asked, handing the datastick out to the human.

Aaron closed his hand around the precious datastick, taking the information it held away from the starat. "Keep your heads down. Don't attract any attention from Amy or the Inquisition. They are both your enemies at the moment."

"Centaura wasn't meant to be like this," Twitch said dully. He breathed in deep and sighed, curling his ears down.

"Let me deal with that," Aaron said, touching his hand to Twitch's shoulder, before turning away. "You just focus on your calculations. They could be more important that you realise."

Twitch forced himself to smile. "I'll get right onto it."

"Stay safe, all of you," Aaron said, looking around the room. The eyes of all starats turned to him for a moment. Only Nick moved as he stood by Aaron's side.

"You as well," Twitch said quietly. He did not move as Aaron left with Nick. The starat bit his lip as his shoulders hunched forward, weighed down with the responsibility he had just given himself. His mind already buzzed with thoughts about how he was to run the calculations. At least they started to drown out the screams.

# chapter eight

Twitch buried himself in his work. For two days he did little else, hunched over his desk with scraps of paper adding to the mess. Most of his calculations were put onto the holographic projector, but sometimes his mind worked better when he was able to scrawl out little scraps and ideas onto physical pages.

The other starats knew to leave Twitch alone while he worked. Occasionally, they went out to the park that bordered the back garden, but never further than that. Twitch remained inside the entire time. When he wasn't working on his calculations on the Denitchev drive, he was tinkering with his synthetic legs; pulling off the panelling and looking inside to see how they worked.

Twitch was slowly getting used to the idea that the synthetic legs were part of him. The process of removing them, and his tail, each night to ensure they were fully charged had become a familiar habit for him. He still hadn't gotten used to waking up without his legs attached, but it was gradually becoming more normal.

Twitch had taken to keeping the news channels on quietly in the background while he worked, hoping to pick up any information about the Inquisition surfacing in Hadrian, but there was little direct news about them. Instead, most of the talk seemed to be focused on the counter-protestors. There had been one instance of violence at one of the pro-Vatican rallies, and the media had turned on those who opposed them, which was a group that called themselves the Resistance.

The news made Twitch uncomfortable, but he kept listening to it. He didn't like how the mostly-starat protestors were being branded as instigators of violence. He suspected there had to be some pressure coming from figures like President Shawn to displace the blame and public focus. He shivered. There had to be a reason behind it, but Twitch couldn't be sure what it was. If the Inquisition's plan was to rip Centaura into subspace and destroy the planet, then why did they care about what the public thought of them? He was sure he was missing something.

A knock at the door distracted Twitch from his calculations. He glanced up, realising that he was alone. He had a vague recollection of David telling him he was going out to the park with the other starats, but he hadn't realised they had all gone. He didn't know how long they had been.

Cautiously, Twitch rose to his feet and approached the front door. He wasn't able to see who was standing there through the main windows in the living room. They hadn't been expecting any visitors.

He opened the door to find Maxwell standing nervously outside. The other starat rubbed at his synthetic palm.

"Maxwell? We weren't expecting you," Twitch said, glancing up the road to see if anyone else had joined him. The street was deserted, with only one empty driverless car parked close by.

"No, sorry," Maxwell said, not managing to meet Twitch's eyes. "We would have called ahead, but we're worried Bakir's office is being bugged."

Twitch's throat felt dry. He tried to swallow. "Even when we were there?"

"I don't think so," Maxwell replied, shaking his head. "But even so, we thought to take some precautions, just in case they link you with Hadrian."

"You think they might find us?" Twitch asked. He took a step back into his home, almost tempted to slam the door closed on Maxwell. His fingers tightened around the doorframe.

"I think we should be open to that possibility," Maxwell said slowly. He flicked his tail. "May I come inside for a moment? I have something I would like to discuss."

Again, the temptation to just close the door welled up in Twitch. He suppressed that desire and stepped aside, giving Maxwell the opportunity to come inside. The augmented starat came inside and stood in the living room, casting his eye around the empty room. His gaze fell on Twitch's desk and the spare legs, as well as the calculations Twitch had started to make on the Denitchev particles.

"Looks like you've been keeping busy," Maxwell said. He rubbed at his palm again, before turning on his toes. "I understand that this must be a difficult time for you. We're not going to ask you for anything more than information, but we need to confirm a rumour that the minister was able to overhear."

Twitch curled his ears down as his head tilted to one side. "What rumour?"

Maxwell lowered his gaze. "That you've uncovered evidence that Captain Griffiths might be alive."

Twitch felt like his tail should have puffed up, but the synthetic fur did nothing. He shuffled back half a step. "Why do you think that?"

"You're confirming the rumour is true?" Maxwell asked, keeping his eyes away from Twitch.

"I'm asking why you think he might be alive," Twitch asked, a growl coming to his voice. Beyond the walls of Twitch's home, there was only meant to be four people who knew about that piece of information, and he didn't expect any of them would leak such crucial knowledge. There must have been someone spying on them. His eyes drifted towards the sensors he had removed from his and William's legs.

"We overheard an SFU message," Maxwell said. He was silenced by a sharp gesture from the other starat.

Twitch grabbed hold of Maxwell's arm and pulled him out into the small back garden, slamming the door behind them. His ears perked up, taking in the sounds coming from over the fence. He thought he could hear David's voice in the park. The air was hot and humid, warmed by the long daylight that had already lasted for three days. He pulled Maxwell to the far end of the garden, putting as much distance as he could between them and the house.

"The sensors I found in my legs might be transmitting sound back to Amy," Twitch said quietly. His blood ran white hot at the thought. Without inspecting the sensors more, he had no idea if his suspicions were correct, but he could think of no other way the SFU could learn about the evidence of Rhys's survival.

"We overheard an SFU message," Maxwell repeated, a little quieter this time. "We don't know where the leak came from, but it suggested that video evidence had emerged, and that a cousin of Amy Jennings had access to it."

Twitch turned to the side and hissed gently. He suppressed a chilled shiver, despite the warm air. "Nessie. Nessie Ulrich. She's Amy's cousin. She's who I spoke to. She's on our side, whatever that means at the moment."

Maxwell lightly touched Twitch on the shoulder with his organic hand. "Alright, thank you. We'll see what we can do to get in contact with her. She's with the Stellar Guard, isn't she?"

"Yeah. Major-General Ulrich," Twitch said with a nod. His shoulders shook as he rested his forehead on the fence. He closed his eyes and took a deep breath to stop a dry sob. He hated the prickling on the back of his neck, constantly making him feel like he was being watched. "You'll keep her safe, right?"

"We're going to keep you all safe," Maxwell said. He didn't sound confident, but Twitch chose not to comment on that. Such thoughts would only lead to a place of darkness and despair, and he had no desire to sink down there again.

Twitch forced a smile to his muzzle as he looked back to the other starat. "Is there anything else I can help you with, or was that all you needed from me today?"

"I think that's all, for now," Maxwell replied. He glanced towards the house. "Keep in contact, please. But be discreet. If you learn anything more, get in contact with me so we can arrange another private meeting."

Twitch curled his ears and glanced up. He was still not yet convinced he could fully trust Maxwell and Minister Bakir, but they had not lied to him like Amy had. They had not tried to kill him like Snow had done to Rhys. This was not the freedom he had been promised on Centaura, and he felt danger closing in around him. "Will we actually be safe though?" Twitch asked quietly. "If Amy is listening to our conversations already, how long will it be until the Inquisition realise what I'm doing? What I've done?"

"Minister Bakir can arrange you and your friends going into hiding, if you'd like," Maxwell said, idly twisting his synthetic fingers around in his palm.

Twitch glanced to the fence, his ears flicking back as he heard David's voice again. If there was any way he could protect his friends and those important to him, then he would have to do so. He looked back to Maxwell and nodded. "If there's any way, please. I don't know if I feel safe here."

Maxwell held his hand out. "Then I'll do what I can. Don't say anything around those sensors, just in case. I'll be back in contact soon."

"Thank you," Twitch whispered. His throat constricted as he thought about how to break the news to David and the others. He bit his lip as he took Maxwell back through the house, his eyes sliding to the sensors. He longed to smash them, but he didn't want Amy to learn that he had discovered them. Instead, Twitch tried to bury himself back into his work until the other starats returned home.

Twitch's head hurt. He couldn't focus on anything as he rested his head in his arms, leaning over his desk. He just wanted to feel safe again.

***

As soon as the other starats returned, Twitch held his finger to his lips and guided them through to the back garden. He stood by the back fence as he waited for them all to gather around him. Ears were curled low. They all knew something had happened, but they all kept to his wishes and remained silent. Twitch opened his mouth, but as he tried to explain, he found the words didn't come.

"What happened, Twitch?" David asked, standing ahead of the others. He held his hands out, letting Twitch take hold of them.

"I think Amy might have been spying on us, through the sensors I found in mine and William's legs. She was recording what we said," Twitch said in a small voice. He stared down at David's feet, his ears plastered against his head and his tail tucked between his legs. He hated how his tail fur remained sleek and still, not displaying his worries or concern properly.

"Then we should destroy them," William said with a growl, already starting to turn back to the house.

"No," Twitch hissed, lunging forward and grabbing hold of William's hand. "We can't. If we destroy them, Amy will know that we know she's spying on us. What's to stop her from attacking us then?" He released the other starat and stepped back.

"You think she would kill us?" Steph asked, her eyes wide. She leaned into Richard's side.

"I... I don't know," Twitch said, his voice trembling as he looked away. He dug his hands into his pockets. "I don't know what she would do, but I know that we can't trust her."

"Then who do we trust?" William asked. His synthetic foot dug up the soil beneath him, tearing large gouges through the mud with his claws.

"Aaron," Twitch said. He tried to lift his tail up slightly, so that it did not linger between his legs. "Captain Rhys trusted Aaron enough to come to Centaura after him. We can trust him as well."

"Minister Bakir," Steph said with a growl. She clenched both fists. "I know she isn't involved in this. She's on our side."

"Each other," Leandro added. He clasped his hands together and looked around the small group. "We may not have many allies, but we will always have each other."

Twitch held his arms out, resting his hands on David and William. The starats all clustered close together in a tight circle, embracing each other and resting their head on the shoulder of the starat next to them. "We've got each other," Twitch said, repeating Leandro's words. He knew it would be important to remember that, but he was scared that it would not be enough. "Maxwell said he'll try and find somewhere safe for us to go, but I'm still scared."

"Why don't we go inside?" David suggested. His hand gently stroked over the back of Twitch's neck. "We don't mention anything about Amy or Hadrian, or anything that we can't control at the moment. I was going to cook some dinner. Let's try and relax for a while."

Twitch sniffed and nodded. He let himself get led inside. His eyes turned immediately to the three sensors on the mantle by the front door, but he forced himself to look away. Instead, his attention fell on the papers strewn across his desk.

Leandro stayed with Twitch in his small workshop, while David and William disappeared into the kitchen. Richard stayed with Steph in the living room with the holoprojector on. Despite David's suggestion that they try to relax, the two starats had a news report on. There had been an incident at the Caledonia space elevator, but Twitch turned his ears away with a soft growl.

"How is this going?" Leandro asked. He picked up one of the many pieces of paper on the desk and peered at the numbers. His ear flicked back as he tilted his head to one side.

"Ugh," Twitch said, rubbing his temples. His eyes again moved towards the sensors. He curled the tip of his tail, but he saw no harm in discussing his work with Leandro. If Amy was able to defeat the Inquisition, then that was better for everyone. "I thought I'd be able to do this, but I just can't work it out right."

"What is troubling you?"

Twitch laughed bitterly and grimaced. "About this specifically, or everything else? Because one answer will take a long time." He pressed the heel of his hands into his forehead and groaned. "I need to know the concentration of Denitchev particles that would pull Centaura into subspace, but the only answers I'm getting are either too low, or so high that there could never be any hope of achieving it."

"What makes you think the low figures are wrong?" Leandro asked. His eyes quickly scanned over the hand-written figures Twitch had written on the loose pages.

"Because if it was right, then they'd be able to do it like that," Twitch said, snapping his fingers. He gritted his teeth. His ears were flat against his head in worry. "It's more of a hope that it isn't correct, because if it is, we're all screwed."

"Why would it be different to the concentration needed on a spaceship?" the grey-furred starat asked. He seemed genuinely interested to know the answer, for which Twitch was glad. David always loved to listen, but Twitch got the impression his partner never absorbed any of the information.

"More mass over a bigger area. It's not a linear equation," Twitch said, trying to make sure his answer was simple to understand. "The amount of particles goes up exponentially. A normal drive will never be able to create enough particles before they decay, but this one should be big enough for it. Or at least, they think so. But if the higher estimate is correct, then it would take them ten years to produce enough of the particles."

"Could they have been producing the particles for that long?"

Twitch shook his head. "Nah. That machine was pretty new. It definitely wasn't ten years old."

Leandro peered over the notes again. "What gave you the lowest figure?"

"I didn't know if gravity would make a difference, as well as mass, so that's ignoring it," Twitch said, slightly distracted as his ears caught sound of talk on the news about another protest forming in Hadrian.

"And this figure here?" Leandro asked, sliding his finger across to another part of the page.

Twitch blinked. "Gravity. That's assuming it does make a difference, which creates the much larger figure."

"Why did you use that number?"

"Because that's what I've always used for gravity," Twitch said. He then clapped his hands to his mouth. "Shit!"

The sudden exclamation brought a flurry of activity from the kitchen. David was almost pushed over as William barged into his back; both starats trying to get into the main room at once. Steph and Richard both twisted around on the sofa.

"Is everything alright?" David asked in alarm. He winced as William's cybernetic foot trod down on his.

Twitch kept his hands over his mouth. His cheeks burned a little in embarrassment; both for causing the fuss, but also a little shame for missing something so obvious in his calculations. "Yeah. Leandro just helped me work out why this was all wrong," he said in a small voice that barely made it beyond his fingers. "I was using the gravity for Ceres, not Centaura. Fuck, I'm an idiot."

"What does it say if you change the number to Centaura's gravity?" Leandro said calmly. He passed the page of notes back to Twitch, who quickly scrawled down a new number and started to run the calculations in his head.

The maths took Twitch a few minutes to work out. Most of the groundwork was already done. It was just putting in the new numbers to fit the formula he had already determined. Not only did he need the concentration of the particles, but he also wanted to know how long it would take the drive to reach those sorts of numbers. That part was guesswork, based on the size of the machine in comparison to the maximum output of regular drives on spaceships, but it would give him a rough figure to work with.

Twitch frowned at the new figure. "Two hundred and twenty parts per million. At that concentration it would take them about... two and a half days," he said. He looked up to Leandro. "That sounds about right, I think?"

Leandro shook his head. "I don't know. This is all nonsense to me, I am afraid to say. I have learned many things, but this is not one of them."

Twitch leaned into Leandro and gently hugged the older starat. "Well, you still helped me realise what I was doing wrong," he said brightly. His tail draped across his lap as he scanned over his notes again. "I should let... You know. I'll tell them about it."

"I am glad I could help," Leandro replied, nodding his head in gratitude. The grey-furred starat smiled, but it was one that never managed to reach his eyes. There was still sadness there, and grief.

"You must miss him really badly," Twitch said. He lowered his eyes.

"I truly hope you never have to feel what I feel," Leandro said. He touched a finger beneath Twitch's chin and lifted it gently. "It is a harsh pain, but it makes the good times feel even sweeter. And it clears my mind for what still needs to be done."

"What do you mean?" Twitch asked with a flick of his ears.

"I mean that we must win at all costs," Leandro said sternly. He patted Twitch on the shoulder and leaned on the other starat's side. "I know what it feels like to be in a hopeless situation. I look around me now and do not see that. I see hope. I see skills that will free you from these evil humans. Please, do one thing for me."

Twitch nodded and stared up at Leandro as the grey-furred starat smiled sadly at him.

"Please, always believe in yourself," Leandro said, his eyes watery as tears formed.

"What if I can't do it?" Twitch whispered, curling his tail low and trying to pull away from Leandro. The grey-furred starat did not let him move.

Leandro's hand rested on Twitch's cheek. "I know you can. You have a strong soul, something that Emile always had."

Twitch whimpered softly. He did not know how he could live up to that. "I can't compare to him," he said, his voice barely louder than a breath. "I tried to be like him, like Captain Rhys. I'm not that starat."

Leandro's muzzle flicked into a sad smile. "No, you aren't. But that doesn't mean you're lesser than them." His hand softly fell away from Twitch's cheek. "Please. Believe in your strengths."

Twitch bowed his head. "I can try."

# chapter nine

The call from Aaron was urgent, though it came with no information. All the human asked was that Twitch came to meet him right away. The location was one Twitch didn't recognise, in a part of the city he had never been to before. He was also asked to come alone. That had been something that alarmed Twitch, as he wasn't sure he wanted to travel anywhere without the comfort of David close by.

In the end, Twitch had disobeyed that final order. David had come along with him, but when they neared their destination, David hung back. He would be far enough away that Aaron wouldn't know he was there, but close by enough that if Twitch needed him, he could be there in just a few moments.

Aaron's meeting place was on the opposite side of the city, not too far away from the space elevator mountains. It turned out to be a small area of parkland, right up against the boundary between suburbia and the endless fields of greenhouses that surrounded the city. A high wall divided the crimson parklands with the vivid green of the hydroponics beyond, though there were several glass windows to look through.

The human was waiting by one of the viewing portals that overlooked the farmlands. He was stood with his back to the wall, keeping vigilant and monitoring the park. He lifted his hand in greeting when he saw Twitch, but he didn't move from where he waited.

Twitch nervously approached Aaron. "What's with the meeting place?" he asked as he neared him. There was no one else around at all. Not even Nick had come. They were completely alone inside the park, with a row of trees obscuring the view to the nearest street. The gentle hum of electricity across the wall tickled at Twitch's ears, but the surroundings were otherwise almost completely silent.

Aaron didn't look down at Twitch. Instead, the human's eyes kept scanning around the park. He held a finger to his lips. "Were you followed?" he asked quietly.

"No. Was that a risk?" Twitch asked, keeping his voice equally quiet. His tail tensed, but the fur didn't puff up like it usually would have. He felt like he had been robbed of a little nuance in his expression with his new tail. It didn't feel like it worked as nicely as his legs.

"It might have been, I'm not sure," Aaron said uncertainly. His face was unshaven, and his hair dishevelled. Twitch had never seen Captain Rhys's friend look so ungroomed. The human ran his hand through his hair. "I didn't want to drag you out here, but I feel like you have the right to be kept in the loop. I haven't been able to confirm anything yet, but I think they know."

"They?" Twitch asked in confusion. A shiver ran down his tail. His mind went back to the conversation with Maxwell. Were people still spying on them? "And what do they know?"

"The SFU," Aaron said. He paused. His shoulders slumped. "Ulrich is dead. We found her a few hours ago. It... it was clean, I think. But..."

Twitch held his hands to his muzzle. Tears sprung to his eyes. "She's... how? Who?"

"I don't know," Aaron replied. His voice was strained as he answered. "I think we have to suspect that whoever she told reported back to Amy."

Twitch felt an icy shiver trickle down his spine. "But she was only going to inform the fleet-admiral," he hissed. His eyes were wide as he looked up to the human.

"Exactly," Aaron said tersely.

"She's working for Amy?"

"Until we can confirm, I think we can only assume so much, yes," Aaron said. He pulled an envelope from his pocket and handed it to the starat. "Don't open this yet. It's co-ordinates for a safehouse with a group called the Resistance. You can trust them. I vouch for them. They'll be expecting you."

"Minister Bakir was going to offer us a safehouse," Twitch said warily. His tail tensed as he looked around behind him. He had been sure he had heard something closer to the road, but he couldn't see anything out of the ordinary. "Who can I trust more?"

"If the Freedom Union were able to get to Ulrich, then it's possible they are able to compromise the government," Aaron replied. His hand slowly moved down towards the pistol at his hip. "They'll be looking for you, and it won't take them long to find you if they're able to act through Bakir. Or if they control her."

Twitch took a deep breath. He stared down at the envelope in his hands and resisted the urge to open it right away. "I should get back then," he said uncertainly. "Get everyone out before... before..."

The starat found he was unable to even finish speaking. His throat tightened up as he struggled to hold back a sob. He didn't know how things had come to this. Centaura was meant to be safe, but he had never felt like he was in so much danger before. It terrified him.

"Did you come with anyone else?" Aaron asked softly. Tyres of a car crunched up against the street on the far side of the native trees.

Twitch nodded. "David is waiting a few streets away."

"Tell him to get back home. We have a new problem," Aaron said. He placed a hand on Twitch's shoulder and provided a little pressure to get the starat to turn around on the spot.

Twitch's hands trembled as he sent David a quick message. He didn't wait to see if he got a response, though he felt his tablet vibrate as he pushed it back into his pocket. He could only hope that David would listen to him and not come after them. He didn't want his partner to willingly run into danger.

Once Aaron saw that Twitch had finished sending his message, he gave a little more pressure to the starat's shoulder. They walked together alongside the perimeter wall, towards a small, closed door beside one of the wide windows. A large sign covered most of the door, advising that only authorised personnel could pass through to the other side. The door was locked, though that didn't stop Aaron. One well-placed bash with the butt of his pistol cracked open the lock, and the door swung open.

An alarm began to sound. Aaron pulled Twitch through the open doorway and into a short, narrow tunnel that cut through to the other side of the wall. A second door blocked the far end, but it wasn't locked. It easily gave way to Aaron's push.

There was nothing but dirt beneath Twitch's feet. A couple of metres away was the closest of the greenhouses. Clear glass protected the precious and valuable crops that were the lifeblood of the system. A mesh fence stood between them and the greenhouses. The starat could hear the gentle hum of electricity thrum through the fence.

"Don't get too close to them," Aaron warned. He kept one hand protectively between Twitch and the greenhouses. "Stay to the path. Now, go."

Twitch squeaked and nodded. He glanced further around the wall. The small path stayed beneath the base of the wall, following around the gentle curve until it disappeared out of sight. A few more paths branched off to go between the greenhouses, though these were blocked off by gates that were locked by a security system.

"Who is there?" Twitch asked. He started to run. His synthetic legs felt strong and capable, but even so, he surprised himself when he was able to easily keep up with the much taller human beside him. He resisted the urge to look back. "Who's chasing us?"

"I don't know. Inquisition or SFU. Both bad," Aaron replied. His breath came sharply.

Twitch wanted to ask where they were going. He wanted to know he could be safe. The first gunshot robbed him off his voice. He squeaked in alarm and lowered his head, though he doubted how much that would help.

A second gunshot followed the first. Twitch wasn't sure where the bullet went. It didn't hit him, and there was no cry of pain from Aaron either.

Twitch glanced back for a moment. There were two humans behind them, but they were too far away to see clearly. He wasn't able to tell if they wore the insignia of the Inquisition, and nor did he recognise them from the meetings with Amy.

The path seemed to never end. It slowly curved around to the left, with the greenhouses remaining on their right. The endless greenhouses. Twitch could see no escape. It could only be a matter

113

of time before someone approached from the front, or the shooters behind found their range.

A pull on Twitch's arm almost unbalanced him. Then the sensors in his legs worked hard to keep him upright, and the starat turned to hurry after Aaron. The human had darted down a path that had branched off to the right. There was no security gate across this one, though it didn't go through the mesh fencing. Instead, it went between two separated sections of greenhouses.

Aaron didn't go far before he stopped and dropped to his knees. At first, Twitch was terrified the human had been shot, but Aaron merely pulled up a grate beside the path to reveal a dark hole beneath.

"Down there," Aaron ordered quietly.

Twitch didn't hesitate. He quickly slipped into the hole and dropped down. In the darkness it was hard to tell just how far he fell, but it was barely a second before he struck the ground. He dropped to his haunches as his synthetic legs absorbed the shock of the impact, before he rolled away to give Aaron space to come down too.

The human used the ladder.

Twitch only saw the rungs embedded into the metallic tube for a few seconds before Aaron sealed up the grate again. Total darkness swallowed up his vision as he heard Aaron slowly clambering down the rungs. The starat barely dared to breath, lest the chasers above know where they had gone.

A bright light flared to life. Aaron had a torch in his hand. "This way," he whispered.

"Will they know where we've gone?" Twitch asked, keeping his voice as quiet as Aaron.

"It might buy us a few minutes if we're lucky," the human replied. The beam of light from his torch swept around the narrow tunnel. The walls glistened with moisture, and there was a small flow of water at the bottom of the rounded shaft.

Twitch followed the human as he picked a direction. The starat had been slightly disorientated in his drop down from the surface, but he had a feeling it was going in the same direction they had been running previously.

"What is this place?" the starat asked. His tail tucked between his legs as he tried to avoid splashing through the small amount of water. His legs were able to detect a slight incline to the passage, down which the water slowly flowed.

"Irrigation overflow," Aaron replied simply. He offered no further explanation.

Twitch curled his ears in as he looked through the darkness. He could see no other light other than that from Aaron's torch, but as the beam swung from side to side, he could see markings on the walls. They were stains, created by a torrent of water. Some were higher than his head.

"Are you sure this is safe?" Twitch asked nervously. He didn't want to think about what would happen should a large flow of water roar down the tunnels. There would be no way out.

"Would you rather be up there?" Aaron asked. The beam of light swung up a couple of times to reveal numbers written by small metallic struts on the ceiling.

Twitch shook his head and snapped his mouth shut. As trapped as he felt below the ground, at least he wasn't being shot at. He could only hope that would continue for a little longer.

A few more ladders leading up to the surface rose from the shallow water. Aaron ignored all of them, but to shine his torch up to read the identification number beside each one. Whatever the human was looking for, he didn't tell Twitch.

Distant shouts and splashes echoed down the long tunnel. The voices were distorted and muffled by the distance, so Twitch couldn't work out what was being said. The tone was unmistakable. Urgent and demanding. Their pursuers had come into the irrigation tunnels.

Twitch looked up to Aaron, but he hadn't reacted at all to the shouts behind them. He had to have heard them. The starat knew his hearing was better than that of a human, but the pursuers were so loud.

The human continued at the same pace. It would have been harsh for Twitch, but for his improved legs. Instead, he was able to keep pace with the long, loping strides of the human. But behind them, it seemed like the chasing humans were getting closer.

A light appeared at the far end of the tunnel. It started as just a tiny pinprick of light, but with every step Twitch made, the light got that little bit larger. Before long, Twitch could see that it was the end of the tunnel as it opened out into the dim light of day.

Another sound made itself known to Twitch's ears. A dull roar that slowly grew louder as they neared the light. Twitch wasn't able to work out what it was.

Then they emerged into the light, and Twitch had a terrifying moment of vertigo as he almost plummeted from the end of the tunnel. It opened onto a sudden drop, though the distance down only about six metres. The broiling waters of a wide river flowed beneath them.

"Down there?" Twitch squeaked in alarm.

"Down there," Aaron replied. The human applied a little pressure to the starat's back, and suddenly Twitch was falling.

The water was icy cold and dirty. Mud swirled around as it was kicked up from the bed. The current buffeted at Twitch's body as he struggled to surface again. His legs kicked against nothing but more water. He wasn't able to find the riverbed, nor the surface and the precious air above it.

A hand grabbed hold of the scruff of his neck and pulled him up. Instinct kicked in, and Twitch tried to struggle against the pull. His fist caught something, but the torrent of water he tried to flail through dulled the impact. Then his head breached the surface.

Twitch took in a deep gasp of air as he struggled to right himself in the water. Aaron still had a firm grip on the back of his neck to offer a little support, but the two were being buffeted by the fast-flowing water, making it difficult to remain in one position. Already, Twitch could no longer see the open tunnel they had jumped from.

Even while he kept one arm wrapped around Twitch, Aaron was able to swim towards the closest shore. It was slow progress. The current kept pulling them further downstream as the river angled around the city. Caledonia rushed by on the northern bank of the river, visible over the gleaming glass rooves of the countless greenhouses that were arranged in neat, orderly lines.

Aaron reached the northern bank and hauled himself up. The muddy ground gave way a couple of times, threatening to pitch them both back into the water, but Aaron was able to maintain his grip on both ground and starat.

Twitch's fur felt heavy as he dragged himself out of Aaron's grip. There was a small strip of open land next to the river, before a mesh fence cut them off from the greenhouses. The starat lifted himself up to his knees and wriggled out of his t-shirt. He let the sodden fabric fall to the ground, not caring how muddy it got. His fur was plastered to his sides. It felt heavy, even as he shook vigorously to rid himself of as much moisture as possible.

"Must you?" Aaron said in annoyance. He wiped his face, only managing to smear mud across his cheeks.

"You didn't say anything about getting wet," Twitch replied. He used his sodden t-shirt as a towel across his face, but he wasn't able to dry off at all.

"I didn't have time, alright?" Aaron retorted.

Twitch grumbled quietly as he tried to shake himself dry again. He wrinkled his nose as he wiped away some of the mud from his nose. It didn't smell too pleasant. "Just feel glad I don't have much fur below my hips, or I'd be naked right now. Unless you're into that."

Aaron's eyes glanced down to Twitch's legs. "Shit, they are waterproof, aren't they?"

Twitch raised a brow. "Bit late to be asking that. But yes, they are. I can't feel any damage."

Aaron rose to his feet and looked around. His clothes clung tight to his body, and they continued to drip even as he took a few steps away from the river. "We should get moving. Dragons tend to lurk around the riverbanks here."

"Oh great. Wouldn't that just be perfect. Chased by soldiers and eaten by dragons," Twitch grumbled to himself. He hauled himself up to his feet and squeezed water out from his t-shirt. His legs still felt stable beneath him, and they moved in their usual smooth motions. He knew he would want to run a careful eye over them once he got home, but he wondered if it would even be safe to spend some time there.

Twitch shivered as he started to follow Aaron. He wanted to check that David was alright, but as he pulled his tablet out of his pocket, he saw that it had not survived the plunge through the river like his legs. The screen was dead.

Until he got home, he had no way of getting in contact with anyone. No way of knowing they were safe. Visions of his home destroyed flashed through his mind. He whimpered softly and lowered his head as he trudged after Aaron. He would have to fight hard to keep the horrible thoughts away.

\*\*\*

Aaron didn't go with Twitch the whole way. The human left Twitch in the suburbs close to the starat's home. Aaron wanted to get back to his house so that he could make sure Nick was safe. While Twitch understood the sentiment, he was terrified about being left alone. His fur was still wet from the river, despite walking for almost two hours in the growing evening heat. He hadn't put his shirt back on, and he kept his head down and ears up as he hurried through the quiet streets.

Finally, Twitch was able to see his house again. It had not been destroyed. There were no enemy soldiers surrounding it. Nothing looked out of the ordinary. No one was waiting around in the street.

Twitch hurried to the front door, which opened before he had a chance to do so.

David stood there. Tears were in his eyes. They said nothing. Words were not necessary They just embraced and enjoyed the physical presence of the other.

It couldn't last though. Twitch pulled back from the hug and looked beyond David's body. The other starats were all there, watching nervously. "We need to get ready to go," he whispered quietly. He hated bringing the bad news, but there was nothing for it. They were all in danger if they stayed.

"Where can we go?" Richard asked. "There is nowhere else for us."

Twitch reached into his pocket, then went cold. He remembered the envelope Aaron had given him, but there was nothing left of it but mush. The paper had been completed destroyed in the river along with his tablet. He flicked his tail nervously. "I don't know."

Steph spoke up. "Let me message Maxwell. He'll know somewhere for us."

"No," Twitch said with a shake of his head. He let the sodden remains of the envelope fall to the floor. "Call Aaron. We have to know where this safehouse is."

"We've already tried calling him," David said, his ears drooping. "And Nick. Neither of them have been answering."

"Fuck," Twitch said, his hands trembling as they cupped the sides of his muzzle. "I don't know if we can trust Maxwell and Bakir. We can't know if the SFU have already got to them."

"Do we have any other choice right now?" Steph asked. She took a step back.

Twitch slowly shook his head as he watched her scamper into the next room. He felt like an idiot. He should have realised that he wouldn't be able to read the note from Aaron. He should have asked the human about the safehouse before they parted ways. Now he had nothing.

David's hand cupped beneath Twitch's chin. "Are you alright?" the larger starat asked.

Twitch took a deep breath. He nodded again. He was scared. Terrified, even. He wanted to be free of it all, but he was able to cope with it for now. "I am, yeah."

"You know you can tell me if you're not," David said quietly. He kissed Twitch on the top of the head and pulled him into another hug.

"I know, yeah," Twitch replied. He said nothing further. There was nothing more to be said. Not yet, at least. Twitch could only hope that things would start to get easier. He didn't know how much more he would be able to cope with, or how long it would take for the realisation of what had happened to catch up.

Leandro placed his hand on Twitch's shoulder. The starat reluctantly pulled out of his embrace with David to turn and face the grey-furred starat.

Leandro frowned. "Should we be looking at escaping the planet, rather than finding a new safehouse?"

"And go where? Terra?" William growled. He approached Leandro and shook his head. "I just got away from that hell. I'm not going back."

Leandro shrugged. He looked to the ceiling. "We steal a ship. My Silver Fox made a life for himself as a pirate. Why can't we do the same?"

"That's not an easy life," Richard added. Only Steph wasn't keeping an interested ear on the conversation. She was busy with her tablet, sending a few messages back and forth. Twitch could only assume it was with Maxwell.

"Better than no life at all," Leandro retorted. He spun on his toes to stare down both Richard and William. "Emile gave his life because he believed Captain Rhys was the best help for us. That did not work out, so it is up to us to save ourselves now. Do we really think we can defeat this threat? We have no allies. No help."

"We have friends," Twitch said. He leaned back into David, who wrapped his arms around the smaller starat.

"And yet none of them will confront Amy. None dare move against her. None will even talk to her and make her see reason. She has already won. Our best chance is to stay well away from this place," Leandro said. He looked around the small group of starats, but there wasn't much support in the eyes of his companions. None were able to meet his eye and agree with him.

Twitch scuffed his foot against the floor. "I just don't think I want to give up just yet," he said quietly. "Captain Rhys would have wanted us to keep fighting."

"And he is not here," Leandro said. He sighed and slumped back against the sofa. He sat down and held his head in his hands. "And nor is Emile. We do not know what they could have wanted. All we can do now is the best we can for ourselves."

"And what of the starats in the empire?" William said. He dropped down to one knee in front of the older starat. "The ones that we vowed we would fight for? Why should we give up on them?"

"We owe it to them to keep fighting," Twitch added. He stared down at the floor. Fighting scared him. He didn't want to do it, but he knew that he had no real choice. He would never forgive himself if he ran away like Leandro suggested. His heart knew fleeing was the safest decision. He craved the safety of that choice. He didn't want to constantly be looking over his shoulder for fear of another soldier with a gun.

Fresh tears came to Leandro's eyes as he looked around the room. His fists clenched tight. "Very well," he said. His voice trembled. "We shall stay and fight. I can only hope that someone will survive to tell our story."

Richard took hold of Leandro's hand. "We will. We all will."

Twitch looked around the small group of starats. They were not fighters or soldiers. They were labourers. Former slaves who had been forced to survive however they could. It was ridiculous to even think they could make a difference, but that would not stop Twitch from trying.

# chapter ten

Maxwell was able to provide them with a safehouse, and a transport to get there. It was located on the outskirts of the city, far from any residential area. The safehouse was isolated and well-protected, something that provided Twitch with a little more peace of mind. He didn't want to leave his home, especially as he had enjoyed the concept of living in a house that he had owned for so short a time. He hoped that he would be able to come back before too long, and he stared at it as it receded in the back window of the car Maxwell had provided for them.

Within two hours of Steph reaching out to Maxwell for help, the starats had arrived at their new safehouse. It did not look homely. The buildings were right on the edge of the endless fields of greenhouses at the summit of a tall hill, and they had the appearance more of a research facility than a group of houses. The three storey buildings were made of concrete and metal, and a large satellite dish dominated the flat roof of the largest structure. A couple of run-down and broken single-occupant cars were parked out the front.

"Are we at the right place?" David muttered as he got out of the driverless vehicle.

Twitch didn't vocalise his concerns, but the same thought had been running through his mind. Then he saw Maxwell at the front doors. The starat spread his arms and beckoned everyone closer.

"I'm sorry it's not too glamorous, but it was the best I can do at short notice," Maxwell said. He grinned wryly and gestured behind him. "Welcome to the Research and Communication Centre for Terran Affairs. It's a shell company, mostly. There's facilities for staff to remain on site indefinitely though, and that's what you need right now."

"We're going to be workers here for a while?" Richard asked. He flicked his ears in confusion as his attention was taken by the large satellite dish above them.

"I don't expect you to do any actual work, but yes, I suppose you will be," Maxwell replied. His laugh wasn't quite natural. "Come on inside and I'll show you around."

Inside the facility was much like Twitch expected. There were conference rooms and research laboratories, though Maxwell never elaborated just what any of them were used for. The doors were all locked, and inside the labs there was little evidence that any of them were ever used with regularity. Only one room appeared to have a lot of use, and that was the communications array. The starats weren't shown around that room, but Twitch quickly glanced inside to see labels that indicated it recorded all communications from the Sol System; both military and civilian.

The most important part of the facility was the dormitories. There were around two dozen beds in total, and Maxwell explained that none of them were currently in use. When the research station had first been built, it had been designed so that the workers would be able to remain at the facility for overnight periods; or longer if they were coming from other parts of the planet.

When the tour was complete, Maxwell took Twitch to the side. David stared after them, but he remained with the other starats. Twitch nervously followed Maxwell, who led him through into one of the rarely used laboratories.

"I am sorry it has come to this. We weren't able to get to Ulrich in time. We found out about her death just before Steph got in contact," Maxwell said. He kept his head low as he closed the door behind them. A lock hissed and clicked as it activated. The starat gestured to the nearest of the half dozen desks throughout the room. "We have something for you."

"Something for me?" Twitch asked in surprise. He turned to see a case resting on the desk, looking much like the ones that had carried his first set of legs. He suppressed a shudder as he thought back to that first time waking up in the hospital, before he had been fitted with his new cybernetic limbs.

"You need to be protected. These will help you with that," Maxwell explained. He slowly approached the desk and rested his hands on it. He didn't look towards Twitch. Instead, he stared down at the desk between his hands.

Twitch tensed. "How much danger are we in?"

"I don't know. No one should suspect you are here, but then no one should have known about your conversation with Ulrich. We want you to be prepared, just in case," Maxwell admitted. He still didn't meet Twitch's eye.

"Prepared how?"

Maxwell clicked open the case. Inside were a new pair of gleaming silver legs. They were sleeker and thinner in design than either of Twitch's other cybernetics. They were completely uncoloured. No attempt had been made to match his fur colour. There were also some additional seams on the panelling, which Twitch couldn't identify the use for. "We had these built for you," Maxwell explained. His hand touched lightly on the surface of the right leg. "Military spec."

"I already have these," Twitch said uncertainly. His tail curled up as he took a step back from the desk.

Maxwell's eyes glanced down for a moment. "I'm sorry you had to go through Hadrian in exchange for those. Amy told you that you had no choice but to go through her. That was nothing more than a lie," the starat explained. He took a seat at one of the chairs around the desk. His tail hung limply through the hole in the back.

Twitch stared, unsure if he had truly heard those words. "A lie?" he hissed, white fury almost blinding him. He forced himself to take a few deep breaths as he rested his elbows on the desk. His toe claws tensed, scraping across the tiled floor with a painful screech.

"There were options for you, but Amy pushed things through so quickly that those options were never given to you," Maxwell explained, not managing to meet Twitch's eyes. "We can't change what happened then. We can only prepare you for the future."

Twitch felt a tightening in his chest as he held his head in his hands. He closed his eyes for a moment and breathed out heavily through his nose. "Why are those better than what I already have?"

Maxwell flicked open the panel on his wrist to reveal the small screen beneath. A holographic projection emerged, providing a schematic of the legs inside the case. With his other hand, Maxwell navigated through the projection, enlarging it so Twitch could see the various labels.

"These are top-of-the-line military prosthetics," Maxwell explained. He gestured with one hand towards the right calf. "Modular weapons are implanted into the limbs, which are designed to be removed quickly and easily, without compromising the structural integrity of the limb. The claws are retractable and sharper than any blade. They're waterproof to greater depths than your current ones and are almost impervious to most standard gunfire."

Twitch jumped back from the desk, only to bump against the wall behind him. "You plan on turning me into a weapon? Captain Rhys was always scared of that. Why would you do the same to me?"

"We have no intention of making you a weapon," Maxwell replied with a shake of his head. "But we want you to be safe and capable of protecting yourself. These will allow you to do that."

Twitch didn't say anything. He couldn't. He didn't trust his voice. Instead, all he felt was a panicked fear rushing through his head. Dizziness threatened his balance, though the sensors in his legs kept him standing upright. An acrid taste burned at the back of his throat as he looked at the gleaming new legs.

"May I show you what these do?" Maxwell asked tentatively.

Twitch bit down on the immediate, furious response that came to mind. He didn't trust himself to open his mouth, unsure if anger or nausea would spill out. His eyes were drawn back to the legs as Maxwell lifted one out of its casing.

"These are lighter and stronger than your current pair," Maxwell said, not waiting for Twitch to speak. He placed the leg down on the desk and ran his hand over the shiny length, the projection from his wrist moving with his arm. "The right leg here had a hidden panel in the thigh. If you push it like this, then it opens to this chamber with a pistol." The starat demonstrated, but Twitch could barely look as he saw the gun emerge from inside. No matter what Maxwell asserted, Twitch could only see a pair of legs that would make him into a weapon.

"The left leg has a dagger and a bullet shield," Maxwell said, smiling at Twitch as his hands moved to press at the toes. "The claws are incredible sharp and durable. They're retractable to preserve their integrity, but will allow you to pack a much stronger kick. They'll keep you safe."

"I don't want this," Twitch said, his voice barely more than a breathy whisper. He swallowed and turned his eyes away.

"It's the only way to keep you as safe as possible," Maxwell replied. He tapped a couple of buttons on his wrist and the holographic projection disappeared. "I know you don't like it, but the minister fears you could still be targeted by the Inquisition, or by the Starat Freedom Union. Whoever neutralised Ulrich could still want you. Minister Bakir wants you to be protected, and so do I. This is your best chance."

Twitch growled. "I don't want this," he repeated, a snarl coming to his voice as anger won out over his nausea. Tears sprung to his eyes. "I'm not a solider, not a weapon to be pointed at the enemy. I killed... I killed someone the last time I held a gun. I don't want to be made into one."

"I know you don't want this," Maxwell said with a sigh. He stayed where he stood on the other side of the desk, both palms flat against the wood. "It's what you need, just for now. When this is all over, you can give them back. You can pretend you'd never had them."

Twitch glared at the other starat. If he could not convince Maxwell to take the legs away, then he would keep his silence. He already knew he would never wear the legs that were little more than glorified holsters for a weapon.

Maxwell scuffed his foot against the floor. "I should warn you too. Never overclock the batteries, alright?"

Twitch flicked his ear and tilted his head, curiosity taking hold of him despite his anger. "Why?"

"They're still a prototype, and some of the kinks haven't been worked out at the highest stress levels. They, uh. Explode." The starat held up his hands to forestall Twitch's squeaked anger and shock. "It can't do it automatically, and you have to clock them to over three hundred percent. There's loads of warnings before you can even get close to that. Just don't be tempted, alright?"

"What if someone hacks into them wirelessly?" Twitch snarled, stepping back from the desk as though the legs were already primed to explode.

"Impossible," Maxwell said, keeping his hands lifted in the air. "The warnings are neural linked. Only the wearer can authorise the overclock."

"Fucking hell," Twitch breathed. His anger spilled over into incredulity. He felt like he was trapped in a nightmare, but there was no waking up from this.

Maxwell smiled nervously as he returned the leg to its casing. He shifted on his feet and glanced back to the other starat. "I should get back to the others and make sure everyone is comfortable," he said. He held his hand for Twitch, who noticed for the first time that Maxwell's cybernetic limb was different to usual. It, too, was lacking the usual fur and natural look. As Twitch gripped it, he felt the unyielding strength in the other starat's fingers. Twitch assumed he was not the only one with an upgrade.

Twitch didn't follow Maxwell out of the laboratory. He stayed inside by himself, and spent some time just staring at the new legs in their case. He couldn't even imagine what it would feel like to turn his legs into weapons. Would he really feel different if he wore them? Nausea swelled anew in his chest just thinking about it. He snapped the lid of the case closed and turned his tear-filled eyes away.

That would never be him.

*∗∗∗*

The research centre was quiet. There was no staff around, and the place had the feeling of an abandoned building. Dust covered most of the walls and floors, and the small kitchen had to be cleaned thoroughly before it could be used. Thankfully, Maxwell had thought to send food supplies through, so they had something to eat, but there was not much else to occupy the starats.

Some of the starats wandered through the facility and began to read up some of the open-access information that was provided there. Not all of it was viewable. Some was locked away behind confidential codes. Most of that had been the military logs that the centre had been able to discover, but the civilian files were almost all available. There hadn't been much to learn. Leandro had tried to find out what was happening in the empire, but details were vague. It was difficult to pierce through the propaganda and deliberately skewed information. Even some of the most recently logged news was woefully out of date.

William had tried to learn anything that had been happening on Pluto, but there hadn't been a single reference to the dwarf planet that he had been able to find. For two full days he worked; sifting through the data for any discussion of it, but there was nothing at all. Not even a mention of the initial raid Captain Rhys had led, which had resulted in the liberation of the Silver Fox. It was like it had never even happened. There had, of course, been no mention of Captain Rhys and the events on Ceres.

Twitch had busied himself like the other starats. He had spent most of his time working on the two broken cars abandoned at the front of the building, finding them to be an interesting project to take his mind off the fears that lurked in the corners of his mind. For the most part, he had been successful. Lost in his work, he had no chance to think about anything beyond the research centre.

Taking a short break from his project, Twitch sat on the bonnet of one of the cars and looked out over the sights that surrounded the facility. The buildings were raised on a hill, so there was an impressive view of the endless greenhouses that spread around the city. For the first time, Twitch could truly appreciate the scale of the massive farms. There was literally no end to them, as far as Twitch could see. Nothing but vivid emerald green crops partially obscured by the gleam of the glass protecting them from the elements.

Long shadows stretched out over the greenhouses as Prox neared the mountains on the western horizon. The day was almost at its warmest, and Twitch had long shed his shirt to sit in just a pair of shorts. Free from the distractions of his repair work, his mind was plagued by thoughts about what was to come, and what was sat beneath his bed. He had been able to move the new legs from Maxwell without anyone learning about the dubious gift. No one knew of them, not even David. Keeping a secret like that from his partner twisted his guts, but he didn't want anyone to know what he had the potential to become.

Though Twitch was often by himself, his ears perked up as he heard the doors open not far behind him. He expected to see Leandro, as the grey-furred starat occasionally kept him company when he needed fresh air. Instead, he turned to see William prowl outside. The other starat growled softly as he pushed the door closed behind him.

"Is everything alright?" Twitch asked, a little nervous at William's obvious irritation.

William jumped in surprise. His ears folded back as he turned to face Twitch, a grimace on his muzzle. "Yeah, fine," he said with a sigh. He rubbed his hands over his cheeks and approached, turning to lean on the car. He tilted his head towards the cluster of buildings. "They're all gathered around the array. Richard thinks he found a reference to the SFU on Terra. They're all investigating."

"Why aren't you?" Twitch asked, flicking his right ear.

William's lip curled. "Why do we need to? We have the head of the SFU right here. We can stop it all right now, but we don't."

"What can we do against Amy?" Twitch asked. He slipped down from the bonnet of the car. His synthetic feet pressed against the rust-coloured grass that covered most of the grounds.

"We know where she is. We confront her. We force her to stop this madness," William said with a growl. His synthetic leg bounced up and down as he leaned his head back against the broken car.

"It's not that simple," Twitch protested. His ears curled down. He gripped onto the tip of his tail and nervously stroked the smooth, synthetic fur.

"Isn't it? They threw Captain Rhys out of a shuttle. They lied to us about how the Silver Fox died. They deserve to come to justice," William said. He tightened his hand into a fist as a growl came to his voice. "We've always seen humans get away with killing and abusing starats. But for a starat to do the same thing? It's a horrible thing for them to forget what we came from. The starats here may have forgotten what it was like."

Twitch sighed and shook his head. He pulled open the bonnet of the car and stared down at the loose wires he had pried apart to see what needed fixing. He wished he knew what could be done, but this was when he needed the knowledge and experience of Captain Rhys to know what to do. What did he know about war and battles like these? He was an engineer; a mechanic. Not a soldier.

"We must do something, Twitch," William said softly. Gone was the growl in his voice. "Captain Rhys had his faults, some of which

I've forgiven him for. He would not have sat around doing nothing, waiting for someone else to tell him what to do. We should not be doing the same."

"I'm not Captain Rhys," Twitch protested.

"No. But you are alike in more ways than just your body," William replied. He reached out to place a hand on Twitch's shoulder. "There is bravery there. And honour. You would always do the right thing."

Twitch pushed away William's hand. He growled softly. "I know you want to fight. You fought with Captain Rhys on Pluto. You're capable of it, but I'm not," Twitch said, his voice choking in his throat. "I tried. I killed. I don't want to do that again."

William bit his lip and turned away. He tucked his hands into his pockets and scuffed his foot over the grass. "I'm sorry, I know. I just... I feel like there's something we could all do, even if it isn't fighting."

Twitch rubbed his muzzle in his hands. "I'll try calling Aaron or Nick again. Maybe they have new information. Perhaps they can tell us more about this Resistance Aaron mentioned," he said. His voice was slightly muffled as he spoke through his hands. He heard William sigh and step away a few paces.

"Perhaps you are right," William said quietly. "Maybe we should be trying to stay out of it. I just feel like we've got a chance to actually help everyone stuck back in the empire."

Twitch rested his hands on the edge of the engine housing. He stared at the mess of wires and batteries that took up most of the space. "Leandro said that maybe we should try to talk to Amy."

"I'm not suggesting we talk to her," William said, the growl coming back to his voice. "There can be no justice for her or Snow. We've seen what they're capable of. We know what they're planning. She still thinks she can trust us. We can get to her easily enough."

Twitch spun around, his claws gouging through the dry dirt. "You think we should just go there and kill her? She gave you your leg back too. Don't you owe her a little bit of mercy for that?"

William snorted in laughter. He patted his synthetic leg. "She used us to get Captain Rhys on her side. That's all it was. Do a couple of favours for him, and he'd do whatever she asked."

Twitch grimaced and pinned his ears back. "But why? Why did she need Captain Rhys?"

"I don't know the answer to that," William said with a shake of his head. He flicked his ears and looked down to the car. "I've been distracting you for too long, I'm sorry. Did you need any help on this?"

Twitch pulled down the bonnet. "No, it's alright. I think I'm done for the day anyway. I'll work on it again tomorrow," he said. He could feel a headache coming on and he didn't want to stay out in the heat for too much longer. With sunset less than twenty-four hours away, the temperature was beginning to get uncomfortable. "Don't wait for me. I'll be inside soon."

William shrugged. "I'll see what I can find for food," he said, stepping away from the cars and approaching the buildings again. His tail drooped low as he trudged back, leaving Twitch alone once more.

Twitch curled his tail over his lap as he watched William leave. Only once the other starat disappeared inside did he allow his head to drop in sorrow and fear. Tears came to his eyes at the thought of what needed to be done. He was not a warrior like Captain Rhys. He could not fight like him, but he still knew that he had to get involved somehow.

"I need your advice, Captain Rhys," Twitch whispered to the crimson sky. "What would you do?"

The sky crackled bright as the electromagnetic shield flared to life. If there was meaning in the erratic strings of light as they arced through the sky, then they were lost to Twitch. There was no answer to his question. He had never felt more alone.

\*\*\*

The sky had begun to darken as the sun approached the horizon, but Twitch knew it would still be many hours before night truly came, and the oppressive temperature would begin to drop. Ignoring the discomfort, he had returned to the cars the following morning, lying beneath one as he attempted to repair it.

Despite some excitement amongst the other starats, there had been no further information about the SFU's activity on Terra, and William had not mentioned his desire to take out Amy. Twitch had been glad of that, not wanting to brood on the darkness that lurked beyond the walls of the research centre.

Twitch lay beneath one of the cars, tongue hanging from his muzzle as he worked. There was not much light to see by, forcing him to work largely by touch and feel. Once he had reconnected the kinetic motors, then all he needed to do was run some power through the engine. He hoped that would be enough to restore them to function.

The final motor popped into place with a satisfying click. Twitch grinned to himself, finally feeling a sense of satisfaction wash over him. He felt better than he had at any stage since Cardinal Erik had first captured him and taken the use of his legs. This was what he was good at, and Twitch was glad to get a chance to repair something.

"Ok, let's see how you work," Twitch said, patting the underside of the engine before starting to push himself out from beneath the car. He furrowed his brow as the movement was not as easy as he expected. His legs were slow to respond.

With a few grunts and wriggles of his hips, Twitch was able to drag himself out and sit up. He placed his hands on his legs. The touch was muted, almost completely numbed. His ears curled down as he tried to wiggle his toes, but was barely able to get any movement from them at all. He swallowed around the lump in his throat.

Twitch's hand scrabbled at the small panel in his thigh, grimacing as he pulled it open. A lone red light flashed above the screen where normally there would have been electrical activity. The starat swore and leaned back against the car behind him. "You're an idiot, Twitch," he muttered to himself. He had not charged his legs overnight. The charging dock was in the shared dormitory, on the far side of the research centre.

Struggling to get up to his feet, Twitch rested both hands on the front of the car, finding every movement to be a challenge. He had no balance in his legs and hardly any sensation. He gritted his teeth together, his furred hackles raised as he tried not to think too much about it. He did not want to be reminded of the mercifully short time when his legs had been utterly ruined by the cardinal.

The front doors of the research centre opened. Footsteps approached. Twitch's ears folded at the thought of being seen so vulnerable, but he forced a smile to his face as he turned his head. Leandro approached.

"Are you alright?" the grey-furred starat asked. He held his hands in front of his chest, his lone ear arched back.

"Fine," Twitch replied, his voice a little higher pitched than he intended. He cleared his throat and tried again. "Just forgot to charge my legs. Didn't realise they went into low power."

"Oh," Leandro said, sucking in his breath. "Was there anything I can do to help?"

Twitch wrinkled his nose and looked around the small courtyard within the boundary walls. Most of the space was empty tarmac, with just the two cars and the tools Twitch had scattered around in his work. "Can you pass me that jump lead, please?" he asked, pointing to the unorganised stack of cabling between the two rundown vehicles.

"This one?" Leandro asked, his ear flicking as he held out the cable. The grey-furred starat's eyes were dull as he looked around the courtyard. "Do you agree with William?"

Twitch ran the cable through his hands, finding the connector port at the end. He tilted his head as he processed Leandro's question. "Agree with him? You mean what he wants to do with Amy?"

Leandro slowly nodded but said nothing. The older starat appeared lost in deep thought.

"I don't want to go and fight her," Twitch said, choosing his words carefully. He flicked his ears down, unsure what conversations Leandro had been having with the others inside. David had not mentioned any arguments when he had last come out to check on him. He glanced down to the open panel in his leg. "Shit. This won't connect to my legs. Was worth a try."

"You think we should talk to Amy?" Leandro asked.

Twitch sighed softly. "I don't think that will work. She's well beyond the point of just being talked to. She doesn't care about the harm her actions will cause."

"I would not be so sure," Leandro said. His ear was flat against his head. He shook his head and held out his hand to take the cable back. "Would you like me to help take you inside?"

"Wait just a moment," Twitch said, weighing up the cable in his hands. He flicked his tail to the side as he glanced between the vehicle and the research centre. A charging port stuck out from the wall, just to the side of the doors. "Can you plug this in over there? I want to see if I've actually fixed them."

While Leandro plugged in one end of the cable, Twitch worked on the other. He had to grimace as he leaned forward, unable to properly balance himself as he did so. Once he got the signal from Leandro, Twitch plugged the cable into the car and flicked the switch beside the port. A green light switched on and a gentle whine came from the engine. Twitch whooped and clapped his hands together, a genuine beam of delight breaking across his muzzle for the first time in days.

"You made it work?" Leandro asked, still standing by the doors. His tail curled around his right leg.

"Yeah," Twitch said brightly. His grin grew wider as he patted the car gently, leaving the power on. "There was still some residual power in the batteries, too. You could drive this to Caledonia and back without having to charge it."

"Perhaps we should do just that," Leandro said quietly, barely loud enough for Twitch to hear him. "We could talk to Amy. Make her see reason at last."

Twitch snorted and shook his head. "No chance. She's dangerous," he said, twisting his hips after realising that his legs no longer responded at all. "Trust me, Leandro. We won't achieve anything if we went to Amy but putting us all in danger."

"Or it could save us all," Leandro said softly. He grimaced and flicked his eyes to the door. "If you'll forgive me, I'll go and get David. My old shoulders may not take your weight if you need help inside."

Twitch nodded. He leaned against the side of the car; not like he could go anywhere while he waited for help. He called out to

Leandro as the grey-furred starat stepped inside. "We're safest if we stay here. Talking to Amy won't do anything."

Leandro hesitated on the threshold. Twitch could feel the cool air-conditioning wash out into the heat of the evening. "I will always do the right thing," the old starat said with a pained smile. The doors closed behind him and hid him from view.

Twitch rested his head back and looked up to the red sky. Prox almost touched the horizon, but there would still be many hours until darkness came. The protective shield crackled, making Twitch shiver. He looked down, not wanting to be reminded of the danger that loomed large because of that shield.

The starat only had to wait a few minutes before David hurried out. He was alone, but Twitch needed no one else. He put aside his worries and pushed a smile onto his muzzle again. "I was an idiot," Twitch said, speaking before David could say anything.

"Nothing new there," David replied, sticking his tongue out. He put his arm just beneath Twitch's, offering some support to the smaller starat.

"Not my fault I'm not used to this," Twitch said, twisting his face and sticking his tongue out as well. "I'd never have thought I would need to plug my legs in to charge. Sounds ridiculous."

"Better than the alternative," David said with a shrug. "Are you able to walk at all, or do you need me to carry you?"

"I'd never stop you from carrying me," Twitch said, smirking as he leaned into his partner.

With a mock sigh, David scooped Twitch up into his arms, only to stumble forward a couple of steps. "Damn, those legs are heavier than I thought," he said with a groan.

"Too much for my big, strong protector?" Twitch said, resting his head against David's shoulder. "Am I going to have to find another one?"

Unable to swat at Twitch, David rolled his eyes and shifted the smaller starat in his arms to find a comfortable position for them both. "I'm not letting you get away from me that easy," he said, leaning down to kiss Twitch's forehead. His voice dropped a little quieter and his smile weakened. "I'm glad you're sounding a bit better."

Twitch smiled, hooking his arm around David's shoulders. "I am, I think. Working with my hands helps," he said. He looked ahead, down the narrow corridor of the research centre. He could not see any of the other starats, though he could hear them close by. "Is Leandro alright? He seemed upset by something."

David's ears flattened. His hands tightened their grip around Twitch. "He and William have been arguing a bit. Both want to go to Amy to stop all this with the SFU, but Leandro thinks we can just talk Amy down."

"He said as much to me as well," Twitch said. He closed his eyes and leaned into David's shoulder, taking in the scent of his partner and feeling comfortable in David's strong arms. "You don't think he'll try to do something stupid, do you?"

David didn't answer for a few seconds. His claws clicked against the tiled floor. "As soon as I've got you sorted, I'll make sure he's not planning anything."

"He's still grieving," Twitch said quietly. His tail drooped, hanging low to lightly brush against David's legs with each step. "He finally got Emile back, only for..." Twitch couldn't even bring himself to finish the sentence.

David turned slightly, using his hip to push open the door to the dormitories. No one else was present inside, though the scents of the others lingered. With no one else to disrupt the scents, they mingled with the dust and did not disperse. It was hard to tell how long the dormitory had been empty before their presence.

Twitch was gently laid down on the edge of the bed. With a soft sigh, he began to unclip his legs. The void of feeling still unnerved him, and he fought hard not to let his tail curl down or his ears to droop. He reached across the drag the charging port closer, clipping both legs into place and leaning back when the small red light started to shine.

Twitch stuck the tip of his tongue out from between his teeth, hissing softly. "It will probably be at least half an hour before I have enough charge to get through to tonight," he said quietly, gently running his fingers through the synthetic fur of his tail. "You might as well go see to Leandro now. I'll be fine here."

"If you're sure," David said uncertainly, taking half a pace back towards the door. The larger starat did not turn around.

Twitch forced himself to smile. The expression came a little easier to his muzzle than it had the last few days. "Trust me."

David's shoulders slumped. He slowly nodded and began to turn, but before he had even taken a single step the door burst open. William hurried in, sliding to a stop and scraping his synthetic claws against the tiled floor. The other starat breathed heavily.

"Is everything alright?" Twitch asked, tensing his hands against the mattress and curling the tip of his tail.

"Leandro just left," William hissed between sharp breaths. His claws scratched at the floor again, digging white gouges into the tiles.

"What?" Twitch yelped, sharing an alarmed look with David.

"He took one of those cars you were working on," William said. The other starat still breathed quickly and harshly. His ears both flattened against his head. "I couldn't get to him in time to stop him. I don't know where he's going."

"He's going to see Amy," Twitch said. He leaned back and grimaced, pinching the base of his tail against the bed. "We have to stop him."

"How?" William asked. He glanced back down the corridor. His tail drooped between his legs.

"Did you finish repairing that other one?" David asked, his attention turning to Twitch. "I'll go after him in that."

Twitch shivered. The second car had not been finished. It would not switch on without an external power source. His eyes flicked down, staring at his mattress as though he could see through it. He knew what lay beneath, hidden and secret. He could let David go without him and hope his partner could finish the repairs to the remaining car, or he could make the decision to go himself. He whimpered softly and closed his eyes for a second. "I'll go."

"Twitch, you can't even walk," David retorted. He stepped forward to gently rest his hand on Twitch's shoulder. "Just tell me what needs to be done if something else needs to be fixed, but we don't have time to argue."

"Exactly, we don't have time," Twitch whispered. He glanced down again, avoiding David's eyes. "Please. Underneath my bed is a case. Can you get it out for me?"

A question appeared to die at David's lips. His eyes narrowed into a frown, before he did what Twitch had asked of him. He reached beneath the bed and pulled out Maxwell's briefcase, the metal scraping as it moved. The weight of the case the settled against the bed as David put it down. Twitch's fingers shook as he unclipped the latches.

"Holy shit," William whispered as the case opened. Both starats stared open-mouthed in surprise, but it was William who was able to find his voice again first. "Are those mil-spec?"

Twitch nodded. He carefully lifted the right leg from its holster. "Maxwell gave them to me. I didn't want to wear them, but..." He looked up, meeting David in the eye and holding that gaze. "I have to be the one who goes."

David grabbed hold of Twitch's free hand and gently kissed it. "Be safe," he said quietly, but did not attempt to argue with his partner. Twitch was grateful for that. He doubted his resolve would last long if David tried to stop him.

The legs clicked on perfectly, without any resistance at all. One at a time they went on, and a few moments later sensation sparked through them. Every movement felt clean and crisp, and otherwise perfectly ordinary. There was no dirty sense of unease that Twitch had been expecting. Not until he stroked his fingers down the smooth surface and tugged at one of the seams in his thigh. There was a soft popping feeling as something disconnected, and Twitch was given a brief glimpse of the pistol inside. He quickly pressed the panel closed again, hoping that David and William had not seen that.

Feeling nauseous again, Twitch quickly stood up. His balance was perfect on the new legs. He could feel every slight change of pressure as his upper body moved. His new sharp claws slowly extended to prick against the tiles before he retracted them again. He took a deep breath. "I should go now."

Again, David made no attempt to stop Twitch. He just pulled his partner into an embrace and held him there for a couple of seconds. When he moved away, David was bravely holding the tears back, but Twitch could still see them in his eyes.

"Be safe," David said again.

"I will," Twitch whispered. He stepped away, moving past William and towards the open doors. His feet were completely silent against the tiles. A thin layer of rubbery pads provided the perfect grip and muffled the sound of his movement.

Twitch did not look back as he started to run. He had lost too much time to Leandro already. So long as Twitch's repairs held, then Leandro would make it to Caledonia in good time. The city's skyscrapers were visible on the horizon.

The charging cable was still plugged into the terminal on the wall. A small victory. Things would have been much more difficult if Leandro had taken that with him. Moving quickly on his new legs, Twitch plugged the second car in, hoping that it was in a similar condition to the first. He tried to power it on. A few lights flickered briefly before fading again.

"Shit, come on," Twitch groaned. He pulled open the door and rummaged through the storage compartment just beside the lone seat. He gasped, barely able to believe his luck, as he pulled out a couple of connection cables. Tossing aside the ones he didn't need, Twitch cradled one in his hands.

Leaving the car plugged in to the main port for the moment, Twitch hunted for a second port inside the cabin. He found one just beneath the dashboard, exactly where he needed it. Feeling a bit of relief flood through him, Twitch connected the cable and let the other end hang over the seat.

David waited in the main doorway. Twitch briefly made eye contact with his partner again, but they said nothing as Twitch unplugged the car from the main wall. There was nothing else Twitch could do. Everything was ready to go. He hurried back into the car without a word and pried open one of the panels in his leg, revealing several sockets and ports. He connected his legs to the car's battery, yelping in shock as a tingle ran up his right leg.

The starat grimaced and gritted his teeth together as he powered on the vehicle, feeling a strange sensation flowing through his legs. The thrum of electricity tingled at his synthetic flesh, and he could feel a strange ghostly echo of sensation coming back from the car, like he could feel the road beneath the tyres.

An artificial voice chimed as the car fully powered on. "Please state your destination."

"Jennings Tower, Caledonia," Twitch replied. The car began to move, its automatic systems plotting a course into the city. Twitch turned his head, looking towards the research centre. He lifted his hand to say farewell to David, but his partner had already turned away.

Alone in the car, Twitch began to feel the fear rising in him again. He didn't know what Leandro planned. The grey-furred starat was putting himself in danger by confronting Amy. Nothing good could come of this. It would not have the happy conclusion Leandro believed it would.

***

The night lights had come on in Caledonia. Prox had almost completely disappeared at last, though the heat of the long day still lingered. The air was muggy and still between the towering skyscrapers. As always, Twitch felt nervous on the busy streets, but he had no choice.

Twitch had not dared to take the repaired car right to the doorstep of Jennings Tower in the middle of the city. He could only hope Leandro had done the same, for he didn't want anything to provide a trail back to the research centre for Amy to follow.

Twitch had not seen Leandro, but he didn't expect to see the starat out on the streets. They were simply too busy to hope for that kind of luck. His only hope was somehow catching sight of the starat at Jennings Tower, before Leandro made the stupid mistake of barging in on Amy and Snow.

The massive letters on the side of Jennings Tower gleamed brightly into the growing darkness as night spread. The harsh white lighting felt almost ominous as Twitch cautiously approached the base of the tower. The foyer doors were wide open, and a steady trickle of starats and humans passed through the doors, both going in and out of the building.

Twitch's tail curled between his legs as he made his way up the steps towards the doors. No one stopped him as he slipped into the air-conditioned lobby. His eyes quickly scanned around the room, hoping against hope for some sign of Leandro.

A flash of grey fur disappeared into the elevators at the far side of the lobby. It had only been for an instant, but Twitch knew it was Leandro. He was sure of it.

One of the starats behind the reception desk called out to Twitch. "Are you waiting for anyone in particular?"

Twitch shook his head. "I know where I'm going," he replied. He tried to sound confident and sure of himself, even swapping over to his impression of Captain Rhys to try and feign that self-assurance. He flashed a smile to the starat. If he looked like he was meant to belong, then perhaps no one would try to stop him.

Even surprising himself, the ploy worked. The receptionist shrugged his shoulders and turned to a human who had approached the desk. A tingle of delight ran down Twitch's spine as he walked away from the desk in the middle of the expansive lobby. He didn't want to walk too quickly, lest he drag suspicion back to himself.

No one tried to stop him as he waited for an elevator. He stepped in with a group of humans and starats. Twitch stared at the buttons and swallowed. A card reader was needed to control the elevator, but he didn't have one. His hand trembled, unsure what to do. As he stared, the light for the top floor switched on. Twitch quickly moved away and waited by the back, watching the others nervously. None even looked in his direction. Not even at his glistening silvery legs.

One by one, the other occupants of the elevator left as it stopped at the different floors. Soon, Twitch was the only one left. He had to take the elevator up to the highest floor. Up to the office of Amy Jennings.

Despite his trepidation about what was built into his legs, Twitch's hand rested over his thigh, where he knew the pistol to be housed. It provided a little comfort that he wasn't going in totally defenceless.

The elevator doors opened out onto the small room before Amy's office. If someone had summoned the elevator, then no one waited for it. Mortimer's desk was next to the closed doors that led through to the office. No one was stood behind it, and the little waiting room was completely empty. Twitch was sure he could pick up on the scent of Leandro. It was fresh too. Only a few minutes old. Perhaps he had been right that he had seen the grey-furred starat in the lobby.

Twitch caught his breath in his throat. The starat could be just on the other side of the doors. He placed his ear against the wood, but he couldn't hear anything on the other side.

Cautiously, he opened the door and peered inside. He could smell Leandro on the still air, but there was no sign of him in the office, which was just as quiet as the waiting room. The lights were all switched off. The only illumination came from the adjacent building and the dying embers of Prox on the horizon.

The light cast a blood red tinge on everything.

Twitch closed the door behind him. His ears strained to pick up any sound, but all was silent and still. He began to doubt himself. Perhaps he hadn't seen Leandro after all, and that he had been so desperate to find him that he had imagined the starat and his scent.

Then he heard something back in the waiting room. The elevator doors had opened again, and a voice drifted into the office. Amy's voice.

Twitch let out a tiny squeak of fear. He didn't want to be caught in here by himself. That was the last thing he wanted. His eyes quickly scanned around the room for anywhere to hide. His focus lingered on a small closet not far from Amy's desk. He hurried across the room and slipped inside, managing to close the door just as the main office doors opened.

There wasn't much room inside the closet. Twitch could feel shelving press into his back, and he struggled not to move lest he knock something to the floor.

"...say why he was here?" Amy asked sharply.

A second voice spoke. Mortimer. "He didn't, sorry. He said it was urgent though. He's in the conference room at the moment."

"Did you let Snow know?"

"I did, but she seemed reluctant to come. She's still suffering from those headaches. Did you want me to insist?"

Amy clicked her tongue. "No, it's fine. Let her rest. I don't want her over-extending herself again."

Through the crack in the door, Twitch could just about make out Mortimer bowing his head to Amy, who he couldn't see.

"I'll hold all appointments for you," Mortimer said. He paused for a moment, and Twitch could hear someone take a deep breath. "Do you smell something?"

Twitch froze. He kept his eyes open, despite the urge to squeeze them closed. If either of them recognised his scent and realised he was here...

"I don't think so," Amy replied. "Make sure no one disturbs us."

"Of course," Mortimer said slowly.

Nothing else was said between the two starats. From his vantage inside the closet, Twitch couldn't see either of them moving, but he did hear two doors open and close. The sounds came from opposite ends of the room. No further noises reached his ears, no matter how much he strained them. No sounds of movement. No soft breathing.

Slowly, Twitch moved his hand down to the side of his leg. His hand pressed against the small panel that housed the hidden pistol. His fur at the back of his neck rose as he carefully opened the panel and pulled out the weapon. It felt strange and awkward in his hand. Bile rose in his throat. He shook his head and bit down on his tongue as he put the pistol back. He could resolve this without shooting anyone else.

After taking a deep breath for composure and to ease his nausea, Twitch pushed open the door. The office was empty. The lights had been switched on, but neither of the two starats remained.

Twitch's eyes moved to the main doors, but he shook his head a little. He knew he didn't want to go that way. Mortimer would have gone back through there, but he didn't care for the assistant. If Twitch wanted to find Leandro, then he needed to go after Amy.

There was only one other door out of the office. Unlike the large, traditional wooden doors that led through to the waiting room, this was a small, automatic sliding door that opened as soon as Twitch approached it. He tensed, but thankfully there was no one waiting for him on the other side. Just a short corridor with a single translucent glass wall at the end. Two doors were perpendicular to the glass wall. The one on the right was partially open. Twitch could see a silhouette moving against the glass.

Twitch crept forwards. He kept his ears partially focussed on what was behind, as he didn't want Mortimer to sneak up and surprise him, but he edged closer to the open door to catch any conversation that was happening inside.

"…not tell us the truth."

Twitch's ears flicked. It was definitely Leandro's voice. His mind raced as he tried to work out what he could do. He didn't want to just barge in and demand Amy let them go. He needed to know what Leandro had planned first.

"I have told you everything you have needed to know," Amy replied coolly.

Twitch could see Amy's silhouette pace back and forth.

"But it was not the truth." Leandro did not sound angry. He sounded calm and measured. Almost disappointed.

"What is the truth, but a sequence of events everyone agrees to believe?"

Leandro scoffed in laughter. "You are sounding dangerously like the humans. What are starats but vermin and soulless slaves? Twisting the truth into a lie is dangerous. You would do well to avoid walking down that path."

"And what path do you suggest walking down?" Even though Twitch could not see her, he could hear the smile on her words.

Leandro did not hesitate. "Co-operation. At heart, we both have the same desire."

"I thought we were co-operating. That was why you came to the SFU," Amy said. Twitch could see her silhouette stop moving.

"Then I learned the truth. The real truth. Not this sequence everyone chose to believe. Not the truth you sold us on," Leandro replied. For the first time, a small growl of anger did come to his voice.

"It is necessary."

"Death is never necessary," Leandro said. His anger gave way into a choking sob. "It is inevitable. But it is never necessary."

"Some deaths are always necessary."

"Some?" Leandro asked. He sounded incredulous. "You would call the loss of billions as 'some'?"

"They don't share our ideals. Most of them never will. We can't trust them."

Twitch closed his eyes and cursed to himself under his breath. He knew he had to do something. He had to go in there and join the other two starats, if only to get Leandro out of there, but he was scared. He was afraid of Amy and what she was capable of.

"I struggled against the empire for years as an equal with Terran humans. There are good people there," Leandro said. The growl was back.

"You were a ship's pet and nothing more."

"How dare you," Leandro hissed. Twitch heard a chair scrape on the floor. "Emile would never..."

"That's the problem with Terran starats. You see equality where there is none, because you have been crushed underfoot for so long. There is no saving you from that," Amy said calmly.

That brought a growl from Twitch. The starat could not hold back any longer. If he didn't step in now, then Leandro would do or say something he would regret. He barged open the door and stepped into the small conference room.

Leandro blinked in surprise and looked across to Twitch. The grey-furred starat was stood behind one of the rows of tables, with his chair pushed back. At the front of the room was Amy. She had been facing Leandro, stood in front of the lectern. She barely reacted to Twitch's presence. She turned on her toes and smiled to him.

"Glad you could join us," Amy said. Her ear flicked a couple of times. "Did you have anything to say?"

"Captain Rhys was the change you refused to believe," Twitch snarled. His hand drifted down to his right leg, lightly brushing over the panelling that concealed his weapon. Amy carried a weapon too. She had a pistol at her hip, still holstered. He had never seen her with one before.

Amy shook her head. She kept her eyes on Twitch. "Captain Griffiths was not our ally. He refused to side with starats, and he presented a danger to our cause."

"He realised what you were doing," Twitch growled. "He never turned his back on starats. He was our friend, and he was helping us. You threw him out of a shuttle when you realised he wasn't on your side anymore."

"I did nothing to him," Amy replied. She sat on the edge of the front row of tables. Her fingers idly toyed with the hilt of her pistol.

"You. Snow. What does it matter which of you did it?" Twitch said. He took a step around closer to Leandro.

"Snow did nothing to him either," Amy replied. She slowly folded her arms in front of her chest.

"I saw the footage," Twitch spat. His muzzle wrinkled up in disgust as he glared to the starat. He couldn't believe he had once trusted her. He had believed her. Now he was utterly appalled by what she had planned.

Amy didn't seem perturbed by the unravelling of her lie. She just shrugged her shoulders and glanced across to Leandro. "Is this what your argument was based on? You learned what we are capable of, and you got scared?" she asked the older starat.

Leandro nodded. "Everyone in the empire deserves the chance to make a change. They deserve the opportunity to change their ways when they learn the truth. Both human and starat," he said. He took a step towards Amy. "Please. They don't deserve to die. Especially not like this."

Amy shook her head sadly. "It is a shame. I really think we could have done a lot of good together."

Leandro took another step forward. He held a hand out to Amy. A hopeful smile came across his muzzle. "We still ca-"

Amy's hand moved quickly. Her pistol came up. Before Leandro could even finish his word, the bullet passed through his forehead.

The grey-furred starat fell back. The smile was still on his face.

Twitch fumbled as he took the pistol from his leg. Shockwaves reverberated through his hand as he squeezed the trigger.

Amy yelped in pain and dropped her pistol. An angry line of red opened up on her forearm as the bullet clipped against her. She laughed as she held her left hand over the small wound.

Words struggled to come to Twitch. His mouth formed them, but nothing came from his throat. He couldn't breathe. His vision was blurred. All he could hear was the cruel laughter from Amy. "Why...?" he finally managed to gasp. His hand shook as he lifted the pistol to aim for Amy's chest.

"He's a pirate. Once he knew he couldn't change my mind, he would do what it takes to stop me," Amy said with a sneer. Her voice had gone cold. She grimaced and gripped her arm tight and tensed the fingers of her right hand.

"You think I won't?" Twitch squeaked. His voice trembled as he tried to hold his hands steady. Both hands gripped onto the hilt of the pistol.

Amy laughed again. "You're not a killer. You don't have the guts to do it," she said. She turned her back on Twitch as she checked on her injured arm.

"You made me one," Twitch snarled. His hands gripped so tight against the gun that his fingers hurt. They still shook. He could barely see Amy as his vision blurred. "You turned me into a killer!"

Amy slowly turned back to face Twitch. "You killed to save your life. You will not kill when there's no threat to you," she said. She held both hands up. Blood trickled down her right arm, but she didn't pay it any attention.

"You don't know that," Twitch gasped. He breathed quickly and heavily. He tried to force his finger to squeeze the trigger, his pistol aimed for her heart.

"Then do it," Amy said. She made no movement for her dropped weapon. She kept her hands spread wide. Her feet stayed planted on the floor, making no attempt to approach Twitch or take the pistol from his shaking hands.

"You deserve it," Twitch hissed. He blinked furiously as he tried to clear his vision. His throat felt raw. He choked back a sob. "You killed him... you... how could you?"

"You're stalling. Kill me or leave. The door is still open," Amy said sternly. She did nothing to stop the blood flowing through the fur on her wounded arm. The crimson liquid dripped to the floor between her feet.

Twitch took a stumbling step backwards. For a moment, his pistol fell. He lifted it again, but Amy had not moved. "Aren't you going to kill me, like you did Leandro?"

Amy scoffed. "Prove me wrong. Become a threat. I don't believe you'll do it. You try to be Captain Griffiths, but you're not."

Twitch whimpered and shook his head. He took another step back. He knew he wanted to do it. He knew he had to. But she was right. He couldn't. He had waited too long. He had given himself the chance to think about it. Ending a life with conscious thought was not something he could do.

With one last apologetic look towards the lifeless body of Leandro, Twitch turned to run. Amy did not follow.

Twitch burst through into the main office, bouncing off the sliding door as it opened too slowly for him. The doors to the waiting room were open, and Mortimer was stood in there. He was unarmed, and the starat took a couple of steps back with his hands raised when Twitch lifted his pistol.

"Easy there," Mortimer said nervously.

"Step back," Twitch growled. His hands still trembled as he held the gun up.

Mortimer stepped to the side, leaving the doorway clear.

Twitch took a step forward, then froze. The waiting room was not empty. Another starat sat on one of the couches. Pink eyes looked sightlessly towards him. Twitch's grip tightened on the pistol.

"Why are you here?" Twitch demanded of Snow. He didn't dare get closer to her.

"I work here. Why are you here?" the albino replied. She rose to her feet, but she kept one hand on the sofa for balance.

"I tried to help... tried to save..." Twitch said, before his throat tightened up. His vision swam again, but he stayed steady on his feet.

"Not everyone can be saved," Snow said softly. She lifted one hand up, and Twitch recoiled. He knew enough about her fearful abilities, though he had never been able to grasp the basics of performing them.

"We can at least try," Twitch said. His voice cracked as he took another step back from Snow.

The albino starat shuffled forward slowly. Her steps were unsteady. "Why try when all we will do is fail?"

"Because it's the right thing to do," Twitch replied. He kept his eyes on Snow's hands, but they remained still. One was outstretched, but she used it only to grab hold of the frame of the doorway.

Twitch flicked his tail. "You hurt yourself when you pushed Captain Rhys out, didn't you? You did too much."

Snow smiled wryly. "Subspace is a dangerous tool. Do too much and it cripples you, as Captain Griffiths learned himself. My injuries are not permanent," Snow explained. She kept hold of the door frame and pushed away Mortimer's offer to provide support. "Do not expect to make any progress in your development. Cybernetics weaken your touch to subspace. You're less organic. More machine."

Twitch tightened his grip. "I never want to use it again. I wish I'd never learned of it," he growled. He was boldened slightly by the knowledge of Snow's continued weakness. He doubted she would dare use her subspace powers to stop him. "Now let me through, or I'll shoot."

A laugh from the side of the room caught Twitch's attention. Amy had caught up. "He won't shoot," she said. She leaned against the wall beside the door through to the conference room. "Let him through anyway."

"Are you sure?" Snow asked, turning her sightless gaze towards Amy.

Amy smiled sweetly. Her ears perked up as she held her wounded arm to her chest. She did not seem to care about the blood she smeared on her shirt. "He's no threat to us."

Snow inclined her head towards Amy. She gestured with her free arm for Twitch to pass through.

Twitch trusted neither Snow nor Amy, but he couldn't bring himself to firing his pistol at either of them. He knew his only way out was to run while they gave him the opportunity. He didn't want them to change their mind and revoke it. Amy's words burned into his mind. He was no threat to them. He never had been.

Twitch ran for the elevator. He didn't look back at any of the starats as the doors silently slid open, but he turned as the doors closed again. He caught a brief look of Amy's predatory smile before she had disappeared from view. A quiet whimper escaped Twitch's mouth as the tears began to flow down his cheeks.

As soon as the elevator reached the ground floor, Twitch began to run again. He wouldn't stop running until he made it back into David's arms.

# chapter eleven

Twitch didn't know how he managed to remember where he had parked the automated car. The vehicle never moved fast enough through the traffic, but it gave the starat an opportunity to attempt to compose his thoughts. He didn't get far. He just kept going back to that horrible moment when Amy had shot Leandro. The light had gone from the starat's eyes in that instant. The image was burned into his memory.

Worst of all the thoughts that passed through Twitch's mind was the realisation that he was weak and cowardly. He could have ended it, right there. He had Amy and Snow at the end of his pistol, but he had not been brave enough to pull the trigger.

A starat was waiting for him when he finally stumbled out of the car at the research centre. David didn't need to say anything. He just pulled Twitch into a tight embrace and kissed him gently on the cheek. The tears that had been trickling from Twitch's eyes flooded out in a series of sobs that shook his whole body.

"He's gone," he whimpered after a few minutes in the arms of his beloved partner. "Leandro, he's gone. She killed him."

"It's not your fault. You did everything you could," David whispered. He closed his eyes and rested his forehead against Twitch's.

"He thought he could reason with her, but she just..." Twitch said, before his voice strangled up again. He gulped down air rapidly as he tried to compose himself. His arms squeezed tight around David, but the bigger starat didn't complain about the pressure. "I could have killed them... I had the chance, but I couldn't..."

David pulled back slightly and placed a finger on Twitch's lips. "But that's not who you are."

"But it was who was needed then. I could have done it. I could have ended it," Twitch whimpered. His fingers tensed against David's arms. He rested his head on his partner's chest. "All those starats on Terra. They could have been safe if I were brave."

David gently lifted Twitch's chin. He kissed the smaller starat on the lips. "We'll have another chance to stop her. You didn't fail, and you are the bravest starat I know."

Twitch scoffed and turned his head away. "Braver than Captain Rhys?"

"Far braver than Captain Rhys."

Twitch whimpered slightly, but he didn't pull his head away from David's gentle grip. "I don't feel it."

David kissed Twitch gently again, before his hands tensed against Twitch's back. "Were you being followed?"

Twitch flicked his ears. A low rumbling sound was starting to build in volume as it approached. He pulled out of David's arms and spun around on his toes. His eyes quickly scanned across the landscape towards the distant city centre, which was mostly open terrain. A single large truck was approaching the research centre. With little else around them but the greenhouses, there seemed to be no other destination.

Another sound filled the air. A soft whirring that seemed to come from somewhere above them. "We need to go," Twitch squeaked.

"Where?" David asked in alarm.

"I don't know," Twitch replied. He turned and started to run for the research centre. "Anywhere."

David hurried after Twitch. The two starats barged through the main doors and ran down the corridor. David's hand on Twitch's arm guided the other starat, and together they found the remaining three of their companions. They had been sat together in the dormitories, perched on the edge of one of the beds.

"What's going on?" Richard asked. He jumped up to his feet. "Did you get Leandro?"

"They've found us," Twitch whimpered. He wiped his face dry as adrenaline kicked in. He had no time for fear and regret now.

"Who have?" Steph asked. She shakily rose to her feet with William.

"Bad guys. Doesn't matter," Twitch replied. He realised then he didn't know who was coming after them. It could have been the Inquisition, or the Starat Freedom Union. It could even have been the military. Somehow, he had become an enemy of all three.

William sucked in his breath. "They'll have us surrounded in no time. We can't go out the main doors."

"What about the back doors?" Richard asked. His eyes flicked towards the corridor leading to the front of the centre, as though fearing armed troops could come through any moment.

"Surrounded," William said simply. He flicked his tail and tapped his synthetic foot against the floor.

"What about that tunnel I found yesterday?" Steph asked. She looked up, her eyes moving from starat to starat. She grasped the tip of her tail in both hands and took half a step back.

"Tunnel?" Twitch asked, his ear flicking up. Marching footsteps echoed down the corridor, but they still originated from outside. There were at least a dozen people out there. An occasional shout came through.

"We don't know where it goes," William said with a groan.

"Do we have another choice?" Steph asked. She let go of her tail to reach for Twitch's hand. She gently pulled on him. "Come on. Follow me."

William opened his mouth as though to protest, but he quickly shook his head and fell into line behind Twitch and Steph. There was no time to gather any of their limited possessions that had been brought from their home in the city. Twitch's ears pinned back for a moment as he thought of his second pair of legs in the charger dock, but he did not turn back. He broke into a run with Steph.

The smaller starat led the way. She hurried out of the dormitory, away from the front doors. Many of the doors they passed were locked, sealed up by the former occupants of the research centre. Twitch had not explored any of them. He had not shared the same curiosity as his fellow starats in seeing what secrets could be learned.

His attention had solely been on repairing the cars parked out the front. His ears folded. If he hadn't done that, then perhaps Leandro would still be alive.

Twitch was not given any time to dwell on that. Steph released his hand as she pushed open a door at the end of the long corridor. Through the windows opposite, Twitch could see they were close to the back of the research centre. There was no movement outside that he could see, but the humans had to be close.

The door led to a small flight of stairs leading to a storage room. Twitch's eyes widened as he looked around. Cleaning supplies were stacked on shelves on three sides of the room. Cobwebs and dust covered most of the surfaces, though there was a small trail of clean footprints through the grime on the floor.

Steph hurried across the room, dragging one side of a free-standing set of shelves. Scrape marks on the floor indicated it was not the first time the shelves had been moved, and Twitch came across to help the smaller starat. Behind the shelves was a reinforced door with a half-rusted lock keeping it closed.

"Is this the only way out?" David asked. The coffee-furred starat was last of everyone, warily looking behind. There were no further noises from the facility above. If the building was surrounded, then no one was making a move to assault it.

"You got a better idea?" Steph asked. She pried open the rusted lock. The screech of metal irritated Twitch's ears as the door was forced open. His eyes widened as he looked down a set of steep stairs descending into darkness. Steph flicked on a light switch. One by one, lights began to turn on, lighting the way to almost impossible depths.

"That's certainly a tunnel," Twitch said quietly. He glanced back. The other three starats gathered just behind. A low whine filled the air.

William glanced up, then roared out. "Go! Now!"

Twitch and Steph hurried down the first few steps. David and Richard came just behind, with William slamming the door after them all. A moment later, the world seemed to explode into fire and debris.

Flames burned all around Twitch as the building erupted in an explosion of twisted metal and concrete. Heat blasted at his fur.

Something sharp struck his arm, and he recoiled. He struggled to keep moving down the stairs.

"Fuck!" William's voice drifted across the eerie sound of debris clattering, and the loud clatter of an engine close by. "Is everyone alright?"

"Hurting, but fine," Steph quickly replied.

"I'm alive," Richard added a few moments later. His voice was pained, but Twitch did not dare to look back yet. Dust drifted in the flickering lights.

"Me too," David said finally. "Shit, what was that?"

"Missile or something. We should go before they realise we're not dead," William replied. He pushed past Twitch and Steph, limping slightly. Blood and dust clung to his fur as he moved further down the stairs.

Twitch paused for a moment. He looked up as David took hold of his hand. The door was a splintered mess of twisted metal. Cracks ran through the walls that had not been there before. The smell of dust and scorched concrete filled Twitch's nose as he allowed himself to be led deeper below ground.

"Quickly, quickly," William hissed from up ahead.

Twitch held his free hand over his muzzle. Smoke was already beginning to descend the stairs, clogging the air and making it difficult to breathe. Muffled noises echoed down to his ears. Footsteps and shouts. The humans had come into whatever ruins of the research centre they had made with their missile attack.

The long descent finally came to an end. Twitch's hand brushed over the seams in his leg, feeling around where he had stowed the housed pistol. His ears curled down. He withdrew his hand.

A long, flat tunnel stretched out as far as Twitch could see. There weren't as many lights on the ceiling, leaving large patches of shadow between the rings of illumination. The walls were dirty and covered in grime, though there were mercifully no cracks to be seen. There was no cover to hide behind, should someone from above realise where they had gone.

Twitch knew he could run quicker. His synthetic legs gave him the pace to easily outrun any starat or human, but he stayed at the back of the group with David. He kept looking back, but he could see or hear no one approaching. Smoke continued to drift through the dark, narrow corridor. The gloom built up behind them, gradually spreading outwards, but not quickly enough to overwhelm the starats.

"What happened back there?" David asked, his hand squeezing around Twitch's as they ran.

Ears perked up ahead, but no one slowed down or turned. Twitch opened his mouth to speak, but only a choked sob made it out. Tears sprung to his eyes, and he knew it was hopeless to try and blame it on the smoke. "Amy didn't agree with him," he managed to force out, his voice thick around the tears and stuffed nose. He wiped his hand over his muzzle.

"Shit," Richard said. His tail drooped as he ran alongside Steph, who almost stumbled and fell.

Leandro's last smile had burned on Twitch's memory. The crimson blood running through his grey fur. The lifeless slump of his body. His vision blurred before he furiously blinked his eyes. There would be a time to grieve and mourn, but first he needed to be safe. Whatever safe was.

"I think we're here," William said. He pointed ahead. A rusted metal ladder climbed up to a hatch in the ceiling. The corridor appeared to go on for another dozen metres before coming to an abrupt end.

"Where is here?" Steph asked. Her ears flicked back as she turned to look down the corridor, back the way they had come. Twitch heard the noise at the same time. A voice shouted, echoing directly down the corridor and out of the smoke. Someone had found the underground passage.

"Doesn't matter," William barked. He pulled himself up the rungs, testing his weight on the rusty bars of metal. "Up, now."

Steph followed directly after William, with Richard just behind her. Twitch's ears strained to hear the pursuing humans. He could only hope that they had enough time to climb up and into the unknown of beyond the hatch. If they were caught down here, then Twitch knew that nothing could save them.

William swore and grunted as he struggled to lift the hatch. For a brief moment, Twitch was terrified that the hatch would not open, but William was able to break through a layer of rust that had swollen the metal joints. The starat quickly disappeared into darkness above.

Twitch let David go up the ladder first. David's muzzle was set into a fierce grimace as he began to climb.

Finally, Twitch had his opportunity. The rungs of the ladder felt fragile to his hands, and the metal creaked alarmingly beneath the weight of his legs. Trying to put fears of falling out of his mind, Twitch focused on the movement of his hands, reaching for each successive rung. His ears pinned flat against his head, but that did not drown out the sound of commands to stop. Human voices called down the corridor. At least three pairs of footsteps. They were almost out of time.

David's hands hooked beneath Twitch's shoulders, lifting him through the hatch and into the dark room beyond. The starat twisted and kicked out at the top of the ladder. With three powerful kicks, he ripped the rusted metal from its supports. The ladder clattered down to the floor and the brittle metal snapped apart. Twitch hoped that would delay the humans a little.

The only light came from the corridor below, and that was quickly extinguished as William slammed the hatch closed once Twitch's legs were out of the way. Twitch's eyes took a moment to adjust to the darkness. Close by, a thin crack of light shone around what appeared to be a doorway.

The faint red-hued light illuminated four close walls. There was not much room, and Twitch stumbled to the side for his hand to brush against a metal wall. The constant hum of electricity filled the small room, powering whatever devices and machinery were housed with the starats. With the hatch closed, Twitch could no longer hear the sounds of pursuit, but he knew they would not be far behind.

A hand pulled at Twitch's shoulder, dragging him away from the metal wall. "Gun. Do you have one?" William hissed in his ear.

Twitch quietly fumbled for the pistol housed in his right leg. It barely made a click as he pulled it free and passed it into William's waiting hands. The other starat crawled away. Twitch could see his shadow move across the cracks of light around the door. Another shadow moved just outside. They were not alone on the surface. Soldiers waited for them.

Twitch crouched down and pressed at his left leg, finding the small socket in his calf. A wrist-mounted bullet shield popped free, looking like a thick bracelet. He tapped William on the elbow and held out the shield for the other starat to take. "You'd better have this," he said quickly.

William shook his head, pushing Twitch's hand back. "Put that on yourself. I want both hands free, so I'll need your help."

Twitch pinned his ears back. "What?" the starat squeaked.

"Please, Twitch. We don't have long," William whispered. He placed a calming hand on Twitch's shoulder for a moment, before turning away. He left Twitch no opportunity to continue his protest.

With his hands trembling, Twitch fitted the bullet shield to his wrist and crept after William. Soft footsteps followed just behind him, but they stopped a few paces away from the only door.

William pulled Twitch forward. "When I push open the door, protect me with the shield on the open side," he whispered in Twitch's ear. "The door will protect us from the other side."

Twitch nodded grimly. He activated the shield with a firm touch of his fingers to the wristband. Almost instantly, the shield extended to a rigid, transparent protective barrier.

"On three," William hissed. A shadow moved outside the door, momentarily blocking the light.

The sounds of pursuit had been silenced by the closed hatch, but Twitch knew they would not have long. He stood in front of William; his right arm raised to protect the other starat with the bullet shield. His wickedly sharp synthetic claws dug into the floor as William started to count down.

"Now!" William barked. In the same moment, he thrust his left hand forward and pushed the door open, a rusted lock snapping. The door slammed open, catching a human on the leg. The human swore and jumped back. At a push from William, Twitch stepped outside. The other starat's pistol lifted. Two shots were fired. The human fell before he could even draw his weapon.

Twitch swallowed down the bile rising in his throat. He quickly turned his eyes away from the fallen human. There were two other soldiers to Twitch's right, both human. Another shouted to the left, behind the door and further up the hill. Smoke and fire drifted across the sky from the ruined research centre, out of sight beyond the open door. To the right, light from the setting Prox glimmered off the nearby river and the greenhouses.

"Stand down. We will shoot," one of the humans said. Beneath their helmets, Twitch could not tell which human spoke. It could have been any of them.

"Stay steady," William growled, ignoring the spoken command from the humans. He kept one hand on Twitch's shoulder. With his other hand, he lifted his pistol and fired twice more.

Twitch couldn't help but recoil from the noise right by his ear. He shied back, almost standing on William's toe. One of the humans fell to William's shots, but the other returned fire. The starat squeaked in terror as his shield thudded with the impacts of the bullets, but nothing penetrated the sturdy barrier.

The remaining human activated his own bullet shield and held it protectively across his body. William hissed in frustration. "Advance forward," he growled, nudging Twitch in the back again.

Twitch's tail curled. His legs would have trembled, but his synthetic limbs remained perfectly steady as he took a couple of paces forward. The human retreated by the same distance, keeping the gap between them steady. Neither William nor the soldier fired their weapon, for that would have been a waste of ammunition.

"Run to him," William barked, pushing Twitch in the back again.

Twitch responded quickly. He wanted to run as far from the soldier as possible, but he obeyed William's command. He ran forward, towards the human. The soldier lifted his rifle and fired twice, thudding shots against the bullet shield, as he backed away. Twitch immediately saw the reason for William's plan. The human couldn't turn his back on them, or else he would lose protection from his shield, but he couldn't retreat as quickly as the starats could run.

William leaped out from behind Twitch. The starat dived for the human, slipping around the side of the bullet shield and grappling directly with the soldier, w combat knife in his offhand. Twitch barely dared to watch, but he was distracted by the sound of footsteps approaching behind. They were heavy, too heavy to be a light-footed starat.

Twitch turned to face a third soldier, also human. He quickly lifted his shield again, protecting his torso but leaving his feet exposed. He didn't worry about those getting struck. His toes dug into the soft mud as he braced himself. He had no weapon. Panic rose in his chest, but he did not call out to William. The other starat had his own problems, and Twitch could hear him struggling behind him.

The human opened fire. A pair of shots ricocheted off Twitch's shield. A momentary spike of pain flared in his right foot. Twitch grimaced and held steady as the pain instantly faded as the sensors in his leg adapted. He could still move his foot without issue. He took a step forward.

This was not the time to freeze and take no action, like he had done in Jennings Tower. If he had taken action then, Leandro might still be alive. He couldn't make the same mistake again. He advanced another step. He needed a weapon, and it took a moment for Twitch to remember that he did have one, in his legs.

Keeping his shield up, Twitch quickly fumbled at his left leg. The panel in his thigh opened, and his fingers grasped the hilt of a small dagger, similar to the combat knife William wielded. It wasn't a gun, but it was something. Holding the blade awkwardly in his hand, Twitch stared at the human soldier in the eye. He tried to ignore the snarls and grunts of pain behind him as William struggled with the other soldier. None of the other starats had come out from inside the small hut, but a few of their shouts drifted from within.

The soldier moved quicker than Twitch expected. He crossed the gap between them in an instant, forgoing his rifle and trying to shove Twitch to the ground. Though the starat lashed out with his dagger, he wasn't able to penetrate the soldier's tough armour. He yelled in terror. His heart burned with each thudding beat that echoed in his ears. The human's arm knocked aside his shield.

For a moment, Twitch felt completely exposed. His hand came up, striking the human on the arm and disrupting his aim. The rifle fired. Two shots struck Twitch's leg. His left foot numbed for a second and threw off his balance.

Twitch stepped back and tried to strike the human across the face with the shield. The human's free hand grabbed the edge of the shield and wrenched it to the side. Twitch yelped as he was thrown to the ground, landing on his back in the mud. The dagger spun out of his grip and landed a metre away.

The starat had no chance to think. He kicked up hard, striking the human in the chest once, and then in the jaw as the human crumpled into a silent heap.

"Oh fuck, I'm sorry," Twitch gasped, rolling over quickly and checking to see how badly the human had been hurt. He quickly looked away, his chest convulsing at the sight of the human's injuries. The soldier's face was a mess of broken bone and blood, and his breath came in ragged gasps.

A pair of gunshots quickly drew Twitch's attention away. He squeaked in terror and scrambled to his feet. William stood above his foe, his pistol aimed at the prostrate human's body. The soldier did not move.

William panted as he looked to the soldier Twitch had brought down. He did not hesitate as he fired another shot into the human's head. The fallen soldier fell still. Twitch jerked back a couple of steps.

"We had to do it," William said with a growl. His lip came up in a snarl, but his tail was tucked low. "If we didn't kill them, then they would kill us."

Twitch's head spun. He knew the truth to William's words. They had to escape, and they still weren't safe yet. He stumbled away, taking a few steps towards the hut. His ears perked up and his eyes widened as he heard David yelp. Richard swore, his voice muffled by the thin metal walls of the hut.

"Shit," William said, having also heard the noises from inside. He didn't move right away. Instead, he crouched beside one of the dead humans and rummaged through his armour. He grinned savagely as he pulled something free from the supply pouch at the soldier's waist. A grenade.

Twitch went cold, memories of the last time he had seen a grenade flooding through his mind.

He did not freeze this time. He hurried after William. They sprinted back towards the hut. The door was still open, casting light across the dirty floor. The hatch had partially opened, with Richard pushing all of his weight down onto the heavy metal structure to stop the humans below from coming up to the surface. A human struggled to push the hatch open, fighting against Richard's weight.

A second human joined the first. The hatch opened fully, knocking Richard backwards. Four shots fired out. Two from William. Two from a human. A strangled cry of pain was quickly stifled.

Both humans fell back into the darkness, but Twitch could hear more coming. Before anyone else could react, William primed the grenade and tossed it down into the tunnel. David leaped forward and slammed the hatch closed. A deep rumble shook the ground. Panicked screams fell into silence.

"Is it over?" Twitch gasped. His heart pounded in his chest. A bitter taste still lingered on his tongue, and his nose wrinkled at the scent of fresh blood in the air.

"No," Steph whimpered. She had crawled to Richard's side, where the starat had fallen after being knocked off balance.

It took Twitch a moment to realise what he was seeing. Richard had been wounded; shot twice by the human's bullets. Once in the belly and once in the throat. There was already so much blood. Steph tried to staunch the flow, but there was no hope.

Terror was in Richard's eyes. The wounded starat tried to speak, but all that escaped his lips was a gasping, trembling wheeze. It was a horrible sound.

Twitch dropped down beside Steph. There was nothing he could do. No way to heal the wounds. No way to go back and save the starat from an undeserved fate. All he could do was kiss the dying starat on the forehead and squeeze hold of his hand. William slumped opposite him, holding Richard's other hand.

By the time Twitch's lips came away from Richard, the starat was gone. There was no life left in those eyes, though there was a haunting trace of the terror that lingered.

Twitch couldn't bear it. He turned away and closed his eyes. Anger and grief filled him in equal measure. He felt like screaming his pain to the world, but he couldn't. Not yet. "We have to go," he said, his voice barely a strained whisper despite the desire to yell.

"Where to? Where's left?" Steph said dully. Her hands and wrists were soaked in blood, but none of it appeared to be her own.

"Aaron," Twitch said. He clenched his hands into fists. "You call Aaron and don't stop until you get an answer from him. He's our only hope now."

"Where do we go until then?" David asked. He scooped Richard's limp body safe in his arms. William still held onto the hand of the starat he had served with on the *Harvester*, his face a mask of tears and grief.

"Away from here. They'll send more after us," Twitch said. He glared out the door, into the red light of Prox. Even the air outside looked soaked in blood.

With William and David carrying Richard between them, Twitch went ahead with Steph. She kept trying to get through to Captain Rhys's oldest friend, desperate for a place of safety. Behind them, beyond the crest of the hill, a violent plume of smoke and ash erupted into the air as more of the research centre collapsed. Sparks lit up the twilight sky. In the far distance, a siren wailed.

Twitch turned his back on the former safehouse. They needed to disappear again.

*** 

The wide river cut through the flat landscape. The waters were dark and murky as it slowly flowed towards the distant coast in the south. The greenhouses dominated the land on both banks, leaving just a strip of a few metres of empty land. Steph announced that they had reached the place where Aaron had said he would meet the starats.

Twitch looked up and down the banks. Both sides were completed devoid of human or starat life, though the air smelled vaguely of cinnamon. On the opposite shore, a herd of dragons clustered together. The six-legged beasts didn't move much. One lifted its head to look across the river at the starats. Its eyes gleamed in the light from the greenhouses. Twitch shivered and looked away.

William stood on a small rise at a curve in the river. He looked around in all directions. His tail curled in between his legs, and his ears flattened down against his head. "Is this the place?" he asked quietly. He turned on his toes to look down at the diminished group of starats. "Will he be long?"

"I've let him know we're here," Steph replied. She stared at the river, barely blinking.

William nodded, then slumped to the ground. He sat back and hugged his arms around his legs, pulling them close to his chest. His tail thumped against the ground a few times, splattering mud and water against himself.

Twitch sunk to his haunches and turned his back on the river. He could hear David setting down Richard's body against the bank, but he didn't turn around. He didn't want to see.

Steph sat down by his side. Her foot had been crudely wrapped in a dirty strip of cloth that had already been stained crimson. She whimpered in pain as she lay back. Her hands cupped her muzzle. "Please tell me this is just a nightmare," she said quietly.

Twitch reached out to take one of her bloody hands in his. "I wish I could say that," he said. His voice cracked as he struggled to hold back tears.

"I just can't believe it," she said. She squeezed his hand and fell silent.

Twitch had nothing more to say. He didn't know what more could be said. All four of the surviving starats had drooped ears and listless tails. Twitch knew their thoughts had to be as dark and brooding as his, but he just didn't have the words to articulate what he felt. Anger simmered away deep down inside him, but the grief and hopelessness threatened to overwhelm all else.

The starat stared up at the stars and just lost himself to his thoughts. He found Sol in the unfamiliar network of stars. He had become familiar with its location in the dark night sky, but he didn't know any of the others. The constellations he had learned from a young age were no more; twisted into new shapes from the different vantage point. Some formed rough approximations of the patterns in the stars, but they felt like parodies of the real thing.

A loud shout shattered Twitch's attention.

"No! Get back!"

Twitch jerked up. It took him only a moment to see what had roused David. One of the hulking dragons had slipped into the river and silently crossed the murky waters. It had emerged on their side of the river, teeth bared. Its eyes were fixed on Richard's still body. David stood over their friend, fists held up, but he had no weapon to wield against the fierce creature.

Twitch jumped to his feet. He tightened his grip around the stolen rifle and aimed it towards the creature. The dragon stood nearly twice as tall as Twitch, and many times longer. Twitch's eyes briefly glanced over its rust red scales and long, flexible tail, but his attention quickly snapped back to the front of the creature. Specifically, the two rows of large, sharp teeth in its mouth.

The creature's breath stank. Twitch gagged on the smell of rotting meat as he neared. The small, bright eyes of the dragon turned to him as he approached, rifle raised. A guttural growl reverberated from deep in its throat.

"Stay back," Twitch barked out, trying to project anger and confidence into his voice. He wondered why he even bothered. The dragon was not a thinking person. He doubted it understood what he said, but maybe the noise and anger would be enough to deter it.

The dragon prowled closer, almost within striking distance of David and Richard's body. A cascade of water drenched the starats as the creature's tail slapped against the river. In the brief moment Twitch was blinded by the spray, the dragon lunged forward.

The creature slammed hard into David, but the starat managed to twist away from the sharp teeth in time, though he was thrown back by a grasping limb. David landed hard, scraping along the ground, before coming to rest with a pained whimper.

Twitch stood over his partner and lifted his rifle. He squeezed the trigger. The gun jumped in his hand with a powerful recoil that disrupted his aim. The dragon's head snapped around to look right at him. The starat had distracted the dragon from Richard's body, but he had only drawn its attention to himself.

Twitch stepped back nervously. He tightened his grip on the rifle and tried to aim again, but the dragon was too quick. Before he could even react, the dragon's powerful tail snapped around and lashed Twitch across the chest. A powerful paw whipped against his legs, knocking the starat to the ground.

Teeth snapped close to his chest. The starat kicked out and struck the dragon on the throat. The creature snarled and growled in pain, but it did not retreat. Its beady yellow eyes were fixed on him.

The dragon prowled forward slowly. It used four of its legs for movement, with the middle pair raised up off the ground. Its powerful claws clenched as it reared up above the starat.

Twitch lay on his back. His toe claws were extended as he tried to kick out and slice the dragon's thick scales with the wicked blades. He fumbled for his dropped weapon, desperate to get a shot in before the dragon attacked.

The starat's fingers closed around the weapon. A brief flash of fur passed across Twitch's vision as one of the other starats tried to attack the dragon with little more than tooth and claw. A lazy swipe of a leg battered them away. The dragon's middle right paw slammed down on the rifle and shattered it, almost crushing Twitch's hand.

Twitch stared up at the dragon. He could see every tooth. The stench of the dragon's breath overwhelmed his nose. Hot air blasted over his fur as the dragon breathed heavily over his face. Dimly, he could hear someone shouting his name. He kicked at the dragon again. This time, he managed to draw blood across the creature's shoulder, but it didn't even react to the wound.

"Fuck," Twitch gasped. One of the massive paws rested down on his chest. Claws squeezed tight, but they didn't crush him. Not yet. He could feel the strength in that grip, but the creature hadn't yet used its full power. He felt dazed as he stared up at the mouth of a ferocious predator. A mindless predator. If anything, Twitch liked the idea of being killed by that thoughtless instinct. It certainly sounded preferable to the vile hatred he had endured before.

The dragon growled.

Twitch closed his eyes.

A loud roar buffeted Twitch's ears. The pressure around his waist suddenly lifted.

Twitch opened his eyes. The dragon still stood over him, but it no longer looked down. Instead, the dragon's eyes focused on something on the other side of the river. Its tail had lifted slightly, and three of its six paws were raised from the ground.

In an explosion of movement, the dragon dived back into the river and charged across to the far bank. The rest of the small herd had whipped up into a loud frenzy too. They had all detected something amongst the greenhouses, and they charged towards the fencing that surrounded the farms.

A voice hissed through the growing darkness. "Quickly. That won't distract them for long."

Twitch looked up to see a new, black-furred starat standing on the low crest. He recoiled in fear. His heart hammered in his chest as he fumbled around for anything he could use as a weapon, before he recognised who he was looking at. Aaron's friend, Nick.

"Hurry," the starat hissed. He snapped his fingers and extended his hand.

As though a spell was broken, Twitch scrambled up to his feet.

David groaned and winced as he rose, fending off an offer of help from Twitch. The larger starat scooped up Richard's body. He wasn't going to be left behind, no matter what.

Nick waited until they had all reached the top of the small rise before he turned around. Twitch stumbled forward to walk alongside the black-furred starat.

"What did you do?" Twitch asked in terrified awe.

"Subspace lure. I've been practicing on this herd for a few days. Glad I got here when I did," Nick replied. He grimaced and glanced back at the three starats who followed just behind; William offering support to a limping Steph.

Twitch took a deep breath. He closed his eyes for a moment, then managed to force a smile onto his muzzle. He glanced across to Nick. "Thank you. You saved our lives."

Nick held his arm around Twitch's shoulders. Twitch didn't need the support. His cybernetic legs were steady enough, despite how unpleasant his head felt. He didn't push the other starat away though. He appreciated the contact, and he couldn't get any from David while his partner carried the body of Richard.

Nick smiled weakly. His ears drooped down in sorrow. "I'm sorry we couldn't help you sooner. We didn't know where you had gone."

Twitch's right ear flicked. "And who is 'we'?"

Nick sighed. "Where Aaron should have taken you the first time. He should have taken us all there. We're going to the Resistance."

\*\*\*

Nick didn't lead the starats far. He took them into an irrigation overflow tunnel that delved down beneath the greenhouses. The rounded floor was completely dry, with no trace of water on the concrete at all. Electric lights shone from the walls every few metres. Loose wires hung down between each of the lights, most of which were suspended from metallic struts embedded into the curved roof.

The tunnel didn't curve once. The long, round shaft remained in a perfectly straight line beneath the greenhouses. Twitch knew the farms were above them, but there was no trace of them below ground. No water dripped down into the overflow, and he didn't even see an access ladder leading up to the surface.

Twitch's tail remained tucked between his legs as he walked behind Nick, just ahead of William and Steph. Their pace was a slow one out of necessity for Steph's injury, and David's grim burden. No one spoke. Not even Nick, though he glanced back occasionally to make sure the others were still following close.

After they had walked far enough that Twitch could no longer see then end of the tunnel whenever he looked back, the shaft came to an abrupt end. At first, Twitch had thought it was a sudden curve or bend in the tunnel, but as they approached, it became clear that the tunnel went no further.

Nick was not disturbed, but nor did he offer any explanation. The starat simply placed his hands on the smooth concrete wall. One hand moved to the right, when suddenly everything shimmered in front of Twitch's eyes. A holographic layer faded and flicked off, revealing a similar concrete slab right behind, but this one had a door in the middle.

Twitch felt a small spike of wonder at the disguised entry, but that brought little more than a small flicker of a smile to his face. He couldn't summon up the energy to produce a wider smile than that.

The door opened slowly. A dark room lay beyond. The light barely lit up anything, but Twitch could just make out a staircase rising through the gloom. Light shone through cracks around a second door about ten metres up.

"Through we go," Nick said. He stepped to the side after going through into the small room. Lights automatically clicked on to illuminate the staircase. The starat pulled the door closed behind them, once all the starats had come through. The door sealed tight with a loud clang, and the click of a strong lock.

"What is this place?" William asked in a trembling voice.

Nick placed his hand on William's shoulder. "Safety."

167

"They said that about the last place," Steph said in a sombre tone.

Nick turned to look at her. "This time it's true. I promise you. No one can reach you here. You are safe."

"For how long?" William asked.

Twitch looked up the staircase. His shoulders slumped. He couldn't yet believe that Nick was telling the truth. Safety had quickly become something unknowable to him. Alleged safety had already cost the lives of two of his friends. Minister Bakir had promised them they would be safe at the research centre, but Leandro and Richard were now dead.

Twitch could not believe Nick. But he could hope.

He hoped they were safe at last.

# chapter twelve

The Resistance base consisted of a small warehouse complex several miles beyond the outskirts of Caledonia. The warehouses looked old and worn down, like they had been long abandoned and then reclaimed. A dozen humans and starats, all heavily armed, came to meet Twitch and his disconsolate group of survivors.

One human, squat like all Centauran humans, with short sandy hair stepped forward from the crowd of armed guards. He did not carry any weapon, unlike his companions. He stood with his hands on his hips, his eyes flicking from starat to starat. "Hand over your weapons, please."

Twitch glanced up to William and David, who stood either side of him, before his eyes turned to Nick. The black-furred starat nodded once.

Though he was reluctant to give up his only source of defence in the face of so many armed guards, Twitch slowly and carefully lowered his stolen rifle to the ground. He also removed the hidden knife from inside his leg, placing the blade down beside the weapon. Beside him, William did the same with the pistol. David and Steph had nothing to relinquish, though Steph did lift her hands to show she carried nothing.

Two humans came forward to retrieve the weapons. Twitch took half a step back, his tail tucked low. He tried to relax his body, but every inch of himself above his hips felt tense and poised for flight. He struggled to keep his hands from tightening into fists.

"These are the friends of Aaron Lee?" the sandy haired human asked, turning to Nick.

The black-furred starat nodded again. "They are. He can vouch for them all. His judgement is sound. Aaron has never been wrong about anyone before, even if I didn't always understand that at first."

The human pursed his lips. "You were all associated with Amy and her Starat Freedom Union," he said, shifting his hands to rest behind his back. "Aaron tells me that your involvement with her was, like his own involvement, a result of being lied to. The same trust we showed him will be shown to you, but understand that we will not accept or tolerate any further communication with any of her associates."

"We will not be falling for her lies again," William spat.

"I should hope not," the human said. He extended his hand out to William, who warily took it. "My name is Michael. For all intents and purposes, I am the one in charge here. It is me who you must convince of your loyalty and trust."

"How can you keep us safe?" Twitch asked. He stared down at the human's feet; his shoulders hunched. He could barely speak without drawing out more tears.

"There is no answer I can give you that will fully satisfy your desire to be safe," Michael explained. He stepped to the side and stood in front of Twitch. He held his hand out, but Twitch did not take it. The human continued speaking, undeterred. "These are dangerous times and standing against the Inquisition and the SFU are dangerous positions to take. I will not guarantee your safety, but know that with the Resistance is the safest you will be."

"And what do you expect of us?" William asked. His voice was as hoarse and rough as Twitch's.

"For now, nothing," Michael replied. He stepped back, towards the armed guards behind him. "You shall be taken to somewhere to sleep. You will be given the opportunity to rest, but tomorrow I will expect to hear from each of you. You will tell me your story and give me any information you might have on the Inquisition and the SFU."

"What about Richard?" David asked. "He deserves a proper funeral. Something to remember him by."

The human did not answer immediately. He lifted his eyes to look at David directly, then down to the body in his arms. "We will ensure that your fallen companion receives the send-off he deserved.

Let us take the burden of his body now so that you can get your rest. We shall prepare a soldier's ceremony."

David whimpered and recoiled as Michael held his arms out. Then Nick stepped forward, coming between the human and starat. "You can trust him," Nick said quietly, placing his hand gently on David's arm.

Twitch's vision blurred behind fresh tears as he watched David reluctantly pass over the body of his fallen friend to the humans. Richard's body was limp and lifeless, but a small corner at the back of his mind still hoped that the starat would start moving again. He did not, even as he was passed to a second human and carried away.

A hand touched Twitch's shoulder. He flinched back, before realising that it was Nick. "Come with me. Let me take you somewhere to rest."

"I don't think I could sleep," Twitch said with a quiet whimper.

"All the same, you need to rest," Nick said insistently. He gently pulled Twitch forward, who stumbled a couple of steps before beginning to walk properly.

Twitch could hear David right behind him, with William and Steph following after. None of the humans, even Michael, came with them. Nick led them across the open courtyard between the warehouses and into the largest of the buildings. Half of the warehouse had been converted into a dormitory, with dozens of beds in rows on one side of a partition wall. Curtains could be drawn around the beds, but otherwise there was little privacy to be had. The facilities were simple and reminded Twitch of those on Ceres. His ears curled down. He had survived Ceres. He could only hope he could get through this as well.

"These here will be for you," Nick said, gesturing to four beds in the far corner of the warehouse. They were all neatly made and looked like they had not been used for quite some time. "I won't be far away, and nor will Aaron when he gets back to base."

William and Steph dropped down onto the closest of the four beds. William's arm rested around her shoulder.

"Can we trust them, Nick?" Twitch asked with a growl. He wiped at his cheeks, which were wet with his tears. His fur felt knotted and clumped, but he did not pay any attention to that. "They speak nicely, but so did Minister Bakir. She promised we would be safe, but Leandro and Richard..." His voice was swallowed up by another pained sob. Guilt forced his ears down against his head, and he turned away from the other starats.

"You can trust them here," Nick said. He stood a few paces away, his tail twitching. He didn't seem sure what to do with his feet as he kept shuffling them back and forth. "Ever since we knew what Amy was up to, we've been here. Aaron tried to get you here earlier, but..."

"It's all my fault," Twitch whispered hoarsely.

"Twitch..." David spoke sharply, pulling his partner around and holding onto both hands. He leaned down and kissed Twitch on the forehead. "None of this was your fault, do you hear me? None of it." David's voice almost broke into a choked sob, but he managed to force the words out even as he furiously blinked away the tears in his eyes.

"Any one of us could have stopped Leandro," William added. His voice was listless and dull, almost a perfect monotone. He stared towards a bank of windows close to the ceiling, which let in some of the last light of Prox before it sunk below the horizon at last. "I perhaps should have. I knew he thought he could speak to Amy. I didn't think he would actually try."

"But Richard died because I didn't shoot Amy when I had the chance," Twitch said, trying to pull away from David. His partner did not let him go anywhere. "I should have shot her. I should have..."

"No, Twitch," David said firmly. He cleared his throat and breathed in deep, fighting away the shakiness in his voice. "You are not a soldier. No one would ever have expected that of you."

Twitch turned his head away and whimpered. Another hand touched his shoulder. He jerked in surprise, looking up to see Nick standing right next to him. The black furred starat smiled in sympathy. "War is shit, especially for those who haven't been brought up in it. I know it's going to be hard not to blame yourself, but you need to understand that these people we fight against are monsters. They don't care about us or our lives." Nick paused and flattened his ears. "It's like being back in the empire, but this time it hurts more because here was meant to be safe from them."

"How many more do I need to see die?" Twitch said, not even wanting to know the answer. Who would he see the life drain out of next? William? Steph? He couldn't stop the whimper when he thought about David dying in his arms. He leaned into his partner, resting his head against the safe comfort of David's chest. David's arms wrapped around him.

"For tonight, no one," Nick said. His hand slowly dropped away from Twitch's shoulder. His feet scuffed against the floor. "I can't make any promises beyond that, but I can promise you that tonight you can sleep in safety."

Twitch couldn't even summon the energy to scoff. He doubted he would be able to sleep. Not with what he had seen. Leandro's final smile and Richard's terror were burned into his mind. He would never be able to forget that.

"If there is anything I can do to help you this evening, just let me know," Nick said hesitantly.

Twitch nodded dumbly as David guided him towards one of the beds. Twitch was grateful to settle down and take the weight off his legs, though they did not pain him or ache at all. It was his shoulders and chest that hurt the most. Some of the pain came from the dragon, but most of it was the emotional turmoil that tied his stomach in knots.

Turning his face to the wall, Twitch curled his ears and closed himself off to the warehouse. He was only vaguely aware of David next to him, one hand gently stroking through his fur. He lay listless and still, not reacting to the touch. Voices murmured, but no words got through to Twitch. His eyes closed, but sleep was not an option.

The seemingly endless night of Centaura no longer felt long enough to Twitch. Even if he lay in bed for the whole thing, he doubted he would be able to sleep. David's hand never once stopped stroking him, but the touch did little to soothe his troubled mind.

\*\*\*

Sleep had finally come, but it had been a troubled sleep for Twitch. He did not feel rested when he woke. He lay in bed with his head beneath the thin blankets as he listened to all the movement around him. Starats and humans quietly roused themselves throughout the dormitory. A few muted conversations were exchanged, but most remained quiet until they left the warehouse.

Twitch could hear a few metallic clangs and crashes from somewhere not far away.

The scent of bacon and eggs soon drifted across the air. That managed to tempt Twitch from beneath his blankets. He smoothed down his wild headfur as best he could, before checking to see if any of the others were awake. He could hear nothing from behind the curtains around the beds, so he slowly slipped out to track down the source of the bacon and eggs.

He didn't have to go far. A massive canteen took up the second half of the warehouse, beyond the partition that split the building in two. Tables were strewn across the open floor, with a small kitchen at the far end.

A familiar face broke out from the crowd. A black-furred starat waved to him.

Feeling grateful for the familiar face, Twitch approached Nick. He slipped past a couple of humans, who apologised for almost bumping into him. The starat held a chair out for Twitch. "How are you feeling today?"

"I don't think I'm ready to answer that yet," Twitch replied. He could feel the dark thoughts of the previous day bubbling around the back of his head. For the moment at least, he could distract his thoughts and avoid thinking about them too hard. Sleep had tempered the worst of those thoughts and his dreams had been mercifully forgotten.

"Will breakfast improve your mood?" Nick asked. He didn't sit down yet.

Twitch breathed in deep. "Bacon and eggs never hurt."

"Then I'll get some for you. Wait here, and I'll be right back," Nick said. His hand lingered on Twitch's shoulder for a moment, before he made his way through the crowd towards the kitchen.

Twitch used the opportunity to look around the canteen. He didn't recognise any of the faces he saw around. The humans and starats were all unfamiliar to him. He had seen no sign of the only two humans he thought he would have seen. Neither Michael nor Aaron had shown their faces for breakfast at all.

The starats were just as unfamiliar. None of them approached him, but Twitch wasn't too surprised. He was a dishevelled stranger whose fur was streaked with mud and even a little blood. He longed for a shower to help himself feel clean once more, but breakfast felt like a bigger priority.

Nick returned a few minutes later. He carried two plates filled with steaming bacon, eggs, sausages, and beans. He placed one plate down in front of Twitch, then took the seat next to the hungry starat.

Twitch ate voraciously. He felt like he hadn't eaten in days. Only then did he realise that he had not eaten at all the previous day. He had been bombarded with distractions that had left him with no opportunity to even think about something as mundane as food. The last food he'd enjoyed had been the simple dinner Leandro had prepared for everyone the night before.

For a brief moment, Twitch's appetite was in danger of being chased away. He tightened his hand around his fork and took a deep breath, before managing to compose himself once again. Leandro would not have wanted him to linger and brood too much; especially not if those dark thoughts came at the expense of a good meal.

The two starats ate in silence, for which Twitch was glad. Not only did it give him a chance to feel a little more awake, but his thoughts also felt a little more composed by the time his breakfast had been finished.

Twitch leaned back in his seat. His belly felt so much better now it had been filled. He hadn't realised just how bad he had been feeling because of his hunger. He took a few moments to take in the sounds of conversations all around. Unless he focused on one particular voice, he couldn't really keep track of what was being said. Everyone's voices melded together into one indistinct chatter of background noise, but Twitch felt soothed by the sound.

Twitch ran his hands over his muzzle. "Is there somewhere I can shower? I feel so dirty still," he said. He grimaced as he glanced across to Nick.

"There sure is," Nick replied as he took hold of the plates. "Go and grab anything you need, and I'll meet you by the dorms in a moment."

Twitch lowered his eyes. "I don't have anything. Not anymore. It's all back at home, and I can't go back there."

Nick hissed softly beneath his breath. "Then I'll sort you out with something. Don't worry, we'll look after you here." He gently patted

Twitch's shoulder. "Give me a few moments and I'll get everything ready for you."

Twitch managed to flash a brief smile. "I won't go anywhere," he assured the other starat.

While Twitch waited for Nick to return, he had another look around the converted warehouse. But for the tables and the large partition wall that ran lengthways down the cavernous room, little had been done to change the appearance of the warehouse. A couple of large fans languidly spun on the sloped ceiling to provide some airflow.

Outside the main doors, Twitch could see part of a small courtyard. Floodlights provided illumination on the concrete, which obscured any view of the night sky. There were no windows on this side of the warehouse walls, providing no other way to look outside. The warehouse reminded him of his accommodation on Ceres. But for the humans sat through the cafeteria and the heavy weight of gravity on his shoulders, Twitch could almost have been back on the dwarf planet. He bit back a fresh wave of nausea at the thought.

Before long, Nick took Twitch back through the dormitories. On the opposite side were a series of doors that Twitch had not noticed before. They led through to the bathrooms and showers, which were all hidden away in individual cubicles. That had not been how things had been on Ceres, where everything was communal and open. The showerheads there had barely worked, providing little more than a slow trickle that took ages to soak their fur. Twitch was glad for something to break the similarities to Ceres.

As Twitch stepped into one of the cubicles, he realised that these were nothing like the decrepit ones back on Ceres. Water cascaded down onto him with pressure, and the temperature was easy to control. He let out a sigh of relief as he stood beneath the jet and felt the dirt, grime, and blood wash away. Nick had provided him with soap and fur shampoo, which he used liberally.

"So, what exactly is this place?" Twitch asked Nick, who had remained just outside the cubicle. "No one really explained it last night, and I didn't want to ask."

"The Resistance," Nick replied. Twitch could see the bottom of the starat's feet beneath the cubicle door. "It's a group trying to fight back against the Inquisition, given the government is doing fuck all about it."

"I've seen some of the news reports," Twitch said. He rinsed off his fur beneath the powerful jet of water, only to start lathering it up with shampoo again. "But what is this place? These buildings?"

"Not sure what they used to be. Just a bunch of warehouses that used to be used for food production, I think. We're out in the middle of the greenhouses here," Nick explained.

Twitch struggled to hear the other starat clearly as water poured around his ears. Everything sounded a little muffled and indistinct. He flicked his ears a few times to clear them. "And no one suspects this place is being used?"

"I've been told it's all off the grid. No external power provided, and no network connections either. All the greenhouses are automated, so no one ever actually comes within visual range," Nick replied. His foot tapped on the tiled floor a few times as he leaned on the cubicle door. "I'm sure they have other security measures too, but I don't know what they might be."

"And you're sure we're safe here?" Twitch asked. He just about managed to keep the tremble out of his voice.

"So long as no one does anything stupid and attract attention to us," Nick said.

Twitch pinned his ears down. Water plastered down his fur as he stood still for a moment. That had meant to have been the case at the first safehouse, but things had not ended that way. Leandro had done something stupid, and Twitch had compounded the error. Amy might have killed Leandro no matter what, but no one could have followed Twitch out of the city if he hadn't run after the older starat.

Twitch sighed and flicked his tail. Everything below his waist was waterproofed, so he didn't have to worry about damaging any of his cybernetics for something as simple as a shower, but as he looked down at his silvered feet, he realised he had a new problem he hadn't considered.

"Hey, Nick? Will there be anything I can use to recharge my legs and tail? My docks were destroyed yesterday," he said nervously. He fought down a sudden panic that he would be forced to go without his legs if he had nothing to keep them powered.

Nick didn't answer for a few seconds. "I'm pretty sure there's something. Do you need it urgently?"

Twitch finished rinsing out his fur a second time, before switching off the water flow. He wiped away some of the moisture on his leg, then dug his claw beneath one of the panels on his thigh to pry it open. Beneath was a small screen, which displayed some of the diagnostics and settings for his legs. The screen also showed how much charge he still had. "Enough for another day, I think," he said, before snapping the panel closed again. He suppressed a small shudder. He still hadn't gotten used to that feeling.

"I'll find you something, I promise."

Twitch started to shake himself dry, before he noticed a fur drier hung on the back of the door. He reached out for the handheld device and flicked it on, waiting for the air to heat up enough to dry himself. His fur slowly puffed out again, rather than sticking close to his body. Out of habit, he lowered the drier down to his legs as well, though they didn't need the blasted hot air to dry anywhere near as much as his upper body. Starat fur retained water remarkably well.

After he felt sufficiently dry, Twitch dressed himself. Nick had provided some clean clothes of his own for Twitch to wear, rather than getting back into his dirty, bloodstained shirt and shorts.

"Feel better?" Nick asked as Twitch opened the cubicle door.

Twitch nodded. "Much, thank you." He squeezed a little moisture out of his tail, which hadn't dried quite so easily. He certainly felt cleaner, though he hadn't fully groomed his fur back into its usual state. He didn't want to keep Nick waiting for too long.

"If you're feeling up to it, I can take you to see Michael again. He's eager to speak to you," Nick offered. His ears flicked back. "He wants to meet all four of you when possible, but you were closest to Amy."

"He's the leader of the Resistance?" Twitch asked, shuddering at even the mention of Amy.

"Just this outpost. There's a couple of people above him," Nick clarified. He held his hand out. "Do you want to see him?"

Twitch considered the offer for a moment. He then nodded his head. "Sure. So long as he doesn't try to throw me into combat again. I don't know if I can deal with that."

"He knows what you've been through. For a human, he's pretty good," Nick said. The corner of the starat's mouth twitched up into a smile. "He's not going to ask you to do anything you don't want to do."

"Then I'll see him. I don't think I gave a good impression of myself yesterday," Twitch said. He took hold of Nick's hand, letting the other starat begin to guide him back out of the bathrooms.

"He wouldn't have taken it personally, don't worry," Nick said, assuring Twitch with a gentle squeeze of the hand. "Come on. Let me take you there. This place actually looks quite nice at night too."

Twitch flicked his tail nervously. He didn't know what to expect out of the meeting with Michael. He could only hope Nick was telling the truth. He really did not want to see combat again. He got the uneasy sense that fighting was only going to be inevitable.

\*\*\*

Nick's suggestion that the warehouses looked nice at night seemed to be correct. A large courtyard sat in the middle of the half-dozen buildings. The tarmac shone in the light from the dozen floodlights. A light mist drifted through the open area, which added an ethereal twinkle to the swirling light.

Four of the warehouses opened out onto the courtyard. Twitch couldn't see anything different between the four buildings. All were coloured the same deep red, and faded lettering was still just about visible on the sides. Two more warehouses, both larger than the four around the courtyard, stretched out beyond the square.

High above, the electromagnetic shield crackled to life. Bursts of light shot across from the east. Prox didn't need to be above the horizon to make its presence known. Twitch paused for a moment to look up at the sky. The stars were barely visible behind the constant action across the shield. He had never seen it so active before. Above the shield, a curtain of light swayed across the sky. The shimmering veil shone green and blue as it rippled from horizon to horizon.

The fur on the back of Twitch's neck rose. He could only imagine what that swirling curtain sounded like. He imagined a gentle flutter of fabric. The display of light certainly looked delicate enough. Unfortunately, none of those sounds reached his ears, no matter how much he strained them. He lowered his eyes again.

Nick led Twitch into the warehouse directly opposite from the first. Inside, the cavernous building had been divided into many smaller rooms, though the temporary walls that had been placed didn't even reach halfway up towards the distant ceiling. The walls were all the same, a dull grey opaque polycarbonate. A narrow corridor wound between many small rooms partitioned off by these walls. The constant whir of two large fans overhead didn't quite do enough to drown out the sounds coming from within the small, partitioned rooms.

"This is where everything the Resistance does in Caledonia is organised," Nick explained. He didn't look back at Twitch as he talked. His hands gestured to the doors as he explained who tended to occupy each one. Twitch took none of the information in as he failed to recognise any of the names.

The two starats side-stepped a human who looked vaguely familiar to Twitch, but he couldn't get a good look at her before they rounded a corner. He flicked and ear and shook his head. He doubted he knew anyone, but for Nick and Aaron. He could only assume he had seen her in his weary state the previous day.

Finally, there was only one door left. Twitch felt like he had been led through a maze, though there had only been a couple of turns made. The high ceiling and low walls had disorientated him slightly, and he found himself still slightly distracted by the curtain of light he had seen outside.

Nick knocked on the final door. He only had to wait a couple of seconds before a voice from inside told them they could enter. Though Nick opened the door, he didn't step through. He moved to the side and gestured for Twitch to go first.

"He doesn't want to see me. It's you he's after," the starat explained. He flicked his ears and scratched over the black headband he wore around his forehead. "I'll head back, but you'll be able to find me if you need me."

"Can I trust him?" Twitch said warily, not approaching the door.

"You can. If you can't trust my word on it, then trust Aaron," Nick said with a nod of his head. He gestured to the door again. "Go on, I promise you that you'll be safe."

Twitch breathed out slowly. He put his hand out to rest against the door. "Can you just check on David, Steph, and William for me please? I don't want them to worry about where I am," he asked.

Nick nodded and smiled. "Of course I can, yes." The starat raised a hand in farewell, leaving Twitch alone to step inside the small room.

A single human sat inside the little office, behind a small desk in the middle of the room. A bank of computers covered the left wall. A longer desk that looked like it belonged in a workshop covered the length of the right wall. Trinkets and devices cluttered the surface of the workshop desk, most of which Twitch didn't recognise. He did see a holographic projector amongst a couple of tablets, and even what looked like a model miniature shield generator. His ear flicked as he dragged his eyes away from the desk and towards the human.

The sandy-haired man was the one who had greeted them the previous day, Michael. Twitch had been too tired, too full of grief to really listen and take in anything the human had said in their brief introduction. For the moment, the grief was held at bay. If he tried not to think too hard about it, he could manage his emotions again.

"Welcome again, Twitch," Michael said. A smile formed a few more wrinkles on his lightly lined face as he gestured to the chair opposite his desk. "I trust you are feeling better?"

"Much, thank you," Twitch replied with a bow of his head. He sat down on the offered chair, only to find that the hole in the back of the seat was a little small for his tail to comfortably rest through. He leaned forward and perched awkwardly on the edge of the chair so there was enough room for his tail to drape behind him.

"I'm glad to hear. Everything you see around you here is because of my ideas, and the work of those who believe what I say," the human said. He spread his arms wide. "I have been worried about the Inquisition for years, but only recently have they become a real and present danger. It is my understanding that you know more about the threat they pose than most?"

Twitch sighed softly and nodded. "I managed to get into their facility in Hadrian. I saw what they're hiding below the surface." He paused and curled his tail beneath the side of his chair. "Last time I told someone what I saw down there, she was killed. I don't know who killed her, but I have suspicions."

"That would be Major-General Ulrich?" Michael asked.

Twitch nodded again. He clasped his hands across his lap. "Yeah. She thought she could trust someone, but it seems they killed her."

"I assure you the same will not happen again. I have heard bits and pieces of the story from Aaron and a few other informants, but I would like to hear it direct from you," Michael said. He rested his hand on a small black box on his desk. "If it is alright with you, I would like to record this too."

Twitch hesitated, before giving his approval for the recording. A little spike of worry filled him at the thought of someone in the Inquisition getting hold of the recording, but he then realised there could be nothing he could do to make them hate him more. They already wanted him dead. He took a deep breath, and once again began to recount the events of Hadrian.

\*\*\*

Twitch lost track of how long he spoke. The human provided him with food and drink throughout to keep him from getting too restless. The drinks were hot chocolates, which put Twitch back in the mind of the time he had received his new legs, and the human woman he had talked to while he waited for David to wake up. That conversation felt like a lifetime ago. A little over two weeks had passed since that safer, happier time.

Michael remained silent throughout most of the conversation, except for the occasions when he called for more food or drink. He rarely interrupted Twitch or tried to speak over him, only speaking for some clarifications or queries about the events. Mostly, he sat and listened.

Twitch didn't hold anything back. He didn't just speak about Hadrian, but he continued on to tell the human everything that had happened in the two weeks since then. His worries about Amy and her plans were all revealed. The words spilled from his mouth with little thought behind them. He had not intended to tell the human everything, but once he started, he could not stop. The words felt good as they came, like each one took away that little bit of guilt, fear, and shame with them. He only faltered when he came to tell Michael about his concerns with the military. He hesitantly accused Fleet-Admiral Bosler of being the one who betrayed and killed Nessie Ulrich.

When Twitch finally fell into silence, Michael clasped his hands and nodded once more. He clicked off the recorder, before he cleared his throat. "That paints a worrying picture, but thankfully we already knew most of those pieces. I shall of course corroborate your story with your companions, but I have no doubt that you are telling the truth." The human paused for a moment, clasping his hands together on the desk. "I think there are a couple of people I would like you to see. Neither of them are here right now, so it will take some arranging, but they will benefit you and also between you I think you can help further our cause."

"I don't have to fight anyone, do I?" Twitch asked. His ears pinned down and he stared at the desk.

"I'd certainly prefer it if you didn't fight anyone here," Michael replied with a laugh. The human smiled as Twitch quickly glanced up to him. "It might take me a few days to arrange the meetings though. Is there anything we can do for you in the meantime to make you more comfortable?"

Twitch's eyes moved down again. His tail draped across his lap. "Can we do something for Richard? He deserves something..."

"Of course. Like I promised yesterday, he will be given a soldier's send off. He died in arms against tyranny. He will be honoured as such."

Twitch managed a weak smile. "Thank you."

"You're under our protection now, Twitch. All four of you. We look after our own here," Michael explained. He rose to his feet, and Twitch quickly followed suit. "We'll keep you updated on any information we gather about Jennings and the Inquisition, but we won't pressure you to take any action you feel uncomfortable with. I know you're not a soldier, and we won't be treating you like one."

"I want to do what I can," Twitch said. He kept his eyes low, and he nervously stroked over the tip of his tail. "But I'm not a starat who can kill someone and be happy with it."

"Few soldiers ever are," Michael said. "But most soldiers are given the choice of whether they put themselves into those situations. You were not, and no one will think worse of you for not wanting to continue."

Twitch curled the tip of his tail as his hands gripped tight around it. He couldn't help but feeling he was taking the cowardly way out. Would Captain Rhys be doing the same thing? He doubted it, but at the same time, he knew that he wasn't Captain Rhys, no matter how hard he tried. He was a mechanic and nothing more than that.

Michael gestured towards the door. "I shall be sure to keep you updated, but for now, I must request that we part ways. I have some meetings to prepare, especially given the information you have provided," the human said. He looked down to the starat and smiled.

Twitch released his tail and smiled back. He bounced on his toes a little. "If there's anything I can do to help..."

"I'll be sure to let you know," Michael said, resting one hand across his chest.

Twitch nodded. He glanced around the small room once more, before holding his hand out to the human. They shook hands and said their farewells. Twitch then hurried out through the door, closing it behind him. He felt a slight weight remove from his shoulders. The Resistance had no expectation that he had to join in the fight against the Inquisition.

There were others who could do the fighting. Humans and starats who had trained for combat. That had never been who Twitch was. He just wished he could ease the twisting in his gut as he thought about standing back from the frontlines. War and fighting terrified him, but so did the thought of being seen a coward. No matter how much he hated the thought, this was still his battle to win.

Once again, he had allies to support him. He could only hope that these allies would not betray him like Amy. Or that their protection was a false security, like Minister Bakir. Twitch didn't know if he could take the heartache of being betrayed again. The Resistance had to be true. He needed it to be.

# chapter thirteen

"For many years, Richard was the only one who heard my voice," William said. He stood with his hands clasped in front of the pyre that had been built for Richard's body in the middle of the courtyard. William managed a bitter smile as he shook his head, his eyes watering with tears barely held back. "We were two starats alone amongst humans in the empire, on a ship with a captain who didn't really care much about us. We had no one else but each other."

Twitch bowed his head as he stood in the small crowd that had gathered around the pyre. So many were people who had never once known Richard, had likely never even seen him alive. It was not the memorial Richard deserved, but Twitch was thankful that there was something. William had been brave and strong enough to stand in front of those strangers and deliver a speech about his fallen friend.

William's voice started to tremble. "Richard is the reason I am still alive. When I lost my leg, he did twice the work on the *Harvester* while I recovered. Without that, I would have been replaced and killed," the starat said, bowing his head and holding his muzzle in one hand. His synthetic toes wiggled, scratching their claws against the stone courtyard. "I owed him everything. I just wish I could have done more to save him."

The starat didn't seem capable of speaking any further. His whole body shook as he looked back at his friend's body, laid to rest on the unlit pyre. "I just... I just... want to talk to him again."

Without even thinking about it, Twitch moved forward quickly. He placed his hand around William's side, letting the other starat lean into him. "We'll all miss Richard," Twitch said quietly, not intending for his words to be heard by anyone but William. His eyes slid to the side of the pyre, to the small table there. "They both will be."

There had been no body to collect, but Twitch had not wanted Leandro's death to go unnoticed. A small urn had been placed in the middle of the table, like the one that would soon contain Richard's ashes. Though the small clay pot would likely always be empty, Twitch hoped that the urn would also provide a memorial for Leandro. His name had been engraved on the base, alongside that of the Silver Fox. They had died in different star systems, but their names would always be together.

William tightened his grip around Twitch. He nodded and shuddered, wiping his eyes with the back of his hand. "Leandro always told us his stories. He had so many of them, and it's impossible to know how many more were lost with him," the starat said, finding the confidence and strength in his voice once more. "If we are to honour him and Richard, then we must never forget those stories and to keep on telling them. No one can forget them."

"I'll never forget either of them," Twitch said, finding some strength in his voice and addressing those gathered to remember the two fallen starats. He nervously looked around the unfamiliar faces at the front of the crowd before quickly lowering his eyes again. "Richard was always so nice. Everyone was his friend. The same for Leandro. I wanted to hear more of his stories, but instead we must simply say goodbye."

"Goodbye, yes," William whispered. The starat extricated himself from Twitch's comforting hold to reach for the fiery torch to the side of the pyre. With the flame held in his hands, William looked over the body of his friend one last time. His voice fully cracked, and the tears streamed down his face. "Goodbye, my friend. I will never stop missing you."

William lowered the torch into the pyre. The flames quickly spread as William and Twitch stepped back. The two starats retreated to the semi-circle of mixed humans and starats, the strangers and friends who had come together to say farewell to Richard and Leandro. The starats would not be forgotten.

The flames lit up the darkening sky. Light and shadow danced across the courtyard as the pyre was engulfed. It was a rustic funeral. Simple and traditional, but a better ending than so many of the starats Twitch had known in the empire. Twitch looked between the pyre and the urn. His vision blurred as William buried his head in David's shoulder.

A quiet voice behind him caught Twitch's attention. He glanced back just as a human hand touched him on the shoulder. He squeaked in surprise and spun around on his toes, raising his hands up defensively. His eyes widened as he looked to the human in front of him.

"Doctor Anthony?" Twitch gasped.

The human didn't respond vocally. He simply crouched down and wrapped his arms around the starat. He squeezed tight, and Twitch's arms rested around the human's shoulders. His head nestled in the crook of the doctor's neck.

"Thank God you're safe," the human said quietly. He leaned out of the embrace and rested his hands on Twitch's shoulders. "I'm so sorry I couldn't do anything about Richard and Leandro. I should have been there for you."

Twitch shook his head. "I don't know if there was anything you could have done," he said, keeping his voice as quiet as Doctor Anthony's. He could hear murmurs of conversation around them, with Steph and David both comforting William.

"All the same, I'm the one who brought you here," the human said. His hand slowly moved down Twitch's arms to squeeze around his hands. "I sold you on an idea that wasn't real. This isn't the Centaura I was promised."

"Perhaps we can still have that," Twitch said quietly. He pulled away from the human's grasp and turned to look towards William, with the flames behind the other starat. They could have the Centaura the human had promised them, but that peace and safety would never feel the same. The price for it would be too great.

"I really hope so," the doctor said. He almost took hold of Twitch's hand again, before he let his arms drop down. He remained crouched, keeping his head at the same height as Twitch's.

Twitch sighed softly. He wiped at his eyes with the back of his hand. The fire still burned fiercely, though a couple of humans had approached the blaze, ready to collect the ashes of the starat who had been rested on the pyre.

"Where have you been?" Twitch asked, tearing his eyes away from the pyre to look back up at the human. "I haven't seen you at all since Captain Rhys's ship came back."

"I'm sorry, I should have been there. I've been trying to learn what's going on. I didn't think you were in so much danger," the doctor explained. He rubbed his cheek with one hand, resting his other hand on Twitch's shoulder. "Shit's fucked, basically. I couldn't have known the Vatican were so strong here. That was never on any of my briefs when I was Centaura's spy. None of the SFU's treachery was, either. Everything I knew about Amy was that she was safe. She was meant to be a good starat to help you all get used to Centaura."

"Do you think we can win?" Twitch asked nervously, almost afraid to learn the answer.

Doctor Anthony sucked in his breath. "It won't be easy, but I think we can. I've got a meeting with Michael tomorrow to let him know everything I've learned. I think there might be a plan going forward, but it's going to be difficult."

Twitch bowed his head. His tail curled close to his legs. He wanted to ask the human what he had learned, but at the same time he wanted to distance himself from anything the Inquisition were doing. They had taken so much from him already; he didn't want to risk losing more.

"What about the rest of Captain Rhys's crew? Have you seen them?" Twitch asked, hoping to avoid Doctor Anthony potentially asking him to join in the fight again.

"Most of them are coming here. As soon as Captain Lee told me about Amy's true intentions, I got in contact with Rhys's crew and started to arrange for them to go into hiding. We couldn't all come at once, in case we raised suspicion," the human explained. His fingers gripped a little tighter over Twitch's shoulder. "Everyone I could find will be coming over the next few days."

A shadow of a smile pulled at Twitch's mouth. "Captain Rhys chose a good crew, didn't he?"

"He did. I hope he's still alive somewhere out there."

"I think he might be," Twitch said. He shrugged away Doctor Anthony's touch and took a couple of steps forward. The fire had started to fade, and the two humans collected the ashes remaining, filling them into a second urn. This urn had been engraved with Richard's name.

William stumbled forward to take the urn from the humans. The starat held it tightly in his hands as he kissed the lid. His tail tucked between his legs as he kept the urn against his lips. He then slowly turned around to look around the gathered crowd; the friends of Richard and Leandro, as well as those who had never known either starat.

Nothing else needed to be said. William had said everything before lighting the pyre. The starat didn't diminish the moment with words. Instead, he just held the eyes of everyone present for a moment, before moving on to the next person. Both of his hands gripped onto the urn.

Hushed silence filled the courtyard, broken only by the wind whistling through the warehouses. The electromagnetic shield crackled silently above.

In the silence, a human moved through the crowd to stand next to Twitch and Doctor Anthony. Twitch glanced across to see Michael. The human bowed his head as he looked towards William, still standing resolutely in front of the expired pyre.

"I would like to pass on my condolences once again, and I hope that this was satisfactory," Michael said quietly. He didn't wait for an answer from Twitch before continuing. "I apologise for discussing business at a time like this, but I'd like you to come see me again tomorrow, with Doctor Sparks. We have a strategy meeting with a couple of others from off-base. I'd like you to contribute."

Twitch shivered. Doubts filled his mind. He had no skill in strategy or planning. His only use had been the information he had learned. He didn't know what more he could do, but he looked up to the two humans beside him. He nodded. "I'll be there."

Michael turned to Doctor Anthony. "If Chekolin is here by then, make sure he comes too. He was Captain Griffiths' most senior officer, wasn't he?"

"After Scott was killed, yes," the doctor confirmed.

Twitch's tail quivered at the thought of seeing more of Captain Rhys's crew again. Almost without exception, the crew had welcomed him as an equal. He missed their presence almost as much as he missed Captain Rhys. Twitch would be glad of the familiar company once again. For humans, they were pleasant to be around.

"Then I look forward to seeing you all tomorrow," Michael said. The human furrowed his brow in thought and looked to be about to say something else, before shaking his head and half turning. His eyes fell on the pyre. He glanced back to Twitch. "I do pass on my sympathies again."

Twitch did not answer the human as he started to walk away, taking a large amount of the gathered humans and starats with him. The crowd quickly began to disperse, leaving just Twitch's friends behind.

William clutched Richard's urn as though it was his most precious possession, which it almost certainly was. The starat stared at Doctor Anthony as though he couldn't believe his eyes. The human crouched to one knee and held his arms wide. William bared his teeth and turned away, slinking back towards the dormitory warehouse. Steph started to follow him, but only made it a couple of steps before she stopped.

The doctor's shoulders slumped, but he made no attempts to stop the starat retreating. Twitch lowered his ears at the doctor's reaction.

"He's just lost his best friend," Twitch said quietly. He leaned into the human's arms, resting his cheek against Doctor Anthony's. "It's going to take time until he trusts people again, especially humans."

"I understand," Doctor Anthony replied with a saddened nod of his head. "I just hope he doesn't fall too deep into grief and blame."

Twitch scrunched his muzzle and forced himself to look away. His tail curled as he suppressed a shudder of distaste. He didn't know how much the human knew of what had happened to the starats. Twitch was certainly aware the same advice could be given to him. Blame for Leandro's death still hung heavy on his mind.

"You're here now though," Twitch said. He forced his ears to lift again, and a bitter smile slowly spread across his face. He looked up to the human. "You and the rest of Captain Rhys's crew. You can make a difference, right? Better than any of us could do."

"We can certainly try our best," Doctor Anthony replied. His smile looked every bit as pained and forced as Twitch's felt. He rose to his full height and looked around the courtyard, though his eyes

190

lingered on the pyre and the small table by its side. "Why don't you tell me a story about Leandro? He sounds like he was a wonderful starat."

Twitch's tail drooped, but he forced the smile to remain on his muzzle. "He really was, though I don't know if I could do his stories justice."

Steph came across to put her hand in Twitch's. "Between all of us, I think we can manage. Leandro deserves his stories to be told. It's what he would have wanted."

Twitch rubbed his hand over his muzzle. Perhaps telling the story of Leandro would help. Just informing Michael of the events that had befallen him had taken a weight off his chest. He hoped the same would be true of telling Doctor Anthony one of Leandro's many stories. He took the empty urn in both hands and lightly ran his finger over the engraved names at the bottom.

The grey-furred starat would not be forgotten. His story would be told.

*** 

A strange tension filled the warehouses. Darkness had truly fallen, and a full night had passed since the funeral and memorial of Richard and Leandro. Twitch had slept poorly, and he had spent most of the night staring at the silhouette of the two urns, where they had been placed next to William's bed in the dormitories.

Twitch's head had been filled of thoughts and worries of what was to come. Darkness clung close to his mind. After a few hours of patchy sleep, Twitch had sat up in his bed, staring out to the windows. He idly toyed with his disconnected synthetic legs in his hands, running his fingers over the smooth, furless surface.

There was no dawn to herald the coming of the day. Instead, Twitch was aware of the new day by the sounds coming from the adjacent kitchens, and the gradual increase from the artificial lights around the compound. Smells of food soon followed, but he couldn't muster up the energy to get something to eat. He just sat back with his head resting against the wall.

"Is everything alright?"

Twitch opened his eyes just as David sat down on his mattress. His partner looked tired, with dishevelled fur that stuck up randomly around his ears and neck.

Twitch shrugged. "I feel awful. But given everything that's been going on, I suppose I could be feeling worse," he replied. He grimaced and leaned into David's side. "I guess I'll go and see what Michael and Doctor Anthony has to say in a bit. Maybe then I'll feel a bit better."

"And if they don't have anything positive to say?"

"We try Sirius?" Twitch said, a bark of humourless laughter following.

"We could try," David replied. His hand gently stroked down Twitch's arm. "No point staying here, especially if we know we can't save it. Might as well run and live somewhere else."

Twitch's tail drooped. "How can we get away? We can't steal a ship. We wouldn't know how to fly it."

"Maybe we can convince Aleksandr. He was Rhys's pilot, wasn't he?"

"And if we can't?"

"I won't just sit around and wait for you to be killed. For all of us to die," David said fiercely. He squeezed Twitch tight and kissed his forehead. "I'd rather run away and try somewhere new."

"Sirius is back in the empire though. It'll be just as bad as Ceres," Twitch said. He felt comforted in David's arms, but the worries weren't chased away. His synthetic tail thumped against the mattress, then curled up around the empty leg sockets on his hips.

"At least we'll be alive," David replied.

"But we wouldn't be free. We might not even be together, if we're in Sirius. They could separate us."

"I won't allow that," David hissed, gripping around Twitch's torso a little tighter, as though someone threatened to split them apart immediately.

Twitch knew they wouldn't be given a choice. He knew David knew that as well. He said nothing, but just enjoyed the company of his partner for a little longer. He had stayed in bed for too long already, and soon he would be expected in the meeting with Michael and Doctor Anthony. Twitch just wanted to enjoy the feeling of being able to relax without the fear of being pursued.

Time didn't slow, though. William had left with Steph for some breakfast, leaving Twitch and David as the last two inside the dormitory. The quietness of the dormitory after everyone had woken and left was nice, but Twitch knew that he was expected elsewhere. He slowly extricated himself from David's embrace and clipped his synthetic legs into place.

As much as he wanted to stay, Twitch reluctantly rose to his feet. His mind, still tired from the poor night of sleep, felt almost overwhelmed by the influx of information that came from his legs. Everything, from the texture of the floor beneath his feet, to the temperature of the air in the room, came through the sensors in his artificial limbs.

"Are you sure you're going to be alright?" David asked. He rested a steadying hand on Twitch as he regained his balance. "I can come with you if you like."

Twitch shook his head. "Thank you, but I'll be fine," he replied. He managed a faint smile. "Just help me find my pants, and I'll be alright to go."

Once Twitch was fully dressed, he began to make his way through the Resistance facility. His stomach growled a little in hunger, and he began to regret his earlier laziness in not getting some breakfast. He could only hope that there was some food in Michael's small office. He still didn't know who else the Resistance leader had wanted the starat to meet. He knew Doctor Anthony and Aleksandr would be there, but Michael had teased someone else Twitch knew. He could only hope this person came with answers to the situation they found themselves in.

The cool air inside the warehouses chilled through Twitch's fur. Prox had sunk below the horizon, but the star's heat still lingered. Twitch couldn't decide which he preferred. The bite of air-conditioning sometimes felt too cold to him. It reminded him of his life on Ceres, where all he had ever known had been air that had passed endlessly through cooling and recycling vents.

Twitch had no guide to lead him through to Michael's office, but he picked his way between the narrow corridors from memory. A faint scent also guided him. Doctor Anthony had passed through the

J.F.R. Coates

warehouse recently, and Twitch could just about pick out his scent amongst the many other smells of human and starat.

Following that scent, Twitch found his way through to Michael's office. A few voices murmured inside, but they quickly stopped when Twitch knocked on the door. When the door opened, Twitch looked around to see several humans inside. He recognised four of the five present; Aaron, Michael, Doctor Anthony, and Aleksandr, the pilot of the *Harvester*. The fifth human was dressed in military uniform like Nessie Ulrich had worn.

The unknown human peered at Twitch inquisitively. "They're right. You do look just like him."

Twitch flicked his ears up. "You knew Captain Rhys?"

The human nodded. "I did. I'm the one who oversaw his time in the Stellar Guard. I am Fleet-Admiral Bosler. Pleasure to meet you, Twitch."

Twitch took a quick step back, but the door had already been closed behind him. His eyes opened wide as he stared up at the human woman, then to Doctor Anthony and Aleksandr. He didn't know how either of them could be associated with the one who had betrayed Nessie Ulrich. Aaron especially knew that she couldn't be trusted, and yet he had been in casual conversation with her.

Before Twitch could do anything, Aaron and Aleksandr both stood between Twitch and the fleet-admiral. Aaron placed his hand gently on Twitch's wrist.

"It's fine, she's fine," Captain Rhys's friend said urgently. "I'm sorry, I should have warned you."

"She... she..." Twitch spluttered, before finding his voice. "She's the one who got Nessie killed."

Bosler raised her hands, which were both empty. She made no attempt to move out from behind the shadow of Aaron or Aleksandr, but she showed no fear to Twitch. "I swear to you, I was not involved."

"How can I trust you?" Twitch growled. He relaxed his hands, no longer struggling against Aaron's touch on his wrists. "She came to you, and she was killed."

Michael spoke before Bosler could deny anything. "Twitch, please come and sit down. You told me everything that had

194

happened to you, but you were not given all of our intel. It seems you have some misconceptions about what Jessica has been doing."

Twitch made no move to sit down at all. "I know what she's been doing. She's been working with Amy or the Inquisition. Doesn't matter which. They're both as bad as each other," he said, a snarl coming to his lips.

"She came to me, yes," Bosler admitted. She took a step closer to the desk in the middle of the crowded office. She leaned against the desk and waited for a few seconds.

Aaron pulled out a chair for Twitch, but the starat still didn't feel like sitting. He waited for Bosler to continue her explanation.

The human hesitated. "She did come to me. She told me everything. I didn't want to believe her, but I knew she wouldn't be lying even before she presented her evidence. I'd always had doubts on Amy Jennings, but I didn't realise…" Bosler paused again. She tapped her fingers against the desk. "If Nessie told anyone else what she knew, then she didn't pass on that information to me."

"Then who killed her?" Twitch demanded.

"That is currently unconfirmed, but the fleet-admiral has provided verified information to clear her name," Michael said. He had sat down behind his desk, but he was the only one who had done so. Everyone else remained standing. "We haven't wanted to look too closely into Nessie's death, in case we arouse further suspicion."

Twitch glared between Michael and Bosler, but he accepted the explanation for the moment. He didn't trust the fleet-admiral, and he had yet to be convinced that she had not been involved in the death of Nessie, but he did trust Aaron. The starat took the chair Aaron had been offering and sat down, but kept his narrowed eyes fixed on Bosler. "Tell me everything then."

Michael gestured to the remaining chairs around the office. The humans took a seat, with Aleksandr and Aaron taking the chairs either side of Twitch. The Resistance leader clasped his hands over his desk. "We're all friends here. We're working together to better the lives of everyone on Centaura."

"I heard that from Amy. Why are you different?" Twitch grumbled. He folded his arms across his chest and leaned back in his chair.

"Because we won't annihilate an entire planet in an attempt to cleanse it. Both Amy and the Inquisition plan that. We merely seek to stop them," Michael said.

Twitch raised his brow. "Then what are you waiting for? Go stop them. I told you where the Inquisition's machine is."

"It's not quite that simple," Bosler said.

Twitch glanced sharply towards the fleet-admiral. He silently snarled. "Isn't it?"

The human shook her head. "If we strike, then we need to be sure we eradicate the Inquisition. More, we need to make sure President Shawn is shown to be working with them. We will be seen as a military coup. We need to show our actions are justified."

"And we need to make sure they don't know we're coming. If we attack and they activate the weapon..." Aaron added. He shuddered. "We need a good plan, and we need protection."

Twitch flicked his ears. He looked around the group of humans as a chill descended into his stomach. "I hope you're not expecting me to think something up for you. I'm a mechanic. This is meant to be your area," he growled.

"You know this machine like few others," Michael said. He appeared to be sweating a little, despite the cool air inside the warehouse, circulated by the large fans on the ceiling. "You know more about how it is modified and what it may be capable of, as well as the signs to look out for if it's nearing deployment."

Twitch groaned and rubbed his forehead with the heels of his hands. His ears pinned down. He looked up to Aleksandr through his fingers. "You have sensors that can detect Denitchev concentration?"

"We've already got some installed around the planet," Bosler confirmed. She pulled back the sleeve of her shirt to show a small wristwatch. She pressed a button on the side, projecting a small holographic display, which showed a pair of numbers. "Twenty-five per million. Very slightly elevated but remaining steady. We've noticed the numbers rise every time Prox goes through some wild storms, like it is now."

Twitch grimaced. "I estimated two hundred and twenty," he said. He ran his clawed fingers through his headfur. His foot tapped nervously against the concrete floor. "Is there any chance I can get one of those?"

Bosler unclipped the wristband and tossed it across to the starat. He fumbled the small device, but he managed to catch it before it fell to the floor. He ran his fingers over the small, smooth holoscreen. Though the projection had been switched off, the numbers were still displayed on the screen. He tightened the band around his wrist, making sure it wouldn't slip off. The adjustable strap moved to its tightest setting, and it still hung a little loosely.

"These will give us warning," Twitch said, rubbing his left hand around the strap. "But I don't know how much that will help us. I can't think of anything that destroys Denitchev particles."

"They do degrade," Aleksandr said slowly. "But not quickly enough for us. It might take years for high concentrations to fade."

"We need something faster, and we know one person who might know more," Bosler said. She looked down to Twitch. "That's why we brought you here. We want you to meet this person, and together you might be able to come up with a solution for us."

"And who is that?" Twitch asked.

"His name is Captain James Herschel. He was the former captain of the Pluto station," Bosler said. She leaned forward in her chair, squeezed into the small space between the desk and the wall. "He was captured in the raid that lost Captain Griffiths."

Twitch's ears flicked up. He looked to Bosler with one raised brow. "He might have been the last person to see Captain Rhys? He might have seen him hit the ground after he fell."

"His memory is the same as ours," Aaron said, quickly dashing those hopes. "None of us can remember what happened. Whatever Snow did, she did it well."

"No one seemed sure what happened to the captain," Aleksandr said. The human scratched his cheek, which didn't look like it had been shaved for a few days. "I had thought it was just shock, at first. I could not really explain it."

Twitch bit his lip and hid his disappointment. "But he knows a lot about the Denitchev drives?"

"He oversaw the design on these enlarged models," Michael confirmed. "We haven't yet questioned him on their use as a weapon, as we wanted to have an expert on them present."

Twitch laughed. "And I'm that expert? I fix them, but that's about all." He looked around the room, but no one else laughed with him.

"I know how to fly with one," Aleksandr said. He shrugged his shoulders. "I would not know how they are built, or how they really work."

"Nor me," Aaron admitted.

Twitch laughed again, this time in disbelief. "Shit like that is why starats don't respect humans in the empire. You treat starats like mindless beasts, but then expect us to do all the things you can't do." He sighed and slumped back in his seat, lifting his hand up to forestall any protests from Aaron and Aleksandr. "I know you two weren't that bad, but others were."

"Do you think this is something you can do?" Michael asked.

Twitch hissed softly as he slowly breathed in. He looked around the group of humans. Two of them he knew and trusted. He didn't know enough about Michael to get a good judgement, and he still had many doubts about the fleet-admiral. If Aaron and Aleksandr believed he was the best person for this task, then he had to believe them. He slowly nodded. "I'll do it. If you need something fixed, it's best to get a starat to do it. Can't trust any of you to get it right."

Michael beamed widely. He clapped his hands together. "Very good. Fleet-Admiral Bosler will lead you all to the captain. Please report back to me with any information you gather."

The fleet-admiral rose to her feet. Both Aaron and Aleksandr followed her up. Twitch remained sitting.

"Why aren't you coming? Isn't this important?"

A smirk spread across Michael's face. "Crucial. But so is tracking the president. I need spies on him every moment of every day. I need to know what his movements are. We can't miss anything that proves his involvement in this plot, so I must coordinate that."

Twitch flicked his muzzle, then rose to his feet. He could feel a slight vibration through the floor, but the sensation quickly dissipated. The starat frowned and flicked his ears, but he quickly moved to follow the humans. His tail remained tucked close between his legs. He had no idea what to expect from the captured human. The captain was from the empire. He doubted the reception would be good.

*\*\*\**

Captain James Herschel had been kept under guard in one of the smaller buildings, which Twitch had not gone into before. Inside, there was just a single room. The human had been handcuffed and left to sit in the lone chair in the room, with his ankles also cuffed to the chair legs. Though he was sitting, Twitch could tell that the captain was probably the tallest human he had ever seen. Edgar Scott, the first officer for Captain Rhys, had been tall as well, but Twitch looked eye-to-eye with this human, even as the prisoner sat down.

The human never looked at Twitch. His eyes solely focussed on the three humans with the starat. Familiarity glared at Bosler from his deep green eyes. Like Aleksandr, his facial hair had started to grow out, with black wiry hair covering most of his lower face. "Come to explain why you moved me here?" he asked the fleet-admiral.

"We told you. We needed an expert in the Denitchev drives before questioning you," Bosler replied. She remained a few steps away from the bound prisoner.

Captain James immediately turned to look up at Aleksandr, then glanced to Aaron and Doctor Anthony standing either side of the pilot. He sneered. "And what did you want to know."

"Not me. Him," Aleksandr replied, jabbing down with a thumb towards Twitch.

The empire human turned to Twitch for the first time. Confusion entered his eyes. A flash of disgust. "How quaint."

Twitch growled, but he knew not to get angry with the human. He needed to remain calm if he could. He took a couple of steps forward, ahead of the three humans with him. "Tell me about these drives. How do we stop them?"

The human blinked. Twitch knew he had probably never heard a starat speak to him in such a way before. "Is this a joke?"

Twitch snarled at the bound human. His tail flicked to one side. He refused to step back and let his human companions come forward and question the prisoner. "Listen to me, human," Twitch growled, lowering his voice to his best Captain Rhys impression. "I am not a mindless beast. None of us are. This is not the empire where you get to pretend that is true. This is Centaura. Do you understand me?"

The human kept trying to look away, but finally Twitch met his eyes fully. Captain James's eyes stared into Twitch's. They watered as the pupils widened. The human's mouth hung open.

Twitch could see a change clearly reflected in the human's eyes. The same thing had happened to Captain Rhys, all that time ago. The prisoner no longer saw a beast in front of him, he saw a person.

"What? How?" Captain James gasped. His breaths came quick and short. He struggled at his bonds.

"Answer my question. How do we stop the drives?" Twitch growled, not wishing to let the human get distracted.

"Why do you care?"

"Because this planet is going to be consumed by subspace if we don't do anything," Twitch retorted. He delighted in the fear that filled the human's eyes. The human turned away and stared at the ground.

"The tech was being developed as a protection against meteor and comet strikes," he said quietly. Shame crept into his voice, and a tinge of red spread across his cheeks. "Then funding came in from the Vatican to develop it faster. The scale they wanted exceeded any meteor, but we didn't question them. You can't question them and live. We just did what they asked."

Twitch glanced back to the three humans behind him. None of them said anything, though Aaron frowned in concern. The starat turned to face the prisoner again. "I don't care how you developed the drives as a weapon. All I care about is how to stop the Inquisition using them."

Captain James shook his head. "Once started, the only way to stop it is to switch it off again, or to prevent the electrical spark that triggers the jump," he said. A frown furrowed his brow as he looked down, staring at his shackled hands in his lap. "I know of nothing that can destroy the particles, apart from letting them degrade naturally."

Twitch clicked his tongue. He had been afraid of that. "So what can you tell us?"

The human hesitated. He lifted his hands for a moment, before dropping them back down into his lap. "I probably deserve these chains for the weapon we created. I thought I was right, and that I was justified in what I was doing. Now I know it was lies, though I don't know how I know that. It feels like a fog was cleared from my mind, and only now can I think clearly. Even you... I look at you and feel confused."

"I meant about the weapon," Twitch said. He wrinkled his nose as he got too close to the captive human. The prisoner had a sharp odour to his body, like he hadn't been given the proper facilities to wash frequently.

Aleksandr cleared his throat. "I recognise that feeling," he said slowly. He approached Captain James and knelt in front of him. "When did you feel like you could think clearly?"

"Not long after arriving on this planet," the captain said. He looked over Aleksandr with interested eyes. "You're from the empire too, aren't you? Everyone's so short here, like my hard-hearted captor." His head tilted in the direction of Bosler, who frowned.

"For me, it was after choosing to accept my captain for who he was," Aleksandr said. He smiled. "He was a starat now, but he was still the same person he had always been. For me, that felt like a mist had lifted, and I saw everything in a different way."

Captain James's eyes widened. "I heard about that captain. He was all over the news for a day or two before everything got silenced. The one who was a starat?"

"This is all very interesting," Bosler said, cutting across the discussion between the two humans. "But how will it help us stop the Denitchev weapon?"

Captain James leaned back in his chair. "There is no reliable way to stop it. Your best chance is to stop them ever using it. Once started, there's not much that can be done. If the particle concentration gets high enough, then any significant electrical charge will trigger it. You get storms on this planet, right? One big thunderstorm, and the planet will jump."

"Alright, so there's no counter," Bosler said. She leaned back against the wall and drummed her fingers against it. "What concentration should we be looking out for?"

Captain James furrowed his brow. His mouth moved silently as he calculated some sums. "Planet this big? You're at what, one point three G? Probably looking at something like two-thirty per million."

Twitch whooped and punched the air. "Thought it would be around that," he said, beaming in delight as he looked around the room. No one else smiled, but that didn't diminish his triumphant grin. "So we just need a way to dissipate the particles."

"It can't be done," Captain James said, shaking his head. "There's nothing we know of that will make the particles degrade faster than their natural rate, and that would be too dangerous."

Twitch looked up to the low ceiling. A small fan spun in one corner, circulating the air through the cramped room. A window sat high in the wall, through which Twitch could see a couple of stars. A pulse of light spread through the electromagnetic lattice that surrounded the planet. Fur stood up on the back of his neck.

"Then we lower the shields," the starat said slowly. His tail arched up as he turned on his toes. He looked up to Bosler. "Denitchev jumps need the shields to work. If there aren't any shields, then nothing happens, no matter how much electricity is pumped through the air."

"One flare from Prox and half of the planet is dead," the fleet-admiral said hesitantly.

"Last resort only. If concentrations of the particles get too high, then we must be ready to drop the shields before the Inquisition is ready," Twitch said, speaking as quickly as his thoughts raced. He knew the dangers. He knew why the shields were there, but he knew that there could be no other choice. If the shields remained up, then the consequences for Centaura would be dire.

"The starat is right. In theory, that works," Captain James said, but no one looked towards him. All eyes remained on Twitch.

"There should be some alarm system that warn people if the shields are down, right? Get inside, and all that. I know we had one on Ceres if the atmosphere was breached. Never really worked, but it was still there," the starat said, the words all spilling from his mouth at once. He felt like pacing, but there wasn't enough room for it. He contented himself with just tapping his foot. "If Denitchev concentration gets above two hundred, then evacuate and prepare to lower the shields. Gets above two hundred and ten, then drop the shields."

Bosler ran her hand over her jaw. She didn't look Twitch in the eye. "I don't like the sound of that. It feels like sacrificing the planet just so we don't let them win. But... I can see how it might work."

Twitch beamed widely. His tail flicked out from between his legs. "It's an insurance," he said. He looked up to the three humans. "It will be up to you to make sure we don't need it though. I can't do military stuff."

Bosler nodded. "We can handle that one, once we get the latest report from Michael. We suspect the president will go to Hadrian once they're ready to move."

"That just leave the problem with Amy," Aaron said.

"We've got her under control," Bosler replied, waving her hand at Aaron nonchalantly. Her mouth tightened into a pursed grimace. "We know who is loyal to her, and who is loyal to us. We're working on removing her influence from the military."

"I can only hope you're successful," Aaron said uncertainly.

Twitch turned back to Captain James. "Is there anything else we should know about these drives?"

The captive human thought for a moment. "Yes. When the drives are this big, things tend to get a bit weird when they're on. Reality can twist a bit. Humans can't get too close, but starats can. If the machine is on, and you want to turn it off, you have to send a starat."

Twitch wrinkled his muzzle. "I don't want to know how you learned that information."

Captain James bowed his head. "I have done many things I am now ashamed of. I once thought they were justified, but now I know otherwise. You have no reason to trust me, but I would like to offer my full service to help pay for my sins."

Twitch opened his mouth, willing to accept that help. Before he could get the words out, Bosler spoke over him.

"We'll see about that. I think we've learned enough for now," she said. She lightly placed her hand on Twitch's shoulder, encouraging him to walk away from their captive.

With a soft sigh, Twitch obliged. He turned on his toes and pushed open the door. He didn't look back to Captain James, and nor did he see if the other humans followed him. Once outside, the starat turned to head back towards the dormitories. He could hear the following footsteps a few metres behind him, and the quiet, murmured conversation between the four humans. His ears pricked up at the mention of the shields.

Ice filled Twitch's body as he heard Bosler whisper to one of the others. "I think we might need him."

Twitch had been dreading that.

Somehow, it had felt inevitable.

He would have to go to Hadrian one last time.

# chapter fourteen

"You don't have to go."

David wrapped his arms tight around Twitch, as though his partner could leave at any moment.

The two starats were alone, on the outskirts of the Resistance base. A wire fence kept them inside the boundaries, and neither had any desire to walk beyond the safety of the fencing. Inside it, they expected to be protected from any harm. They couldn't be sure if the Inquisition or Starat Freedom Union were still searching for them.

Twitch had been afraid to tell David exactly what had happened during the meeting with Michael and the other human leaders of the Resistance. For a full night, Twitch had struggled to sleep on the knowledge that he could be called to go to Hadrian in any assault made on the Inquisition. No one had told him he had to go, but nor had he spoken to any of the humans about what he had overheard.

"I think they need me," Twitch replied. He lay back on the ground, looking up to the unfamiliar stars. His head rested on David's chest, with his partner also sprawled out on the ground, a small distance away from the closest of the buildings. In the distance, Twitch could hear some of the humans and starats moving around the complex, but nothing sounded urgent. Everyone seemed relaxed; even happy. Knowledge had begun to creep in through their spy networks and channels. A bigger picture had started to form.

The Resistance knew now that the Inquisition had moved to their final preparations with their weapon beneath Hadrian. Fleet-Admiral Bosler had reported that several shipments of Denitchev crystals had gone missing. President Shawn was expected to make a state visit to Hadrian, though no official explanation had come from his office

J.F.R. Coates

that justified the trip to the southern city. No one had heard anything from Amy Jennings or Snow. Everything had fallen quiet from Jennings Tower in the middle of Caledonia. None of her known partners had gone off-planet, and her attempts to ignite the war between Centaura and Terra had been silenced. The Resistance no longer viewed her as an active threat, though no one understood why.

Twitch knew not to trust Amy. He expected her to still be plotting her attempts to strike at Terra. He doubted that anything Leandro had said with his final words had managed to sway Amy. She and Snow would stop at nothing to do what they believed to be right, but Twitch also knew why the Resistance could not keep watch on her. The bigger threat to Centaura was the Inquisition. Once that threat had been dealt with, then they could turn to bringing Amy to heel.

"Why would they need you?" David asked, pulling Twitch's attention back from his musings.

Twitch didn't answer at first. He just watched the stars, and the occasional spark of light as the shields lit up. Despite his worries about the future, he felt relaxed. He enjoyed the quiet company of David.

"They'll need a starat who knows how to turn the drive off," Twitch said quietly, finally answering his partner. He thumped his tail against the dirt ground. Close by, a few tendrils of a native plant writhed in the gentle breeze. The starat's eyes dropped down from the stars to look at the bizarre foliage. He had never experienced plant life on Ceres, but he had learned about native Terran species. The sticky, bioluminescent tentacles were nothing like anything that lived on Sol.

"If you're going, then I'm going too."

Twitch sat up sharply. He looked down at David, who remained lying on his back, partially propped up by his elbows. "Why would you want to come as well?" Twitch asked in surprise.

"Because you're there. I won't let you out of my sight." David reached up to cup one hand around Twitch's muzzle. "I want to protect you, but I can't do that if I'm not by your side."

"It will be dangerous."

David smiled sadly. "And yet you will still go. If you're going to be brave, then so can I."

"Is it bravery?" Twitch asked with a twist of his muzzle. He met his partner in the eye, not looking away. "Or is it stupidity?"

"There's often not much of a line between them," David said softly. He leaned in and kissed Twitch on the forehead. "But a brave idiot is still brave. You know this is going to be dangerous, but you're still going to choose to go there."

Twitch slowly lowered himself to rest his head back on David's chest. His partner's hand held him close. No matter what, Twitch knew that he would always have David by his side, protecting him when necessary. "I just wish we could sit this one out and let people like Aaron and Nick sort it all out."

David chuckled. "Are you sure you could do that? You've always been helping starats, even back on Ceres. If there was the chance you could make it better for someone, you'd go and do it."

"Yeah, I suppose so," Twitch mumbled. His ears folded down in embarrassment.

"And besides, I think you're too nosy. You'd want to know what was going on in Hadrian if you weren't asked to go. You started this, so you're going to have to be there when it ends," David said. He stuck his tongue out as he looked down at Twitch, who could only grumble in protest.

Twitch turned his head to look back up at the stars. His ears and cheeks burned slightly in a deep blush, and his tail flicked around nervously. Everything David said had been true. He hated how right his partner had been. He wanted to be safe. He wanted to leave the fighting behind, to go somewhere quiet and out of the way. But he knew he would never let himself do such a thing.

A beep from Twitch's wrist interrupted the calm silence.

Twitch glanced down to look at the sensor. He switched on the holographic projection to read the number it displayed. The reading was no longer the same. Instead of exactly twenty-five over a million, the concentration had started to very slowly rise. The change was so small to be insignificant and could have been in response to Prox's moody nature, but it wasn't worth taking that risk.

"We have to go."

Twitch deactivated the holograph as he leapt to his feet. He held his hand out for David.

The calm feeling that had pervaded the facility faded quickly. Twitch knew a few of the leaders had their own Denitchev sensor. Knowledge of the small raise in concentration would already have spread through the Resistance. Twitch knew that he would be summoned soon.

The courtyard between the warehouses remained calm and organised, but an urgency had filled movement of everyone passing across. Orders barked from one end to the other, and boxes of equipment were carried out of storage and placed in an organised pile in the middle of the empty space. Twitch stared around from the edge, recognising a few more faces amongst the humans. More from Captain Rhys's crew had arrived.

The Resistance moved quickly and efficiently. The fleet-admiral and Michael had clearly been planning for this. Twitch could only watch with wide-eyed admiration at everything. He squeezed David's hand tight. "We should go and see what we can do to help."

"I think they've got everything alright," David replied. He leaned into Twitch slightly. "If we're going to be going as well, then we need to make sure we have our stuff prepared. Are your legs alright?"

"Charged them overnight," Twitch said with a nod. He rubbed one hand over the smooth skin of his left leg. Slowly, he was getting used to the thought of having inorganic limbs. They were becoming a part of him. He looked down at his wrist sensor again. The reading remained at just above twenty-five, but it had not yet dropped again, like it might if the rise had been in response to a flare from Prox. Instead, the number continued to slowly tick up.

A voice called out across the busy courtyard. Twitch looked around as he heard his name. His ears fidgeted as he tried to work out where the sound came from, before he saw Fleet-Admiral Bosler with her hand raised. Aaron walked with her.

With David staying by his side, Twitch scampered through the crowd. He bumped into a couple of humans by mistake. He expected to hear a shout of frustration, but none came. Only apologies.

The fleet-admiral didn't stop walking as Twitch caught up with her. She kept moving towards the northern warehouse, which housed Michael's office. "We have a difficult thing to ask of you," she said.

"You want me to come to Hadrian," Twitch said, before the fleet-admiral could say it. He took a deep breath. "I'll do it, but I'm not there as a soldier. I'm a mechanic, and nothing more than that."

If the fleet-admiral was surprised Twitch already knew what she wanted to ask of him, then she showed no sign of that emotion. She didn't even look down at Twitch. "I understand. If we succeed, then that will be the last we ask of you. We will be grateful to you, but we understand you are not a soldier."

"You know this place better than any of us," Aaron explained. He did look down to Twitch. The starat could see the worry in Aaron's eyes. "Most importantly, you may be needed to shut this thing down. You've seen this machine before, and that gives you the advantage no other starat has."

Twitch bowed his head. "I understand."

"We'll be transporting everyone to shuttles in one hour. Make any final preparations and be ready then," Bosler instructed. Her hawkish eyes looked around the busy square as she walked. She stopped just outside the door to the warehouse. She turned on her heel and looked to Twitch and David. "This is when we fight for our planet. If I don't have the chance to say so later, I am glad to have starats like you on our side, and I apologise for any doubts you had over my involvement in Nessie Ulrich's death. She was a great starat too, and her loss is felt in times like this."

The fleet-admiral held out her hand.

Twitch tentatively took it. He still hadn't been convinced by her, but everyone else seemed to trust her. For now, that would be enough for Twitch.

"Fleet-Admiral, a word please?"

A voice Twitch didn't recognise called out across the courtyard.

The fleet-admiral pulled her hand away from Twitch. "Excuse me, I have to go. Captain Lee, please inform Michael I'll be with him soon," she said. She started to move away, before pausing for a moment. "Remember, one hour until we leave. Don't be late."

"I'll be there," Twitch said. He watched her back as she disappeared into the crowd. While she left, Aaron remained.

"We can trust her, Twitch," Aaron said.

The smile on Twitch's muzzle faltered slightly. "Captain Rhys thought that about Amy."

"This isn't the same. I promise," the human said. He looked up to the dark sky. "I hope he's still out there."

Twitch's smile returned. "He will be. He's Captain Rhys. He'll be fine."

Aaron returned the smile. "I'll see you on the shuttles." He waved farewell and pushed open the warehouse door. He slipped inside without another word.

Twitch glanced up at his partner, squeezing tight around David's hand. "We'd better make sure we're ready to go as well."

\*\*\*

Twitch lost count of how many gathered together to leave the Resistance facility. Over one hundred humans and starats were present, with more due to join them on additional shuttles from different hideouts spread across the continent.

Two military transport shuttles landed just beyond the perimeter fence. Fleet-Admiral Bosler hurried to meet someone who stepped out of the closest. A quick conversation followed, before the gathered supplies were loaded onto the shuttles. The waiting soldiers began to board.

Twitch hung back with David, William, and Steph. The four starats had all agreed to travel to Hadrian together. They owed it to each other, and to the two who they had lost. Even Steph, who had no skills in combat, had refused to be left behind. She would be staying back from the front lines, assisting in communication.

The shuttle interior was sparse and simple. A row of seats backed onto the side walls, with a large open space between them. At an order from the fleet-admiral, Twitch strapped himself into one of the seats, with David and William either side of him. A small hole in the back of the seat provided room for his tail to sit comfortably.

The shuttle began to vibrate as the engines started. The doors closed, blocking away any external view. Twitch couldn't see any evidence of a pilot's cabin inside the shuttle. He couldn't be sure whether the craft was fully automated or piloted.

By the time the shuttle lifted from the ground, all but one was seated. Fleet-Admiral Bosler remained on her feet, both hands wrapped around a couple of straps descending from the ceiling. She and Michael had shared leadership from this outpost, with the other human present on the second shuttle.

"Attention please!"

The last lingering conversations immediately fell silent as the fleet-admiral called out. All eyes turned to her as the shuttle ascended. Twitch could feel the vibrations through the craft, though he had no windows to look out of.

"You know why we're here. You know where we're going," the fleet-admiral called out. Though the roar of the engines reverberated through the shuttle, Twitch could clearly hear every word the human said. Her voice had a power to it that he had heard in few humans. "We will rendezvous in Hadrian and gear up on the ground. Our target is below ground, meaning heavy weapons cannot be brought with us. It is also beneath civilian homes, meaning orbital bombardments are impossible. We are forced to go on foot. It is no hyperbole to say the fate of our planet depends on us. I expect total dedication and commitment. Quite simply, we must win this battle. Do I make myself understood?"

A chorus of, "Yes ma'am," echoed around the transport shuttle. Twitch remained quiet through it all. He looked around the shuttle and saw mostly men – mostly humans – cheering to each other. None of them truly knew what they were going to face. Twitch had no knowledge of battle, but he had seen the battlegrounds. The claustrophobic confines of the dark underground cavern did not strike Twitch as a good place to wage war.

The starat looked down at his wrist. As he had been doing every five minutes, he pressed the small button on the side to read the projected numbers.

Just over twenty-six. The numbers rose slowly, but the pace was beginning to increase, ruling out any coincidental natural event from Prox. Twitch had not yet worked out how long they had before the numbers were critical. Hours, still. But not enough of them to feel comfortable.

Twitch covered the small screen with his hand. He closed his eyes and leaned back. The shuttle vibrated against his head, chattering his teeth and feeling like he was being shaken. He stayed there for a few seconds before leaning forward again.

The starat felt sick. He had promised himself we would not get involved anymore, but here he was, on the shuttle again, after willingly choosing to break that promise. He didn't want to sit alone in Caledonia and wait for the end of the world, but nor did he want to hear the screams again.

He would do anything to purge those memories from his mind, but they only came back stronger.

This time, they were different. Instead of watching a human fall to his death, the positions were reversed. Twitch's mind played a scene of him falling. Screaming.

A hand squeezed around his.

Twitch looked up to his partner. The pain in his gut didn't go away, but just looking into David's warm eyes soothed his dark thoughts.

No words needed to be said. They were together, and they always would be. So long as they had each other's backs, nothing bad could ever happen to them.

Or so Twitch kept telling himself.

# chapter fifteen

The skyline of Hadrian lit up the horizon. The shuttles had landed a short distance outside the city, at a military barracks that played host to the dozens of shuttles coming from across the planet. Despite the sheer number of shuttles and soldiers arriving, there appeared to be a calm organisation to everything. Inside the outer perimeter walls were large camps providing the arriving soldiers with equipment they would need in the coming battle. Neat lines had formed, with human and starat alike corralled by their superiors.

Once disembarked from the shuttles, Twitch was guided to an armoury. Body armour in his size was found and fitted, though he refused the offer of a rifle. If he needed a weapon, then he had the pistol housed in his right leg. He picked up some spare ammunition for that, just in case. The fur on the back of his neck prickled as he was shepherded out of the armoury a few minutes later. The flexible armour over his clothes was so light he could barely feel its presence. His helmet was clipped to the resource belt around his waist.

But for the mask of terror that had been plastered over his face, Twitch was sure he probably looked the part of a soldier. The more he looked around though, the more he believed everyone else felt the same fear as him. He could see it in their eyes. Human and starat alike were scared. They fought hard to hide the emotion. Voices were loud and brash, and they charged around quickly to their designated muster points. But in their eyes, Twitch could see that fear.

Twitch waited for the other starats to come through the armoury. As he did so, he listened to the conversations around the barracks. Rumours swirled in hushed tones. Some questioned why so many

213

had been left behind. Nearly one third of the military strength available to Fleet-Admiral Bosler had not been chosen to join the assault.

Twitch thought he knew the answer. Those left behind had been those loyal to Amy Jennings, and not to the leaders of the Stellar Guard. He shivered at the thought. There had been so many.

"Twitch!"

The starat turned to see Steph pushing her way past a few humans. She had been kitted out in body armour, but Twitch couldn't see any trace of a weapon. She pulled Twitch into a hug, squeezing her arms tight around his chest.

"I'm not going with you. I'm staying here," she said. She rested her head on his chest, and he gently stroked between her ears. "They're putting me on comms, so I'll be able to keep track of you."

Twitch laughed. "I wish I could do that too. No one will be shooting you here."

Steph curled her ears against her head. "You'll be needed down there," she said quietly. She tightened her embrace around his chest. "I'm glad there's something I can do to help."

"You'll be keeping us all safe," Twitch encouraged.

A shadow of a smile spread across Steph's face. She nodded, then gave Twitch a quick kiss on the cheek. "I'll do my best. I should head back though. Just wanted to say goodbye and good luck."

A blush spread across Twitch's muzzle from the kiss. He grinned bashfully. "I'll be fine. I've got you and David looking after me."

"You'd better be fine," Steph said. She squeezed her arms around Twitch one last time, before breaking away and scampering off the way she had come. She crossed paths with David and William as they approached.

David carried a large pack on his back. He rolled his shoulders as Twitch began to walk alongside him. He didn't seem capable of hiding the nervous smile on his face, and his tail quivered in excitement over something.

They had been given their muster point. Aaron would be their direct commander, something that Twitch was glad of. He would have someone he knew and trusted giving the orders.

"What's with the bag?" Twitch asked, giving in to David's obvious excitement and asking the question he could tell his partner had been waiting for.

"They're trusting me as a field medic," David replied, a slight squeak coming into his voice.

"Wait, really?" Twitch said in shock. He laughed and leaned into his partner, grinning from ear to ear. "That's really good news. I'm so happy for you."

"I'm worried I won't do a good job," David whispered quietly.

Twitch shook his head and growled a little. "Nonsense. You've been looking after injured starats for years. You always did a good job then. Why not now?"

David wrinkled his nose. "Because then I didn't have people shooting at me while I was trying to help."

Twitch stumbled and missed his footing. "True," he admitted. He placed his arm around David as they walked. He grinned. "I'll just have to protect you then."

"Thought that was my job."

Twitch lifted up on his toes so he could kiss David's cheek. "It's for both of us."

On the other side of David, William sighed softly. "Keep an eye out for me as well, if you can."

Before either David or Twitch could answer, a black-furred starat hurried up to William's side. "Heard you needed someone to watch your back?" Nick asked, slapping William lightly on the shoulder. "If the position's vacant, then may I step in?"

"The last person watching my back died when I was meant to be protecting him," William growled.

Nick took a hasty step back. "I'm sorry, I didn't mean to-"

"So you'd better not die on me," William continued, jabbing a finger against Nick's chest, while wrapping his other arm around the confused starat's shoulders. "Promise me that?"

Nick's eyes flicked across to Twitch and David, before back to William. "I have no intentions of dying. I trust you to have my back, if you can trust me to have yours."

William looked over Nick. His mouth flicked up into a small smile. "Will be good to have a wizard around."

Nick ran a hand over his forehead. "I'm not a wizard. It's not magic."

"Seems like magic to me," Twitch said. He extended out one hand and waved it around. "You make stuff happen with a thought. That's magic, isn't it?"

"You know you could do it too," Nick said, turning his attention to Twitch.

Twitch grimaced. "Nah, not me. I tried a few times, but it just hurt my head. You and Captain Rhys are the best ones at it."

"So long as I never have to go up against Snow," Nick replied. He shuddered and gripped the tip of his tail. "She's something else entirely."

Twitch chuckled nervously. "Yeah, if she's there then we're screwed. If you're a wizard, then she's a sorcerer."

"I'm not a... Ugh, never mind," Nick said, rolling his eyes.

Twitch managed a giggle. He had never fully understood the subspace manipulation that Captain Rhys had been able to learn. The concept had eluded him almost completely. Trying to do it had just given him a few bad headaches, and all he had achieved was to touch that white void briefly. He adored watching someone manipulating subspace. No matter what Nick claimed, it was magic to Twitch. He looked forward to seeing what Nick was capable of.

The four starats were amongst the last to reach the muster station. All around the perimeter wall of the barracks, groups of around forty gathered together, all clustered around a single commander. Aaron had been given direct control of one group, and Twitch looked up to the human as he waited for the last few to arrive. This was the human who Captain Rhys had been closest to, and Twitch felt he understood why. The two were quite alike.

A friend of Captain Rhys's would always be a friend of Twitch's.

Twitch's ears focused on Aaron as the human started to speak. He struggled to tune out the voices of the other nearby commanders.

"Be alert," the human warned. "We have intel of Inquisition forces in the streets of the city. If we can, we would like to avoid skirmishes on ground, as any second lost on the surface gives us less chance below.

"Our target is the Holy See Church, which is the only confirmed access directly to the underground cavern. This will likely result in us being first on the scene. We must be prepared for a fierce defence, but remember that defeating the defenders is not our primary objective."

One human raised his hand. "If I may ask, sir. What is?"

Aaron pointed to Twitch. "He is. He's the one who knows how to disable the weapon down there. We must get this starat into a position where he can disable the drive." The human looked to his wristband sensor. "We're approaching thirty per million. If it reaches two hundred and ten, then the planetary shields come down. We can't let it get to that stage. Current projections give us a few hours."

Twitch felt a little numb at being singled out. His tail flicked nervously as he felt almost forty pairs of eyes look to him. He felt like cowering behind David, but he managed to keep his back straight. He looked back up at Aaron, not letting his gaze move to the others.

A shout from Fleet-Admiral Bosler silenced all lingering orders coming from the commanders. Her voice echoed through the loudspeaker systems around the barracks. "We act on no one's authority but our own. Loyalties have been divided. Amy Jennings and President Shawn act on violence and genocide. You are all here to do what is right. We seek peace on Centaura, but to achieve that peace we must strike out against those who would destroy it."

A small pause followed, but no one spoke. The fleet-admiral continued a moment later. "Our first objective is to destroy the Denitchev drive, no matter what. After that, we can deal with the Inquisition and the ramifications of our coup. To all of you, good luck. You fight for a better future."

A cheer broke out around the barracks. It started small, before spreading into a wordless roar. Fists raised into the air. Twitch joined in. He couldn't even hear his own voice amongst the noise, but that didn't matter. He never expected to make a difference. All that mattered was contributing his own, small part.

The order to move out followed the war cry. Most squads filtered towards transports, though some remained on foot. Though the church was a known entry point to the caves below, other leads were being followed to gain access through alternate routes. Some of those entry points were believed to be close to the barracks, but Twitch wouldn't be seeing any of them. Instead, he was going back to the church. This time, he would not be only with David. They would have the support they needed, but Twitch still wanted to be anywhere but there.

Twitch held onto his tail as he approached the ground transport.

Screams echoed through his mind again.

***

Despite Aaron's warnings, there had been no opposition in the streets of Hadrian. The armoured transports rolled through the streets without any blockade to divert them. Unlike the civilian vehicles, the armoured transports were manually driven. Any automated vehicles that got too close to the transports slowed and cleared the road, automatically pulling to the sides.

Twitch watched everything from his seat, peering out the reinforced windows. A small crowd had gathered on the pavements, watching the procession with interest and ignoring the broadcast request to evacuate the area. Aaron stayed at the front of the transport, warily looking out the front windows.

"Stay alert," the human said, lifting one hand up. "We're almost at disembark."

The streets were familiar. Twitch could remember walking down them with David. They weren't far from the church, and only a few minutes later, the call came to halt. The transports shuddered to a stop, and the back doors opened. Two-by-two, the soldiers disembarked. Guns were raised, but no one confronted them.

"All clear," one human called out.

Twitch hopped out of the transport next to David. They were the last two to disembark, just after Aaron. His heart thudded as he stared right at Tyler's house. The security cameras still littered the front of the house.

"This is definitely it," Twitch said quietly. He took a moment to adjust his helmet, which pinched against his muzzle a little too tightly.

The transports had been parked to block off the road. No traffic could approach, and the vehicles themselves provided a little cover should anyone assault them. Twitch felt almost like he was caught in the middle of a trap, and he warily turned around on the spot.

Opposite Tyler's house was the church. Nothing had changed. The bright green colours of the fake foliage still looked out of place amongst the dirty greys and reds of the street. The stonework of the church gleamed bright, and the stained-glass windows shimmered in the streetlights. The doors were closed, but a couple of lights shone from inside.

Aaron signalled towards the church. But for four who would remain behind with the transports and guard against a hostile force approaching the rear inside the church, everyone advanced towards the closed doors. Aaron took the lead position. He hammered on the doors. No response came from within.

"Open up!"

Something smashed inside the church, but no one called back to Aaron.

The human thumped his shoulder against the wooden doors, but they held firm. He tried a second time, with the same result. Before he could try a third time, Nick stepped up beside Aaron's side. The starat pushed down on the handle. The door swung open.

Rifles were raised, but there were no immediate threats inside. The pews were empty, with no worshippers present. Always in pairs, the soldiers advanced into the church. One covered right, the other covered left.

A noise came from one of the side rooms to the right of the church, where Twitch and David had once hidden.

No shots were fired, but an immediate response came. Rifles were aimed at the closed doors. Bullet shields were extended, though Twitch had a few troubles with his.

Aaron barked out commands. "This is the Stellar Guard. Step outside, hands visible."

An angry voice came through the closed door. "This is a house of God!" The male voice spluttered with rage and disgust, but no one opened the door.

Aaron gestured for someone to kick the door down. The lock splintered from the force of impact, and the priest inside the side room shrieked in terror.

Twitch didn't recognise the priest. He cowered before the four soldiers who swept around the small side room. Only the priest was present inside.

"Out," Aaron barked. "Escort him to the transport and keep him there."

The priest did not allow himself to get taken. His deep green robes swirled as he took a few steps. His red face quivered. Tears filled his eyes, but his mouth twisted in anger. He jabbed a finger towards Aaron. "May Veritas find it in his heart to forgive you for what you have done here."

"It's what's down below that Veritas will need to forgive," Aaron said, starting to turn away from the priest.

The priest blanched white. "What are you talking about?"

Aaron didn't look back to the priest. "Someone escort him outside," he said harshly. He gestured with one hand towards the altar at the back of the church, with the two archways behind the stone slab.

The priest had nowhere to run. He posed no threat to anyone as he was taken outside by two soldiers, and the front doors of the church closed behind him. His outraged yells continued even after the doors closed. One at a time, the other three side doors in the church were opened, but none were occupied.

Twitch remained in the middle of the squadron. He let others sweep through the rooms, ensuring that no one was lying in wait to ambush them. He didn't want to risk himself, and no one seemed like they were about to force him forward.

Two at a time, they began the descent down the narrow staircase. The small room beneath the church looked exactly the same. The last time Twitch had been there, he had been scared but excited for what was to come. The memories of what came after now disturbed him. He wished he could return to that time, before he had heard the screams of a dying man.

A nervous energy filled Twitch as Aaron opened the hidden passage. A bitter taste filled his throat. His fur prickled with unease.

The only thing that comforted him was the presence of David by his side.

"It's really quiet down here," William whispered.

The starat's hushed voice sounded almost like a roar to Twitch, only matched by the thudding heartbeat in his ears.

Twitch's ears flicked in irritation. At first, he couldn't work out what had bothered him, but then he heard it. They didn't walk in total silence. A low hum filled the air. A rumble and a vibration rippled through the stone beneath his feet. Twitch knew what that had to be. He glanced down to his wrist. The numbers continued to rise as the machine churned out more Denitchev particles into the atmosphere. Every second wasted was another second closer towards defeat. Twitch doubted they had hours.

A few gasps of awe rippled around the group as they stepped out of the narrow path and into the cavernous chamber, on top of the wooden platform close to the ceiling. Everything had been lit up bright. The floodlights that had illuminated the cavern had been made redundant. Twitch couldn't see just what had created the light, as his eyes watered every time he looked up.

The Denitchev drive thrummed with power. Twitch could feel the vibrations through his chest. Sparks flashed and crackled up the sides of the megalithic structure. The crane in front of the machine moved slowly, feeding ever more Denitchev particles into the hungry mouth of the drive. Whatever sabotage Twitch had wrought on the device had clearly been fixed.

An acrid tang filled the air. Twitch felt on the verge of sneezing.

"Is that... cinnamon?" William asked.

Nick wrinkled his muzzle. "Yeah. It means they're getting close."

Aaron didn't give the order to progress. He held his fist up, silently commanding to halt. His eyes focused on the distant ground. Twitch's attention followed his.

The prefab buildings remained, seemingly unchanged, though there were more barricades and defensive walls in place. Around the small compound, the Inquisition had gathered a small army. Twitch couldn't be sure, but he thought there could be over a thousand humans down there, waiting for them. The starat's eyes drifted back up to the drive. He grimaced. They didn't want to waste too much time having to fight their way through.

"We're too exposed up here," Aaron said quietly. He gestured for Twitch to approach him, and the starat hesitantly came up to the human's side. "Where do you need to get to?"

Twitch pointed to the base of the drive, right in the heart of the defensive structures. "The only way to turn it off is on the machine itself."

"I was hoping you wouldn't say that," Aaron said quietly. He took a couple of steps away from the soldiers and exchanged a quick conversation with some of the other commanders across his radio. The one-sided discussion sounded urgent to Twitch, and a decision appeared to be quickly made. Aaron turned back to face his squad. "We need to get down to the ground and get into cover. Reinforcements are coming through alternate entries."

A mumble of understanding rippled around Twitch. The starat tucked his tail close to his legs. He didn't want to go down there, not with so many humans willing to shoot him. He doubted David would be able keep his promise down here. No one would be safe. Twitch would be foolish to rely on David now, because that would be asking his partner to do the impossible. He had to keep himself safe.

A few distant shouts drifted up from below. Twitch couldn't make out what was being said, but it sounded like the harsh shout of orders being given. If Aaron had been hoping for an element of surprise, then that had been robbed away already.

No shots were fired as they descended the walkway. Though Aaron had been worried about being exposed high up, the protective barrier on the side of the winding path gave enough cover to dissuade any distance shots from below.

"Here we are again," David said. He crouched down by Twitch's side, making sure his head was below the level of the guard wall. Aaron had the most trouble out of anyone to do the same. The Terran human had over a head advantage in height compared to even the tallest Centauran human.

"Why aren't they moving at all?" Twitch asked. Every time he caught a glimpse of the cavern floor, he could see that the human defenders had remained in formation just in front of the prefab buildings, safely within the interior of the protective walls. They made no attempt to advance.

"Because they don't think we can do anything against them," Nick replied. He followed right behind Twitch and David, with William by his side. The four starats had found themselves together, close to the rear of the formation. As the least experienced present, Twitch couldn't imagine that had been a coincidence. They were the most vulnerable, and the most needing protection from those with training.

"With this many, I don't think we can," David said tersely.

"There's more coming," William said. "I only hope they get here quick enough."

Twitch glanced up. More were already coming from the church. He didn't know whether it would be enough. He doubted it would be. What mattered was finding a way to get close to the Denitchev drive and shutting the machine down before Centaura could be destroyed. His heart thudded loudly. They were so close. His head couldn't wrap around it all.

If they failed, all would be lost. Twitch couldn't even imagine it. Looking up at the sky and seeing only the white void of subspace. The vision that came to his mind's eye was like a surreal dream. He could only hope that the dream never became a reality. He struggled to focus his thoughts.

They didn't need to defeat all the humans down there. All they needed to do was find a way to switch off the drive, to stop it from streaming Denitchev particles into the atmosphere. If they could do that, then they would save the planet.

It seemed such a simple plan. Turn off the monstrous device that loomed over the expansive cavern. Twitch felt like laughing to himself. The absurdity of the situation hit him hard. Only a starat could get close enough to the drive to switch it off, and only he had the practical knowledge of the machine to have a good chance of succeeding.

"If only we had this the first time," David said quietly. He gestured one hand to the soldiers in front of them. "We might have been able to properly destroy it then."

"Amy probably learned something from what we did," Twitch said bitterly. His muzzle twisted at the thought. She had seemed like the saviour, but in reality, she had been little better than the Inquisition. Her target had just been somewhere that wasn't Centaura.

The walkway touched down against the rocky floor of the cavern. Rough outcrops of rock provided a little cover, but there was not enough for nearly fifty people to gather behind. Some remained on the walkway, while others hurried into cover and crouched down. Twitch was one of the last to make the dash across open ground, following right behind David. Nick and William came after them, but no one else made the run.

Aaron looked around the small group, around half of their total numbers. Beyond the rock cover, Twitch could hear orders to advance.

Splinters of rock exploded close to his head as the first round of shots were fired. Twitch cowered in the shadow of his partner.

The battle had begun.

# chapter sixteen

Twitch didn't know what to do.

Inquisition forces had been advancing, but they had been held off for the moment by return fire. Orders were barked out. Twitch struggled to obey them. He didn't want to lift his head out of cover. His pistol had been pulled from his right leg, along with the bullet shield from his left. The shield was raised, but his pistol remained unused.

The noise threatened to overwhelm Twitch. His senses couldn't keep up with the light and noise. Rock cracked and exploded around him. Voices cried out; some giving orders and others howling in pain.

Twitch sat with his back against the rock, clutching tight onto his weapon. His eyes were wide as he looked towards the walkway. He didn't belong there.

"Twitch. Twitch!"

A voice broke through the fog of his thoughts. David called his name.

Slowly, Twitch turned his head. His partner had moved towards the edge of cover. Humans and starats wearing Stellar Guard uniform poured past them. They had begun to advance.

Dimly, Twitch was aware that reinforcements had arrived. Some had come from the church above, but more had arrived from other entry points around the cave. A quick glance up told Twitch that none had approached the Denitchev drive.

David held out his hand to haul Twitch up to his feet. Together, the two broke free from cover and hurried after the others. Twitch could feel the heat of a couple of shots pass close to his legs, but nothing hit him.

The perimeter fence had been upgraded in the time since Twitch had last seen it. Instead of wire mesh, the fence had been reinforced with sleek panels of protective barriers that resisted any gunfire. Occupied guard posts provided a place for defenders to repel any assault. Most of the defenders had fallen back behind the walls, leaving the Stellar Guard to circle around and prevent any escape.

Twitch hid behind his transparent bullet shield, which was secured tight to his left wrist. He felt it judder a few times as he repelled a couple of shots, but he kept the shield stable in front of his body. David stayed to his left. William and Nick crouched to his right.

Aaron tried to gather a force to charge on the sealed gates, but they couldn't get far. No matter how hard they tried, the spray of bullets that came from above forced them back with cracked shields. A few didn't make it to safe lines.

More and more of the Stellar Guard arrived in the cavern. Most came from the train tracks, with a few more descending from the church. None circumvented the walls or got close enough to the drive.

Twitch looked down to his wrist. Seventy. He didn't like how quickly that number was beginning to rise. The first projections had expected a few days before the numbers reached critical, but that was being steadily revised down. Even the multiple hours looked optimistic. "We're running out of time."

"What can we do?" A new voice surprised Twitch. Human, not starat. He turned to see an unexpected face; Commander Simon Briggs, one of Captain Rhys's crew.

William spat at the human. "What are you doing here?" the starat snarled. "Going to stab us in the back?"

The human kept his eyes facing forward. He made no attempts to meet William's eye. "I'm here to help," the human said. He held out his hand for William, who didn't take the offer. "I'm here to start redeeming myself for what I did before."

Nick scoffed. He kept both eyes on the defensive line ahead of them, his head only slightly above cover. "Why would a human change like that?"

Simon briefly looked to Nick. "I look back now, and I feel like someone else did all those horrible things. I can't justify those actions to myself. I know they had all been me, but it feels like another's thoughts had told me to do so."

David cleared his throat. "Can we save this until later?" he asked, peering around their cover to look towards the sealed gates.

"You're right. How else can we get through?" William asked, ignoring the human behind him. The starat's eyes scanned across the wall, and then up to the towering drive behind.

Twitch flicked his ears. Everything looked so different, he could barely remember what was where. He knew the drive backed onto the far wall of the cavern, protected on three sides by the rocky alcove it nestled in, but he couldn't recall any way to clamber up and around. The only way was to punch right through the defending garrison, but they were well protected.

A loud rumble filled the cavern. Twitch looked up to see a few lights shining at the top of the drive. Red and green flashed in a hypnotic display. He stared up at them for a few moments, before realising that the sound had not come from the drive.

Artillery fire began to rain down on the assaulting Stellar Guard. Shells whistled over the wall, crashing down with terrifying explosions of rock and fire. The heat of the closest blasts roared over Twitch, but his shield protected him from a few pieces of shrapnel.

Aware of the new danger, Aaron ordered a return fire. The Stellar Guard had not been able to bring much heavy weaponry down through the narrow tunnels, but everything they had was fired in response. The perimeter wall stood firm, but the hail of bullets ceased as the defenders took cover.

"Advance forward!" Aaron bellowed, his voice barely audible to Twitch over the concussion boom of another explosion.

Twitch didn't want to move from his small patch of cover, but he knew he had to keep moving forward. Simon moved first; the human leaping out into danger before the starats could do so. David coaxed Twitch on, and with the three starats around him, Twitch rose and began to follow the advancing human.

William and Nick led just ahead of Twitch. They in turn followed a group of a dozen people who ran directly for the sealed gates, amongst whom they soon lost sight of Simon. Bullet shields were raised above their heads for protection, but no shots came down from the walls.

Charges were put in place against the gates. Shields locked together as human and starat took cover, preparing for the blast. Twitch closed his eyes at the last moment. Even still, his eyes were seared by the fierce light that erupted. Shards of the gate scattered all around them, thudding against the shields. Some scratched against Twitch's helmet and down his back.

"We're through!"

The call of triumph was almost immediately suppressed by a loud roar from within the compound. An armoured anti-grav tank eased up to the tattered remains of the gate, drifting through the smoke with its turrets spinning around in preparation to fire.

Twitch didn't hesitate. He dived to one side, rolling towards the wall to press his back against it. The other three starats all followed right behind him, thudding against the wall with a nervous glance upwards.

Some humans reacted in time. Those who did not had no chance. The spray of heavy bullet fire from the tank ripped through shield and armour with ease. Twitch couldn't tell if anyone he knew had been caught in the line of fire, and nor was he able to tear his eyes away from the bloody scene. He breathed heavily as he reached to open his radio channels.

"Aaron, if you can hear me, we need help by the gate," Twitch said, surprising even himself that he was able to keep his voice steady. He closed off the channel to Aaron when there was no immediate reply.

The tank slowly edged forward from the gate. The survivors fired a few futile shots, but nothing breached the thick armour panelling. Twitch glanced at the vehicle, hovering about a metre above the ground, in terror. The main turret faced directly out. Four more secondary turrets slowly rotated. One turned towards Twitch.

The starat acted quickly. He rolled forward, closer to the tank. He hoped to get too close for the turrets to reach him, and the spray of heavy gunfire kicked up dirt just behind his tail. The hum of the anti-grav motors almost overpowered the constant thrum of power coming from the Denitchev drive.

Lying flat on his back, Twitch kicked up hard, striking his feet against the underside of the tank. The impact reverberated through his legs, the powerful kick denting the poorly armoured underside of the tank. The brightly glowing panelling flickered, and the entire vehicle momentarily veered to the side. Twitch struck again and his foot ripped a hole through the anti-grav panels. Sparks washed over the starat as a couple of small explosions ruptured deep within.

The starat's ears flicked as voices shouted, coming from inside the compound. Twitch lifted his shield above his head and scrambled back as the tank began to slow and sink.

A whining whistle filled the air.

Twitch swore as a missile arced towards the tank. He hurried back, unable to get to his feet quickly enough. The armour breached and ruptured. The tank listed to one side, veering towards Twitch.

Flames licked around the punctured hole in the side of the tanks armour. Sparks crackled as an intense heat scorched at Twitch's fur.

"Shit," Twitch squeaked, holding his shield up to protect his head and torso.

The tank exploded in a deafening ball of light and fire. Shrapnel thudded against Twitch's shield. Cracks snaked through the protective barrier, but it held. He screamed as he felt something slice against his leg. Sensors quickly shut down the pain, but tears still came to his eyes. The concussive blast pinned him against the wall, and he slowly slipped down to his haunches as smoke billowed all around.

A familiar voice reached Twitch's ears. "Twitch, are you alright?" David called out through the smoke.

"I'm fine, you?" Twitch gasped out in reply. He felt winded from the blast, but the only damage had been to his legs. He crawled across to find David.

His partner seemed unhurt, but William had been sliced across the cheek and shoulder. The starat whimpered as David started to clean the wound.

"You need to go on," David urged, not looking away from the wounded starat in his care. His voice shook. "I have to stay here. They might need me."

"I can't go on alone," Twitch squeaked in terror. Already he could hear footsteps all around. Shouts and commands began to regain order. The Stellar Guard started to press forward and claim the advantage. They needed to hold the gate.

"Take Nick," William said with a grimace, pushing the black-furred starat forward.

"I'm meant to have your back," Nick protested. He held his hands over his nose as he struggled not to breathe in the acrid smoke from the ruined tank.

"Go, I'm fine," William growled, pushing Nick again.

Nick relented. He lifted his rifle and glanced to Twitch. "You know where to go?"

Twitch's tail curled tight. He didn't want to leave David behind again, but he knew he had no chance. David had his own responsibilities to deal with. He trembled as he rose back to his feet. His right leg felt a little unsteady for a few moments, but it supported his weight. He felt down with a couple of fingers to find a gash just above his knee, but nothing appeared to be broken.

The Stellar Guard advanced through the smoke. Gunfire crackled, and soldiers from both sides fell to the ground. Twitch chose his moment to run. He waited for a brief lull, then ran through the gates, following behind a human. Nick shadowed him.

Before anyone could see him, Twitch veered away from the main cluster of combat. He hurried behind the cover of the prefab buildings. He kept his head low, only looking up to make sure there were no humans ahead of him. Between the perimeter wall and the buildings, Twitch had found a small calm place a little distance from the battle.

Gunfire rang loudly around. Twitch jumped every time he heard something close by, but for the moment, he felt like he and Nick had broken through without being seen by the enemy. On the other side of the buildings, he could hear the Inquisition defenders preparing their new line of defence, but it didn't extend all the way around to the perimeter wall.

"You need to get to the drive, right?" Nick whispered, coming up to crouch alongside Twitch.

"As quickly as possible," Twitch replied. His wrist sensor read over seventy-nine. Already, the machine was nearly halfway to completion, and it seemed to be getting faster. The number ticked over to eighty and continued to rise.

"Then we'd better keep moving. Stay behind me," Nick said. He took the lead, but he glanced back to make sure Twitch followed him.

Twitch didn't let his eyes wander from the black-furred starat. His hands remained tight around his rifle, ready to use the weapon if anyone approached.

A voice crackled in Twitch's ear. "Where are you?"

Twitch recognised Aaron's voice. Ahead of him, Nick paused for a moment and held his hand up to his ear.

"I'm in the compound with Nick," Twitch replied quietly, knowing the mouthpiece of his helmet would be able to transmit his voice back to Aaron. "We're close to perimeter wall still."

A moment of silence followed. "We'll try to draw them away from the drive. Be safe in there."

Twitch giggled as panic and fear gripped his heart. "Safe? I don't think that's happening."

"I'll keep him away from trouble, Aaron," Nick added. He reached out his hand to encourage Twitch on. "I'll let you know if we need anything from you. Just keep them close to the gates for now."

"Wilco."

Twitch was left in silence again. He took a deep breath and quickly looked back. No one had followed them. Ahead, the perimeter wall arced around to the left, but didn't directly approach the drive. That lay halfway between the outer compound walls as they intersected the cliffs. At some point, the two lone starats would have to move away from the relative safety of the perimeter walls. Between them were half a dozen buildings and over a hundred Inquisition soldiers.

"Where on it do you need to go?" Nick asked. His eyes kept flicking around, responding to little movements Twitch couldn't see. The tang of cinnamon filled Twitch's nose every time he looked towards the darker-furred starat.

Twitch flicked his ears and wrinkled his muzzle. The cinnamon scents tickled at the inside of his nose, irritating him. "I'm not too sure. If I can't get in at the control room at the base, then pretty high up, I think. Most of the critical systems can only be accessed right at the top."

"Fuck. That'll take a while to get up. How long do we have?"

Twitch glanced to his wrist. Eighty-four already. "Half an hour, if I want to be safe. This is getting quicker and quicker each time I look at it."

"Then we'd better get you up there. Come on."

Nick led the way. He followed around the wall for a dozen metres, before pausing. Ahead of them, the wall cut out into the inner compound. A door, partially open, provided access to a stairwell that led up to one of the defence platforms just above.

Twitch couldn't see anyone up on the platform. He couldn't smell any humans close by, but his sense of smell had been utterly overwhelmed by the cinnamon scent of subspace.

The door slammed open. A lone human stepped out, his weapon already raised.

Twitch lifted his shield just as his nose was assaulted by a fresh burst of cinnamon. Metal twisted and screeched as the door ripped from its hinges and slammed into the side of the human.

Three shots thudded into Twitch's shield before the human fell to the ground. He did not rise, covered in the smoking remains of the broken door.

Nick stumbled and dropped to his knees. He took in several deep breaths and tensed his fingers.

Twitch tried not to think about what he had just seen. Instead, his eyes focused on the twisted metal hinges that had once held the door to the frame. A little wisp of smoke drifted upwards on the light breeze. "That was you?" he asked the other starat in awe.

"Yeah," Nick replied, a weak smile on his muzzle. "Just don't ask me to do it too much. Takes a lot out of me."

"Still cool though, Mr Wizard," Twitch said. He helped Nick back up to his feet. The black-furred starat stumbled, but he found his balance quickly. There had been no one else following the first human, who Twitch tried not to think about. At least they hadn't screamed out in their dying breath.

Twitch peered out between two buildings. The narrow gap between them was empty, barely wide enough for one starat to pass through without brushing up against the walls either side. Through the gap, Twitch could see the base of the drive, surrounded by a guard of about two dozen humans.

"Do you think we can get past them?" Twitch asked. He looked back to Nick, who frowned in thought.

"Not without a distraction," Nick said. He placed his hand on Twitch's shoulder as he looked around.

Twitch could feel the heat in Nick's hands. They felt like they burned, the blistering heat coming through the armour covering Twitch's shoulder.

Nick pointed to another of the buildings, just opposite from their position. "Looks like an ammunition hut. I might be able to cause an explosion there. When it happens, get ready to run in."

"What about you?" Twitch asked, a little squeak of fear escaping his mouth.

Nick shook his head. "If I do something that big, I probably won't be able to go anywhere in a hurry. I'll only slow you down."

Twitch flicked his ears. His eyes turned to the building beside the ammunition hut. A deep growl came from within. His eyes widened as he remembered what he had heard in there during his last terrifying visit to the cavern. He placed his hand on Nick's wrist and pointed to the second building. "Pull the door off from that."

"Why?" Nick said warily, but he lifted his hand anyway, tensing trembling fingers as he prepared his mystical ability.

"Dragon," Twitch said, shuffling back half a step. Further down the hill, towards the gate, the fighting looked to be growing fierce. Twitch quickly turned his eyes away.

233

Nick wrenched his hand back. He didn't just rip apart the door to the dragon's compound. Another quick pull released the dragon's bonds, and the six-limbed reptile began to slink out of captivity. Shouts from the drive guards attracted its attention.

"Think that's a good enough distraction?" Nick panted. He held onto Twitch's wrist and began to pull him forward, ducking behind cover as they followed the dragon's prowling progress.

The guards opened fire on the dragon and started to retreat. Their bullets did not appear to affect the hulking creature at all, as it snarled and snapped its great jaws. It continued its relentless approach, beady eyes fixed on the Inquisition guards.

"Shit," Nick muttered. Twitch quickly saw the reason for his distraction. Four humans had broken away from the rest of the force down the hill, sprinting to reinforce those facing the dragon. The black-furred starat pushed at Twitch. "You keep going forward. I'll deal with these ones."

"What about the dragon?" Twitch squeaked.

"It's not going to attack you. Not until it kills all the humans first," Nick said. He lifted his rifle and turned his back on Twitch, putting his focus towards the humans down the hill. "Now, go. Quickly. I'll buy you time."

Twitch ran. He kept to the shadows so he would be harder to spot. He did nothing to draw attention to himself, like attempting to shoot any of the humans who struggled to stay away from the dragon. Chaos had been sewn by the vicious creature, and Twitch could hear a change in the gunfire further back. He dared not look to see how Nick held back the reinforcements.

The dragon split apart the defensive force at the base of the drive. The creature chased six away down the hill, but three remained at their posts. Those who had escaped the dragon's wrath did nothing to chase after those unfortunate enough to remain in the creature's path. All three looked down the hill, standing directly between Twitch and the ladder leading up to the scaffolding. Their faces were obscured by their helmets, and their armour appeared thick enough to repel Twitch's shots. All had been able to keep hold of their weapons in the chaos.

The starat checked the sensor on his wrist again. Dangerously close to ninety already. He didn't have time to wait, but he also knew that if he approached the guards, they would easily be able to pick him off. He couldn't count on shooting them, for he wasn't accurate or quick enough with his pistol.

Twitch knew he was all on his own now. He quickly looked back. By the gate, he could see the skirmish raging. Soldiers struggled to get a good shot off, and no one appeared to be winning the fight. There was no one else running up the hill to help those guarding the drive, and there was no sign of Nick or the reinforcements. No one from the Stellar Guard had broken through to help him.

Twitch cautiously crept through the shadows, edging closer to the three remaining guards. He could only hope that something further happened to distract them. He got close enough that he could hear them speaking to each other, even over the sounds of gunfire.

"…that fucking creature. How did it get out?"

"Are you sure we're outside the exclusion zone?"

"I think so."

"Stinks here. And that noise."

Twitch flicked his ears. He looked up to the drive. As he drew nearer, he began to hear more sounds coming from within. A dull whine and throbbing rumble filled his ears, and the scent of cinnamon had only been growing stronger with every step.

The starat set his pistol. He peered around the corner of the final building, looking across the empty gap towards the guards and the gate. The three humans seemed more concerned with their conversation than keeping watch.

"Where do we even go anyway?"

"When?"

"When this thing is ready to pop. We have to go somewhere, right?"

"Father Nichols said he'd lead us to safety when the time is right."

"Wasn't Father Nichols bitten by that dragon?"

"Ah. Shit."

The third guard, who had remained silent, waggled a finger in the direction of the other two. "Veritas will show us the way. He kept us safe from the dragon. We are his blessed chosen."

Twitch stayed low. The fence he had once broken through remained, but there was nowhere to hide while cutting through it again. If he approached it, the guards would see him. He doubted they were paying so little attention for that.

An explosion blasted through the air. It came from above. Fire spat out from near the top of the drive. The blaze didn't last long, only for a few seconds. All three humans looked up. One removed his helmet and squinted into the brief flash of light. He clicked his fingers in the direction of one of his companions.

"Go and find Father Nichols. Or anyone else who can tell us where we're going."

One of the other guards nodded his head. He retreated away from the open gate and started down the hill. That left just two to deal with, but Twitch knew that he would still struggle with a pair of guards. Even one might be too many for him.

The lone guard who had been sent down the hill keeled over and slumped to the ground. Blood spread from his body as he lay still.

Twitch stared in shock. He hadn't heard a gunshot.

The remaining guards had seen their fallen companion too. They shouted and raised their weapons, aiming down the hill.

Twitch backed away, keeping close to the buildings and creeping further up the hill, hoping to avoid their attention. He no longer had any cover, with just a couple of crates to keep himself obscured, and he remained behind them as much as possible.

Nick stepped out of the shadows further down the slope, from next to the dragon's broken cage. His rifle was raised, but he stumbled with each step. His hands clearly shook with exhaustion. The dark-furred starat was not alone. Two human soldiers walked by his side, both in the armour of the Stellar Guard.

The guards abandoned their posts to chase down the soldiers.

Twitch took his chance. He ran hard and fast, sprinting across towards the unguarded gate. His movements didn't go unnoticed.

He was not the only one with reinforcements. Four returning guards had evaded the dragon. Twitch felt a couple of impacts against his legs. He stumbled as he ran. He tried to keep upright, but the sensors in his legs failed for just a moment.

The starat struck the ground hard. He rolled a few times and came to rest on his back just beyond the open gate. His pistol skittered a little further as it dislodged from his grip. The closest ladder up to the drive was just a few metres away, but before he could rise to his feet again a human stood over him.

Twitch stared up at the wrong end of a gun. A small whimper escaped his lips. The guard sneered.

"I'll be glad to be rid of your lot," the guard spat.

Twitch kicked up hard. His legs moved faster than he believed possible, cracking into the human's right knee. He felt bone shatter and splinter in the impact.

The human screamed as he fell backwards. Twitch kicked again as he fell, this time striking the human across the ribs. The scream of pain was silenced as ribs fractured. A choking wheeze was the only sound the human made as he collapsed backwards.

Twitch breathed slowly as he scrambled up to his feet. The guard had been disabled, but more were coming. Three more humans, all bleeding from slashed claw wounds on their faces and torsos, advanced with rifles raised.

They all fired together. Twitch instinctively lifted his bullet shield in time, feeling his arm judder from the impacts. He backed away, retreating closer to the ladder. Two guards followed him. One remained by their fallen companion.

The air felt thick. Twitch struggled to breath in. His lungs were choked by the cloying smell of cinnamon. He fumbled and reached back for the ladder as his vision clouded a little.

"Step back from there," one of the advancing guards bellowed. His voice sounded muffled to Twitch's ears.

Twitch's hand found the ladder. It felt buttery.

One of the guards took another step forward. Almost immediately, he dropped his rifle and fell to his knees. His hands clenched around his head as he let out a piercing, shrill scream of terror. Blood dripped from his nose. Another human yanked him back, but the screams did not stop.

Twitch turned and began to climb. The ladder felt like it shouldn't support the starat's weight, but each rung held firm as he ascended. He pulled himself up onto the first level of the scaffold and took a moment to look back.

The guards had tried shooting. None of them dared to approach, but their bullets never got close to the starat. Of the four who had chased after him, two were lying on the ground; one with a broken leg and ribs, and the other still bleeding from his nose and twitching fitfully.

Twitch shook his head and tried to clear his thoughts. Patches of white imprinted on his vision, covering up the reality that lay beneath. The sensor on his wrist read ninety-six.

Everything blurred as Twitch moved his head. Time seemed to move both slowly and quickly at the once as he stared at several imprints of his right arm. Though he moved it, the arm appeared to remain where it was for a few seconds before the image faded away.

He squeezed his eyes shut. The white streaks in his vision remained, clear even through the darkness of his eyelids. His hand rested against the side of his helmet as he activated his radio.

"Can anyone hear me?" he whispered quietly.

A distorted voice answered. "I can hear you, Twitch. Where are you? Do you need help?"

Twitch took a moment to work out who had spoken. He couldn't recognise the voice through the distortion. It might have been Aaron. "I'm on the drive. Don't come here. No humans. Captain James was right. It hurts them."

"Are you sure you don't need help?"

"I don't think anyone can," Twitch said. He opened his eyes once again as he realised that he was wasting time. He looked up and tried to ignore the streaks of light across his vision. He needed to climb up and find a way to shut the machine down, but the drive had been built to run just once without a shut-off. There would be no big red button to press.

Static filled Twitch's ears. The radio had failed. Twitch removed his helmet and clipped it to his belt. Without it on his head, he knew no one would be able to speak to him. There was nothing anyone could say to him now. No one could help him. He was truly on his own.

Feeling like his legs were stuck in treacle, Twitch began to ascend again. He knew that he just needed to keep going up.

# chapter
# seuenteen

Reality swirled. It twisted and howled around Twitch. He struggled to trust his senses. Metal that should have been hard and rigid felt soft to the touch, and bright lights flashed in his eyes that appeared to have no source. Even when he flung his arm in front of his face, the lights pierced through his flesh.

Up, Twitch continued to climb. Up spongy ladders and through bursts of white darkness and black light. Shadows shone brightly, and Twitch waved away illusions that danced before his eyes.

Another starat walked beside him. The starat mimicked his every move. He walked with him. Climbed with him. Stumbled and swayed with him.

The companion split and doubled. One walked to his right, the other to his left. Both appeared ghostly and translucent. One walked on wasted legs, and the other had withered arms.

"Captain Rhys?" Twitch whispered, staring to the starat on his right.

The starat with the withered arms just smiled and said nothing.

Twitch could no longer see the ground, or indeed anything of the cave. Around the drive, he could see nothing but flashing light and the eerie void of subspace. He shivered. The air had chilled around him.

A cloud of shimmering steam drifted up from his mouth. The mist sparkled with colours Twitch had never seen before. He extended his hand to brush through the mist, watching it dissipate through the blurred sweep of his arm.

He had lost track of how far he had climbed. He tried to focus, but nothing made sense to his mind. Everything all looked the same. Colourless metallic panels stretched out one side, with a couple of ladders leading up. A grilled floor provided the support beneath his feet, and Twitch felt like he bounced with every step.

Twitch blinked. When he opened his eyes, he saw the world upside down. He squeaked in fear and lost his balance. He fell up. His chest slammed against the floor, and his fingers gripped tight against the metallic lattice.

A voice whispered.

Twitch's ear flicked and he looked down at the void of white below him. Shapes swirled in the light. A burst of cinnamon overwhelmed his senses, and he felt like gagging. He squeezed his eyes closed again.

"I can't do this," Twitch groaned. He grimaced. His head hurt. Nothing made any sense. He didn't even know where he was supposed to go.

A thought reached out to him. Wordless, but still understandable. Encouragement welled within him, rising from a place he did not know.

Twitch's eyes snapped open. Above him, Captain Rhys held out a withered hand. He took hold of it, and he was wrenched up to his feet. The apparition faded into smoke, but the starat did not feel alone.

He held his hands up. They glowed in the light streaming in from subspace. The drive was ripping space open, even before it had completed its purpose.

The holographic projector on his wrist had somehow switched on. One hundred and thirty-seven and rising quickly. The number shone bright even against the backing of subspace.

Twitch curled his tail in close to his legs and took a few stumbling steps forward. He felt unsteady. Gravity seemed to shift direction every few seconds, making it difficult to know where to place his feet. He swayed like a drunkard as the sensors in his legs struggled to compensate, but he kept his eyes fixed on the ladder a few metres in front of him.

A shimmer of light danced in the air just before the ladder, only to skip upwards as Twitch approached. The starat wrinkled his muzzle and held an arm in front of his nose to block the spicy smells that washed off the light's wake.

He climbed the ladder and emerged into nothingness. Reality crumbled around him as an endless white plain stretched on to infinity in all directions. He could see nothing else, but for his own body. The floor beneath his feet had vanished entirely; even the ladder he had just climbed from.

Slowly, he slid his left foot back, only to lurch and lose his balance as he found the gap in the floor he had climbed through. His feet were still grounded in reality, but his mind and senses had been ripped away into subspace. He barely dared move.

A tendril of darkness swirled around him. Twitch couldn't say where it had come from. The sliver of darkness didn't seem to be connected to anything, but it reached out to towards him. Twitch's hand raised, but they didn't quite touch. Once more, an emotion planted into his thoughts, one that translated itself into a single feeling.

It was an offer to help.

Twitch nodded. "Help, please. I don't know if I can do this."

The thoughts roared in his mind. Something, somewhere, agreed to help him.

The tendril disappeared in a wisp of smoke.

Twitch whimpered softly. He could go no further, not without seeing the way. He had failed. His wrist sensor had stopped working too, preventing him from seeing how much longer he had left before the machine had completed its work. The screen displayed just static.

Another voice filled Twitch's mind. He didn't know if it was real. He couldn't be sure of anything anymore, but David's voice echoed inside his head.

"You can do it, Twitch. You're strong. You're capable. So much more than you know. I believe in you."

"I'm always better with you by my side though," Twitch whispered into the white void. He shuffled forward a couple of steps. His arm extended out to the side, trying to find something to guide him, but he found nothing.

"I'm always beside you, though," David's voice replied. He laughed. "Even if I'm not physically there, you'll always have me."

"You make it sound like you're dead," Twitch replied, a little giggle escaping his lips despite his worries. "Are you a ghost haunting me?"

"Dead? No," David's voice said. A breath of wind brushed across Twitch's muzzle. "A ghost? Perhaps."

"I don't understand."

"You don't need to understand. You just need to follow. Trust me."

Twitch held his mouth open, about to question what he had to follow, before he saw the dark imprints before him. They looked like footsteps through the void.

"Trust you? Alright," he said quietly. He took a tentative step forward, placing his foot exactly in the dark footprint. He felt nothing from his legs. Everything below his waist felt numb, and a little terror grew in his chest as he remembered the helplessness he had felt lying in bed after Cardinal Erik's attack. But his legs still moved, even if he couldn't feel them.

If his legs moved, he could walk. And if he could walk, then he could follow the footsteps as they appeared in front of him.

Twitch didn't know how far he walked, or how long it took. He counted dozens of steps, but they all faded into each other in his mind. They didn't go in a straight line either, but they twisted and turned around hidden obstacles. Sometimes they climbed invisible ladders.

The footsteps stopped. Twitch stood still where the last of them faded into the void. He extended his hands out in front of him, and he was surprised to feel a glass screen against his palms.

Darkness pulsed out in a radiating web of blackness, originating from his hands. The webbing wrapped around a computer terminal, outlining the shape but none of the details. But for one thing.

Twitch broke out into disbelieving laughter. There was a big red button.

The bright colour hurt Twitch's eyes. The vivid light didn't belong in the empty expanse of subspace, but there it sat.

"It can't be that easy," Twitch muttered to himself. Nothing could ever be that simple.

The starat brushed his hand over the button. His fingers passed right through it. The button faded into swirling shadow, which drifted down and reformed as a vertical black footprint at the height of Twitch's knees.

He knew what to do. He had nothing to brace himself against, but he lifted his leg and smashed his foot hard against the footprint. His numbed legs felt nothing, but for a moment the white void flickered into darkness and smoke before snapping back.

Twitch gasped. In that brief moment, his senses had been dazzled by reality. He hadn't been sure what he had seen, but he had ruptured a panel protecting what he assumed to be a critical control console.

He kicked hard again. And a third time.

Subspace splintered around him. The white veneer fractured and burst apart into reality.

Twitch yelped and covered his face, but nothing struck him. The splinters of subspace were consumed by light and colour before they could reach him.

He took a step back, only to suffer a terrifying lurch as his foot dropped. The starat leaned forward and grabbed hold of the broken terminal. With a horrified look down, he realised that he was stood on a narrow walkway that perched precariously on the side of the drive. Nothing but half a metre of metal separated him and a plunge of a hundred metres right down.

"Oh fuck," he squeaked. He pulled his leg up and knelt on the narrow walkway.

A little smoke drifted up from the terminal. Numbers still flickered up onto the broken screens. Twitch could see diagnostics flicker up briefly, before the screen faded to darkness.

"Is it done?" he asked himself, but he already knew the answer to that. He could still feel the machine rumbling against his body. The power supply had been disrupted, but backups would be online before long. He had only disabled the drive briefly, not shut it down. He had bought himself a few more minutes.

The sensor at his wrist worked again. One hundred and eighty-nine. So close to Fleet-Admiral Bosler activating the emergency protocols of deactivating the shields.

"Where now?" Twitch muttered. He hauled himself up to his feet and tried not to look down. He didn't want to be reminded of the terrifying plunge. Instead, he looked up. The top of the drive wasn't far away, just a few metres above his head. Beyond the drive, the rocky ceiling of the cave was cast in dark shadows. A lattice of pipes from the drive crossed across the rock. Most delved upwards and out of sight, though some disappeared into the shadows to the sides of the cave.

Twitch bit his lip. He knew he still had to find a way to shut the machine down for good. "Come on, Twitch. You know what to do," he hissed to himself. He had spent so long working on regular Denitchev drives that they were second nature to him. His ears perked up. He knew how to shut the drive down. "The shutoff valves should be just up there."

Twitch reached up. His fingers found a few small crevasses to dig his claws into. He hauled himself up, kicking against the machine to create a few dents in the metal. They were rudimentary footholds, but they provided him with enough grip to release one hand from the small cracks. If he could get to the top of the machine, then he would be able to access the maintenance shutoff valves that were present in any standard Denitchev drive. He could only hope that this one possessed the same emergency shutoffs.

Aware of the plunge below him if he got things wrong, Twitch slowly began to climb the last few metres of the drive. A soft beeping filled his ears, coming from the sensor at his wrist. He didn't know if the noises were an alarm from the high concentration of Denitchev particles, or if the numbers had started to rise again. He didn't dare pause to look.

Inch by inch, Twitch edged his way up. His vision remained mostly clear, but a fog of white began to encroach around the corners of his vision. He could smell nothing but choking cinnamon.

Twitch almost lost his grip when his right hand reached up and found nothing to hold onto over the edge. He let out a terrified squeak. Nothing near the edge provided anything to give him an anchor point, but he managed to hook one elbow up and use that as leverage to haul himself onto the flat surface atop the drive.

His arms shook and he felt like curling up into a ball, but Twitch knew he had no time to sit and rest. He clambered up to his feet and quickly scanned around.

Though most of the standard drives had several outputs pipes in the corners of their upper surface, this only had the one. A massive output pipe as wide as four starats lying head-to-tail emerged from the centre of the drive, which quickly split apart into the myriad of pipes above. They would then go on to vent the particles into the atmosphere.

Twitch flicked his ears. The machine was not standard design, just blown up to its incredible size. He could only hope that the maintenance shutoffs were still present, or else he wouldn't have much chance to switch it off. The Inquisition wouldn't have wanted any easy way to turn off their terrifying machine, after all.

The surface beneath his feet had many small protrusions, and Twitch had to be careful not to trip and fall. Valves and bundles of wiring took up most of the space, with only a few small patches providing flat areas for walking. Nothing looked critical enough to waste time on damaging.

Subspace started to bleed into reality again. White patches swirled around Twitch as he stumbled for the output pipe. The vast metal structure curved away from Twitch. He placed his hands on the smooth surface, feeling the burning heat even before he touched it.

"There has to be some way to disconnect this," Twitch muttered. He kept his hands on the pipe for only a few moments before the heat forced him to remove them. He found nothing as he walked around the circumference. Where there should have been a hatch to access the shutoff valves there was flat metal.

Twitch grimaced. He looked down at his legs. The smooth, shiny surface had been scratched slightly, with one large gash just above his knee. They had taken damage, but they had held up well in function.

The only way Twitch could see in was to break the pipe. He had no tools to rip through metal, but he didn't need them. He sat back in front of the pipe and braced himself with his hands. With both legs raised up off the ground, he kicked hard several times. The metallic surface buckled with each impact, the crash of metal breaking echoing and reverberating off the rocks above.

A frantic hiss filled Twitch's ears as a small crack ripped open. Steam poured out, washing over Twitch's feet. The steam burned for a moment, but the pain sensors in his legs quickly deactivated. The acrid smell of burning cinnamon accompanied the steam. Twitch knew what it was: a concentrated jet of Denitchev particles. He tried not to breathe any of the superheated gas.

Two more kicks and the metal buckled entirely. A large square the size of Twitch's torso broke away and clattered down the pipe. Twitch heard the shorn metal crash and bang all the way down.

A new problem quickly emerged. Twitch leaned in towards the hole, but he quickly had to recoil away as searing steam jetted just above his body. While his legs could withstand the heat, his organic body could not. Even without direct contact, the heat was uncomfortably high.

Forced to lean back, Twitch held his hands over his nose to protect himself from the Denitchev steam. He swore beneath his breath. The stream of Denitchev particles leaking into the atmosphere had barely slowed at all.

A low, deep alarm echoed through the cave. The noise rumbled through Twitch's body, feeling like he was being shaken from the inside. He had never heard the sound before, but as it sounded constantly, he realised he knew exactly what it was. He didn't need to look down at his wrist to realise the Denitchev concentration outside had reached two hundred. The emergency evacuation alarm had sounded.

The planetary shields would soon be deactivated.

Twitch had to shut off the machine.

"How do I do it?" he squeaked. He tapped his feet nervously against the drive. He couldn't go down into the drive, not without something to protect himself from the heat and steam. His armour was not suitable for that. He squeezed his eyes closed as he struggled to recall the inner schematics of the drives. Assuming this one had been built the same way, his memories could dredge up a solution.

If he could find something to create an explosion deep within the drive, then perhaps that could work. Throwing a bomb or a grenade down the pipe would create a chain reaction that would destroy the drive from the inside. Twitch's ears folded down. Only one problem with that plan: he had nothing he could rig to explode.

Despite the heat, Twitch felt cold. He looked down and stared at his legs. They were military spec. Twitch had once vowed never to wear them because of how dangerous they were. Maxwell's warning echoed in his ear. Never overclock the batteries because they could explode.

Twitch knew what he had to do.

Twitch opened the control panels on each leg. He quickly scrolled through the menus on the miniature display screens until he found the battery settings. Taking a deep breath to prepare himself for what he was about to do, he began to raise the battery output. He gasped at the increased flow of sensation that flooded through him. After a few seconds of sustained changes, the first warning flashed up. Twitch dismissed it.

A second warning flashed up, more urgent than the first. Again, Twitch dismissed the notification without reading it. Twitch could hear a quiet whine within his legs as the battery output lifted beyond the safe settings. The starat was tempted to throw the legs down the output pipe right away, but he grimaced and raised the settings higher still. He didn't want to risk the chance of the legs taking too long to explode as Maxwell had warned.

Twitch raised the settings to the highest possible level the small screen terminal would allow him. Every movement of his toes made him shudder and groan. He grimaced at an itch at the back of his mind. A spark of electricity pulsed up his spine and back down to his legs again. A green light flashed on his legs, confirming the final command to overclock the batteries far beyond the safe levels. Twitch knew now that he had little time to waste.

The starat scrambled to find the latches that disconnected his legs. He grimaced as he pulled them away; the hypersensitive feelings instantly vanishing to nothing. He hated the void of sensation beneath his hips but for his tail, but he knew it was necessary. With both legs tucked beneath his arm, he crawled towards the pipe and held his breath. The steam blistered over his fur, easily creeping in between the gaps in his armour. He whimpered in pain, but he could not allow himself to recoil.

Once he felt like he was close enough, Twitch lifted himself as high as he could, before tossing both legs down into the pipe. He let out a small whimper; both in pain from the searing heat, but also the mental agony of losing his legs once more. He could hear them clatter all the way down, before a loud crash echoed up from the very bottom.

Twitch dropped back, falling away from the ruptured pipe. He rubbed over his muzzle, trying to soothe the burning sensations that prickled at his face. He crawled backwards, dragging himself along on his elbows. He breathed quickly as he strained his ears, waiting desperately for that explosion to come.

For a few horrible seconds, Twitch thought he had been unsuccessful, and that he had wasted his legs for nothing.

The drive shook. A rumble growled up from deep within the massive machine. Flames spat out from the ruptured vent, charring the scent of cinnamon and bringing with it the smell of burning metal. Hardly any sound accompanied the flames, but for a deep rumble and grinding of metal coming from far within the drive.

Twitch dragged himself away. He stared in awe as flames filled the pipe, roaring up towards the surface in a fierce conflagration. Already, he could see the network of smaller pipes above begin to steam and smoke. He swore quietly to himself. He didn't know how long he had before the pipes began to rupture and rain fire and debris down onto him.

White streaks swirled around Twitch's vision, but they were fading. A sensation of satisfaction washed over the starat, one that did not come from his own mind. He looked up. A hole through reality shone through, beyond which Twitch could make out a darkened distortion. A shiver ran down his spine. He thought he could see an eye in the darkness.

Twitch turned away. He had bigger problems to deal with, like getting down from the drive before the whole thing collapsed around him. He didn't know how he could do that, not without his legs.

The starat struggled to drag himself along. His loose, empty shorts snagged on the twisted metal of the drive, and his belly scraped against the rough surface. He reached the edge of the drive, and he stared down at the terrifying distance to the cavern floor. Only a narrow walkway ledge provided anything to drop down onto. Before his confidence could fade, he wriggled and twisted his body around to lower his hips and tail over the edge.

Another loud rumble shook the drive. The entire structure lurched a little before settling back into position.

Twitch squeaked in terror as the sudden movement dislodged his grip. His left hand slipped from the edge, and his tail thrashed around helplessly in the air. He could feel his fingers sliding closer to the edge, before he managed to find another handhold.

With his heart racing fast, he slowly lowered himself down, feeling around with the tip of his tail for the walkway. Without his legs, all of his weight pulled down on his arms and shoulders, which quickly began to ache. A small whimper escaped his muzzle. He didn't know how he could climb all the way down.

His tail touched the walkway, and he dropped down the last few centimetres. He struggled to find his balance, before leaning against the wall of the drive. He rubbed his shoulders and grimaced.

"Alright, Twitch," he muttered to himself. "You've gotten yourself into this mess. How do you get out of it again?"

Unfortunately, he didn't even know which way to go. He had come to the walkway partially in subspace, and he had no way of retracing his steps – the loss of his legs notwithstanding. Instead of making a decision, Twitch just slumped back and draped his tail over his bare hips. His fingers idly toyed with the loose fabric of his empty shorts.

A constant vibrating rumble lightly shook Twitch. He could feel the metal heating up behind him as the fires inside the drive lit up. He wondered how long he had left. Would it hurt when everything exploded?

The starat slowly unclipped his helmet from his belt and pulled it over his head. His ears scrunched inside slightly, and almost immediately they were filled with the frantic words of Aaron and David.

"Are you there?"

"I'm here," Twitch said, cutting across the repeated question.

"Oh, fuck, are you alright?" David said frantically, his voice tight and high pitched.

"I'm fine," Twitch said, leaning back against the wall and closing his eyes for a moment. "I think I stopped it."

"I think you did too," Aaron said, cutting across David. "Are you able to get back to us?"

Twitch shook his head, knowing that no one could see him. "No. I'm stuck up near the top on a walkway. I don't think I can get down." Even knowing he was stuck and helpless, Twitch's voice was calm. He had done what was needed of him.

"I think we can see you," Aaron said. His voice faded into silence.

Twitch had to laugh. He didn't know what difference that would make.

"Hold on tight, Twitch," David said quietly.

The walkway lurched. Metal screeched and twisted a few metres either side of Twitch. He yelped and gripped tight onto the metallic lattice beneath him, for all the good he knew that would do. With a blinding flash of white light, the walkway snapped away from its supports.

It didn't fall.

Not quickly, at least. The walkway slowly descended, like wires gently lowered it towards the ground, but Twitch could see nothing that provided any support. Flashes of white light, tinged with golden streaks, swirled around the twisted strands of metal at either end.

Twitch barely dared to move. His chest tightened in fear. Someone had hold of the broken fragment of the walkway with the mysterious subspace powers, but Twitch didn't know how they worked. He was scared that if he moved too much, he would end up plummeting to the ground anyway.

As he got closer to the ground, he began to see a little more around the darkened cave. Fighting appeared to have stopped, with the invading Stellar Guard having overwhelmed the defending Inquisition forces. A couple of small skirmishes still took place, but these were quickly being quelled.

At the base of the drive, Twitch could see a couple of figures. Three starats stood with two humans. One starat had his arms raised into the air. Nick had hold of the walkway, but there was still such a long way to descend.

The walkway shook and shuddered. Metal screeched as the platform scraped against the side of the drive. All Twitch could do was hold on for dear life, scared that any movement would send him pitched over the side and down to his death. He knew that Nick wouldn't be able to catch him with subspace.

The distance below never seemed to diminish, though Twitch knew it had to be getting smaller. He swayed with the movement of the broken walkway, struggling to remain upright. His tail couldn't do much to keep him balanced, not without his legs as well.

Voices slowly started to drift up. A familiar voice called his name. David shouted for him, not using the radio. Twitch pulled off his helmet. He wanted to shout back, but he didn't trust his voice just yet.

As the walkway got closer to the ground, the more erratic the movement became. It shuddered the jerked, before dropping the last few metres to land with a crash on the rocky ground. Twitch screeched in terror, bouncing and thudding hard off the stone as he rolled clear of the twisted metal.

Nick slumped to the ground at the same moment, a couple of metres away. William dropped to his knees beside the black-furred starat, while David quickly ran across to crouch by Twitch's side.

"Are you hurt?" David asked, gently placing his arms around Twitch's shoulders.

Twitch leaned into David's comforting grip. "I'm fine, I think. I... I did it. But it might... we need to go."

David looked up. A deep growl came from within the drive, quickly followed by debris falling from the higher reaches. "I think you're right," he said quietly. He wrapped his arms a little tighter around Twitch's shoulders, before lifting the smaller starat up into his embrace. "What did you do to your legs this time?"

Twitch buried his head in the soft fur of his partner's shoulder. "Kinda dropped them down a big hole. They stopped the drive though. It's all finished, they can't use it now."

"You need to be more careful with them," David whined, but a small smile touched his lips. "I can't carry you everywhere."

"You can't?" Twitch giggled, despite himself. He hooked one arm around David's shoulder. "What's the point of you being all big and strong if you can't carry me around all the time?"

David rolled his eyes. He turned around. "William, do you have him?" he asked the other starat, who had been trying to lift Nick back up to his feet.

For the first time, Twitch could see the two humans who had joined the starats. He didn't recognise either of them. He had hoped to see Aaron or Fleet-Admiral Bosler, but neither were present. He weakly waved to the two humans. One returned the gesture, but the other just turned on her heel, hands gripped firmly on her rifle.

"What happened?" Twitch asked, turning his attention back to David. "Did we win down here too?"

"We did. I think when they saw the drive fail a lot of them gave up heart," David replied. He held Twitch tightly in his arms, not letting his partner drop. But for a few scattered shouts coming from further down in the compound, there appeared to be no signs of fighting left.

Bodies still scattered around the ground, and Twitch tried his hardest to avoid looking down at them. He didn't want to think about those whose deaths he had contributed to. He kept his focus on David's head, just above his own. "Where is Aaron now?"

"He's with the fleet-admiral, negotiating surrender from President Shawn."

Twitch flicked his tail. His head buzzed at the thought. "So, he was here? We got him?"

David hoisted Twitch up a little to kiss him on the lips. "We got him. It's over. You finished it." His arms squeezed a little tighter.

Twitch managed to peer over David's shoulder. The drive seemed to have stabilised and didn't appear in imminent danger of collapsing. A couple of rumbles emanated out from within, and the growl of internal motors powering down still reached Twitch's ears, but the crashes of falling debris had quietened. No more explosions sounded out from within. The spark of power generators and wiring still crackled, but the massive cave sounded eerily quiet without the constant thrum of the drive irritating Twitch's ears.

With his arm still wrapped around David's shoulder, Twitch allowed himself to close his eyes and rest his mind. He had nothing more to worry about. David's protective arms comforted him, and the Inquisition could no longer threaten them.

Twitch opened his eyes just for a moment, to look down at the sensor on his wrist. Two hundred and one. The concentration of particles in the atmosphere was still far too high, and the air still had the faint tinge of cinnamon to it, but the numbers were no longer rising. Someone else could deal with the problem of reducing those numbers back down to natural levels. Twitch had done his part.

He deserved a rest.

# chapter eighteen

A team of engineers and mechanics had been sent into the caves to ensure the drive could not power up again. The invitation had been extended towards Twitch to join them, but he had flatly refused. Even if he hadn't destroyed his legs in the process of deactivating the deadly machine, he still wouldn't have gone back there. He never wanted to see a Denitchev drive again, large or small.

Someone else could deal with the mess now. He had done his part.

Instead of staying close to the drive, David carried Twitch towards the magtrain station. A gathering of humans and starats processed the captives taken from the Inquisition, under the watchful eye of Aaron. He directed everything, ensuring that none of the captives made an escape towards the surface.

Twitch couldn't see Fleet-Admiral Bosler or President Shawn amongst the organised chaos.

"More for medical?" a human soldier asked, approaching the four starats.

David flicked his ears back. "Nick first. He needs it more."

Twitch got a brief look at Nick as William limped past. The black-furred starat looked to be unconscious, though his limbs twitched a little as he was carried by. Some of the fur around his fingers had been singed away, leaving behind a few angry red welts on his skin.

"Will he be alright?" Twitch asked nervously. He looked up to David, who looked tersely towards the unconscious starat.

"They'll look after him. He'll be fine, I'm sure. He just needs some rest," David said quietly, watching as the human directed William towards a medical tent that had hastily been erected.

Aaron passed command over to another human as he hurried towards his injured friend. A few quiet words were exchanged between Aaron and William.

"Do you need to go and help them?" Twitch asked, squeezing his fingers a little tighter against his partner's shoulder.

"I need to stay and help you," David countered with a shake of his head.

"I can look after myself this time. Others need you more," Twitch said. He tried to squirm free of his partner's grip, but he couldn't manage to break free. He felt a human hand on his shoulder, and he looked up to see Aaron standing with them.

"I'll keep him safe," the human said, addressing David. He held his arms out.

Twitch looked up to his partner and nodded. The arms wrapped protectively around his body loosened as he was passed over to the human.

"Where will you be?" David asked, uncertainty still in his voice.

"He'll be by my side the whole time. He'll be safe, you have my word," Aaron said, shifting Twitch's body a little so that he was pressed up against the human's chest. "He'll get to sit in on me speaking to President Shawn."

Twitch's ears perked up. "That sounds exciting," he said brightly, though internally he was conflicted. While he wanted to see the president's downfall, he didn't want to hear the excuses the human might make for betraying his planet and potentially handing human and starat over to the Vatican.

David leaned in to give Twitch another kiss. "I'll see you soon then. Be safe, please."

Twitch smiled. "I will. You go save other people this time, and I'll see you soon." He waved goodbye to David, and he tried everything to keep the smile from slipping as his partner turned away. He just about managed to do so, even keeping the tears hidden. He had barely had a chance to see David again, and once more they were being parted. He knew David had important responsibilities to deal with, but he felt scared. He had been terrified on the drive, and fears of dying still lingered in his mind. He knew he could trust Aaron, but he didn't feel comfortable expressing his feelings to the human just yet.

He remained silent, holding his tongue and letting the fear and worry swirl around inside his mind. He would need to push that deeper, so he didn't threaten the mask of aloofness on his face, but he found the task harder than usual.

Half a dozen more humans came onto the magtrain with Twitch and Aaron, all soldiers in the Stellar Guard. None of the prisoners came with them, though plenty of guards remained to ensure no one could attempt an escape.

Aaron spoke to a few of the humans as the train sped its way underground. Twitch kept his ears down, not paying much attention to what was being spoken around him. Most of what he picked up sounded like updates coming from the field, with reports on the offensive that had just been concluded. No one attempted to include Twitch in the conversation, and he made no efforts to insert himself into the discussion. He just wanted to put the whole battle behind him.

Familiar corridors followed the train. Twitch knew he had come through these corridors once before. Back then, he had been running for his life, desperate to avoid capture from those who would kill him. The memories were hard to repress, even if he knew he should feel safe in Aaron's arms.

After a short walk, ascending several flights of stairs and flanked by the half-dozen other humans, Aaron reached their destination. A pair of double doors opened out onto a conference room. A flickering holographic projector dominated one wall, while most of the floor space had been taken up with a circular table.

Three humans and one starat were already present in the room. Twitch recognised two of the humans, the ones in the middle. Fleet-Admiral Bosler stood beside President Shawn, who was the only one of the four sat down. His hands, resting on the table, had been cuffed.

At least two dozen could sit around the table, but only ten were present. Including the president, eight were human, with only one other starat beyond Twitch. He did not recognise the other starat, who had received a small cut above her eye. Dry blood stained her fur.

Aaron gently placed Twitch down in one of the vacant seats, before sitting down beside the starat. Everyone else, including the humans who had followed Aaron inside, took a seat too, with the exception of the fleet-admiral. She alone remained standing.

The president stared at his cuffed hands. Not once did he look up.

"President Shawn," the fleet-admiral barked. He still didn't look up at her. He gave no indication he even heard her, but Bosler didn't wait for any acknowledgement. "I am relieving you of duty as president of Centaura. The duty of my command stipulates that I must protect Centaura from any threat, even those that come from within. You have been deemed a threat to our planet and its people. You acted against Centaura with enemy powers and sought the destruction of those you pledged to protect and serve. Do you have anything to say in your defence?"

President Shawn spoke in a low, emotionless voice as he stared down at the table. "I acted on behalf of a greater power than any human could aspire to attain."

"You were not elected to serve any power other than that of Centaura," Fleet-Admiral Bosler countered. She folded her arms across her chest as she slowly paced back and forth behind the president's chair.

"I serve the only power that matters. The power that deserves our undying love and devotion. I serve the Almighty, who gave us Veritas to show us the way," the president said, finally lifting his eyes to look up at the ceiling.

"And what of those who chose not to follow your Inquisition? You'd have killed us all without a moment of hesitation?" the starat opposite the president growled. Her fist clenched, and she narrowed her eyes in the president's direction.

"Those who truly believed had already been given the means to salvation," the president replied, keeping his eyes up to the ceiling. "Those who do not believe were lost souls already. Their sacrifice was necessary to cleanse our universe of the filth that had spread through it."

"It seems like you're the filth here," the starat growled.

Fleet-Admiral Bosler held her hand out to the starat. "Sergeant, please. Let me do the talking."

The sergeant growled, but she leaned back in her chair and folded her arms. Her fingers still flexed, but she said nothing else.

Aaron leaned in close to Twitch and whispered in his ear. "That's Sergeant Jen Taylor. She was one of the commanders leading an assault team down. She took some heavy losses, unfortunately."

Twitch nodded and curled his tail over his lap. He struggled to remain upright in his chair, without his legs to provide any balance or support. He rested his arms on the table, using them to hold himself up.

"Religious fanaticism has no place on Centaura," Fleet-Admiral Bosler said calmly. "It has no place anywhere in this system. Every belief the Vatican of Mars tries to sell us is outdated and archaic. The people of Centaura are not swayed by such arguments."

"I found enough support here," the president said, finally looking down to survey those sat in front of him. His eyes lingered on Twitch.

"We estimate what, fifteen thousand? Is that all the support you could manage for this puritanical mission?" the fleet-admiral asked. She paused her pacing. "This was an infiltration mission by the Vatican, and they were lucky beyond belief that we had elected a president willing to go along with their hateful plans."

"We are dooming humanity. I had no choice," the president snapped. He tried to pull at his cuffs, but they held firm.

"You say nothing of starats," Twitch said quietly, speaking before any of the humans could say anything. A small sneer came to his muzzle. "Are we what dooms humanity?"

The president mirrored Twitch's sneer. For a brief moment the mask of a politician dropped, and a veneer of hatred revealed itself. "You go against nature. You are an affront to the Almighty. Yes. You were part of what doomed humanity, but do not think you were worthy of that sole title. Centaura had long rotted away from the careful eye of the Vatican."

"The way I see it," Aaron said slowly, drawing attention to himself from the president, finally taking his angry gaze away from Twitch. Aaron paused and frowned, before starting again. "The way

I see it, is that Centaura has flourished away from the Vatican and Terra. As someone who served the empire for so long, I can tell you that I feel free and happy here, like I had never done back on Terra. There is a background anger permeating everything in the Sol System that I can't explain. Here, I finally felt free of that."

President Shawn spat in disgust. "Bullshit. Only on Mars can a human feel free and at peace with himself."

"Have you ever been?" Twitch asked quietly. While before, the fleet-admiral had rebuked Sergeant Taylor for speaking, now she stood back and let Twitch and Aaron question the president.

"To Mars? Of course," the president replied sharply. "I took the pilgrimage as thanks shortly after my election victory. I came back with renewed vigour for what needed to be done, but it was only this last year that I realised there was no saving Centaura from its own degeneracy."

"And so you would have sentenced millions of lives to death," the fleet-admiral said. She leaned against the back of one of the vacant seats.

"I will not apologise for doing the right thing for our Almighty," the president said, his voice beginning to rise in volume. "Veritas would have praised me as a saint."

"I'm sure you'll have plenty of time to ruminate over what you could have done had we been a little later," the fleet-admiral said. She pushed away from the chair and turned her back on the president. "General Campbell, as the only other person of equal rank here, do you consent to stripping President Shawn of his office, and installing myself as the temporary leader of Centaura?"

One of the humans who had come in with Aaron rose to his feet. His grey beard twitched as he used one hand resting on the table to help support himself. "Fleet-Admiral Bosler, I offer my consent and support to this action. I recommend your appointment as interim-president, until this crisis can be resolved."

"You won't be supported in this," the president growled, but only Twitch paid any attention to the deposed leader.

Fleet-Admiral Bosler turned to the five others who had come in with Aaron. "Send word out to Caledonia informing parliament of our actions here. Parliament is to be suspended until we can question everyone for their loyalties. I want to know how deep this corruption went. I also need command sent to Network Central. All traffic to and from empire-controlled territories are to cease. Deploy the Stellar Guard to enforce this. Centaura is on lockdown until further notice."

"Understood ma'am."

All five humans rose to their feet and bowed to the newly-installed interim president. None of them said anything further. None of them needed to. Twitch could see that they all believed their commanding officer, and they would move quickly to carry out her orders.

Once the door had been closed behind the departing officers, Bosler turned to Twitch. "I didn't expect to see you so soon, but I would like to express my thanks to you for everything you have done for us, Twitch," she said, ignoring the deposed president for the moment. "If there is anything we can do for you, then please just let us know. Without your actions today, this would not have been a victory. Millions across the planet would have died without the shields to protect them."

Twitch bowed his head and curled in his ears. His thoughts buzzed at the praise. "Some new legs?" he asked in a small voice. He looked up to the fleet-admiral. "I know they were a gift already, but I had to sacrifice them to destroy the drive. Without them, I'm helpless. I can't do anything."

"We'll make sure you get something quickly. It won't be anything custom, but we'll have spare cybernetics in reserve," Bosler said. She quietly murmured something in the ear of the other human stood with her, watching over President Shawn. A quick, quiet conversation took place before she addressed Twitch again. "We'll have something for you within a couple of hours. Is that acceptable?"

Twitch flicked his ears up in surprise. "Of course, yes," he said quickly. He didn't want to make Bosler think he was ungrateful or impatient for some replacement cybernetics. He felt happy enough that something would be done for him. They didn't have to be instant.

Bosler nodded her head. "Captain Lee, I would request your presence in the forward command centre in half an hour. We need to work out how to mop up any lingering Inquisition forces."

"I'll be there, ma'am," Aaron replied, bowing his head towards the fleet-admiral. "Is there anything else you want of me?"

"Until then, no thank you, Captain. See to Twitch. I'll deal with the president," Bosler said. She gestured towards the doors.

Twitch curled his tail as Aaron lifted the starat up into his arms again. As he was carried away, Twitch looked back towards President Shawn. The human stared down at his hands, fingers clenched. His shoulders had slumped. That human had come within minutes of destroying Centaura and irrevocably changing the human species. Twitch had put a stop to that.

The starat sighed and leaned into Aaron's shoulder. Finally, they could have some peace again.

# chapter nineteen

Twitch finally got the chance to relax. He no longer needed to worry about any fighting that could start breaking out around him. He couldn't yet put his feet up and rest, but only because his promised new cybernetic legs hadn't come through yet.

David hadn't come up from tending to the wounded, but Twitch had been reunited with the other starats. William and Nick had both recovered with only minor injuries. The black-furred starat was still a little dazed, but he had been declared fit after his collapse from overexerting his subspace powers. The three starats didn't speak much as they enjoyed the chance to just sit and enjoy a cold drink.

Twitch felt dirty. His fur was grimy and messy. He couldn't wait to enjoy a long shower to wash away all the dirt, as well as the patches of blood. Not all of the blood was his, and Twitch didn't know whether to be thankful or horrified about that. He tried not to think about it too much, but every time he reached for his cup, he could see the stains there. His ears pinned down low.

William placed his hand on Twitch's. "We did it. We won," he said quietly.

"What about Amy?" Nick asked, his voice hoarse. He moved his hands gingerly as he recovered from his subspace exertions.

William brushed the black-furred starat's concerns away with a wave of his hand. "She's nothing compared to the Inquisition."

Twitch smiled weakly. He looked around the large room, in which other soldiers had been permitted to come and rest. The room appeared to usually be used as a cafeteria, with a small, currently vacant kitchen off to one side. Twitch couldn't be certain if they were in the same building from which he and David had escaped on their previous visit to Hadrian, but he could see the city outside the windows that lined the room.

Conversation murmured all around the three starats, even as they remained mostly quiet.

Twitch glanced down to the sensor around his wrist, mostly out of habit. The number had not been going down, but nor had it been rising. He thumped his tail against the back of his chair. Someone else could deal with the issue of removing the excess particles from the atmosphere. Over time, they would degrade, but Twitch doubted Bosler would be satisfied with that. The amount of electricity needed to jump the planet with the current concentration was still immensely high, more than that of any natural thunderstorm, but should someone else decide to construct a Denitchev drive within atmosphere...

Twitch shuddered and shook his head. He didn't want to go down that mental road. Instead, he wanted to forget everything he had experienced over the last few weeks. He tried to force his ears up. "I hope my house is still alright. I'm going to need some of that whiskey I still have there."

William and Nick both smiled and laughed.

"I think we could all use some of that," Nick said. He sighed and leaned back in his chair.

William tensed as a human approached them. Twitch recognised the stocky man with the greasy black hair. They had briefly met down in the caves. Simon Briggs. The man had a deep cut across his cheek that had been stitched back together. He gestured to an empty seat around the starats' table. "May I sit here?"

William growled, but Twitch nodded.

Simon warily took the seat. He placed a hand over his injured cheek. "A starat did this," he said, before his eyes widened. He hastened to clarify. "The stitches, not the cut."

"Good for you," William said, his muzzle twisting into a silent snarl.

The human clasped his hands together and rested them on the table. "I don't deserve your forgiveness, but I can at least try to explain why I did some of the things I did," he said slowly. He didn't look up at the starats. "It was like a fog being lifted from my mind. It didn't happen at once, but I know exactly when it began to clear away."

"When we left the empire?" Twitch asked, leaning forward slightly, partially for support on the table, but also because he was interested to hear what the human had to say. Neither William nor Nick seemed to care. They both growled softly and leaned closer to each other, William whispering something in Nick's ear.

Simon shook his head. "No, before then. When I made the decision to talk to Richard, Veritas keep him. But that moment, that conscious decision, changed me. I started to see starats as people, and not slaves or objects. I started to lose my love for the Vatican, and to the empire. By the time we got out here, I had to wonder why I had ever been in love with them in the first place."

Twitch flicked his ears. "You aren't the only person to go through something like that. The same thing happened to Captain Rhys when I first spoke to him."

Simon opened his mouth to answer, but he was interrupted before he could begin.

"You're trying to tell us you abused me and Richard because someone else was thinking for you? That I lost my leg because humans didn't know how to control themselves?" William snarled. He curled back his lip and scraped his claws against the table. "Because it sounds like you're making up bullshit excuses."

Simon grimaced. "It sounds absurd, I know. But it's the only way I can explain it."

Twitch stared down at the table. Thoughts slowly trickled through his mind as he tried to process what Simon had told him. His ears flicked and pinned down. "It sounds like what happened to Captain Aaron," he said slowly, looking up to stare at William. "When he got back from Pluto. His thoughts had been changed. Same as yours. You forgot what happened to Captain Rhys."

"That's not the same," William growled. He jabbed a finger towards Twitch. "Don't go taking his side. You don't know what it was like."

"I had Captain Jacques. I know exactly what it was like," Twitch replied coolly. His hackles rose, but he kept himself from snapping at William. "I know you got used to Captain Rhys looking like me.

He didn't suffer like we did, but remember I lived through everything like you."

"It doesn't sound possible," William said. He didn't meet Twitch in the eye.

"We've seen a lot of shit that I would never have thought possible," Twitch replied, his ears remaining pinned down low to his head. He looked across to Nick, whose brow was furrowed in thought. "What do you think? Can someone influence the thoughts of an entire star system?"

Nick laughed nervously. "If they could, we should be rightfully fucking terrified of them." He ran his hands through his cheek fur. "Only person I can think to ask would be Snow, and I don't think that would be a good idea."

"No, we'd best not do that," Twitch said with a shake of his head. He tapped his fingers against the table and glanced back to the human. "Would going back there make you start thinking we're animals again?"

Simon stared at Twitch with his mouth hanging partially open. He then shook his head from side to side. "I don't think so. I went back there with Captain Griffiths on the Pluto missions. I felt nothing. No relapses. No desires to defect back to the empire. Whatever it was, it no longer had a hold on me."

"I don't believe you," William growled. His muzzle twisted. "And I certainly won't forgive you."

"I'm not going to plead for your forgiveness," Simon said gruffly. He leaned back in his chair and crossed his arms over his chest. "I just wanted the chance to say sorry again, now that we're not being shot at."

"It is appreciated," Twitch said, speaking before William could growl at the human again.

Simon pursed his lips together. The movement pulled at the cut on his cheek, but he seemed to show no sign of pain from the injury. "I should leave you to it. I don't want to take up more of your time," he said, before rising to his feet. He hesitated for a moment, then looked back to William. "When all of this is sorted out, if I'm assigned back to the *Harvester*, or the *Freedom* I think they call it now, I would love it if you continued to work with me. You worked as hard as three of us, but this time know that you'll never be overworked again."

William didn't answer. He didn't even look up at the human, who simply shrugged his shoulders and started to walk away. The starat's claws dug into the table, and he breathed deeply. "Fucking asshole," he whispered.

"He's trying his best, same as Captain Rhys," Twitch said quietly.

"Would you ever forgive Captain Jacques? Or Cardinal Erik?" William growled.

Twitch felt a shiver up his spine. His tail curled in tight around his hips. "No. No I couldn't."

William jabbed a finger towards Simon, who had retreated to the far side of the room. "That man, that specific man, abused me and hurt me for years. Captain Rhys did what most humans did: he ignored us and treated us like dirt, but there are some, like Commander Simon, who took pleasure in harming us. I can't forgive that."

Twitch sighed and bowed his head. "We're all just a little bit broken, aren't we?"

"There's not a starat from Terra who hasn't been," Nick said. He rubbed his hand over the headband he wore just beneath his ears. "Some more than others. Some physically, but almost all of us mentally. I was lucky to have someone like Aaron by my side, but he couldn't protect me from everything."

"You as well?" Twitch asked.

Nick sighed. He pulled down on his headband slightly, revealing a streak of pure white fur that ran around the side of his head. He quickly snapped the band back into place. "Got a scar when I was stolen away from Aaron as a kit. They sliced me up pretty bad. I think they wanted to prove a starat brain was too small to hold rational thought. I was lucky Aaron found me when he did."

Twitch didn't know what to say. There never was anything that could be said. Nothing made the abuse better. Every starat knew what another had gone through. All he could do was reach out to hold onto Nick's hand.

"At least now things will start to get better," William said. The growl had left his voice, and he looked up towards the ceiling. "We stood up to the Vatican and won. Centaura is for us."

"Yeah, we beat them. We won," Twitch said, managing to force a smile onto his face. Something prickled at the back of his neck, but he tried to ignore those dark thoughts. They were a remnant of the horrors he had been forced to witness, nothing more.

Things could finally go back to how they were before Cardinal Erik so violently changed Twitch's life. He would soon have some legs again, and then he would be able to walk away from all this violence and war.

Twitch just wanted to go home.

***

The fleet-admiral had been true to her word. Twitch's replacement legs had come quickly. The cybernetics looked almost identical to the set he had used to destroy the Denitchev drive. The left ankle felt a little stiff and they were a little bit too short, but otherwise they seemed to work perfectly.

Even better for Twitch, David had returned not long after his legs, and his partner came with news from Steph. Along with Nick and William, they would be among the first to be transferred back to Caledonia. Several shuttles of non-critical personnel would be flown back overnight, with only communication staff and a garrison to maintain control of Inquisition forces remaining while the drive was fully decommissioned.

The starats managed to get a little sleep while they waited. Twitch couldn't remember his dreams when he woke, but he couldn't shake the feeling that they had been about something dark and foreboding. He had Captain Rhys's voice in his ears too, but he couldn't grasp any of the words the former human had spoken.

By the time Twitch emerged, blinking, into the brightly lit city, all thoughts of the dream had faded from his mind. A shuttle had landed in the middle of an adjacent park, with a crowd of curious civilian onlookers clustered around a temporary barrier that had been placed on the pavement. No one but Stellar Guard soldiers were permitted to approach the shuttle amongst the waving tendrils of foliage.

Twitch was waved forward by a familiar face. He grinned as he hurried forward to greet Aleksandr. Captain Rhys's pilot appeared to be unscathed from the fighting below ground. "I hear you did us good down there?" the human said, tightly squeezing his hand around Twitch's.

"I guess I did, yeah," Twitch replied with a grin. He felt a little more refreshed after his rest, and his thoughts had a bright tinge to them. Optimism started to return. The Inquisition had been defeated, and Fleet-Admiral Bosler would be the one to clean up their mess. He would no longer be needed to do anything.

Aleksandr led the starats onto the shuttle, where other familiar faces were ready to greet them. Doctor Anthony sat next to Simon, and a couple of others Twitch knew from Captain Rhys's crew, but couldn't remember the names. Others, Twitch didn't recognise at all. Almost fifty people were in the shuttle, with the four starats being the last to come on board before the doors were closed.

David took a vacant seat next to Doctor Anthony. "Thought you'd be asked to stay back," the starat said to the doctor.

Doctor Anthony turned in his seat to wave to the newcomers. "I thought they would, too. Seems they have enough doctors," the human replied. He patted David on the shoulder. "I saw you working before. You did great."

David's ears pinned back in his embarrassment from the compliment. He mumbled a quiet acknowledgment.

"Guess we are all getting to go home early," Aleksandr said. He took one of the vacant seats, with Twitch taking the window seat by the pilot's side. "It will be nice to get that vacation we were all promised."

"You were promised a vacation?" Twitch asked in surprise. He didn't look back at Aleksandr, instead staring out the window to see the park outside. The shuttle began to shake as the engines fired up.

"Yeah. Captain Griffiths was meant to be off duty for three months when we got here," Aleksandr explained. "That meant his whole crew too. Then all of this happened. We weren't meant to go to Pluto either time."

Twitch curled his tail over his lap as the shuttle started to rise. There wasn't much room to manoeuvre between the tall buildings of Hadrian, but the shuttle didn't need much. It rose vertically until it cleared the skyscrapers, then started to streak away to the north. Twitch gripped the armrests on his seat hard, with even the internal dampeners unable to fully negate the effects of acceleration on his body.

"What about you, Twitch?" Aleksandr asked, distracting the starat from his watch on the receding ground. "You will be coming to the *Freedom* when we're re-commissioned?"

Twitch shook his head. He still stared out the window. In the growing darkness outside, he could see less and less. Soon, only the reflections from inside the shuttle cabin were visible. He could clearly see Aleksandr looking at him. "I can't do it, no," he said quietly. "Not without Captain Rhys."

"That is a shame. I think you'd advance far on a military ship," Aleksandr said, but he didn't otherwise press the matter.

"I'm not a soldier," Twitch said with a shake of his head.

"No, but you're a great mechanic. It's more than just shooting people and fighting," Aleksandr replied, but he didn't press any further.

Twitch sighed to himself and continued to stare out the window. He could see Aleksandr lean back in his seat and close his eyes, ready to pass the time by resting. Twitch didn't think he could sleep. He felt refreshed after his rest in Hadrian, and now he just felt anxious to be home.

The stars were bright outside the window. The automated computer of the shuttle beeped occasionally, but no one seemed concerned by anything. The battles were over. Peace had come to Centaura again.

Twitch remained awake for the full journey. Nothing but darkness passed by the window, but still Twitch stared out.

A little conversation had rippled around the shuttle as stories of battle were passed around. Some gloried in how many enemies they had killed, a conversation that made Twitch wish he could pin down his ears and ignore everything around him. Thankfully, no one asked him how many he had killed.

Time ticked away, until finally, Twitch could see the lights of Caledonia in the distance.

They were almost home.

There was no warning.

One moment, the shuttle was flying. The next, a deafening roar filled Twitch's ears. Three loud explosions tore through the shuttle. Flames erupted, and the craft began to plummet from the sky.

Twitch didn't even have time to scream.

# chapter twenty

Twitch jerked awake.

Flames lit up the night. Hot air brushed over his fur. Voices urgently spoke.

Someone nudged at his shoulder. "Are you alright?"

Twitch's eyes focused. David crouched over him. "I think so?" Twitch replied. He looked around. He was still sat in his seat, but also lying on his side. Twisted metal arched around him. "What happened?"

"Shot down," David said tersely. He helped Twitch unbuckle himself from his seat.

Twitch hissed in pain as he stumbled up to his feet. His ribs ached, but he didn't think any of them had been broken. He stumbled out of the broken rows of seats. The smell of fire and blood filled his nose.

The starat was forced to clamber over still, motionless bodies. His ears pinned flat to his head as he crawled around Commander Simon, who had slumped forward in his seat. The human did not respond to Twitch's touch. Twitch was frozen in the horror of the moment. Fire burned around him, but he did not move. Then a hand closed around his shoulder and pulled him away.

Twitch fell into David's chest. His partner had a small cut to his face, but otherwise didn't seem harmed. With his partner's help, Twitch stumbled away from the burning wreck of the shuttle. He felt dazed as his eyes fell on the sight of Doctor Anthony crouched next to a human with a broken leg. The doctor had already set a splint around the wounded leg so the human could be moved.

The starat could feel bare dirt beneath his feet, and a gentle wind blew at his face. There was no shelter of trees or buildings close by, though on the horizon he could make out the lights of Caledonia.

"We have to keep moving," Aleksandr called out. Everyone looked towards the pilot. "They'll be looking for survivors. We have to go."

"Who are they?" Nick demanded.

Aleksandr looked up to the dark sky. Lights moved amongst the stars. "Military. Hurry."

"But we're with the military?" Twitch said. His ears flicked as he frowned, trying to sort through his thoughts. Everything above his hips ached, and his vision hadn't fully cleared yet. He felt like he swayed on the spot. William pulled him on, following after Aleksandr. David lagged towards the back of the survivors, helping Doctor Anthony with the wounded.

Twitch got a first proper look at their surroundings. They had crashed in a large, open space with just dirt beneath their feet. There were no buildings or greenhouses; just flat, open ground that looked like it had been purposefully cleared. Dotted around in the darkness, Twitch could just about make out the silhouettes of some tall, tendril-like trees.

One of those small groves was their destination. Engines rumbled in the air above the fleeing group. As Twitch glanced back, he could see bright spotlights shine down on the burning wreck of the shuttle.

Twitch's heart hammered as he ran. He kept easy pace with Aleksandr, having to pull William along with him.

The grove of native trees loomed high as the surviving group limped and staggered into the sheltering darkness beneath the swaying tendrils. Underneath the canopy, the stars above were completely obscured. Sticky sap oozed down the swaying trunks, with small tendrils smearing the gunk over anyone who got too close.

Twitch wrinkled his nose as he peered back out, standing alongside Aleksandr and a couple of Centauran humans. "If we're military, and they are, why did they shoot us down?" Twitch asked, his voice trembling. "Did they think we were Inquisition?"

"Not all of us went to Hadrian," one of the local humans said. He looked out towards the downed shuttle with a grim expression. "Some remained behind. It was never officially justified who stayed and who went out, but we all knew the reason. Those left behind had shown loyalty to Amy Jennings and her organisation."

"You are saying she did this?" Aleksandr whispered. The spotlights over the shuttle began to sweep a little further out, shining brightly around the open terrain. Voices called out over the constant rumbling of the engines.

"It seems like it," the other human replied. "I caught sight of a missile lock just before the explosion. We were targeted from orbit."

"Did you see which ship?" Aleksandr asked.

The human nodded. "The *Freedom*."

"That was Captain Rhys's ship," Twitch squeaked in shock. "How could they be able to use that ship?"

"I think Amy has been recruiting defectors from Terra to fill out her numbers, as well as to gain control of her own armada," the human said. His hand moved down to the pistol at his hip. "I don't think we're safe here."

"How far are we from the suburbs?" Aleksandr hissed quietly. He kept a wary eye on the shuttle. Soldiers had come to the ground, but none approached the copse yet.

"Five minute run, if no one interferes with us," the other human said.

"Then get moving," Aleksandr said tersely. Twitch thought he could hear a little bit of Captain Rhys in the pilot's voice.

The other humans obviously heard the same thing. "Sir," was the brusque reply. A salute followed, and the humans who had sunk to their haunches rose back up to their feet again.

Progress through the trees was slow. The alien plants grew close together, and their sticky sap slowed movement further as human and starat alike tried to avoid brushing against the waving tendrils.

Twitch and Aleksandr remained at the rear of the group, casting worried glances back to make sure they weren't being followed. No lights shone through the trees yet, but Twitch knew it couldn't be long before someone noticed their tracks leaving the downed shuttle.

The starat struggled to get things straight in his head. He couldn't imagine why Amy had done this. He knew she had plans to disrupt Terra, possibly utilising the same weapons the Inquisition had tried to use on Centaura, but he had never known she had ambitions for her home planet. If she had turned part of the Centauran military on itself, then Twitch didn't know what could happen next.

"Should we send a message back to the fleet-admiral and warn her what's happened?" Twitch asked quietly, looking up to Aleksandr.

The human shook his head. "We can't. All our long-range comms gear was on the shuttle."

David placed his hand on Twitch's shoulder. "Hold on, I'll see if I can call Steph," he said, pulling out his tablet and flicking across the screen. He wiped away some of the blood on his cheek with the back of his hand as he waited for some response to come from Steph, but there was no answer.

"Shit," Twitch muttered to himself. He curled his tail between his legs as he followed the human. In the distance ahead, he could see the edge of the trees. Beyond, the lights from the nearest suburbs shone bright. No patrolling shuttles or soldiers stood between them and the streets of Caledonia.

"Keep trying to get hold of them," Aleksandr said quietly. He peered out through the sticky tendrils.

"What do we do until then?" Twitch asked. He couldn't see them just sitting around and hoping they could reach Steph and the fleet-admiral. They had to do something. They had to get a warning to the fleet-admiral and the rest of the military, on the far side of the planet.

Aleksandr sucked in his breath. "We have to get to a barracks, or parliament. Doubt we'll get a message out from anywhere else, not with all the encryption they're using in Hadrian. Civilian frequencies won't do," the human said. He paused by the edge of the trees. "We need to find Amy before her soldiers can find us."

"How do we do that?" Twitch whispered. He nervously stroked his tail.

"We'll work that out soon. First, we need to get to safety," Aleksandr said, lightly placing his hand on the starat's shoulder. "Are you ready to run?"

Twitch took a deep breath and nodded. He had no choice. If he stayed back, he would be captured by the SFU. Amy would not show any mercy this time. He ran after Aleksandr and the other humans.

The lights of the suburbs seemed so far away. They never appeared to get closer, but behind them, the spotlights never swept in their direction. No one had noticed their escape.

A low fence blocked easy access out of the empty fields and into the streets of the city. Most were able to clamber up easily, but those with the more serious injuries had to be helped up and over. Twitch lingered for a moment at the top of the wall. He could see the flames from the shuttle in the distance. Torchlight swung back and forth across the great gap; an empty void of cleared land between the suburbs and the surrounding greenhouses.

"Land cleared for a new suburb," one of the Centauran humans explained. Her hand raised up towards him, offering a helping hand down. The starat knew he was able to leap down with ease, but he accepted her assistance. He dropped down to the ground and found himself on the edge of a pavement. A quiet, two lane road stretched out to the left and right. Houses lined the road. Some lights were still on, but most were quiet and dark.

"We shouldn't stay here. Let's keep moving, then we can work out a plan," Aleksandr said.

Everyone turned to Aleksandr like a leader. They followed his commands, and no one questioned him. The small group followed his lead and made their way down the road, trying to put some distance between them and the crashed shuttle.

A few curious eyes looked at them from inside the houses. They would certainly have been alerted by the shuttle crash, but no one approached them. No one offered help, until one starat finally scampered out from her front door to stand by the front gate of her garden. She beckoned Twitch closer.

"Is it true? Has President Shawn been deposed?" she whispered.

Twitch nodded. He was surprised news of that had travelled so far already.

"Was he really going to do all those awful things?"

Again, Twitch nodded. He curled his tail in close to his legs. "How do you know all this?"

The starat's ears flicked back. "There was an emergency broadcast on the holonetwork, just after the evacuation warning. Amy Jennings said she had taken control of government with parliament's backing, as there was no one else to step in. Is that right? Can she do that?"

"I don't think so," Twitch replied uncertainly. "Did she say where she was?"

"Parliament building, I think," the starat replied. She took a step back from the gate. "Will there be fighting?"

Twitch's ears flattened against his head. His shoulders and tail drooped. "I hope not. I've seen enough of that, but you might want to stay inside where it's safe just in case."

The starat continued to back away. Without another word, she turned and fled inside her house. Twitch remained still for a moment, before he hurried after the group, not wanting to be left behind. He caught up to Aleksandr and tugged on his sleeve. "Amy's taken control of the government."

"Then we can only assume she will move quickly against any other returning shuttles," Aleksandr said. He didn't break stride at all. "She will move against the fleet-admiral too. Amy will know Bosler would most likely take command after Shawn."

"So what do we do?" Twitch asked nervously. He didn't like the thought of having to take action again, so soon after he believed he was done.

Aleksandr didn't answer. He just pursed his lips and lowered his head. No one seemed too sure where they were going, other than back towards the city. The skyscrapers loomed on the horizon, shining bright against the darkened sky.

The wounded humans couldn't go any further. Doctor Anthony called out to Aleksandr from the back of the group, and the pilot called a halt. A small park provided a little shelter from prying eyes, and the wounded were given a chance to rest. The pause also gave Aleksandr the chance to discuss matters with a few other humans. Twitch intentionally sat away from them, not wanting to be involved. He sat and watched David and Doctor Anthony help the wounded.

William sat by Twitch's side, though Nick had gone amongst the group of humans planning their next move.

"It just can't be easy, can it?" William said quietly. He stretched out his legs as he sat back on the park bench, leaning his elbows on the table behind him. "Now we've got to deal with Amy and Snow."

"Why didn't Bosler see this coming?" Twitch mused. He scratched behind his ear.

"Shawn was the bigger threat," William said, shrugging his shoulders. "We had to deal with that first. Maybe she didn't think Amy was going to move for Centaura. Everything suggested Amy didn't care about Centaura, and that Terra was her only target."

"I suppose so," Twitch sighed. He looked up to the night sky. Stars twinkled, and a few ships gleamed bright as they passed overhead in orbit. The shield crackled briefly, but mostly remained inactive. "You think they want a war with Terra?"

William shook his head. "They want to destroy Terra, just like the Inquisition was trying to do here. There won't be a war. There will be extermination."

"Captain Rhys is still over there," Twitch said, still trying to hope that the former human was still alive and fighting.

"Those humans would never lift a finger to save us," William said, a small growl entering his voice. He then sighed and closed his eyes, lying back fully on the table. "But that doesn't mean we can't try. We have to stop Amy."

"We've already stopped one genocidal maniac. What's a second one on top of that?" Twitch said quietly. He thumped his head back on the wooden table. "We're all by ourselves though, aren't we? If we can't get hold of everyone back in Hadrian, then it's up to us."

"All up to us. Hurt and alone," William said. He laughed and rubbed the sides of his muzzle. "I'd like to say we're something other than fucked, but I can't see what we can do."

"We keep going like Leandro and Richard would have wanted," Twitch said. He squeezed his eyes closed to push back the tears that threatened to well up. "They wouldn't want us to stop."

William's hand found Twitch's. "We'll make them both proud of us."

Twitch hoped he could do so. He feared that he would instead join Richard and Leandro in death.

\*\*\*

"If we can capture Amy and Snow, then perhaps we can force the SFU to stand down," Aleksandr said. The pilot looked around the small group. He did not look confident as they walked through the quiet streets. Doctor Anthony had remained behind with those who had been injured in the shuttle crash. Of the fifty who had boarded the shuttle in Hadrian, only fifteen were still fit to walk.

Twitch flicked his ear and frowned. "How do we get to them? They're not going to just let us walk right into parliament."

The streets remained empty as they began to make their way closer to the city once more. Twitch briefly wondered why, but then he remembered the evacuation alarm, warning everyone to stay indoors should the shields be deactivated. He doubted people wanted to be outside until they had assurances the dangers had passed. Given the added insecurity of Amy's declaration, he wasn't surprised few dared to be out. He knew he would have hidden away as far as possible, had he not been so deeply involved.

"We have to try, at least," William said with a growl. He walked just beside Twitch. A shadow of his old limp had returned to his gait, though he had earlier refused Twitch to take a look at his cybernetic leg. He glanced across to David. "Have you been able to get hold of Steph yet? We could really use some advice from her or the fleet-admiral. Some backup would be nice."

"Nothing yet," David said, shaking his head. His tail drooped as he tried contacting Steph again, but the call failed almost instantly.

Twitch flicked his ears as a thought came to his mind. He grabbed hold of David's hand to get the attention of his partner. "Do you think Minister Bakir might be able to help us?"

"Can we trust her?" David replied quickly.

Twitch shrugged his shoulders. "I don't know. She never seemed to want to trust Amy when we saw her."

David didn't answer at first. He kept his hand tightly held onto Twitch's as they cautiously followed the humans ahead. The city had gradually been getting closer, and there had been no sign of any pursuit from the crashed shuttle. "I think if Amy doesn't trust Bakir, then she won't be in a position to help us."

"I suppose you're right," Twitch said quietly. He sighed and lowered his head, staring down at the ground. The roads felt eerily quiet as they walked. But for the occasional rumble of a shuttle engine overhead, all was silent.

"She was someone Richard always trusted," William added. He choked slightly as tears came to his eyes, then cleared his throat. "But he was always frustrated at how little she was able to do, because of people like Shawn."

"We really need to get in contact with the fleet-admiral," Twitch said, looking up to his partner with a grimace. "She has to know what Amy has planned."

David nodded and pinned his ears down. "I know, but there's nothing. I don't know if she's just not answering or if the signal's being blocked."

"Or if something bad has happened there," William whispered.

Twitch tried not to think about that possibility. He took a deep breath and looked towards the city skyline. The loudest sound in Twitch's ears was the rapid beating of his heart. "If it's all got to be up to us, then we've got to do what we can."

William scoffed and laughed. "Never fought I'd fight to try and help people on Terra."

"Nor did I," Nick said. The black-furred starat moved a little further head of the others, closer to the small group of humans. He turned and walked backwards for a few paces. "Let's go and save two planets in one day. Think the empire will like us then?"

Twitch did not have an answer to that. He doubted the humans of Terra would even know they had been saved by a band of starats. His eyes lifted, towards the bright buildings of the city. Somewhere in the centre of those skyscrapers was Amy and Snow. Somehow, Twitch would make them pay for the pain they had caused him. They would come to justice.

# chapter twenty-one

Caledonia was just as quiet as the surrounding suburbs. The city streets were almost completely deserted. Those few that did wander between the tall buildings looked confused and scared. None lingered when the group of soldiers approached, fleeing indoors wherever they could.

There was no sign of any occupying force at first, and Twitch had to doubt the information he had been given. Then he saw the first barricade.

The outdoor shopping mall had been blocked off entirely. A garrison of guards were posted at the blockade, all heavily armed. There was one Terran human amongst the twelve starats. Aleksandr guided his small group off to the side before they got close enough to be seen or questioned. At the far end of the mall, Twitch had briefly caught sight of the gleaming lights of parliament building.

"We'll need to find a way past that barricade," Aleksandr said quietly. He crouched down in front of the closed doors of the deserted train station that overlooked the top of the mall.

"Couldn't we go around? There is another street parallel to the mall," David said, speaking just as quietly as the human.

"Then we have to get past the barricade blocking that road," Aleksandr replied, not looking back to the starat.

Twitch glanced up at David as his partner grimaced. The two of them had been to the station once before. They had met with Minister Bakir and gone to return home, but a group of humans from the Inquisition had chased the two starats, threatening to capture them both. Twitch's tail drooped at the memory, and he leaned into David for comfort.

The pilot looked around the group. He bit his lip and tapped his fingers on his forehead. The way to the centre of Caledonia had been easy and unchallenged, but Twitch knew there had been no plan in mind. Everything was reactionary, adapting to the situation in front of them. Now that they had come across a more concrete obstacle to overcome, the lack of plan had stalled their progress entirely.

Nick cleared his throat. "I think I have an idea, but I don't like it."

"Let's hear it," Aleksandr said.

Nick took a deep breath. "Only we can go through. Us starats. They'll let us past."

"Why would they do that?" Aleksandr asked. He held his hand over his mouth, his fingers idly scratching beneath his nose.

Twitch's breath caught in his throat. He looked into Nick's eye as he realised what the other starat had proposed. "We're Starat Freedom Union," he whispered. He gripped hold of his tail in both hands. "They'll let us through."

"Are you sure?" Aleksandr asked. He looked around at the four starats present. "What if they have records of which starats don't work with her?"

"Then no one will get through," William said with a shrug.

"We have to try, at least," Twitch said, nodding. He then crouched down, plucking at the panels on his leg to make sure he had a weapon close by, just in case. A pistol was housed inside his right leg, but he did not remove it just yet. He glanced either side of him. Nick and David were stood by his side, with William a couple of paces away. "Are we ready to go now?"

"No, but there's no point delaying," Nick said. The starat grimaced. His ears had flattened down against his head.

William hissed softly. "I don't think any of them will know who we are. I don't recognise them." He squinted slightly as he scanned over the barricade. "None of them seem to have any tablets on them, so they might not have access to a database of banned starats."

Aleksandr frowned. The human didn't question them. "Is there anything you need from us then?"

"Just find a different way in and try to catch up," Nick said. He held his hands on his hips and tapped his foot against the ground.

Aleksandr took a step back from the starats. "We'll do our best to find another way in," he said.

Twitch started to move towards the barricade, then paused after just a couple of paces. He looked up to Aleksandr. "We'll keep trying to get in contact with Fleet-Admiral Bosler. She needs to be warned that she's sending people back into Amy's trap." His eyes then slid to the buildings behind the human. He could just about make out the large lettering down the side of Jennings Tower. His ears flicked. "Don't follow us, though."

"Are you sure?" David asked, pre-empting the protests from the other starats.

Twitch smiled weakly. He pointed to the distant Jennings Tower. "That's where you need to go. She'll have information there. You might even be able to contact the fleet-admiral if we can't get through."

Aleksandr straightened his shoulders and followed Twitch's gaze towards the skyscraper with Amy's name emblazoned on the side. The quickest route passed right by the blockade at the top of the mall. The road beyond was perfectly empty, with no civilians present. Twitch shivered. Everything felt too eerie without the usual crowded nature of the city. Before coming to Centaura, he had only experienced large crowds on his brief trip to Sydney on Terra, but now he felt uncomfortable without one where he knew there should be a lot of people.

"We'll give you five minutes," Aleksandr said. He peered around the corner of the station, towards the barricade. "We'll move in should things go wrong. Once you get through, we'll take a circuitous route to Jennings Tower and see what we can do there."

Twitch held his hand out to Aleksandr. The human took it. "I hope it doesn't come to a fight. There's a lot of them," he said nervously. He tried to force a confident smile onto his face. "Good luck."

"You too, Twitch. We'll see you soon," Aleksandr replied. His hand squeezed tight around the starat's.

"Yeah, I hope so," Twitch replied. He tried not to think about what would happen should the guards at the barricade not believe them. He took the lead, with Nick, William, and David following right behind him. The humans all remained behind, out of sight from the barricade guards.

They hadn't even crossed the street before weapons were raised. Twitch kept walking, despite the firepower aimed right at him. He didn't want to show weakness or fear. He had to look like he belonged.

The one human guard in the middle of the barricade shouted out. "Halt there! No further."

Twitch tried to summon his best Captain Rhys impression. "Stand down. We're SFU," he barked, not hesitating in his stride. He didn't look to see if the other three starats had held their nerve.

The human guard pushed forward and removed his helmet. He gestured for his company to lower their weapons, though they only did so hesitantly. "I never heard about any returning agents."

Twitch shrugged his shoulders. "I called it through. Have to report back to Snow." He flicked a brief smile onto his muzzle. "Wouldn't want to keep her waiting, would you?"

The human took a step back again. "No, sir. Better get going then. If you see Miss Jennings, inform her that we've met with no resistance here."

"Thank you," Twitch said, masking his grin and nodding his head in the human's direction. "Better keep your eyes and ears alert. We wouldn't want to be caught by surprise."

The human nodded. "Of course. I'm looking forward to putting this mess behind us and move on," he said, gesturing with one hand down the empty mall. "Best hurry, before Snow gets impatient."

"Most appreciated, thank you," Twitch replied. He scampered forward, trying to look urgent, but not desperate. They still needed to keep up the charade until they were safely inside the parliament building. At least now, beyond the first barricade, they would look more like they belonged. They had convinced the outer checkpoint that they should be let through, and that would give credibility to their presence.

David placed his hand around Twitch's waist as they walked down the deserted mall. "That went surprisingly well," the larger starat murmured, once they were out of hearing range of the barricade.

"I hope the rest goes just as well," Twitch replied. He flicked his tail. He got the feeling the barricade was the easy part. The hard part had yet to come.

The outdoor mall gently sloped down towards parliament. Twitch nervously glanced around. He could hear the footsteps of soldiers somewhere close by, in the adjacent streets. He forced his tail to remain out behind his legs, rather than tucking in between them. He didn't want to broadcast his worry back to the soldiers at the barricade, in case they were looking back.

The myriad of shops were dark, with the doors pulled closed and locked. No movement came from within them. Even Ceres had felt more crowded than the deserted mall. But for the occasional light twinkling in the tall skyscrapers above, Twitch might have thought the Inquisition's plan had worked anyway. He knew people were still alive, holed up in their homes in fear of what was happening. He had to remind himself that most people on Centaura had no knowledge of what had taken place in Hadrian.

Twitch couldn't be sure if he was the right starat to bring an end to things, but he knew someone had to try. He had gotten this far, at least. That had to mean something. Someone had to bring peace back to Centaura, for this was not meant to be a planet of war and fear.

Twitch didn't pretend to understand how President Shawn had managed to get into a position of power, and then use that status to fuel the Inquisition. There were so many gaps in his knowledge that he didn't even try to see the bigger picture. All he saw was humans and starats both trying to use fear to gain control over Centaura. First it had been President Shawn, but now Amy and Snow had used the situation to get control of the planet.

The burden of potential loss of life had been shifted away from Centaura. Now, the empire and Terra was in the line of fire. Even though Twitch had suffered so much under the empire's heel, he couldn't sit back and watch Amy annihilate an entire planet.

At the far end of the mall was the parliament buildings. The fur on the back of Twitch's neck rose as he looked towards it. The fate of Centaura had fallen on his shoulders. Twitch knew it did not matter if he thought he was ready or not. He had to succeed, no matter what. This would all come down to him and his small group of allies.

***

If the streets of Caledonia had seemed quiet and eerie, then the parliament buildings were anything but. The small park surrounding the large domed building teemed with soldiers constructing defensive fortifications on the edge of the roads. Massive concrete slabs were being installed, providing cover for the defending soldiers.

Twitch pinned his ears down. He knew there could only be one reason why the Starat Freedom Union were trying to fortify the government buildings. They expected an assault from the surviving military forces under the command of Fleet-Admiral Bosler.

No one bothered the four starats as they approached. The soldiers were all focused on getting their defensive fortifications into place. One soldier barked angrily at Twitch, but it was only to get the starat to hurry up and get behind the fortifications. As soon as the four starats slipped inside the barrier, another concrete slab was lowered into place, sealing off easy entry from the mall.

Twitch curled his tail as he scampered into the park. David and Nick hurried right behind him. William moved slightly ahead. The four starats appeared like they belonged, and no one had questioned their presence at all. Twitch's heart hammered loudly in his chest, fearing that any moment someone would look at them and realise that they didn't belong amongst them. He felt invisible again, a feeling he hadn't suffered since he had left Ceres with Captain Rhys.

Ceres felt like so long ago now. A distant memory that barely applied to him.

"What's the plan?" Nick murmured. In the noise of construction, Twitch could barely hear the other starat. They paused in the middle of the park to quickly talk, partially hidden by a tall, red stalk-like tree. Sticky sap dripped down from high tendrils, and Twitch stepped aside to avoid some of the fluid landing on his shoulder.

"We go in and find somewhere quiet so we can try to send a message to the fleet-admiral. If we can't, we find Bakir to see if she can help. And if we can't find her, then we find Amy or Snow,"

Twitch said quietly, speaking quickly as he warily watched some soldiers emerging from the parliament building doors.

"They'll probably find us pretty quickly," David cautioned.

Nick growled softly. "Then we make sure we move quickly, before they can stop us."

"I don't know if I like this," David warned. He placed his hand on Twitch's shoulder. "There's too many risks. We could get ourselves killed."

"No different to Hadrian," William said brusquely.

Twitch shivered as a cold tingle ran down his spine. He hated the thought, but he knew it had to be done. They had to stop Amy.

"Come on," he said, speaking around clenched teeth. He took a step forward before he could reconsider what he was doing.

The group of soldiers who had just come from the parliament building stepped aside for Twitch and his small group. They didn't even give the starats a second glance.

The doors to parliament were open. Warm air soaked out into the cool night, and the lights inside were brightly lit. The activity inside was just as busy as the park outside. Everyone Twitch saw was a soldier. Soft conversation murmured around them as orders were passed around and strategies concocted. They all wore the unmodified uniform of the Stellar Guard.

Six guards stood apart from the rest. They guarded the doors at the far end of the opening foyer, beneath the balcony level that stretched around most of the cavernous room. Twitch had never seen those doors open before, but he knew they led into the central chamber where most of the planet's governance was enacted from. The six guards protecting the door were heavily armed, and no one approached them.

Twitch flicked his tail nervously and turned away from them quickly, instead looking up the stairs towards the upper level. "We should get up there," he whispered.

"You've been here before?" Nick asked, warily staying close to Twitch's side.

"Twice. We came to see Minister Bakir. I hope she's safe," Twitch said.

"Probably safer than we are," David muttered.

William moved on ahead, slowly hauling himself up the stairs. His cybernetic limb moved stiffly, especially around the knee. Twitch knew he would have to take a look at it once everything was over.

Nick followed William, before he darted to one side at the top of the stairs. He placed his hand on a small map of the building on the wall, showing the fire escape points. He traced his finger around and tapped twice on it. He waved Twitch and David over to him. "Here, I think. Follow me."

Unlike the main foyer below, the wide corridors of the upper level were mostly empty. The doors to the right were all closed, and Twitch tried to avoid the portraits of the historical presidents on the left wall. He didn't like how their eyes seemed to watch him.

Despite his desire to keep his eyes forward, he found them attracted to the last frame. The final portrait had been defaced. Twitch slowed as his eyes were drawn to it. President Shawn looked out from the picture, but writing had been scrawled over in big, red lettering: TRAITOR.

"He got what he deserved," William growled, slowing down with Twitch to look at the defaced portrait.

"She must have used his plot to force her own way into power," David said. The larger starat moved forward a few paces, looking a little further around the curved corridor. He waved his hand, beckoning the other two forward. "I can see her."

Twitch nervously followed his partner. A few metres beyond the last portrait, the wall opened out into a massive window that continued to follow the curve of the corridor. From the height of Twitch's hip all the way to the ceiling, the window provided a perfect view into the chamber on the inside of the parliament building. The chamber was packed full of people; both human and starat.

Rows of benches curved around the inside of the chamber, all staggered in height so the lowest were right in the middle. The highest, closest to the outer walls, were only a couple of metres lower than the bottom edge of the window. A dividing walkway split the otherwise perfect circle, leading to the closed doors at the opposite end. In the middle of the chamber, in the centre of the circle of seats, was a raised plinth and a lectern.

Amy stood on the plinth, gesticulating as she gave her speech. She slowly turned on the spot so she could look to all sides of the crowded chamber. Twitch couldn't hear a word she spoke.

"We should keep moving," David said, tugging on Twitch's hand.

Twitch pulled back. "Wait, just a moment."

The starat's eyes quickly scanned through the chamber, looking for any familiar faces. There were two people he searched for, but he could find only one of them. Minister Bakir was sat at the far side of the chamber, right up against the wall. Maxwell was not with her, but that wasn't who Twitch was eager to see. The absence of Snow in the chamber filled him with worry.

"Snow isn't in there," he said slowly.

"We'll worry about her later. Come on," David said, giving Twitch's hand another pull.

This time, Twitch allowed himself to be led away. He quickly looked away from the chamber, his eyes wide as he stared ahead. He would have felt a lot more comfortable if Snow had been in the chamber with Amy. He half expected to see the albino emerge from around the gentle curve of the corridor, but the way ahead remained empty.

"I don't think we've got long," Twitch said. None of the others answered him. They all had to know that they were short on time and opportunities. Twitch could only hope that they were able to get done what needed to be done. One small message to the fleet-admiral was all that was needed. If she was warned of the dangerous situation in Caledonia, then she would be able to formulate a plan to deal with Amy's insurrection. Until then, everyone remained in grave danger. A scattered return to Caledonia could easily be picked off by the SFU ships in orbit.

Nick continued to lead the way. He hurried around the curved corridor, keeping his eyes on the wall to the right. He finally found the door he had been searching for, and he scampered across to open it.

Inside the small room were several screens and holographic projectors, all switched off. A single table was surrounded by several chairs. Nick pulled William and David inside, leaving Twitch to close the door behind them.

"What is this place?" Twitch asked. He crouched down in front of the screens, running his hand lightly over the control panels beneath them.

"Media room," Nick replied simply. He had crouched down beside Twitch, reaching behind the control panel. "There should be broadcasting equipment in here. If you can't get hold of Steph, I might be able to configure this to reach the fleet-admiral."

"How long will it take you?" David asked. He kept his eyes on the door, and the small screen on the wall beside it. The screen showed the corridor outside, which remained empty.

"Five to ten minutes, I think?" Nick said uncertainly. He pulled out a small tablet and switched on the large screens. Static flickered across it for a few moments, before with a few presses on the tablet, Nick got the screen to show a camera viewing of himself. The starat grinned, and his mirror image on the screen repeated the gesture half a second later.

"Do you need help?" William asked.

Nick peered beneath the camera and crawled into the small space underneath. "No," he replied, his voice muffled. "No space for anyone else. Just tell me if the screen goes dead."

Twitch watched Nick working with interest. The other starat had been able to set up the screens to record a message, but the more important part was getting the media centre to broadcast the message to the required recipient. He needed to be able to get in contact with the fleet-admiral, but Twitch didn't like the look of the frustrated frown permanently etched onto Nick's brow whenever he briefly emerged, nor the angry swish of his tail.

Twitch didn't interrupt Nick. He let the starat work as he occasionally turned from the tablet to change the input settings beneath the screens. Nothing seemed to make him satisfied, even as he got Twitch's help to unplug a few wires and reconnect them elsewhere.

Eventually, Nick growled in frustration. "I think they've blocked the Resistance frequencies. I'm not going to be able to get through to Hadrian."

Twitch perked his ears up. "We may not need to," he said slowly. He looked around the small, cramped room. "This is a media centre, right? They broadcast from here. Interviews and stuff."

"Yeah..." Nick said uncertainly.

"Can't we just broadcast to the holonetwork?"

Nick shook his head. "This doesn't control the holonetwork. Without someone at the network patching us in, we'll just be sending a message into the void."

Twitch sighed and sat down in one of the chairs, resting his elbows on the table. "Alright. So we can't do that. Was worth a try. Still nothing from Steph?"

"Nothing," David said with a sigh. His tail flicked at the tip as he sat on the edge of a table, his feet dangling over the floor. His tablet rested on the table by his side. There were no new notifications.

"Do you think something has happened there?" William asked nervously.

"I hope not," Twitch said. He stared down at the floor, but before he could go too far down that dark path of thoughts, a buzzing vibration filled the room.

All four starats stared at the tablet by David. A new incoming call flashed up, coming from Steph.

"Could they trace the call?" William asked.

"Probably, but that doesn't matter. We have to speak to them," Nick said quickly, pushing back William and giving David a little space.

"The SFU know what we need to say anyway," Twitch said. He shrugged and flicked his ears up. "Worst case, they learn we're here and find us a little quicker. Better answer it."

David swiped his hand across the tablet to answer the call. "Hello?"

Steph's bright voice came through the speaker. "David! Oh, I'm so glad you're back safe. Sorry I missed your calls. We're pretty busy as we clear everything up here. Should be on our way back in a few hours. Can't wait to see you again," she said. Twitch could hear several loud noises coming from her end of the call, with humans shouting indistinctly to each other.

"It's a trap, Steph," Twitch said, breaking through her excited babble. "We need to speak to Aaron or the fleet-admiral, urgently."

A moment of silence came through the call. "What's happened? Are you alright?" Steph said, her voice immediately sober and quiet.

"We're fine. For now. But we need to get a message to the fleet-admiral," Twitch said. He placed his hands on the table as he spoke, looking nervously up to the small screen beside the door. A chill ran down his spine, though the corridor outside remained empty. He glanced across to Nick, who shuddered.

"I think she knows we're here," the black-furred starat whispered.

Steph didn't give any indication she had heard Nick. "I'll see if I can find her. Give me a minute, alright?"

Twitch curled his tail up. "I don't know if we have that long."

"Are you sure? Then tell me. I can pass the message on," Steph said quickly.

Nick rose to his feet. He placed his hand on the door and closed his eyes. A burst of cinnamon filled Twitch's nose for a brief moment, before fading into nothingness once more. Twitch couldn't be sure whether the smell came from Nick, or from some other source. The thought bothered him, and he glanced down nervously at the tablet on the table.

"We were shot down," Twitch said, speaking quickly so he could get everything out before they were interrupted. "Amy and the SFU have defected and locked down the capital. The military that got left behind have all sided with her. She has control of the government and at least the *Freedom*, possibly more ships. I don't know how, but I think she's trying to take control. Everything is being fortified."

"Shit, are you sure?" Steph asked. Her eyes were wide. She glanced around, looking for something that Twitch could not see.

David moved to Nick's side, peering at the monitor of the corridor. With his partner in the way, Twitch could no longer see the screen. He tried to put it out of mind. He focused on the call with Steph.

"Yeah. I don't know what we're going to be able to do here, but we're already in parliament," Twitch said, his tail curling at the thought. He forced his ears to remain upright, not wanting to portray his worries to Steph. "Just tell the fleet-admiral that this is a trap. She has to be aware of it."

"I'll tell her. I'll find her right now and tell her," Steph said. "Stay safe, Twitch. We'll get to you as soon-"

Sudden static cut through Steph's voice. Twitch's eyes widened as he stared down at the tablet. The call had been severed, and the starat didn't believe it had anything to do with what the Steph had done at her end, and Twitch knew he hadn't touched anything. Something or someone had interfered with the call.

Nick barked out the words Twitch had been dreading. "We have movement."

William slid off the table, positioning himself between the other two starats and Twitch, also keeping himself in the way of the door.

"How many?" Twitch asked.

"Six guards and one unarmed starat," David replied. "Amy."

The door opened. Amy was framed in the doorway, flanked by her guards. Rifles were aimed at each of the starats.

"Well isn't this a delightful pleasure to see you again," Amy said brightly. She held her hands out wide. "I think it would be a good idea if you came out with me, rather than hiding away in this tiny little box. Don't you think?"

Twitch knew they had no choice. His hand moved down to his hip, brushing lightly over his shorts. Beneath his clothes, he could feel his furless synthetic skin. He doubted his ability to pull a weapon free before he was shot. His hand slowly rose again, clenching into a fist and staying firmly in front of his chest.

"We'll come," Twitch said, when no one else seemed likely to break the silence. William had been baring his teeth in a silent snarl, but he had failed to vocalise anything.

"Good. I'm sure you'll want to see what I'm building here. Nothing crude and crass like the Inquisition, which you so helpfully exposed for me," Amy replied. She took a couple of steps back, then spun on her toes to lead the four following starats through the corridor, arcing further around the wide circle.

Twitch glanced back a couple of times. The guards remained a couple of paces behind them, keeping their rifles loaded and raised. There was no chance of escape, and nor did they have an opportunity to fight back. The moment they showed any sign of aggression, Twitch knew they would be shot. He had no desire to know what that felt like.

None of the starats dared to approach Amy. They all stayed a few steps behind her; close enough that she knew they followed her, but not close enough that they posed an immediate potential threat. Twitch knew she had to have some plan to counter them. Snow had to be around somewhere close by, ready with her mystical powers.

Halfway around the massive circling corridor, a flight of stairs on the right side led up to a higher level. Amy led the four starats up to the top, which opened out into an expansive, ornate office. Large windows looked out into the city, with the park just below. Twitch could just about see the defected military completing their ground fortifications around the parliament buildings. The windows shook as a military shuttle roared close by.

Amy took a seat at the desk in front of the windows. No one else was present in the room, but another starat came up the stairs behind Twitch and closed the door for them. Twitch looked around to see Mortimer. His usual bright smile wasn't present, and he stood in solemn silence in front of the closed door.

"Well, Twitch and David. It is lovely to see you again. And of course, you both as well, Nick and William. I see you found Hadrian successful," Amy said casually. She gestured to the seats in front of her desk. "Why don't you take a seat?"

"I think I'd rather stand," Twitch replied quickly. He wanted to remain on his feet, ready to react to anything Amy might have prepared for him. David and Nick both remained standing too, unmoving despite Amy's offer. Only William approached one of the seats. He perched on the edge of the chair, his legs tensed and ready to move.

Amy smirked as she looked over Twitch. "With those new legs, I'm not surprised. Taken a nice upgrade from what we gave you. Didn't you like them? We worked so hard to get them for you."

"I found they monitored where I was a little too much for my liking," Twitch said with a growl, ignoring David's hand that went across his chest.

Amy barely even blinked. She just tilted her head to the right slightly. "We just wanted to make sure you were safe. William, too. I see you decided to keep your leg, though I understand Twitch tinkered with that as well."

Twitch scoffed and crossed his arms over his chest. "Keep us safe? Bullshit."

"Is that so hard to believe?" Amy asked, still with that same slight smile.

William shuffled nervously. Twitch could see him stare down at his cybernetic leg.

"Given I was just shot down out of the sky by your order, yes. I find that very hard to believe," Twitch growled. He refused to look at Amy, annoyed by her constant smirk. Instead, he focused his attention on the city outside the windows. Still, no one walked the streets but for the soldiers patrolling around the parliament parklands.

"We had no way of knowing you were on that shuttle. If you'd have kept our cybernetics, then we would have," Amy said.

Twitch spun around and snarled. "Don't turn this on me. If you'd have kept spying on me, I'd have been locked up somewhere in Caledonia while my friends were off dying."

Amy shrugged her shoulders. "Not that it matters now. The government just voted to elect a new President to lead Centaura in this emergency situation."

"Yourself?" Nick asked bitterly.

Amy giggled. That giggle soon turned into a full laugh. "Me? Don't be so silly. Things aren't so crazy that they'd elect someone who isn't even a government official. Every time that's happened in the past, only chaos and destruction have followed. There are countless stories of it happening on Terra. No, they're smarter than that. I needed someone pliable who I could trust to do my bidding."

Twitch took a step back and frowned. This wasn't what he had expected. "Who?"

"President Bakir will lead Centaura into a glorious new future, free of Terran fear," Amy said.

Twitch took another step back. His head spun. "Minister Bakir? That doesn't make sense. She would never do that!"

"It's amazing what someone will do when given the offer of power," Amy said, leaning back in her chair. She hooked her arms behind her head and flashed her teeth to Twitch. "With me as her top advisor, she has already been briefed on the Inquisition's threat, and how they received backing from the Terran Emperor."

"But it came from the Vatican," Nick said. He began to advance on Amy. She lifted her hand. Nick halted as though he had been grabbed. He took a deep breath and hissed quietly. "You're lying to her so you can start your war."

"I'm starting no war, Nick. I'm finishing one, once and for all."

Nick ran his hands over his muzzle and growled. "You know nothing of what it's like over there."

"I know enough. You said it yourself, Nick. The humans there are bastards who mistreat starats, and the starats themselves are too weak and afraid to fight back," Amy said calmly. She turned to look right at Twitch. "I know you are, no matter how much you might protest it. Terran starats will never be free. There is no option but to exterminate them along with their oppressors."

"I never said they should all be killed," Nick growled.

William clenched his fists. "I have as much reason as any to despise the lot of them," he snarled. "I lost a leg to their mistreatment, but the human who did that to me died on the shuttle you shot down. I will never forgive him, but I never wished that death on him. Just as I will never wish death on any human in the empire."

Amy sat back and clasped her hands together. "Your devotion is admirable, but that is the problem. No empire starat can truly be free from their control or influence. They must be destroyed."

Twitch growled and bared his teeth. "There are other ways. You keep speaking as though they're all without hope, but that's not true."

"It's too late," Amy replied. "I have already placed agents throughout the Sol System, ready to act at a specific time. Only my command can prevent their actions, and nothing you can do or say will make me give that order."

"Fuck," Twitch said. His head spun. He felt dizzy, but his cybernetic legs kept him stable. "When?"

Amy barked in laughter. "I'm not going to tell you what my plan is. What kind of idiot do you take me for? Even in the unlikely event of your Resistance friends coming back and taking me prisoner, I don't want you to know how to unravel my plans."

"Please, you can't do this," Twitch said. He felt like dropping to his knees in front of the other starat, but he already knew that nothing he said would change her mind. He should have seen this coming a long time ago, from those first meetings with the Starat Freedom Union. He, like Captain Rhys, had believed she held the best interests of starats in all three settled systems at heart. She did not. He should have shot her when she killed Leandro.

David placed his hand on Twitch's shoulder and pulled him back, away from Amy's desk. "What will you do with us?" David asked.

"I'll keep you safe, don't worry. That has always been my goal; to minimise loss of life here, especially with starats," Amy said with a shrug. "You'll always be weaker mentally than starats born here, but you're Centauran enough for me."

Amy snapped her fingers to Mortimer. "Take them down to the bunker for safe-keeping."

Mortimer opened the door. "If you'll come with me then."

Twitch hesitated for a moment. He didn't want to go, but he also didn't know what to say. A rifle pressed into his back as one of the guards gave him some additional motivation to move. He stared at Amy for a few moments, before slowly turning on his toes. The starat behind the desk gave him a little wave as he followed Mortimer.

Amy's voice chased him out of the office. "Soon this will all be over. We will have peace for everyone."

Twitch folded his ears. There would be peace, but the cost for it would be far too great. Billions would be killed, of human and starat alike. Twitch had already fought for Centaura. He never thought he would need to fight for Terra too, but he didn't see any way that he could help right now. He had done what he could. Fleet-Admiral

Bosler knew about the second coup that had taken place. He could only hope that she would be able to come up with a plan to dislodge Amy from her position of power in time, because he would never survive long enough to stop Amy from carrying out her plans.

Then something would need to be done about Terra.

As Twitch descended the stairs back down to the corridor, he felt tears forming in his eyes. He needed to cry, but he just about managed to hold back. After everything he had already fought for, after everything he had already lost, there was still so much more to do. He just wanted to stop, but until the last battle had been won, he couldn't rest.

More than ever, Twitch craved the support of Captain Rhys. He would know what to do in such a situation, but the former human still hadn't come back. Twitch's ears couldn't get any lower, but his mood darkened to black.

Twitch knew he had to accept the obvious.

Captain Rhys was lying dead on Pluto, killed by Snow.

Captain Rhys wasn't coming back to save them.

Twitch held onto David's hand, so he didn't feel so alone. David pulled Twitch closer. The two walked side-by-side, with Nick just ahead of them, and William behind.

All six of the armed guards came with them. Mortimer was taking no chances.

For the first time, Twitch felt truly hopeless. They were beyond the reach of any allies. If they were to make a difference, it had to be from their own efforts. At least he still had David by his side. If he didn't have his partner, then Twitch knew his mood would be darker still.

The knowledge that Captain Rhys wouldn't be coming back hurt him, but what hurt more was the revelation that Minister Bakir had betrayed her ideals and sided with Amy. Twitch's tail thumped angrily at the thought, but a little seed of doubt wormed into his mind. His eyes sharply flicked towards the curved window on the inside of the corridor.

He had seen Minister Bakir in the crowd. His ears perked up slightly. He had little knowledge of how the Centauran government worked, but he doubted that the president would sit right up at the back of the great chamber. They would be in the middle, close to the lectern Amy had been speaking from.

Twitch suppressed the instinctive intake of breath. He kept his head low and tried to put the thought out of his mind, lest Mortimer and his guards realise he had seen something new.

Amy had lied.

But just what had she lied about, and why?

Twitch knew he needed to find out the answer to that, and quickly.

# chapter twenty-two

Underneath parliament was a network of small, narrow corridors. Several locked doors gave the obvious impression that these routes were not for public access. The walls were cold, grey concrete, with exposed lighting fixtures overhead. There was none of the pomp and glamour of the parliament building above.

Twitch felt nervous. No one would know where they were so deep underground, and they wouldn't be able to get another message out to Steph, even if Mortimer hadn't already confiscated David's tablet and their weapons. Mortimer had not asked for the pistol hidden in Twitch's leg, and Twitch had not been about to volunteer the weapon.

Finally, Mortimer came to a halt. He stood outside an airlock, which he wrenched open. Air hissed into the chamber beyond. "Through you go. You'll be safe down here."

"Looks more like we're being hidden away until we can be killed," Nick muttered darkly.

Twitch wasn't sure if Mortimer was meant to hear that, but Amy's assistant raised his brow. "If we wanted to kill you, we'd have done it already," he said in surprise. "Didn't you listen to Amy? She wants to save as many lives as possible. Especially starats."

"Except for those on Terra," David said bitterly. His eyes narrowed as he looked down at the smaller starat.

"A necessary loss. Now, please hurry. I'd hate to get demanding," Mortimer said. He gestured towards the airlock again and took a step back nearer the group of guards.

Twitch glanced into the airlock. Beyond the second door he could see a flash of movement, coming from within the bunker. He thought he saw brown fur against the small transparent panel towards the top of the door. At least one other starat was already inside. He tugged on David's hand. "Come on. Let's just go."

This time, David didn't protest. He stepped into the airlock with Twitch, with Nick and William both reluctantly following a moment later. The four starats stood close together as the outer door sealed closed with a hiss. There was barely any room for the four of them to stand, even pressed up close to each other. Mortimer remained in sight until the door completely locked closed.

Only then did the inner door open. Twitch quickly stepped through it, finding himself in a large room with several other doors at the far side. The lights were bright, shining down on several crates of supplies scattered haphazardly through the room. He was curious about what lay beyond the other doors, but before he had chance to explore anything, his eyes fell on the lone figure who had already been in the room.

Twitch had been right. A starat was present. Minister Bakir's assistant, Maxwell, stood before them. His shoulders were hunched over, and he cradled his cybernetic arm in his other hand. His synthetic hand had been ripped from his wrist, leaving exposed wiring hanging from the shattered end.

"I'm sorry to see you here," Maxwell said, keeping his eyes dropped to the ground. He shuffled backwards and turned away. "This is not a good place to be."

"What happened to you?" David asked, hurrying up to Maxwell's side and coaxing his damaged arm free. There was nothing David could do to fix it. He couldn't fix machines and computers. That was Twitch's area, but even he couldn't do anything without the missing hand.

Maxwell laughed bitterly, without humour. He glanced up to the ceiling of the bunker. "Amy happened. She dragged me away from the minister and threw me down here."

"Why?" Twitch asked, casting a nervous glance towards the door.

"I didn't fall for her lies," Maxwell said. He pulled away from David. "Come on through. I'll try and explain everything I know."

Maxwell led the starats through the central of the three doors opposite the airlock. The door led through to a second room which had the appearance of a communal living area. From his brief glances to the other two doors, he could see a kitchen to the right, and dormitory to the left. With all that, Twitch expected there to be the facilities for a longer stay, but everything still seemed sparser than he had anticipated. If this had been where President Shawn's loyal ministers had set aside to potentially see out the Denitchev drive's displacement of Centaura, then Twitch had been expecting somewhere far more comfortable.

The injured starat slumped into a seat. He tapped his remaining fingers on the table. "Amy waltzed into parliament yesterday and presented evidence the president had been involved in a conspiracy to destroy Centaura. Arguments were had. Traitors were weeded out and removed. Some twenty ministers were taken out and placed under arrest for being a part of the president's plot. They'd have come down here when it all happened, but it never did."

"We stopped that," Twitch said quietly. He took a seat opposite Maxwell. "The president was stopped and taken prisoner. But what happened here? What did Minister Bakir do?"

Maxwell sighed. He dropped his head. "We were called in to see Amy and that albino, Snow, just after the first special session. Amy offered the minister to become the new president in Shawn's place, but she refused. The minister didn't trust Amy. There was a confrontation," the starat said, lifting his broken cybernetic arm. "I don't know what happened next. Everything got foggy and I woke up in here."

William bared his teeth. "Snow used that memory thing again, the same thing she used on me on Pluto." He glanced to Twitch. "I don't think Minister Bakir is the one in control of all of this, no matter what nonsense Amy may have peddled us."

"Alright. So, what do we need to do now?" David asked, spreading his hands wide. His tail curled up in resignation.

"What can we do?" Maxwell said, sounding despondent. He thumped his wrist down on the table, the loose wiring in his cybernetics spilling out. "I tried the door. It's sealed closed. I can't open it from this side. It will only open from the outside, and there's no other way out."

"I can get us out," Nick said, shrugging his shoulders. He held his palm open, letting a small crackle of subspace flicker into being. "That door can be manipulated, same as anything else."

"I think they might have thought about that," Twitch said warily, but Nick scampered back out into the other room without a word.

Twitch hurried after him. William half-heartedly rose to his feet, though the other two remained sitting. Twitch stopped by the door, staring as Nick placed his hands on the inside of the airlock. The scent of cinnamon came quickly to the bunker, soon followed by the sizzle of burned fur.

Nick yelped and jumped back, cradling his arm close to his chest. The door remained sealed closed.

"Are you alright?" Twitch asked, quickly closing the gap between the two starats and pulling Nick away from the door.

"I don't understand. That should have worked," Nick said. His ears had curled forward in confusion. "It's like... Someone was already touching them through subspace, but that's not possible. She couldn't know when I was going to do that. She'd wear herself out too quickly."

"You think Snow stopped you?"

"I know so," Nick said warily. He looked around the bunker, but no one else was present but the two of them, with Maxwell and David still in the adjoining room. "I thought I felt her there, and that's what burned me. But... she isn't here."

"Are you sure?" Twitch asked nervously.

Nick shook his head. He took another step back away from the door. "I think she's coming though."

Twitch pulled Nick back through to the middle room. He quickly explained what had happened to the other three, waiting expectantly. The cybernetically enhanced starat did not seem surprised by Nick's failure, but they all expressed concern that Snow could be on her way. To Twitch, that meant only one thing. Snow had come to finish the job Amy had started.

"We need to get out of here," Twitch said, but he just slumped down into a seat and looked up to the ceiling. The bunker had been designed to protect its occupants against the void and vacuum of space. The only way in or out was the airlock, and they already knew that couldn't be breached from the inside. They were locked inside until someone from the outside chose to release them, or until Snow's hold on the door was lessened.

"What more can we do though?" David asked.

Twitch shrugged his shoulders. "I don't know. Something. Anything."

"We've already told the fleet-admiral the situation," David continued. He placed his hand on Twitch's knee. "I honestly don't know what else we can do other than wait for her to lead the liberation."

"And if she fails? We just wait for Amy to destroy Terra?"

"Then we do what we can when we're let out," David said softly. He lifted his hand up to cup against Twitch's chin. "I want to do something, too. I really do. But we're powerless here."

Twitch sighed. He leaned into the touch of his partner. "I'm sick of being powerless. I've been that way all my life, and I finally thought that was starting to change."

"You're not powerless, Twitch," Nick said. The black-furred starat still held his burned hand close to his chest, and he tentatively flexed his fingers open and closed. "You stopped the Inquisition."

Twitch pinned his ears down. "I had help."

"And you have help now. We're in this together," William said. He managed a smile as he leaned back against the table, keeping his cybernetic leg lifted from the floor. "This isn't over yet, no matter what Snow and Amy might think. We can't let them get away with this."

Twitch looked around at the starats with him. All four looked scared. He could see it in the set of their ears and the constant flick of their tails. But, at the same time, he could see determination and confidence there. Four of their number had come from the empire, with only Maxwell being a native Centauran. If Amy believed them weaker because of where they had been born, then Twitch knew they would prove her wrong.

If anything, Twitch believed they were stronger. He had survived things that no Centauran starat would be able to imagine. He had been abused and tortured almost since the day he had been born. Because of that, he had to work hard to ensure that every starat was given the same opportunity at freedom as he had received. That meant saving their lives, even if it also meant saving the life of the human oppressors. The death that Amy had planned for Terra was too cruel, even for them.

Twitch breathed out slowly. "Alright. But I'm not going to be sitting around in here and doing nothing but wait," he said, gripping the tip of his tail in both hands. "There has to be a way out of here. If this was meant to be used to protect parliament in subspace, then there has to be some way to communicate to the outside."

Maxwell pinned his ears down. "I tried that already. All outbound communication is frozen," he said, flicking his tail to the side. He bit down on the tip of his tongue. "Inbound communication still seems active, but no one knows we're down here."

"Then we can't call for help," Twitch said. He frowned and stared at the airlock door. One ear perked upright. "If we can't break through that door with subspace, then we do it the old-fashioned way. I know how to override a lock."

"How long will that take you?" Nick asked, warily eying the door as though it was going to hurt him again.

Twitch shrugged and swept his eyes around the small bunker. "Without any proper tools, it's hard to say. Within the hour."

David put his hand on Twitch's shoulder. "I know you can do it," he said with a smile.

Twitch smiled back. He swished his tail to the side and stretched his arms above his head. It was time to get to work. One way or another, he would get that airlock door open.

Before Twitch could begin, Nick pulled back on his arms. The black-furred starat continued to stare at the airlock door, almost seeming to look right through the solid metal. "Wait," he whispered. He stepped forward, moving in front of Twitch. Shadows moved on the small glass panel. Someone was outside. Twitch already knew who.

The door opened. A solitary figure came through. The doors sealed shut behind the albino. She stood with her hands behind her back, looking sightlessly around the bunker while she waited for the five starats to stand in front of her.

Twitch's fingers tensed as he slowly moved down to his hidden pistol. Snow lifted her hand and waggled her finger.

"You might think you outnumber me," the albino said, speaking in her gentle, soft voice with a hint of light rebuke, "but you do not outpower me. If you even think of attacking me, you will be dead long before you can lay a finger on me."

"What do you want?" Nick snapped. His teeth were bared.

"Such aggression," the albino said, shaking her head. The shadow of a smile touched her muzzle. "I merely came to give you something."

"And what's that?" Twitch demanded. He stood directly in front of David, feeling the comforting presence of his partner looming over his shoulder. He didn't trust the albino, but nor could he see any option other than to stand warily and listen to what she had to say. He didn't want to put her bravado and confidence to the test.

Snow pulled her other hand out from behind her back. She carried a small clay pot, which she cradled gently. She took a couple of steps forward, not seeming to worry about the recoil from the other starats at her approach. "I thought you deserved to have this."

The albino remained still as she held the pot up, raising it into the air before the five starats. Twitch cautiously reached for it.

"What is it?" David asked.

"Your friend, Leandro," Snow said. She released her grip on the urn as Twitch took it into his hands. "We handled him with respect and care, you have our word on that."

"Oh, fuck off," William snarled. He tried to push past Twitch, but Nick held him back. "You do not get to come here and bring us Leandro as though nothing happened."

Twitch's throat tightened. He clutched the urn close to his chest. Tears welled in his eyes. "She killed him… she killed him with no reason. This does not make up for that."

"Amy should not have done that," Snow admitted. She kept her sightless eyes raised high, seemingly watching something just above David's shoulder. She did not even appear to notice William's anger. "But she did, and on her behalf I apologise. I hope this small gesture helps ease the grief a small amount. I mean that with all sincerity."

"If you mean it, let us leave so we can give Leandro our proper respects," David said with a growl. His hand tightened around Twitch's shoulder.

Snow shook her head. Her pink eyes dropped down. "No. For your safety, I ask you remain here. A battle will soon be waged above us. I have a part to play in it, but you do not need to risk yourselves. Amy truly wants you to remain safe."

"Our friends will be up there, dying," Nick said, jabbing his finger towards the ceiling. "Just like we could have done in that shuttle you had shot down."

"They are welcome to set down their weapons. We will give them the opportunity to do so," Snow said. She clasped her hands together and smiled. "We are happy to work with the fleet-admiral and the remainder of the Resistance. After all, we have only the best interests of Centaura at heart."

Nick growled. "Save the bullshit. We're not on board with your schemes, and we never will be. This is about power, pure and simple. You and Amy want it, and you're willing to do anything to maintain it."

"Power is safety, Nick," Snow replied softly. "Starats have been unsafe for too long. We are simply giving them that safety."

"By murdering billions. By murdering people like Captain Rhys," William growled. He crossed his arms and turned his back on Snow, who merely shrugged her shoulders.

"No matter what you believe, you will still be treated with respect, so long as you stay out of our way," Snow said. She started to turn on her toes. Her tail flicked around, sending a waft of cinnamon scent towards Twitch. "Stay in here, and you will be safe. Try to escape, and you will feel our wrath. The choice is yours. Do not force our hand."

Snow stumbled as she started to walk. She growled to herself and regained her balance, an irate flick of her tail giving away the emotions that never came to her face. She didn't look back at the five starats behind her, and nor did she say anything else as she stalked towards the airlock doors. They opened to her touch, but then closed again before Nick could chase after her.

The black-furred starat yelped and recoiled as the doors snapped closed, almost taking an arm with them. He hissed at the closed door, peering into the transparent panel that looked into the central chamber of the airlock.

Nick didn't turn around until the outer door of the airlock had closed. Twitch could hear it hiss as the doors sealed shut, keeping them trapped within the bunker once more.

William growled to himself, but Twitch could only focus on the urn in his hands. He could barely believe he had it. When Richard had been cremated, there had been a memorial for Leandro as well, complete with a small, empty urn as remembrance for the grey-furred starat, whose body had never been recovered.

Now Twitch had that, returned by the very same starat who had taken Leandro's life. He didn't know what to feel. His mind felt like it was being ripped apart by confusion and doubt. He had watched Amy kill Leandro in cold blood. The old starat had not seen the attack coming. Amy did not deserve to be trusted again, but she – through Snow – had returned Leandro's ashes. It did nothing to repair the damage done, but in that small moment, he could at least be relieved that Leandro had been returned to them in some way.

In a daze, Twitch slipped back into the other room and sat down. He gently placed the urn on the table, staring at it. The urn was simple, being made of clay. Leandro's name had been etched around the sealed lid. The clay itself had been painted dark, inky black. Small pricks of light splashed across the darkness, looking to Twitch like a starry night sky.

David followed Twitch, though the other three starats all remained in the other room. The larger starat placed his hands on Twitch's shoulders. "Are you feeling alright?"

Twitch realised tears had wetted his cheeks. He sniffed and nodded. "Yeah, I think so. Just a shock, that's all."

"I know, it's tough. We all miss him, but I feel like we've barely been able to grieve him," David said sadly. He rested his head against Twitch's. "Both Leandro and Richard. One day we'll be able to sit down and properly think about them, but everything has just been too... I don't know."

"Crazy? Chaotic? Insane?" Twitch offered. He smiled weakly and rested his cheek against David's.

"I knew I was signing up for all that with you, but I didn't expect it quite like this," David said with a chuckle.

"Need to keep you excited," Twitch said. He nuzzled in and gave David a quick kiss. "But a little less excitement in the future, perhaps."

"Deal," David replied.

Twitch tried to keep his smile, but every time he looked around and saw the bunker around them, he felt it waning. "We just need to fix this mess first, and then we can have a nice, relaxing life with nothing to worry about. No humans to boss us around. No one threatening to blow up the planet."

"How did we live without that constant excitement, though?" David asked. He sighed and shook his head.

Twitch thought his partner looked tired. David's ears didn't perk up all the way, despite the smile on his face, and his coffee-coloured fur wasn't as sleek as it usually was. Both of them looked messy and untidy, with stains of blood and dirt still smeared over their arms and legs.

"I'm sure we could find something. Live out in a nice house somewhere, adopt a couple of kits," Twitch said, sticking his tongue out.

David froze entirely. His mouth hung open and his ears pinned back. "Kits?" he asked slowly. "Never thought you'd want kits."

Twitch stuck the tip of his tongue out between his lips. He shrugged and spread his hands wide. "They can't be as difficult as any of this stuff. They'll be a breeze."

David gently ruffled through Twitch's headfur. "I think that's perhaps a conversation for another time."

"I just want something to hope for again, to look forward to," Twitch said quietly. He didn't dare look up at David. He didn't want to see the sorry or pity in his partner's eyes. His mind swirled with fear for the future, especially if it was one in which Amy and Snow held power. He feared for when she might turn her wrath to someone closer to Twitch's new home. He feared for his friends; new and old. David and Steph were the starats he had known the longest, but newer friends like William and Nick were fast growing important to him, and he had already lost Leandro, Richard, and Captain Rhys.

David held onto Twitch's hands, both gripped tightly in his. "I will protect you, no matter what the cost. I won't let anything bad happen to you."

"Just don't let anything bad happen to yourself," Twitch replied. He wriggled his hands out of David's, only to pull the larger starat into a hug. "You're more important to me than anyone or anything else."

David kissed Twitch. "I promise. Nothing will happen to me. Now, why don't you get started on that door, and I'll see if there's any tools that you can use."

Twitch took a deep breath to clear his mind. He looked towards Leandro's urn and sighed softly. "Alright. Let's get started."

***

The bunker was well-stocked with food and supplies necessary for several weeks, even if the bunker had been filled with a dozen people. A few personal belongings had been placed in the dormitory: pictures, trinkets, and locked tablets had been scattered around the beds. As far as Twitch had been able to tell, the owners of all the belongings had been human; likely the ministers who would have been sheltering in the bunker when the drive had gone off.

After Amy's takeover of parliament, and the Resistance foiling Shawn's plans, those belongings had been abandoned as the ministers had been taken into custody. Twitch had suffered a brief moment of worry as he wondered what had happened to those humans. He had quickly put the thought from his mind as he knew he could do nothing to help them, and that they had been plotting with Shawn and the Inquisition to destroy the planet. He had little sympathy for them after that.

Food supplies were simple, but enough to last for a long time. Twitch hoped not to learn just how long. They had never been given any estimation of just how long they would be locked in the bunker, but Twitch wanted to get out long before Amy decided to free them. The starat tried not to think too much about what might happen if Amy and Snow were defeated without anyone knowing where they were, and he was unable to break the airlock door. He could only hope that if that happened, Nick would be able to use subspace to rip open the door; that Snow's protections would fade in time.

Twitch had lost track of time, but he did not think he had achieved his one hour estimation. He had lowered the power settings in his legs to extend their life, having found no recharging points for them through the bunker. That had left him almost immobile, moving only when necessary. He spent most of the time sitting in front of the airlock door, prying open the panels on either side as he tried to access the electronics of the lock. William and Nick kept him company of most of the time, while David rested with Maxwell in the other room. They talked of the stars.

"I never saw them," Twitch said, his tail draped across his lap. He had a screwdriver in his hand, one that David had been able to find in the back room of the bunker. "I never left Ceres before Captain Rhys took me away."

"I couldn't imagine being stuck on a worse place," Nick said, sticking his tongue out. He held a few other screwdrivers and rolls of tape, but Twitch had not needed any of those yet.

William grimaced in sympathy. "At least the *Harvester* went to different places. I got to see Terra and the Jovian moons. Even Mars looks nice, if you ignore all the bigots who live there."

"Did either of you ever make it as far as Sirius?" Twitch asked, pausing in his work for a moment to glance between the other two starats.

William shook his head, but Nick nodded. "Once," the black-furred starat said. He twirled the roll of tape around one finger. "Aaron was deployed out on Cymru for six months a few years back."

"What was that like?" Twitch asked. He leaned forward, ignoring the numbness in his legs. The low power mode made him uncomfortable, but he didn't want to take the chance of being stuck in the bunker without any ability to walk.

Nick exhaled slowly. "It was like nothing I'd ever seen before," he said. A smile broke across his muzzle. "It's a binary star system. The planets all orbit around both stars."

"I always thought the CGP was around a binary star as well," Twitch said. He glanced up, though there was no chance of seeing Prox above.

"Nah, the binary stars are still a long way from here. Prox very distantly orbits around them," Nick said. He tapped the spare screwdriver against the floor. "On Cymru there was two suns in the sky. It was absolutely beautiful."

"I'd have thought that got really hot," William said in distaste. "That's definitely the worst part about Centaura. Apart from the Inquisition and everything."

Twitch leaned forward a little more, digging in deeper with his screwdriver. Through a bundle of cables, he thought he could see what he had been searching for. A small, capped box that would contain the dead switch to force the airlock to open. It was in an awkward position, and he struggled to shift himself so he could reach.

"I want to go out there sometime," Twitch said. His imagination ran with the thought of two suns in the sky. Prox was a marvel in and of itself, and Twitch loved the eerie twilight glow the red star gave to the planet, but to have two suns in the sky sounded like it would take his breath away.

The conversation was interrupted. A low beeping started to fill the bunker, distracting the starats in an instant. Twitch pulled away from the door, holding his hands up. "I didn't do that," he said, his ears flicking back and forth as he tried to find the source of the noise.

Nick quickly found what beeped. He padded towards the corner of the room with the communications array. A red light flashed in time with the beeping.

"Why's it doing that?" Twitch asked nervously. He remained sat on the floor, not wanting to put unneeded power through his legs.

Nick flicked the array screen on. The beeping stopped instantly, and the red flashing light switched itself off. Static formed across the screen, before flicking to black. The starat sighed and started to turn away, before the screen abruptly switched on once more, this time in full colour with an image of a group of humans. At the front of the group was Aleksandr Chekolin. This time, Twitch did rise to his feet. He leaned on William for support as he struggled to regain his balance with many of the sensors switched off in his legs.

The *Freedom's* pilot clapped his hands together and laughed. "We did it, good work! Twitch, William, Nick. So lovely to see you all again."

"How?" Twitch asked, his mouth agape in wonder. He had not expected to see Aleksandr there. "Where are you?"

"Amy's office. We broke in just like you asked and have been monitoring communications since. We caught reference to some starats locked up in the bunker below parliament and have been spending a while trying to get in contact. It finally worked," Aleksandr said, beaming brightly. The humans behind the pilot showed a mixture of exhaustion and elation.

"There was no security?" Nick asked, a flick of his ears giving away his confusion.

"Not as much as I expected, but there was some resistance," Aleksandr said. He lifted his right hand up, which had been heavily bandaged. Red stains still leaked through around his thumb. "We have not gone without injury, but we have been able to secure the office from anything but drone strikes. For that, we don't have any protection, but there is nothing to do about that."

Twitch grinned to himself. "We were able to get a message out to the fleet-admiral. They're warned of the situation here, but Amy is expecting an attack. She's fortifying things here. I think she's got more planned that we don't know about."

"Politics goes over my head," Aleksandr admitted. He brushed his uninjured hand over his stubbly facial hair. "All we can do is give the top dogs the best information we can give them and let them fix this mess. Any idea on numbers?"

Twitch wrinkled his muzzle. He looked to Nick.

"That we saw? Several hundred, at least," the black-furred starat said. He leaned back to support his weight on the table behind him. "And Snow. She's worth hundreds by herself, I think. I dread to think what she can do."

Aleksandr frowned. "If politics confuses me, then her even more so. I still don't know how she can do all these things, and I do not think I want to know." The human paused for a moment, turning to look out the window behind him. Streaks of light appeared in the sky, visible against the static movement of the stars and the gentle glow on the horizon as dawn neared. "I'll pass that information on to the fleet-admiral, but I feel the battle is going to begin very soon. Last I heard, they were already moving into position around the capital."

Twitch flicked his ears and furrowed his brow. He had not expected the Resistance to make their way back to Caledonia so soon. "How long have we been stuck down here?"

"I can't tell you for sure," Aleksandr replied. He glanced down to his wrist. "But it's been nearly five hours since we parted ways."

Twitch glanced to Nick again. He then looked back to Aleksandr. "I hadn't realised it had been so long. We're trying to get out of here. I don't know what we can do, but we'll be trying to do something from back here."

"Just keep yourself safe if you can," Aleksandr said. He turned to quickly exchange words with one of the humans with him, before looking back to the screen. "Amy must have been planning this for a long time. She will have thought of everything."

Twitch growled quietly. "Then perhaps it's time we do something she won't expect."

Aleksandr held his hand up. "I know you want to be like Captain Griffiths, but remember you aren't him. Don't try something just because it's what the captain would have done."

"I know," Twitch said. His ears both flicked up and he straightened his back. He held his screwdriver up and gestured it in the screen's direction. "I'm just doing what I do best. I fix what is broken."

Aleksandr's mouth pursed into a tight line. "Just stay safe, Twitch."

"I'll do my best," Twitch said, saluting the human with his screwdriver. The screen went dark. Twitch turned to face his two companions. "I'll have this door opened in a few minutes. Can you make sure the others are ready to leave?"

"What's our plan when we get out there?" Nick asked.

"Stop Amy," Twitch replied, a grim smile set on his face.

Nick lifted his brow, then sighed. "A perfectly detailed plan. Perhaps Maxwell has some insight to her targets."

"Just go and get him, and I'll have the doors ready to open," Twitch said, turning his back on Nick. He crouched back down in front of the door and tried to remove the problematic panel. He didn't want to delay for much longer. They had already lost so much time stuck down in the bunker. He had no way of knowing what state the parliament building was. He doubted he and four other starats would be able to take Amy or Snow captive, but he had to try and make some difference. With any luck, Amy might not even realise that they had escaped from the bunker.

Nick returned a few moments later, with the other two starats with him. David rubbed his eyes and yawned, while Maxwell was still busy slipping his shirt back on, clumsy with only one working hand to complete the task.

"We're breaking out?" Maxwell asked, his head still hidden by his shirt before he pulled it down.

Twitch finally managed to unscrew the panel to reveal the hidden switch. It would take just a moment to open the door, but he did not press it yet. Instead, he leaned back and turned to face the other starats, perfectly balanced on his haunches. "We're getting out of here. I can open the doors right away."

Maxwell frowned. "Where are we going?"

Twitch pressed his hand against his thigh, feeling for the panelling in his synthetic limb. He found a small latch and pulled, opening a small segment. He gritted his teeth, always finding the sensation bizarre. He pulled the pistol out, testing its weight in his hands. He held it awkwardly in his hand as his smile hardened into grim determination. "To stop them. However we can." Twitch swallowed down the nausea that threatened to build within him. "Sometimes to fix things you have to cause a bit more damage."

The weapon was a different model to the ones he was used to. He could find no evidence of ammunition, or even any way to reload the pistol. The muzzle had been flattened slightly from the top, squashing it down into a more elongated shape. A large, bulky chamber at the back of the pistol contained most of the weight, with a small switch on the rear panel. Twitch couldn't be sure just what it did, but he was sure that once he squeezed the trigger, something would happen. He had to trust that the fleet-admiral had given him something that worked. She would have known there was still potential danger to face.

William held his hand out. "Do you want me to carry that?"

Twitch shook his head. "No. I'm ready to do this. I can do this."

"If you're sure," William said hesitantly. His hand remained raised for a few more seconds, before dropping it down to his side.

Twitch felt like he should say something more before opening the door. This would normally be the time Captain Rhys would say something inspiring to his crew, getting them ready for the upcoming battle. "The starats were given a chance to protect Centaura from Terra long ago. Now it's our turn to fight for the starats still stuck on Terra," he said, not letting himself think about the words that came to his mouth. He simply spoke what came to mind. "I wish we didn't have to fight the starats of Centaura to make that happen, but we fight for the billions back home."

Nick stepped forward. "For the starats back on Terra," the black-furred starat said. "One way or another, starats are going to die. Let's make sure it's Amy and not us."

Twitch looked around the small group. They all looked scared. Maxwell was missing a hand, and everyone else had small injuries to deal with. David held Leandro's urn in his hands. Of them all, only Twitch carried a weapon. None of them were going to give up. Twitch could see that in their eyes.

Before his resolve had a chance to fail, Twitch turned again. He reached into the gap he had made beside the door. He hesitated for half a second, before flicking the switch. Both airlock doors snapped open.

Twitch took the first steps out of the bunker and glanced in both directions. The narrow, concrete-walled corridor was dark and empty. Muffled sounds echoed down from somewhere above their heads.

"No point delaying this. Let's go."

# chapter twenty-three

Twitch struggled to recall the route back up to the government building from memory. The maze of corridors below ground all looked the same to him, and he could determine little purpose from most of them. The corridors were all named and labelled, but using terms that meant nothing to him, or a sequence of numbers that probably had some meaning to those who worked there.

Finally, after what felt like an hour trying to retrace their steps, Twitch pushed open a door to find himself back up on the main corridor that circled around the parliament chamber. The noises were louder now, with the occasional shout and deep rumble echoing through the empty corridor.

"Sounds like they've started without us," Nick said, creeping up to crouch by Twitch's side. The two starats looked out through the corridor, but they could see nothing in either direction. All was clear.

"Where to now?" Nick asked.

Twitch wasn't sure, but he was provided an answer from one of the starats behind him.

"We should go to the president's office," Maxwell suggested. "There might be a clue to see what Amy has done with Ceri."

Twitch flicked his ears. "Ceri? That's Bakir?"

Maxwell nodded. He pointed with his cybernetic arm, grimacing as he seemed to realise anew his lack of hand. "It'll be just this way."

"Should we split up, perhaps?" William asked.

Twitch shook his head quickly. "No. We'll be safer together. More eyes to watch each other's backs."

"We can cover more ground though," William said.

Twitch turned to stare William down. "No. We're safer together. If we're going to help the fleet-admiral, then we need to be safe. We can do that without splitting up."

William didn't offer any further protests. He lowered his eyes and nodded, letting his tail droop.

Twitch led the way. The carpeted floor beneath his feet felt soft, but nothing else gave him the same feeling. The walls were cold and austere, and the curved window that ran around the inside of the corridor was darkened. No lights came out from the chamber inside, and only the occasional flashed reflection gleamed off the clear glass. Twitch's fur stood up on the back of his neck every time he looked towards the windows.

The wide, open corridor felt oppressive, as though the entire building was trying to warn him that he didn't belong. Occasional rumbles continued to sound, sometimes accompanied by a slight shaking of the building beneath Twitch's feet. The starat knew those could only be one thing: explosions.

Maxwell briefly took the lead as the starats hurried up a flight of stairs; the same stairs Amy had taken them up a few hours before. Twitch slowed slightly as he picked up a scent in the air, but he couldn't quite place it. Someone had come up – or down – the stairs fairly recently, but he couldn't tell which direction they had gone. He felt like he should know the scent, but he couldn't quite place it. He knew it wasn't Amy, and he had never picked up any natural scents from Snow.

David barged open the door at the top of the stairs. Nothing stirred inside the office, even as Twitch stepped ahead of the others with his pistol raised. As far as Twitch could tell, nothing had changed since he had last stood in almost exactly the same spot, but for the scene outside.

Twitch cautiously approached the window that overlooked the park. His eyes widened as he looked out across the battle scene laid out through the city. Amy's SFU had bunkered down behind the barricades to protect themselves from the ground troops that poured through the streets of Caledonia, with anti-air gunners providing support to keep the military shuttles at bay.

The military had parliament surrounded, but Twitch doubted that was a particular concern for Amy. She had been planning for this, and Twitch knew she had to have expected to be surrounded.

Twitch glanced up towards the sky; difficult to see with the curve of the building above the window. He could see more flashes of light illuminating the sky. The battle was being fought in the air too, above the city. How much further would the combat go? Did Amy have control of any ships in the fleet protecting Centaura?

With his eyes moving back down to the ground, Twitch tried to work out what was going on in the combat below. He was sure strategy and tactics were in play, but he didn't have a military mind. He couldn't make sense of what he saw. Chaos was all he could see.

Twitch turned from the window. Nick and Maxwell were both rummaging through the large desk in the middle of the room, while William and David kept guard by the doorway, listening out for any approaching footsteps. His eyes fell to David's hip. Leandro's urn had been secured to his belt, resting inside a spare holster they had found in the bunker. How they could use the experience of Leandro now. He would know exactly what to do. He would have a plan to defeat Amy and Snow.

"There's nothing here," Maxwell growled, thumping his wrist down on the desk in frustration. "Amy's cleared it all out already. If Ceri was here, I don't know where she is now."

"All those ministers we saw before. They have to still be somewhere, right?" Twitch mused. He took a couple of steps away from the window. "There hasn't been any opportunity to evacuate them, but Amy won't want them in harm's way. She has to be keeping them somewhere, promising to protect them."

Maxwell shook his head. "There's nowhere. Just the bunker."

"Well they have to be somewhere," Twitch replied. He leaned over Maxwell's shoulder to see what the enhanced starat had been looking at. He had been right. Everything had been cleared out of the desk. Nothing remained at all. No paperwork or tablets had been left behind, cleared out in a hurry. Twitch could see small claw marks left in the wooden desk, the peelings clearly recent.

Nick tapped his claws against the desk. "I think there's something strange in that chamber in the middle of the building. I felt something before, but I don't know what."

"I think I felt the same thing. Like something was watching me, but I couldn't see anything," Twitch replied. He shivered at the thought of it.

"Perhaps we should try there," Nick suggested. His fingers gripped tight around the edge of the desk.

"That's the speaking floor. There's no way to keep the ministers safe there," Maxwell protested with a shake of his head. "The room can't be properly secured, not in a military fashion. The lights were all switched off. No one would be comfortable in there."

"All the same, I think something is in there," Nick said. The black-furred starat looked up at Twitch, before his eyes slid past to peer directly out the window. "We should move quickly anyway. We're vulnerable in here. One mis-directed missile…"

Twitch immediately understood, and he backed away from the window a little further, as though those few extra steps would make all the difference. "We should go then. Check out that chamber and see what's in there. We might find someone who can help us."

"Or try to kill us," Nick muttered.

Twitch had been trying not to think too hard about that possibility. He didn't know how he would be able to tell apart friend from foe. Nor would anyone they came across be able to tell if he was with the Resistance or SFU. He doubted anyone would ask questions first. They would shoot to kill, and he would have to do the same.

Disappointed by their failure in the president's office, the five starats made their way back towards the stairs, but Twitch paused. Once more, he picked up the light scent of a starat in the stairwell. "Anyone else smell that?" he asked.

Maxwell's eyes widened. "That's Ceri," he whispered hoarsely. "She was here."

"When?" William asked. He had been leading the starats down the stairs, but he paused and looked back up.

Maxwell wrinkled his nose. "About an hour ago."

"Do you think you can follow it?" Nick asked. He flicked his ear. "I don't think my nose is strong enough to pick it up properly."

"I can try," Maxwell said nervously. He took a couple of steps further down the stairs, pushing past William. Once he reached the bottom, he pushed open the door to step back out into the corridor.

Everything remained quiet, but for the occasional rumbles of explosions coming from the battle outside. The walls of parliament building were thick enough to resist any impact, and the sounds struggled to get through to the wide corridor. Twitch had to admit, the place felt a little like a fortress. He understood a little more why Amy had not been worried about being cornered inside.

Twitch hurried forward to walk with Maxwell. The starat closed his eyes every few steps and breathed in deep through his nose. Twitch had quickly lost the scent of Minister Bakir in the chaotic air of the corridor. So many people, human and starat alike, had walked through the halls that every scent blended into the other. He had no hope of picking out just one scent amongst them all, but Maxwell seemed confident.

Maxwell led them around to a set of double doors on the inside ring of the corridor, at a break in the curving window that looked into the central chamber. Maxwell twitched nervously as he stood outside the door. "The scent ends here," he said uncertainly. "She went in there. Someone might be there after all."

"Are you sure?" William asked. He placed his hand on the door, but it didn't open. There were no handles or locks visible, nor control panels to the side.

"I mean, I don't know if she's still in there, but she went in about an hour ago," Maxwell said. His eyes flicked back and forth down the corridor. "This door is controlled from inside though. You can't open it from the outside. It's one of the fire doors to evacuate the floor."

Twitch swished his tail. He looked down at the pistol in his hand. "I've got a way that will get us through."

William and Maxwell both backed away from the door, giving Twitch a clear shot. He raised the pistol up and squeezed the trigger. Nothing happened. He frowned and stared down at the pistol.

"You have to flick the switch on the back too," Maxwell instructed.

Twitch did as the other starat suggested. He pressed on the switch with his thumb, and immediately the pistol began to whine in a gradually increasing pitch. An amber light shone above the switch, which soon changed to green. Over the next ten seconds, the whine grew louder and more frantic in pitch, before, with a quiet click, the pistol fell into silence again. The green light changed back to amber, and then to red. Twitch exhaled slowly, only then realising he had been holding his breath.

"Alright then. Easy enough to understand," he muttered to himself. He positioned his thumb over the switch again and swung his arms up to aim the pistol. He pressed the switch and waited for the whine to reach its peak; the green light shining on his fingers. He squeezed the trigger again, bracing himself for the recoil that never came.

The pistol remained perfectly steady in Twitch's hands as it fired a bright beam of light from the elongated muzzle. Twitch's aim had been true, though he couldn't have expected the light to do so much damage; the door blasted apart in an instant, breaking in the centre with the two broken panels sliding back into the frames.

With a quietening whine, the pistol clicked again, and the indicator light went red. Twitch remained perfectly still. He could feel a little heat radiating out from the bulky box on the back of the weapon, but otherwise felt nothing out of the ordinary from a regular pistol.

"Well, that's new," William said in awe. "When can I get one of those?"

"They're prototype models. I didn't know any had been issued yet," Maxwell said, sounding equally at awe. "But come on, quickly. If Ceri is in here, they'll know we're coming now."

Twitch moved forward first. He kept a wary, respectful eye on his pistol now, keeping his thumb away from the priming switch. His mind swirled with ideas about what could be making the light-like ammunition work. He assumed it was some kind of energy weapon, but he hadn't thought such things were possible. The proof was right in front of him, with the smoking ruins of the broken door. Even still, he barely believed it.

Feeling like he wielded a power beyond his understanding or control, Twitch stepped forward into the darkness. Light was suppressed. Twitch blinked a few times, but he couldn't clear his vision. All could see was blackness pressed up close to his eyes, though his arms and hands remained visible, raised up in front of him with the red light of the pistol almost blinding. He bumped into a second door, but this one swung open easily, without the need to use the pistol again.

Beneath his feet, Twitch could feel the floor slowly sloping downwards. Voices murmured around him; indistinct and vague. Most sounded human, though there were certainly some starats amongst them. He could hear nothing of William, though he knew the other starat had followed right behind him.

Twitch's breath sounded deafening to his own ears. Electricity crackled over his fur, bringing most of his hair up on end. Cinnamon filled his nose.

Whispers filled Twitch's mind. Thoughts that were not his own swirled around, forcing his own out. Formless ideas threatened to distract him, but still Twitch placed one foot in front of the other, making his way down into the middle of the chamber he could not see.

Twitch pinned his ears down, as though that could stop the whispered thoughts sneaking in. The action helped for a moment, but soon they returned; less formless this time.

*"Resist no more. Snow is the rightful ruler of Centaura, with Amy by her side. Submit to her and allow peace to reign."*

Twitch growled to himself and shook his head, trying to dislodge the idea. The albino was here. She was trying her mind tricks on him. He had to ignore them.

Light suddenly burst into being around Twitch. He shielded his eyes as the darkness faded to nothing.

The starat found himself in the centre of the chamber, at the lowest point, just beneath the raised podium. Twitch was briefly aware of a crowd of humans and starats sat in the seats around the chamber, but his eyes were immediately drawn to the podium itself.

Snow stood there, atop the podium. She had her back to Twitch, but he knew the albino was aware of his presence. Her focus was on the rift of light in front of her. A rend had been made in real space, like a claw had sliced through the fabric of reality. Twitch's ears flicked at the constant static crackle that emanated from the tear.

Through the rip, Twitch could see the pure white of subspace, but there was something more in there. Darkness swirled, and Twitch got the impression of countless eyes watching him.

Twitch had heard Captain Rhys talk about those shapes of darkness. Entities, he had called them.

"I should have known you'd find a way out of there," Snow called out. She didn't look back, but Twitch knew she didn't need to. She could sense him just as well without even needing to turn her head.

"What are you doing here?" Twitch asked. His voice trembled as he tore his eyes away from Snow for a moment. He looked around the chamber to peer at the sea of faces. Humans and starats all sat still, their mouths moving in their quiet chant. Now that Twitch had heard it for himself, he recognised their words as the voice that had tried to worm into his mind.

"Control," Snow said simply. She held her left hand out towards the rift. "Now, if you'll excuse me, this part if very complicated, and I'd appreciate it if you didn't interfere."

Snow's right hand thrust out towards Twitch. Before he could react, he felt something hard slam into his chest. He was thrown back to the floor, and darkness swirled around him again.

Twitch tried to rise, but he felt weakened by the blow. His head spun, and his thoughts were quickly overcome by the whispered mantra running through his mind. His eyes rolled back in his head, and he slumped limply to the floor.

What point was there in resisting? Snow, with Amy by her side, would bring peace back to Centaura. He could allow them that.

***

Thoughts returned slowly to Twitch. His senses followed just after.

Twitch found himself still sat inside the government chamber, in the front row of seats. A starat sat beside him, but he didn't look to see who it was.

Snow remained on the podium. Her body appeared tense as she struggled with the open rift. Dark tendrils extended out; wispy strands of subspace that appeared to be constantly on the verge of disintegrating.

The albino starat hissed in her struggle with the entity, and she stumbled back against the edge of the podium. As she did so, one of the tendrils lashed out beyond her. The translucent wisp of dark subspace coiled around a human sitting opposite Twitch.

The human immediately stopped chanting that constant repeated phrase. He jerked and tensed rigid as his eyes opened. He mouth a silent scream as the atoms that constructed his body were torn apart by the encroaching subspace. In a moment, there was nothing left of him.

Alarm jolted through Twitch, but he couldn't bring himself to do anything. Snow knew what she was doing. She risked everything to save Centaura. He had to trust in her.

The albino starat had the entity back under control. She gritted her teeth, both hands in position to encircle the rift. "Come on, you fucker. Listen to me now."

Twitch's mind buzzed as he watched the conflict between reality and subspace. He could only hope for one winner. He needed Snow to win, so that she could spread her peace across the planet and rid Centaura of the war that had threatened to tear it apart.

Snow screamed in exertion. Twitch wanted to help, but he didn't know how. All he carried with him was a pistol, but he had to wonder why he even had that. He didn't need it. There were no enemies here. Once Snow had wrested control of the entity, there would be no more enemies on Centaura. Everyone would have to kneel to such power and strength. There would be peace in Alpha Centauri, and soon that would spread to the empire. None could withstand Snow and Amy.

An itch of a dissenting thought tickled at the back of Twitch's mind. He breathed in deep. The cinnamon air burned at his lungs.

The albino starat reached out to grab an obsidian spike.

Twitch looked down at the pistol resting on his lap. Feeling like he moved within a dream, his hand slowly moved to brush the weapon to the floor, but before he could do so, he paused. His eyes were distracted by something else. A pottery urn had been tucked in a holster at the belt of the starat sat next to him.

The starat frowned as his thoughts started to well up again, fighting against the constant chant of Snow's voice; echoed by the hundreds of murmuring voices within the chamber. Why had someone brought an urn to such a place?

Twitch's arm fought against a hidden energy as he moved. His hand trembled as he plucked the urn out of its protective holster. The starat beside him did not move. Twitch's fingers brushed over the name engraved there. Leandro.

Leandro.

The starat who had killed Leandro.

Twitch's thoughts wrenched back to reality with a painful snap.

Snow was no saviour. She was the monster threatening to tear apart worlds.

Twitch's eyes flicked to the entity within the rift. His tail curled slightly as he leaned forward in his seat. He didn't know how Snow was doing it, but she had been manipulating his thoughts, and she continued to do so to everyone else within the chamber. How long before she controlled the thoughts of everyone on Centaura? The entity had to be a part of her plan, but he didn't know how to stop something like that.

Snow, on the other hand, was part of his reality. He knew how to stop her. His heart quailed at the idea, but his head knew there could be no other way.

Twitch lifted his pistol and flicked the switch on the back. The low whine filled Twitch's ears, blocking out the murmur of voices and the light crackle of the rift.

The light shone green.

Snow started to turn, her eyes widening in shock.

Twitch fired once.

One shot was all he needed. The bright beam struck her in the middle of the chest.

Snow fell back over the far side of the podium.

She did not scream.

A hand grabbed hold of Twitch's wrist and pulled him back. "What the fuck did you do?" Nick yelled, his face twisted in anger. "She was our only hope!"

Twitch wrestled with Nick, trying to keep the pistol away from the other starat's grip. "She's still in your head, listen to me," he gasped, but two big, heavy arms wrapped around his chest and dragged him away.

He turned to see David holding him. Disappointment and anger filled his partner's eyes. "How could you?" David choked.

Twitch tried to struggle, but David's hold on him was too strong. "David, please!" he gasped out, struggling to breath in the tightness of his partner's grip. Tears welled in his eyes at the sight of David's disappointment. "Trust me."

David's mouth opened. His ears curled. Doubt lingered in his eyes. "Can I?"

"Yes," Twitch said quickly. He freed one arm, resting his hand on David's chest. He didn't have any time to waste. He didn't want to think about what might happen with the entity without Snow's control. "She's in your head. Think of Richard. Of Leandro."

"I..." David hesitated. His grip slackened slightly. His voice dropped to a whisper. "I trust you."

Twitch immediately turned his head. The black-furred starat stood a couple of paces away. His jaw was still set in anger, his eyes blazing fury. He needed to convince Nick. "Close the rift, please."

William had moved around to the far side of the podium, crouching down in front of Snow's still body. He held his hand over her sightless eyes.

Around the chamber, ministers were beginning to rouse, evidently confused by the struggling starats in front of them.

Without Snow's control over the rift, the white light surrounding the entity began to destabilise. Dark tendrils began to emerge once more, tentatively reaching out into reality. Twitch didn't want to see them touch anyone else, after what had happened before. He cried out for Nick's attention once more.

"Close it, please!"

Nick jabbed a finger into Twitch's chest. "Why should I listen to you after that?"

"Please," Twitch pleaded. He broke free of David's arms. "If you don't, we're all dead."

"Listen to him," David said firmly. "We can deal with this afterwards."

Nick's attention flicked up to the rift. "Shit," he muttered, before jabbing Twitch in the chest again. "I'm not finished with you."

The starat growled as he clambered up onto the podium. He held his hands up, much like Snow had done, and furrowed his brow in thought. The tendrils of the entity began to retreat as the rift gradually closed.

Twitch watched with wide eyes. He dropped down to his knees, his ears and tail held low. He could only hope that this worked, or else he didn't know how to explain himself. If his theories were wrong, then he could have done more damage than he could ever have feared. David's hand gripped his shoulder tightly.

Nick screamed out in pain. Cinnamon filled the air as the rift crackled and shrunk. Nervous humans and starats backed away from the podium, towards the doors at the top of the chamber. Only Nick, David, and Twitch remained where they were. Even William had begun to back away from Snow's still body.

With one, final shockwave, the rent in reality sealed closed. The entity withdrew completely. Nick's hands clasped together, and for a few moments he stood still and panted, before he spun around and snarled at Twitch.

"Now, you listen here," he growled, but before he could say anything more, the expression on his face changed. His ears pinned against his head and his eyes widened. He staggered back and stumbled against the lectern, which had been charred black by the subspace rip. "Holy shit."

The grip around Twitch's shoulder slackened. He stood up, unsteady on his feet, Twitch backed away from the starats. Moments earlier, anger and hatred had been in their eyes, but now confusion had replaced those emotions.

"Are we good?" Twitch asked uncertainly, not yet sure if the starats believed him again.

David shook as he approached Twitch. Once more, Twitch found himself in the arms of his partner, but this time it was a desperate, needy hug; not the tight grip it had been before. "I doubted you, I'm so sorry," David whispered, pressing his muzzle into Twitch's neck.

Twitch's arms slowly tightened around David's body, his free hand stroking lightly through his partner's fur. "You didn't have a choice, it's alright. She got into our heads. It's over."

Twitch and David weren't the only two embracing. Over David's shoulder, Twitch could see Minister Bakir and Maxwell share a brief moment in each other's arms too.

Reluctantly, Twitch broke away from David and nervously approached the minister. She quickly stepped back from Maxwell and brushed down her dress.

"It seems we're indebted to you, Twitch," the minister said. She looked around the chamber, where most of her colleagues were speaking quietly to each other. "Though I will admit, I still don't know what I just witnessed. One moment I felt like I was in a fog, and the next, all this." She spread her hands out, gesturing to the room as a whole.

Twitch scuffed his foot against the floor. He felt like he was still trying to work everything out too. "I think Snow was controlling everyone, or at least, influencing their thoughts. Making everyone think she deserved to be the one in power. I think she was using that entity to help do that."

"I don't understand how," William said uncertainly, approaching them both. "She burned herself out trying to cover up Captain Rhys's fall from the shuttle. How could she do this?"

Twitch had no answer to that, but Nick did. "The Denitchev particles. There's so many of them in the air, it makes anything to do with subspace so much easier. She needed the Inquisition to nearly succeed."

"It's not over yet," Minister Bakir said grimly. "There's still Amy to deal with, and she can rule with an iron fist even without Snow by her side."

"Is it true she made you president?" Twitch asked, still not quite convinced that he could fully trust her.

Minister Bakir glanced at Maxwell, then turned around to quickly gaze around the chamber. "I think she did, but everything is hazy. It's hard to explain."

"We can worry about that later," Maxwell advised. He placed his hand gently on the minister's elbow. "Parliament is under attack. We have to do something."

"We're not soldiers," Minister Bakir said. She held her hands on her hips as she looked around the chamber. "But I think I know how we can stop this."

Twitch took a step back, retreating into David's arms once more, as Minister Bakir rose to the podium, where Snow had stood just moments earlier. She clapped her hands together and held her arms up in the air, gathering the attention of everyone who still lingered. Twitch couldn't tell just how many had already left, but the chamber still seemed mostly full.

"We have been lied to and deceived," Minister Bakir called out. No one spoke a word but her. "We have the chance now to put things right and show this insurrectionist her place. Will you stand by my side as we confront Amy Jennings and tell her she has lost?"

"We just walk out there, into a warzone?" one human replied.

"Into the warzone? No. Amy won't be there. She'll be watching it all from somewhere safe," Minister Bakir said calmly. "Once we confront her, she will stand down. We are parliament, and she is not."

Twitch flicked his tail. He couldn't be sure that things were going to be so easy, but he was willing to trust Minister Bakir and follow her. He stepped forward and lifted his voice. "I'm with you."

One at a time, the starats around Twitch all followed him, pledging their support towards Minister Bakir. The support rippled around the chamber, before everyone had agreed to follow the starat.

"Together we stand against this injustice," Minister Bakir said. She turned on the spot and descended the podium steps, her tail swishing high behind her. She walked at the head of a tightly packed crowd of human and starat, with Twitch pushing his way through to the front to stand just behind the minister. He wanted to see this; he wanted to know everything would work out.

The minister marched towards the main doors of the parliament chamber. An uncertain, uneasy group of humans and starats followed her. Twitch glanced back, expecting to see David right behind him still, but his partner had fallen back in the crowd. He felt a little vulnerable suddenly, despite the pistol in his hand.

The doors pushed open to the main foyer. From there, Twitch could see the battle raging just outside. He could hear the explosions and feel the slight shake of the floor from each one. He quailed as his fear threatened to overwhelm him, but he got a hand on his back to keep moving forward. He glanced behind him to see, not David as he had hoped, but William.

For a moment, Twitch thought the minister was going to just walk out through the front doors and into the middle of the combat zone. Instead, she made her way to the small welcome desk in the middle of the foyer. Twitch hurried after her, while most of the ministers remained as far back as possible, in a position of relative safety.

Minister Bakir slipped in behind the computer terminal. Her hands moved quickly through the holographic display to pull up the menus she needed, then opened an emergency broadcast to the local holonetwork. Twitch could only stand and watch, keeping a wary eye on the main doors. He could see movement near them, but no one came through. He didn't want anyone to interrupt the minister's work.

"I've never ended a war before," the minister said, a nervous smile on her usually composed muzzle.

"I hope you never have to again," Twitch replied quietly. "You know what to say?"

"I think so," Minister Bakir said. She cleared her throat, then activated the emergency broadcast system. A loud siren cut through the gunfire outside. Twitch couldn't see if anyone was distracted by the sudden noise, but the sounds of gunfire didn't cease.

The minister spoke clearly and slowly as she addressed the city outside. The echoes of her broadcast voice reverberated through the open foyer. "Enough of this fighting. This is President Ceri Bakir, recently elected by parliament to replace President Shawn, who has betrayed all Centaura has stood for over these many years. He was not the only one to betray our ideals. The usurper, Amy Jennings, has lied and deceived us all, and has attempted this coup against the will of our people.

"As the rightfully voted leader of our government, I urge for the fighting to cease, and for peace talks to begin. This insurrection is unbecoming of Centaurans, and it must end here.

"By order of your president, lay down your weapons."

Minister Bakir shut down the emergency broadcast and slumped back in her seat. "How did that sound?"

Twitch grinned. "Presidential. I think. Never actually heard a president speak like that, but I imagine that's what they should sound like."

"Now we'll just see how soon they react," the new president said.

Twitch flicked his ears and looked outside. He couldn't hear much from outside anymore, but he did hear footsteps from above him, on the balcony level that ran around most of the foyer.

A starat ran down the stairs. Anger blazed in Amy's eyes. "What are you doing?" she yelled. She appeared to be unarmed, and without any bodyguards for support. She advanced on Minister Bakir, ignoring Twitch and his pistol, even as he raised his weapon.

President Bakir slowly rose to her feet. She stared Amy down. "I am ending this farce of a war, and this attempted rebellion."

"I'm doing this to protect you. To protect all of us," Amy hissed. She slowly turned her attention to the gathered onlookers, clustered at the back of the foyer. "You're meant to be loyal to me, to the protection of Centaura under my rule."

"A rule fabricated by lies and deceit," President Bakir retorted, maintaining the calm level of her voice. "It is over, Ms Jennings."

Amy's face twisted into a snarl. "Over? This isn't over. Snow! Deal with them!"

David stepped forward from the crowd. He carried Snow's body in his arms. Twitch thought she looked so weak and vulnerable now. He suppressed a shiver of guilt. She had been anything but weak, and there had been no choice but to take the shot.

A deathly silence filled the foyer as David approached the small desk. He placed the albino's body down carefully at Amy's feet.

"You gave us back Leandro," Twitch said quietly. "It is only fair we return Snow to you."

Amy dropped to her knees. Tears fell down her cheeks. "What have you done?" she whispered, before her voice rose into a shriek. "What have you done? We were going to save this planet! We were going to protect it! You've ruined it all!"

The doors at the front of the foyer opened. Shouts came through from outside, quickly followed by a dozen soldiers with rifles raised. Twitch readied himself, standing by the president to offer what little protection he could, before a familiar face came through. Fleet-Admiral Bosler stood in the doorway, her eyes narrowed as she surveyed the foyer.

"Amy Jennings, this is a pleasure," the fleet-admiral said coldly. She turned her attention to the starat. "Under your authority, President Bakir, I would like to take Ms Jennings into custody."

President Bakir's muzzle flicked into a quick grin. "You have my permission, fleet-admiral. I understand we have an extensive debrief later too, on the fate of my predecessor."

Fleet-Admiral Bosler nodded. "Once I've dealt with the mess Ms Jennings has left us, I'll be happy to advise you of everything that happened in Hadrian," she replied. She clicked her fingers and pointed to Amy. At once, four of the soldiers who had come in with her lowered their weapons and advanced on the starat.

David moved quickly to stand behind Amy, making sure her routes of escape were blocked off. Realising this, Amy didn't resist her capture. "You think you've won?" she growled, glaring right at President Bakir. "You think you've stopped me? My plans are already in motion, and there's nothing you can do to stop them. One day, you will thank me for making you safe from Terra's tyranny."

"You can tell me all about it in questioning," Fleet-Admiral Bosler said, turning her back on Amy to address a couple of humans by her side. "Keep her safe. Don't give her any opportunity to get away. Understood?"

"Yes, ma'am." The humans all saluted the fleet-admiral, before they led Amy away. One of the humans scooped up Snow's body to take the albino too.

Twitch didn't watch them go. He had no desire to see either of them again, nor listen to Amy's attempted justifications for her actions. He slumped back against the desk and closed his eyes. David's comforting hand rested on his shoulder.

"It seems we have you to thank again, Twitch," the fleet-admiral said, her voice much softer again.

Twitch grinned weakly. "Just doing what I can. Is everyone still fighting out there?"

The fleet-admiral glanced to the doors. "Not for the moment. The president's address caught most of Ms Jennings' forces off guard. I don't think peace is fully secured yet, but once they learn of their leader's capture, I think they might think differently."

"I won't keep you, if there is more to do out there," President Bakir said. She nodded her head towards the fleet-admiral and offered a quick salute.

Fleet-Admiral Bosler returned the salute. She then turned on her heel and made her way back outside. Twitch could hear her voice bellowing out commands long after she disappeared from view.

President Bakir held her hand out for Twitch. "Likewise, I'd like to thank you for everything you have done, Twitch."

Twitch bowed his head. "I'd say it was nothing, but it was so much. I think I'm not going to try being Captain Rhys again. He can be him, and I'm just going to be me."

"And I hope you can do so in peace," the president said. She squeezed his hand for a moment, before she released her grip. "We've got this now. Maxwell will find somewhere for you to rest, and then, when this is all cleared up, we'll make sure you get home safely."

A deep relief spread through Twitch's body. He felt like a physical weight had been removed from his shoulders. "President Bakir, I don't think anything sounds better than that. I just want to go home."

Twitch turned at Maxwell's light touch on his shoulder. With one last wave goodbye to the new president, Twitch followed her assistant. Nick and William walked to his right. At his left was David. Together, they had done it. Their fight was over. Now was the time to leave the rest of the battle to those who knew what they were doing.

Twitch couldn't wait to go home. Perhaps this time he actually could.

# chapter twenty-four

Nearly two weeks had passed. Ten blissful days of freedom and relaxation for Twitch to try to forget everything that had happened since Captain Rhys had been forced to leave Centaura on that last mission, not to return. Forgetting was hard, but at least Twitch felt at peace with his environment. He could still hear the screams in his mind; and vision of the deaths he had seen and caused played on the inside of his eyelids, but he could sit in quiet peace in the garden without having to look over his shoulder for the next threat.

Twitch had spent most of the time either sat in peace or building a small shrine in the garden. He was proud of his work; creating a remembrance out of stone for the starats who had not made it through the war. The urns of Richard and Leandro sat inside the shrine. The spare urn, which had been used to memorialise Leandro initially, had been placed there too. Both names of Leandro and Emile, the Silver Fox, had already been engraved onto that first urn. Twitch had left those names be. In name, at least, the two would remain together.

But for a few messages finalising details, and returning belongings left behind in military bases, Twitch had received no contact from the Stellar Guard or the government. The only people he had spoken with had been David, William, Steph, and Nick. He had briefly seen Captain Aaron, but they hadn't spoken in that short interaction. Doctor Anthony, too, had visited David, but Twitch had remained in the garden. The human doctor hadn't come outside to see him.

Twitch leaned back in his chair and stretched out his legs. Prox shone on his face as the crimson star descended towards the horizon after another endless day. Hot air sweltered, but a gentle breeze blew on Twitch's face, keeping him comfortable.

The starat wore his first set of cybernetics, finally repaired of the damage they had sustained during his first visit to Hadrian. Though they had been a gift from Amy, he had no issue wearing them. His only other intact cybernetics were the military-spec limbs, and he had no interest in using those. The second pair gifted by Amy had been lost in the destruction of the research centre. He enjoyed having fur on his legs again.

The delightful scent of a pie cooking in the kitchen attracted Twitch's nose. David and William were working together, and Twitch occasionally heard their voices drifting through the window, over the murmur of the holograph Steph had on in the main room. He had deliberately been avoiding that, not wanting to catch sight of the news. The trials of Amy and President Shawn were expected soon.

Then the doorbell rang. Twitch barely moved. He expected Nick. They had invited the other starat around for dinner, but the new voice he heard did not sound like Nick at all. Twitch flicked up his ears. He recognised them, and so he wasn't surprised to open his eyes and see Maxwell come through into the back garden.

The smile was already waiting on Twitch's face. He rose to his feet and pulled Maxwell into an embrace. The other starat had fixed his cybernetics too, and he wore a gleaming hand on his wrist.

"You're a hard starat to get in contact with," Maxwell said with a wry smile.

Twitch nodded vigorously. "I needed time to just recharge and be myself again," he admitted. He swept his tail from side to side. "Can you believe it's nearly two weeks since anyone has tried to kill me?"

"I understand that," Maxwell said. He put his hand on the edge of the doorway. "We thought it was best to give you the time you needed to properly recover."

"And yet here you are," David said, speaking before Twitch could say anything. The larger starat loomed over both of them, wearing nothing but shorts and a tea towel draped over his shoulder.

"Here I am," Maxwell said quietly. He bowed his head.

"How is President Bakir doing? Is she liking her new job?" Twitch asked brightly, speaking quickly as he sensed a growing point of tension between Maxwell and David. He wanted to diffuse it before it had chance to grow.

Maxwell laughed. "Liking is probably not the right word. There's so much to be done to clean things up, and she's facing a bit of resistance from Amy's and Shawn's old supporters, but she's getting through to them. She's running again in the emergency elections she called, so perhaps she'll be able to stay there for a full term."

"That's good. I thought she would make a good leader. I told you she'd be president, that first time I saw you," Twitch said with a grin.

"You did say that, yes," Maxwell said. He didn't look at Twitch, instead staring out across the small garden, still with his head bowed low. "Some kind of seer, are you?"

David laughed this time. "He barely talks sense at the best of times. Sometimes he's got to get lucky."

Twitch pinned his ears down and stuck his tongue out. "Maybe I can make my way as a seer and predict everyone's future. I can already see your future. Tonight, we're gonna..."

David hastily put his hand over Twitch's mouth, who broke down into a series of muffled giggles.

Maxwell's ears turned crimson as he blushed deeply. He stammered and looked away. "I, uh... should say why I'm here."

Twitch managed to pull David's hand away from his mouth. "I can see the same thing in your future too, if you'd like."

"No, that's quite alright," Maxwell said, but Twitch didn't think he sounded completely certain of his refusal.

Twitch grinned widely and gently nudged David in the ribs. There might be potential there. David responded by lightly squeezing his hand around Twitch's shoulder.

"Well, what were you here for?" David prompted, before Twitch could embarrass Maxwell further.

The flustered starat took a few moments to compose himself. His eyes kept flicking back to David and Twitch, no matter how many times he tried to look towards the little pond by the shrine. "We need your help."

Twitch's smile slid right off his face. He felt David's grip tighten around his chest. "Why?"

Maxwell held his hands up. This time, he did manage to look towards the pair, but his eyes quickly moved away from what Twitch knew had to be a fierce gaze coming from his partner. "It's nothing dangerous, I swear. There's no attacks. We've just had an... incident. We need your advice on how to proceed."

Twitch flicked his ears and glanced up. He could only see the bottom of David's chin right above his head. He looked back down to Maxwell. "What situation?"

"I can't tell you here. It's wrapped under a lot of confidentiality. We need to go to Net Central," Maxwell said, scuffing his foot on the patio.

Twitch sighed softly. "Is there at least time for dinner first? You're welcome to stay too. David always makes extra."

Maxwell opened his mouth, and for a moment Twitch could tell he was going to insist that there was no time to waste. Then his shoulders slumped. "That would be lovely, thank you," he admitted.

"Excellent. Let me make sure William and Steph have everything ready," Twitch said brightly. Any worry of what Maxwell had in store for him could be delayed, and any delay on future concerns was a welcome one for Twitch. He could enjoy the present a little longer, and that helped keep the darkness at bay.

Soon, some of those worries might start flooding back.

For now, there was only pie and friends.

\*\*\*

Maxwell remained quiet. He had barely spoken during dinner, except to praise the quality of cooking. After then, he had taken Twitch away from his quiet home and into a car waiting for them. Their destination was the space elevator on the outskirts of Caledonia; a place Twitch had not visited since his journey up to Captain Rhys's ship with Major-General Ulrich. That had been the last time Twitch had seen her, and the sorrow of her loss threatened to overwhelm him.

Twitch distracted his thoughts by trying to start a conversation with Maxwell, but the other starat remained tight-lipped about the purpose of the journey. He kept deflecting questions by saying the information was confidential and couldn't be spoken about outside of a secure location.

Eventually, Twitch gave up trying, but he had been able to take up most of the time it took to reach the space elevator. The two starats were quickly waved through security, using a pass Maxwell carried with him to give them priority access through the queues.

From there, the two starats slowly rose in the elevator. Twitch tried to look out the lone tiny window, but he had to compete with a cluster of excited kits for the best vantage point. After some stern looks from the parents, Twitch reluctantly conceded the view. Instead, he had to content himself with just watching the holoscreen, which projected a simulated view of the planet below onto one of the elevator walls. Maxwell studiously avoided both window and holoscreen.

After the space elevator, Maxwell led Twitch through to the shuttles that would carry them across to Network Central, the middle of the great web of satellites that circled the planet. Twitch nervously flicked his tail as he sat in the shuttle, waiting to dock. The crowds from the elevator had thinned out, with many different destinations across the planet and system.

"Will President Bakir be here?" Twitch asked, speaking quietly as he leaned across to Maxwell's seat beside him.

"I can't tell you that," Maxwell replied curtly.

"I think she will be. If she wasn't, someone else would have come to get me," Twitch said, grinning as he watched Maxwell's expression. He didn't give anything away. "Perhaps Captain Aaron would have. Or Aleksandr."

This time, Maxwell did react. He flicked his ears down in brief confusion. "Why do you do that? Only use first names? But only for some people. You always say Bakir, but never Ceri."

Twitch shrugged his shoulders. "If I don't know their first name, I can't use it. Never knew Bakir's first name was Ceri until you told us the other week," he said. He paused for a moment and furrowed his brow. "Never really thought about why I do it. Guess it's a respect thing."

"How do you mean?"

"Growing up on Ceres, we never had any respect for any human. We also don't have last names, so I suppose it's a way to bring them down to our level, even a little bit," he said, speaking slowly. "It's petty, but it's all we had. I guess now I'm here and safe, I should start trying to use surnames. Suppose I should get one for myself. Make it all official."

"I can't even imagine what life must have been like back there," Maxwell said sombrely.

"I hope you never have to," Twitch replied.

"And yet, you still fought to save the humans who did that to you."

Twitch smiled. "Just because they were shit to me, doesn't mean I should let them die. It was the right thing to do."

"Just for that, you're a stronger starat than I think I could ever be. I honestly couldn't say I would have done the same as you," Maxwell said. The starat squirmed in his seat, before bracing himself as the warning lights flashed up at the front of the shuttle, alerting the sparse occupants that deceleration and docking was soon to commence.

Twitch turned his head to the front of the shuttle and gripped the armrests tight. The deceleration process of the shuttles was still a little uncomfortable as the weight pressed on his chest. He had grown used to the stronger gravity on Centaura, but acceleration and deceleration was still when it caught him out.

The process took just a few minutes before the green light shone, letting the passengers know that the shuttle had safely docked. An automated voice informed them that they had arrived at Network Central.

Twitch wasn't given any chance to look down on the planet through the wide windows around the shuttle bay. The red planet looked beautiful in the brief glimpse he got, with the light of Prox twinkling off the ocean between the two continents. After that, it was nothing but small and bright corridors away from the windows around the edge of the satellite.

Their destination was a large conference room. As soon as Maxwell opened the door, Twitch nearly crowed in delight. He had been right. President Bakir was present. Almost everyone who had led the defence against Amy and the Inquisition forces were there.

Aaron, Fleet-Admiral Bosler, and a couple of other humans were sat around the table in the middle of the room.

One face did not belong. Twitch came to a sudden halt as he stared numbly at the face from his past. The human looked the same as he always had; an unruly wisp of white hair framing a lined and weathered face. Admiral Nigel Garter peered over the top of his glasses the same way he always did.

Maxwell closed the door behind them.

President Bakir rose to her feet and greeted Twitch with a shake of his hand. "I'm so glad you came. I believe you know this man?" she asked, sweeping her hand towards the admiral.

Twitch nodded. His throat felt dry. He tried swallowing. "I do," he said, only a hoarse whisper escaping his mouth.

"He said he has a message for us, but he requested you be here to listen to it with us," the fleet-admiral explained.

Twitch looked to the admiral. "Me? Why me?"

Admiral Garter glanced to President Bakir. She gave a small nod. He cleared his throat before speaking. "Captain Griffiths specifically requested it of me."

Twitch squeaked. "Captain R... Captain Griffiths? He's alive? He's ok?"

"When I left him, the answer to both of those questions was yes," the admiral said softly. He looked around the table of the most powerful people on Centaura. "But he has pleaded for help."

President Bakir nodded again. "You have the message for us, then? Or is there anyone else you need to witness this?"

Admiral Garter shook his head. He reached into his shirt pocket and pulled out a small, flat disc. He placed the device down on the table, in the middle of all the onlookers. At the press of a button, a holographic projection emerged.

Twitch recognised the figure that rose from the hologram. His own face looked out at him; his own body stood there, but Twitch knew it to be Captain Griffiths. Rhys was alive.

Rhys stood with his arms held behind his back, out of sight so no one could see the injuries he had suffered. The once-human straightened his shoulders. "I don't know who will get this message.

Fleet-Admiral Bosler. Major-General Ulrich. President Shawn. To whoever Admiral Garter finds, I beg that you listen to me. Terra stands on the cusp of annihilation, with multiple sources threatening everyone here. One comes from Centaura, from within your own. There is a plot by Amy Jennings to destroy the planet, obliterating the lives of billions. There is an opportunity to stop her here, but I cannot do it alone.

"Terra will not listen to me. Terra has its own problems that are more important than the words of a lone starat, if they were even likely to listen to me. I knew of only one person I could trust to send to you, and that is Admiral Garter. He is one of my closest allies. You have my word, for all that counts, that he means you no harm. He will explain the situation here in greater detail than I can through this message. He will answer your questions.

"There is a chance here to stop Amy's madness. But it is more than that. There is also a chance to stop this war and bring peace between Terra and Alpha Centauri, and I believe it can be done without a long, drawn out conflict. Neither system wants that. But for this to happen, I need your help. Please, send your fleet to Terra. I will lay down the foundations, and I await your arrival."

The hologram faded. Silence followed the words of Captain Griffiths.

Admiral Garter spread his hands on the table. "If there is anything you would like to know, please ask. He needs your help."

President Bakir ignored the admiral. She turned to Twitch. "You know this admiral?"

Twitch nodded. He looked to the other starat, not daring to look at Admiral Garter. "I do, yes."

"Is Captain Griffiths right to trust him?"

This time, Twitch did flick his eyes briefly to Admiral Garter. His breath hitched in his throat. He nodded again. "He is."

President Bakir turned away. She paced a couple of steps closer to the closed door. Her brow was furrowed in thought as her ears curled down. "Fleet-Admiral, what do you make of this information?"

"If Captain Griffiths is right, and there is an opportunity to break the hold of the emperor on Terra, then it is not one we should miss," the human said slowly. She kept her eyes fixed on Admiral Garter as she spoke.

The president nodded her head. She turned to face the human closest to the admiral. "Captain Lee, what about you? Can Terra feasibly be taken on?"

"If Captain Griffiths suggests there is an opportunity, then that means he's seen something that we haven't yet learned," Captain Aaron said. His mouth flicked into a smirk. "It would be my advice to listen to him."

"And you, Twitch?" the president asked, turning to the surprised starat.

"Me? I'm not a strategist," Twitch said, shuffling back and scuffing his feet. He grasped at the tip of his tail.

"All the same, there is no other starat present here who has lived in the empire," President Bakir said with a smile. "You have an insight that none of us share."

Twitch bit down on the tip of his tongue. He released his grip on his tail. His right ear slowly curled down as he thought. He met the eyes of Admiral Garter, hoping to understand more about the events in the empire, but the elderly human had his focus fixed on the president.

The starat thought back to his time on Ceres. What would he have done if there was word of a fleet from the CGP invading? There would only have been one answer. "There are billions of starat slaves in the empire, waiting for the opportunity to break free. If you give them that opportunity, then they will fight for you. There is an army already waiting for your arrival."

President Bakir snapped her fingers. "That is enough for me. Fleet-Admiral Bosler. Please prepare the Stellar Guard for imminent departure. Once we learn more about this opportunity from Admiral Garter we can send the fleet." The starat grinned widely. "We're going to Terra."

CPSIA information can be obtained
at www.ICGtesting.com
Printed in the USA
BVHW041701091121
621185BV00016B/1005

9 781922 061737